PRAISE FOR
ANNE GRACIE AND HER NOVELS

"[A] confection that brims with kindness and heartfelt sincerity. . . . You can't do much better than Anne Gracie who offers her share of daring escapes, stolen kisses and heartfelt romance in a tale that carries the effervescent charm of the best Disney fairy tales."   —*Entertainment Weekly*

"I never miss an Anne Gracie book."
          —*New York Times* bestselling author Julia Quinn

"For fabulous Regency flavor, witty and addictive, you can't go past Anne Gracie."
          —*New York Times* bestselling author Stephanie Laurens

"With her signature superbly nuanced characters, subtle sense of wit and richly emotional writing, Gracie puts her distinctive stamp on a classic Regency plot."
          —*Chicago Tribune*

"Will keep readers entranced. . . . A totally delightful read!"
          —RT Book Reviews

"The always terrific Anne Gracie outdoes herself with *Bride by Mistake*. . . . Gracie created two great characters, a high-tension relationship and a wonderfully satisfying ending. Not to be missed!"
          —*New York Times* bestselling author Mary Jo Putney

"A fascinating twist on the girl-in-disguise plot. . . . With its wildly romantic last chapter, this novel is a great antidote to the end of su⁓⁓⁓."
          —*New⁓⁓⁓⁓⁓⁓⁓⁓⁓⁓⁓⁓⁓⁓⁓⁓*mes

Titles by Anne Gracie

Merridew Sisters

THE PERFECT RAKE
THE PERFECT WALTZ
THE PERFECT STRANGER
THE PERFECT KISS

Devil Riders

THE STOLEN PRINCESS
HIS CAPTIVE LADY
TO CATCH A BRIDE
THE ACCIDENTAL WEDDING
BRIDE BY MISTAKE

Chance Sisters

THE AUTUMN BRIDE
THE WINTER BRIDE
THE SPRING BRIDE
THE SUMMER BRIDE

Marriage of Convenience

MARRY IN HASTE
MARRY IN SCANDAL
MARRY IN SECRET
MARRY IN SCARLET

The Brides of Bellaire Gardens

THE SCOUNDREL'S DAUGHTER
THE RAKE'S DAUGHTER

The
Rake's
Daughter

ANNE GRACIE

JOVE
New York

A JOVE BOOK
Published by Berkley
An imprint of Penguin Random House LLC
penguinrandomhouse.com

Copyright © 2022 by Anne Gracie
Penguin Random House supports copyright. Copyright fuels creativity, encourages
diverse voices, promotes free speech, and creates a vibrant culture. Thank you for buying
an authorized edition of this book and for complying with copyright laws by not
reproducing, scanning, or distributing any part of it in any form without permission.
You are supporting writers and allowing Penguin Random House to continue to
publish books for every reader.

A JOVE BOOK, BERKLEY, and the BERKLEY & B colophon are
registered trademarks of Penguin Random House LLC.

ISBN: 9780593200568

First Edition: July 2022

Printed in the United States of America
1   3   5   7   9   10   8   6   4   2

Book design by George Towne

With thanks to my friends and writing buddies, Kelly Hunter and Carol Marinelli, who kept me company during this difficult time with laughter, support and endless stories.

And to the word wenches whose friendship and advice is gold: Mary Jo Putney, Patricia Rice, Andrea Penrose, Christina Courtenay, Nicola Cornick and Susan King—thank you.

And to my readers, with many thanks for buying, reading and recommending my books, and for the many lovely emails you've sent me.

Prologue

❧

Studley Park Manor
Hampshire, England
1808

For the first eight and three-quarter years of her life, Clarissa Marie Studley had given nobody any trouble. The servants at Studley Park Manor all agreed: Miss Clarissa was a most agreeable child—quiet, biddable and obedient. No bother at all. You barely even noticed she was there.

But several days before her ninth birthday, she changed. Radically.

And the servants knew exactly who to blame.

The change had come unexpectedly, as change usually did, with the arrival one afternoon of a dusty black traveling carriage. It pulled up in front of the house, and a soberly dressed man of about thirty years stepped down.

A Studley Park groom came running but the gentleman waved him off with a curt "No need. I won't be long."

"Don't move," he ordered an unseen person inside the carriage. He marched up the front steps and rang the doorbell with a hard yank that set the interior bell jangling horribly. And when the butler answered, the visitor demanded—not asked—to see Sir Bartleby Studley, in quite the same brusque tone in which he'd spoken to the groom. If not harsher.

It was a warm summer's day and Clarissa was playing in the garden. Nanny, who was supposed to be watching her, had fallen asleep under the shady oak, and Clarissa, tired of endlessly bowling her hoop back and forth along the path, heard the carriage arrive and was intrigued. Visitors didn't often come to Studley Park Manor.

She wasn't supposed to venture out of Nanny's sight but, curious as to who the caller might be, she ran to the front of the house and peeped around the corner. All she saw at first was the traveling chaise with a bored-looking coachman sitting atop it.

She was about to return to Nanny when the sound of voices raised in argument drifted out through an open window. Papa and a strange man. Shouting.

Her whole attention on the source of the shouting, she crept closer and just as she was almost underneath the window, she stumbled and almost tripped. And stared at the small black-clad girl crouching under the window, almost hidden by the shrubbery, eavesdropping.

"Who are y—" she began.

"Shhh!" The girl jumped up, clapped her hand over Clarissa's mouth and pulled her down into the shrubbery.

Clarissa was about to object to this rude treatment when, with her hand still clamped over Clarissa's mouth, the girl jabbed a fierce finger at the window and hissed, "Listen."

"She's your bastard and your responsibility," the strange man was shouting. "You ruined my sister and disgraced my family, and now that the child's mother is dead—"

"The child is not mine."

"She *is* yours," the man insisted. "My sister was a virtuous girl until you seduced her."

Clarissa's papa snorted. "So you claim."

"There's no question that she's your daughter—wait until you see her. She's sitting in the carriage—anyone with eyes in their head can see the resemblance. You'll have to admit paternity then, and you'll damn well take responsibility for the raising of her. Because I refuse to take on the raising of another man's bastard."

"What's a bastard?" Clarissa whispered.

"Me," the other girl whispered back. When Clarissa shook her head in bewilderment, the girl added, "It's something bad."

Clarissa glanced at the black clothes the girl was wearing. Was that because she was bad? She didn't look bad, but the clothes weren't very nice. "That man said you were Papa's daughter."

The girl nodded. "He told me that, too—that he was bringing me to my father. He says he's my uncle—my mother's brother—but I think he hates me." She pulled a face. "Sounds like they both hate me."

"But if you're Papa's daughter," Clarissa said slowly, "and I'm Papa's daughter, that must make us . . . sisters."

The girl turned her head and stared wide-eyed at Clarissa. Clarissa stared back. The girl didn't look much like Clarissa, with her dark curly hair and brilliant green eyes, but she did look a lot like Papa.

"Well, I'm not taking her back with me." The words came from the open window. "I have a decent, respectable family to worry about, and I won't pollute them with a bastard child. She's yours, Studley—you can do what you damn well like with her."

Clarissa heard her father say, "I'm off to London this afternoon. I'll dump the brat in the first orphan asylum I come to."

The two girls exchanged glances. *An orphan asylum?* Clarissa had heard about them. Betty, the little maid of all work, had come from an orphan asylum, and every time she made a mistake—even a small one—she was terrified she'd be sent back. Papa was going to put this girl—her sister?—in one of those places?

Suddenly she knew what to do. She grabbed the girl's hand. "Quick, come with me. I'll hide you."

Hand in hand the two little girls took to their heels, running like rabbits to Clarissa's favorite place in all the world—the old walled garden.

"What are y—" The girl gasped as Clarissa dragged open a rusty gate set into a high brick wall and thrust her through it. She followed and pulled it closed after her. "What is this place?" the girl asked, looking around her in bemusement.

"Nobody ever comes here," Clarissa panted. "They won't look for us here—it's my secret place. Nobody even knows the gates are unlocked. I found the key last summer. Come this way, where we can sit down and talk." She led the girl to a circular arbor over which pink roses flowed in a tangled waterfall of color and fragrance. Inside, a wooden bench was set around the walls. It was a perfect hidey-hole.

The girls sat, breathing in the scent of roses and gazing at each other in silence. Clarissa had just one thought in her head—could this girl really be her sister? She so wanted her to be. She had always longed for a sister. "What's your name?" she asked.

"Izzy. Isobel, really, but Mama always calls—called me Izzy."

Clarissa eyed Izzy's black clothing. "Is your mama . . . ?"

"Dead, yes. That man, my uncle"—Izzy jerked her head in the direction of the house—"I met him for the first time today. He came to Mama's funeral and told me he was Mama's brother and that I was leaving."

"Leaving where?"

"Home. Mama and I live—lived in a little cottage on the outskirts of the village. I didn't even know she had a brother. Or that I had a father. Oh, I knew people called me a bastard, but I always thought a bastard was a person who didn't have a father—and I didn't have a father. But he—my uncle—said I was my father's responsibility. And so he brought me here." She eyed Clarissa cautiously. "Do you really think we're sisters?"

Clarissa thought about everything they'd overheard. "Yes. I don't look like Papa—everyone says I take after my mother—but you, you look like Papa, except for being a girl. You have his eyes and his hair and—"

"His *hair*?" Izzy tugged a long spiral of dark hair. "This horrid stuff?"

"Horrid? I think your hair is beautiful. Like elf locks. In fact, for a moment when I first saw you, I thought you might be an elf . . . but you're not, are you?" Izzy had an elfin look about her, with her pointy chin and wide green eyes and the tumble of dark, silky corkscrew curls. Clarissa had to spend an uncomfortable night with her hair in rags to get even half that number of curls.

"No, I'm not an elf."

"I've never seen an elf," Clarissa said sadly.

"Me neither. Though I wouldn't mind being one if I could do magic."

"Yes, and I'd be one, too. Or maybe a fairy. Wouldn't that be fun?"

"Yes! I could turn my uncle into a toad," Izzy said, and they both laughed.

After a moment, Izzy sighed. "What are we going to do? I can't stay hiding here forever."

"Not forever, but for a while," Clarissa said. A plan was forming in her mind. "I'll have to go now—Nanny will be missing me—but I'll be back as soon as I can."

Izzy glanced around the deserted garden. "But what will I do? They'll be looking for me."

Clarissa nodded. "I know, but they won't think to look in here. And Papa has very little patience, so he'll end up leaving everything to the servants as he usually does. He was about to leave for London when your uncle's carriage arrived, so he'll probably go soon anyway. And you can leave the servants to me." She grinned. It was just like an adventure in a story. "Are you hungry? I'll bring you some food later if I can, but you must hide here until it's safe. Then I'll come and fetch you."

Izzy frowned. "And then what?"

Clarissa hesitated. "We *are* sisters, aren't we?"

Izzy nodded. "I think we must be."

Clarissa had prayed for a sister all her life, but she needed to be sure. "Yes, but do you *want* to be my sister? It's quite lonely here," she added honestly. "There's only the servants, and most of them are old. And I'm not allowed to play with the village children."

Izzy pulled a face. "Where I come from the village children are not allowed to play with me."

"Why not?"

Izzy shrugged. "Because my father didn't marry my mother."

"No, he married my mother. But that's not your fault."

"Doesn't matter now, and I don't care what they say." She grinned at Clarissa, an elfin smile full of mischief. "I've always wanted a sister, too. And I like you."

"Good. I like you, too, so from now on you're going to live with me, and we will be sisters together and play as much as we want." Clarissa couldn't keep the smile from her face. She darted forward and hugged Izzy. "Now, here's the key to the gate. Lock it when I leave so nobody can get in even if they want to. I'll come for you as soon as I can. I shan't be long."

She returned to the house and found servants busily scurrying thither and yon, and her father standing in the hallway bellowing orders.

Nanny pounced on her. "Where have you been, child? I've been beside myself wondering where you were. Bad enough that one child has gone miss—" She broke off. "But never mind about that, come away upstairs. There's a nice glass of milk and some of Cook's best shortbread waiting for you."

Clarissa didn't move. "Who's gone missing, Nanny?"

"Oh, nobody, no one of any account. I'm sure it's all a misunderstanding and that fellow took the child away with him after all."

"What child?"

"There is no child," Papa snapped from the hallway. "It's all a lot of nonsense. I've had enough of it. I'm off." He snapped his fingers, and a footman ran out the front door and whistled a signal to the grooms.

Clarissa heard her father say to the estate manager, Mr. Edwards, "Find the brat and deal with her."

"What should I do with her, sir?"

"I neither know nor care." The carriage arrived, the luggage was swiftly loaded and a few minutes later Papa was driving away. Without even saying goodbye to Clarissa.

He rarely did. She was a disappointment to Papa; she'd always known it. He'd told her to her face, more than once. She was plain and unattractive. She was dull like her mother. She was no use to anyone. And she should have been a boy.

But it didn't hurt so much now, because now she had a sister. And she wouldn't ever be lonely again.

She went upstairs with Nanny, drank her milk, ate a piece of shortbread, slipped the rest into her pocket and added an apple. Then, telling Nanny she'd left her book in the garden and would be back in a minute, she ran downstairs and took the food to Izzy.

Izzy ate hungrily, and when she had finished, Clarissa smuggled her upstairs via the servants' stairs. She settled her in the nursery bedchamber with a couple of books and some more shortbread. Nanny, who was in her sitting room knitting by the window, didn't notice a thing.

It wasn't until evening, after Clarissa had eaten her supper—slipping half of it into a napkin for Izzy—and gone to bed that the deception was discovered. Nanny came to check she was sleeping and found curled up in the bed two little girls, instead of one.

She gave an almighty shriek, and within minutes several servants were crowded into the bedchamber, exclaiming and speculating.

Nanny, recovering from her shock, said firmly to Izzy, "Now come away, child. You don't belong here."

But the two girls clung to each other, and when Nanny reached for Izzy's hand, Clarissa flung her arms around her sister, and shouted, "Don't touch her! She's my sister and I'm keeping her!"

Nanny and the other servants stopped, shocked—Clarissa never shouted—and eyed one another cautiously.

And when a footman went to grab Izzy, intending to drag her away by force, the two girls fought and scratched like furious little cats, and Clarissa proved she could out-shriek Nanny any day.

The footman retreated. Nanny and the other servants tried to reason with her, but Clarissa dug her heels in and refused to give up her sister, repeating, "Izzy is my sister and I'm keeping her!"

Finally the estate manager was summoned to deal with the problem. Nanny turned to him. "What shall I do, Mr. Edwards? Miss Clarissa will make herself sick if she keeps carrying on in this fashion."

Everyone waited for him to speak.

Mr. Edwards looked at Clarissa, tearstained and desperate, clutching her white-faced sister to her. He eyed Izzy thoughtfully, and said, "That child is the master's get and no mistake."

"Yes, but what do we do?" Nanny repeated.

There was a long silence, then Mr. Edwards spoke. "He did say he didn't care what I did with her."

"But what does that mean?" Nanny wailed. "We must do something."

Mr. Edwards glanced at the two little girls huddled on the bed. "Let her stay. When the master returns, he can decide. I won't be responsible for tossing a child out into the night."

"No, no, of course not," Nanny murmured. "But what should I do?"

"Leave them be for the moment," Mr. Edwards said. "There's been enough upset tonight. We'll make the necessary arrangements in the morning."

"No arrangements. She's my sister and I'm keeping her!" Clarissa said again.

Mr. Edwards smiled. "Nobody's taking her anywhere, child. She can stay here until your father comes back. He will decide what to do."

Clarissa could hardly believe it. Papa didn't visit very often. "Promise?"

"I promise. Now go to sleep," Mr. Edwards said. "Both of you."

Six months later Sir Bartleby returned to Studley Park Manor for one of his infrequent and irregular visits— what was the point, he often said, when he had an estate manager to run things, and no son to interest him.

Even so, since Mr. Edwards was away at the time and none of the servants could rouse sufficient courage to broach the matter, it was almost a week before he realized his bastard daughter was living in his house.

He'd been riding back from paying a call on a neighbor, a juicy widow, when he noticed two small girls, one dark, one fair, playing on the side lawn. He frowned. His daughter was not permitted to play with peasants.

He returned to the house and sent for the nanny. And discovered who the dark-haired child was. In a rage, he ordered the wretched brat brought to him. But though the servants searched high and low, there was no sign of her.

He then sent for Clarissa and demanded she tell him where the other girl was. Pale and trembling, Clarissa answered in a small, firm voice. "No, Papa."

He could hardly believe his ears. He frowned, but moderated his voice. "Now be sensible, Clarissa. That girl is nothing to do with us. She's an orphan. She belongs with her own kind."

His daughter regarded him solemnly. "Izzy's mama is dead, but so is my mama. Does that mean I am an orphan, too?"

He could barely repress his impatience. "Of course you're not an orphan, you stupid child. I am your father."

"But if you are Izzy's father, she cannot be an orphan, can she?"

Big as a bull and just as angry, Sir Bartleby shouted, "I am not that—that *creature's* father! And I won't have her in my house. Now, where is she?" He slammed his fist on the desk before him.

Clarissa flinched, but with a white, set face she stared him down. "Izzy *is* my sister, Papa. She looks just like you. And I won't give her up."

"How dare you defy me, you miserable child!" He rose from behind his desk, stalked around it and loomed over her with a raised fist. "Tell me at once where she is or else . . ."

Clarissa braced herself.

The door flew open, and a small dark-haired whirlwind burst in. "Leave my sister alone, you big fat bully!" Izzy flew at him and butted him hard in the stomach. Then while he was still wheezing, trying to get his breath back, she grabbed Clarissa's hand and the two little girls fled.

They were not seen for the rest of the day.

Sir Bartleby shouted and stormed and ranted. He offered

the servants bribes, and when that didn't work, he made threats. But nobody could—or possibly would—produce either girl.

The estate manager, when he returned, tried to reason with him, pointing out that apart from her irregular birth, the child was essentially harmless, and that she was company for Miss Clarissa. Who had been very lonely with only servants for company, and mostly elderly ones at that.

Sir Bartleby snapped at him to mind his own damned business.

Night fell but the girls did not appear. When morning came, still with no sign of them, Sir Bartleby gave up in disgust. "Let her keep the brat then, if she must," he growled. "But she's not to set a foot outside the estate boundary—not to attend church or go into the village. She's not to mix with local people at all—especially not the gentry." He glowered at his servants, adding, "And if I ever lay eyes on the misbegotten little bitch, I'll make her sorry she was ever born."

He called for his carriage and returned to London in a filthy temper. The first thing he did on his arrival in the capital was to send for his lawyer.

It was another year before he made another visit to Studley Park Manor, and for the whole of his time there he did not acknowledge either daughter. He did not send for Clarissa. He did not speak to her or even look at her; in fact, he gave orders to the servants that the girls were to be kept out of his sight.

No problem there—the girls had as little desire to see him as he to see them, though it did grieve Clarissa that her father was even more set against her than ever. But she had a sister now, and that more than made up for it.

Life with Izzy was full of fun and excitement. They spent hours every day in the walled garden, playing games, creating make-believe fairy villages and gathering rose petals to make perfumes and potpourri. In wet weather they created cozy nests in the attic and read books and played games of make-believe.

On hot days they splashed and cavorted in the lake, squealing with joy and delight, dressed only in their chemises. Until Izzy, Clarissa had never swum in her life. Never even paddled.

They climbed trees. Clarissa had never even thought of doing such a thing, but now they nestled high in the branches, gazing out over their domain, captains of a pirate ship, or princesses in a tower, prisoners of an evil wizard, and once, hiding from a pack of wolves.

They made friends with the shepherd who let them feed an orphan baby lamb, and oh, the fun of holding the tiny woolly creature with its wiggly tail as it greedily sucked down the milk.

They discovered a blackberry patch and returned to the house with scratched arms and stained and torn dresses, their mouths purple with blackberry juice.

At Izzy's instigation, they learned to ride, secretly at first and bareback, because of Sir Bartleby's restrictions, but then Clarissa fell off and broke her arm. Forbidden to ride again, Clarissa said with apparent placidity, "Very well, but only until my arm has healed."

In despair, Nanny sent for Mr. Edwards, who, after interviewing the two girls, arranged for them to have riding lessons. "No use penning them up," he told Nanny. "They've tasted freedom and there's no stopping them now. Besides, riding is a useful skill for a lady and better they be taught properly."

Sir Bartleby's visits became more infrequent than ever, and when he did come, the girls simply avoided him. He never even mentioned Izzy, acting as if she didn't exist. And as the girls grew older and he brought guests with him to go hunting or shooting, the girls learned to avoid them, too.

The walled garden remained their retreat. The servants knew their secret now, but they never told.

For the next ten years, Clarissa and Izzy grew up, side by side, as close as two sisters could be.

And then Sir Bartleby died.

Chapter One

❧

I'm sorry, my lord, it may well be a mistake, but it's definitely legal."

"It's definitely a mistake, and I don't want any part of it," Leo, Lord Salcott, said firmly.

The lawyer, Melkin, tightened his lips. "I'm afraid you have no choice, my lord. Sir Bartleby Studley's will quite clearly stipulates that his daughter Clarissa is to be taken under the guardianship of Josiah Leonard Thorne, sixth Earl of Salcott—which is you."

"I understand that," Leo said impatiently. "But he meant my father, not me. My father was also named Josiah Leonard Thorne. It's a family tradition—the firstborn son of each generation is given the same name, but Papa was known as Josiah while I am called Leo. Presumably if I choose to follow the tradition, my first son will be called Joe by his school friends, and his son will be Leo."

"Indeed, my lord. Nevertheless, *you* are the sixth Earl of Salcott," Melkin said gently. "And thus the will stands."

"It's perfectly clear to me that he intended my father to be the girl's guardian. He simply made a mistake, that's all.

He was probably drunk at the time and forgot that Papa was the fifth earl, not the sixth."

"Possibly so, but your father predeceased him by several months, and it cannot be denied that all the legalities have been met." The elderly lawyer tapped the document with a bony, ink-stained finger. "Miss Clarissa Studley is, for better or worse, your responsibility until she is married. You could, of course, contest the will in the courts, but that would take time and money, and in the meantime you would still be responsible for the young ladies." He gave Leo a shrewd look, then added, "My advice is just to accept it."

Leo blinked. "'Ladies'? What do you mean 'ladies'? I thought there was only one daughter."

"Yes . . . and no." The lawyer cleared his throat. "Miss Clarissa Studley refuses to be parted from her, er, relative, and thus your duties will effectively extend to both girls."

"What the devil is an er-relative? Some kind of companion, I presume."

Melkin pursed his lips. "It's rather irregular, my lord, but the second girl is Sir Bartleby's natural daughter."

"You mean I'm also to be landed with one of his bastards? As well as his legitimate daughter? Damn the old lecher."

The lawyer winced slightly at Leo's plainspokenness and sifted through the documents before him. "I wondered whether it might have been some private agreement, my lord," he murmured. "Between your father and Sir Bartleby."

A private agreement? That'd be right. He sighed. His father had made all kinds of arrangements he'd never told Leo about. Untangling his spendthrift parent's tangled affairs had taken Leo years. He thought he'd finally broken clear of them. Apparently not.

Though acting as guardian for two young women was a new one to him. Lord, how his friends would laugh.

He'd never had much in common with his father, and he'd disliked most of his father's friends, especially Sir Bartleby Studley. How spoiled would these girls be?

"I suppose if Studley has provided for the girl—"

"No provision my lord. Not so much as a penny."

"*What?*" Leo was shocked. "Then what the devil was he playing at, to sire a child and make no provision for her support? He wasn't a poor man."

"I cannot speculate, my lord. It is most irregular." He pursed his lips and added apologetically, "The cousin who inherited Studley Park Manor allowed the girls to see out their mourning year in their childhood home, but he is about to get married and has served them notice to vacate the house."

"And?" Leo prompted. He disliked the look in the man's eye.

"And thus Miss Clarissa Studley and her, er, relative will be coming to London. To you."

"To me?"

The lawyer shrugged. "They have nowhere else to go."

Leo swore under his breath. It was one thing to oversee financial arrangements for a pair of young women, quite another to have them landing—in person!—on his doorstep.

He had a good mind to walk out and catch the next boat back to the continent. But he was nothing if not a realist. He'd dealt with every other problem his father had left him with, and he could deal with this.

He perused the documents in front of him. "Very well then, surely we can find the funds to pension the er-relative off. Studley should have done that in the first place." Leaving the girl without means of support was an utter disgrace.

Melkin nodded. "That would seem the best solution, my lord, only where would the money come from?"

"How is she currently supported?"

"By Miss Clarissa Studley, my lord. She intends to share her own fortune with her—"

Leo frowned. "Can she do that?"

"No. Miss Studley's inheritance doesn't come to her until she is married, after which it will be in the control of her husband, so there's no danger there. In the meantime, the trust that her maternal grandfather set up pays for whatever she needs, including an allowance for pin money. It's a very generous allowance, and she shares it equally with her half sister. And since Sir Bartleby left nothing to either girl . . ." He spread his fingers in a helpless gesture.

Leo's own fingers curled into fists. "So in effect Miss Studley is supporting her father's natural daughter as her father did not?"

He could barely believe it. A disgrace for a young girl— both young girls—to be put in such a position. The sooner Leo made arrangements for the half sister, and freed Miss Studley of the burden of her support, the better.

Melkin produced a sealed letter. "Sir Bartleby left this private letter for you in which, I presume, he explains."

Leo broke open the seal and read the letter. It was dated shortly before Studley's death.

Salcott, apologies for leaving my bastard brat to your offices, but I have been unable to pry her loose from my daughter. The witch has her claws in deep. Isobel has shown every sign of being as immoral and manipulative as her whore of a mother. Perhaps in London she will finally fulfill her aim of becoming a courtesan. Even as a young girl, she was attempting to work her wiles on my guests.

I trust you will find more success than I in freeing my daughter from her unholy influence.

Yours etc.
Studley

Leo read the letter again. It left a nasty taste in his mouth. For a man to talk so about his own daughter, illegitimate or not. Still, she must have done something to provoke such vitriol. And a deathbed request was not something to take lightly.

But Studley's cheek was unbelievable! He should have dealt with his own dirty blasted washing, not palmed it off on another man, let alone a man whom—assuming he'd intended the task for Leo's father—he hadn't seen in a decade or more. Leo's father had been bedridden for the last ten years of his life.

But now things began to make more sense. If the bastard daughter had immoral tendencies and was planning to set up as a courtesan—and if the man knew she was battening on her sister—Leo could understand why Studley might be reluctant to settle money on her. Though it was still wrong.

He crumpled the letter in his fist. *Immoral and manipulative*, was she? As it happened, he was well acquainted with the designing kind of female, and dammit, it would definitely take money to get rid of her.

And Studley had left Leo with no option but to pay her out of his own pocket.

He hoped the man was roasting in hell.

He sat back, eyeing the documents broodingly. "So, two girls, one legitimate and with a fortune, one without name or means. Regardless of any moral failings she may have, the illegitimate girl nevertheless has a right to some support. Studley raised her in his own home along with his legitimate daughter, so it's poor form to simply toss her out in the cold with nothing. No wonder she depends on her half sister for support."

Melkin nodded. "Quite so, my lord."

"Now, what the devil am I supposed to do with Miss Studley?" It was a rhetorical question, spoken half under his breath, but the lawyer thought he was asking for advice.

He beamed at Leo. "Introduce her to society, my lord. Get her married and off your hands."

Leo stared at the man, appalled. "Introduce her to *soci-

ety? You mean take her to balls, routs, the opera? *Almack's*?" He couldn't think of anything worse. He'd fled to the continent to escape all that society fuss and bother.

"Exactly, my lord. You will, of course, need a suitable female not only to chaperone her, but to sponsor her in society."

Curse it. He didn't know any suitable females. Nor any unsuitable ones—not in England, at any rate. "You're not suggesting I get the er-relative to be the chaperone, are you?"

Melkin looked shocked. "Oh, no, no, no, my lord! Quite unthinkable. That girl cannot, of course, have anything to do with polite society."

Leo pondered the problem. The illegitimate girl would be no problem—he'd pay her off and make it clear she was not to batten on her half sister any longer. Whatever she did after that wouldn't bother him.

But the other one . . . he was damned if he'd squire her to ton parties and balls. He'd entered that circus once and had no intention of doing it again. No, Miss Studley's social life was a task for a woman.

"I suppose I'll have to hire someone." Yet another expense he'd have to cover.

The lawyer kept a prudent silence. He tidied the documents, tucked them into a folder and said diffidently, "I believe the girls will be arriving in London quite soon, my lord."

Leo, who had been lost in thought, glanced up sharply. "What? Already?"

"A year has passed since Sir Bartleby's demise, my lord. Had you not been absent from England for the last year, it would not be such a surprise to you. "

"I was traveling," Leo reminded him. The faint reproach in the lawyer's voice was irritating. Dammit, Leo had been entitled to his time away. During the last decade or so his schoolfellows had traveled, had adventures; some had joined the army, others ventured to exotic foreign countries. Leo had barely left the family estate.

His father's apoplexy twelve years before had forced him, then aged sixteen and trying to decide between a commission in the army or university, to abandon all his plans and take on the responsibility for his father and the family estate.

His father's debts had seemed crushing at first, but through hard work, and with good advice, Leo had gradually managed to turn things around. The estate was profitable now, and his investments had paid off.

And so, after his father's death eighteen months ago, he'd made arrangements for the business of the estate to be carried on while he took himself abroad for a little taste of freedom. His own version of The Grand Tour—post-Napoleonic Europe, Greece, Turkey, Egypt. He'd enjoyed every minute of it.

And then, to come home to this debacle!

Melkin consulted another letter. "According to this, Miss Clarissa Studley and her half sister intended to leave for London at the beginning of the week." He glanced at Leo. "Which means, if they left on time—though ladies, you know, often do not—they should arrive tomorrow or the next day."

"*'Tomorrow or the next day'?*"

"I'm afraid so, my lord. You'd better alert your housekeeper to prepare bedchambers for them."

"My housekeeper? I don't have a housekeeper. I don't have any staff in town at the moment, just my valet." On his return to London he'd called in to see his man of affairs and discovered that the Bellaire Gardens house, which had been rented out for the last ten years, was now vacant. The agent was of the opinion that whether Leo intended to take up residence there or lease it out again, the house was in dire need of refurbishment and, when Leo inspected it, he had to agree.

He was temporarily camped in the dusty, empty house until the renovations could begin. In the meantime his valet, Matteo, who was more majordomo than mere valet, was currently making it habitable—for himself and Leo, not a pair of pampered young ladies.

"Oh dear me, no," the lawyer said. "They cannot stay with you unchaperoned—not with your being a bachelor. It would be easier if you were married. I don't suppose . . ." He ended the sentence on a faintly hopeful note of query.

"No. I have no marital plans, not now or in the foreseeable future," Leo said firmly. He had no desire to tie himself down, and he certainly wasn't going to do it for the convenience of two unknown females.

"But as their guardian, you will, of course, make suitable arrangements."

Leo shrugged. "They can stay in a hotel."

Melkin looked shocked. "Oh, that will never do, my lord. A respectable young lady, unchaperoned except by her illegitimate half sister, alone and unprotected in a London hotel? Oh no, no, no!"

"Then I'll hire a maid to chaperone them."

The lawyer shook his head. "A maidservant would give Miss Studley neither the respectability nor the consequence required." His beetling gray brows twitched in thought. "Is there no female relative you could prevail on to assist you, my lord?"

"No, there's only—" Leo broke off as a thought occurred to him. "Now I come to think of it, I do have a female relative in London—my aunt Olive—and as it happens, she also lives in Bellaire Gardens, a short step across from my own house."

The lawyer's brows snapped together. "You don't mean Lady Scattergood, do you, because I hardly think—"

"Aunt Olive will be perfect. She will enjoy the girls' company, and the location couldn't be better. They can stay with her and still be close enough for me to supervise." He could scarcely keep the satisfaction out of his voice.

He'd had quite enough of responsibilities being heaped on him unwanted—since the age of sixteen—and he didn't want any more. He wanted to get back to his life—his own life. Not continue dancing to dead men's tunes.

"But, my lord—"

Leo rose. "Anything else, Melkin? No? Then thank you, I'll be off. I have arrangements to make."

He left the building, pleased with himself. It was all but settled. He'd make the er-relative a handsome allowance—hang the expense; let the girl depart with some dignity—and give the other girl to Aunt Olive. His aunt was hardly the social type, but he was sure she'd enjoy a bit of youthful company.

Yes, Studley's will had thrown him at first, but now Leo had it all under control.

He returned to the house in Bellaire Gardens to find it a hive of activity, with women scattered about the place, scrubbing and polishing, and men up ladders, washing windows, stripping paper off the walls, and more. And at the center of all this activity was his valet, Matteo, apparently in his element.

"There is only one room fit for you at the moment, milor'," Matteo greeted him. "I will bring tea"—he eyed Leo closely—"or per'aps this is a day for wine?"

Leo had come across Matteo living on the streets of Naples, and employed him initially as a temporary guide and then later as valet and general factotum. He had made himself increasingly indispensable, and when Leo was moving on, heading for Greece and Turkey, Matteo had begged Leo to take him, too. An orphan with no living relatives, he assured Leo he was free to follow milor' anywhere.

Within weeks, Matteo had more or less taken charge of all Leo's travel arrangements and had proven his mettle in ensuring the cleanliness of Leo's accommodations, finding delicious—and safe—local food, and was able to produce reliable transport and good local guides, even when he didn't speak the language.

And now, in London, Matteo had taken one look at the house, shuddered comprehensively and set out to find cleaners. And had obviously found them, though how, Leo had no idea.

Leo shook his head. "I'm going to call on my aunt."

Matteo brightened. "You have the aunt here in London, milor'? Oh, that is good. Is not good for a man to have no family. She live far, this aunt?"

"Not far. Just across the garden." Leo gestured to the back of the house. The houses of Bellaire Gardens were built around one large private garden square. Invisible from the street, access to the shared garden was only gained through the back gate of each house.

He allowed himself to be persuaded into a glass of wine and a plate of sandwiches in a room that had somehow become a haven of cleanliness and peace. Thus fortified, he braced himself for the interview with Aunt Olive. Matteo, insisting that an aunt must be paid due respect, had somehow procured a large box of sweetmeats, a good bottle of sherry and an extravagant bunch of flowers, and thus armed, Leo rang the front doorbell.

Her butler, a desiccated ancient clad in dusty black, eyed him with weary indifference.

"Afternoon, Treadwell," Leo said, and then when the butler didn't respond, he added, "Lord Salcott, here to see my aunt Olive," in case the man was as senile as he looked and had forgotten him. It had been more than a year, after all, since he'd last visited.

Treadwell sniffed. "I am aware of who you are, my lord. I will ascertain whether my lady is at home." He gestured

at Leo to wait, then took himself upstairs with a slow, spidery gait.

Leo waited. He was quite certain Aunt Olive was at
home. She hadn't left the house in years, but whether she
wanted to see him was quite another matter. Leo might be
her only nephew as well as head of the family, but Aunt
Olive was a law unto herself.

Eventually Treadwell reappeared. "M'lady will see
you now."

As Leo and the butler approached his aunt's favorite sitting room on the first floor, a flurry of barks greeted them.
His aunt had always been a passionate dog lover.

Treadwell opened the door with a majestic gesture.
"Lord Salcott, my lady."

The minute Leo stepped inside, a pack of small scruffy
dogs surrounded him, yapping and growling and sniffing.
One of Aunt Olive's more endearing qualities was that she
took in abandoned dogs, usually bitches, invariably mongrels and rarely the kind of pretty creature that most ladies
were attracted to.

Resigning himself to the probable ruin of his boots, and
bracing himself for a nip or two, Leo carefully waded
through the whirlpool of little dogs, set his gifts on a side
table and bent to acquaint himself with the little creatures.
He'd always liked dogs. While his hands and boots were
being thoroughly sniffed and licked, he said, "Aunt Olive,
how delightful to see you. You're looking very well, I
must say."

His aunt, tall, gaunt and angular and swathed in several
colorful Indian shawls, sat enthroned in a large chair inlaid
with mother-of-pearl decorations. She eyed his gifts with
dark suspicion. "Those are for me, I suppose, which means
you want something of me. The answer is no."

"You don't even know what I want."

"No, and I don't care. Men bearing gifts are never to be
trusted. Treadwell, put the flowers in water at once. Why

people cut flowers when all they do is die is beyond me. And leave the bottle here," she added sharply as the butler moved to take the sherry as well. "He drinks," she said to Leo.

Leo didn't blame him.

His aunt waved him to a seat. It was occupied by a skinny little dog with a bandage around one leg. Every other seat in the room was occupied by a dog. Leo approached the chair indicated. The little dog snarled a warning.

"She's new," his aunt said. "Hates men. Name of Biddy. Pop her in that basket."

The poor little creature was so thin her bones were almost breaking through her skin, and there were raw scrapes on various parts of her body. From a kicking, no doubt. She had good reason to hate men, Leo thought.

He crouched down in front of the chair. "Well then, Biddy, you've been in the wars, haven't you?" he said softly. He extended his hand to the scrawny little beast, who sniffed it warily, growling quietly. Eventually she suffered him to pat her and Leo, deciding her hostility was mostly bluff, scooped her gently off the chair and settled her in the basket nearby.

"*Hmph*. Animals always did like you," Aunt Olive said gruffly. "She's bitten my butler numerous times—whenever he makes a sudden movement or moves too quickly."

"I wouldn't have thought Treadwell was capable of sudden moves. Or rapid anything," he said dryly.

His aunt raised her lorgnette. "Are you maligning my staff, young man?"

"Aunt Olive, would I do such a thing?"

"*Hmph!*" But her mouth was twitching in the effort not to smile. "Well, nephew, what is it you want?"

"Advice," he said, deciding on impulse to take an indirect approach.

She sniffed. "That'd be a first. What about?"

He explained how, because of Sir Bartleby Studley's mistake, he'd been lumbered with the guardianship of two young women.

"Studley? Ghastly man. Should have been drowned at birth," his aunt said when he'd finished. "Mind you, I said the same of your father. A pair of weasels if ever I met them. What are you going to do with these gels, then?"

He explained the problem of the er-relative.

She bristled. "One of Studley's bastards, eh? Vile lecher that he was, no doubt he peppered the kingdom with them." She narrowed her eyes at Leo. "I suppose you think that makes the gel an undesirable—well, I won't have it, you hear? She's not to be blamed for having a swine for a father, and if you think I'll be party to—"

"No, I'll be dealing with the pair of them. Apparently, the legitimate daughter, Clarissa, refuses to be separated from her sister." His aunt didn't need to know that Leo had every intention of separating them as soon as he could. It was his duty as Clarissa's guardian.

"*Hmph*, well, that shows the gel has spirit, at least. So, what do you want of me?"

"The thing is, Aunt Olive, being a bachelor, I need a reliable lady to chaperone the girls and take them around."

She gave him an incredulous look. "And you imagine I might be such a female? I assure you, I'm not."

"No, but I thought you might know of someone." His aunt might no longer attend social events, but she had a wide acquaintance throughout the country with whom she conducted a prolific correspondence.

She eyed him suspiciously. "To what end?"

"I plan to introduce Miss Studley to society. Marry her off as quickly as possible."

His aunt's brows almost disappeared. "Introduce an innocent young woman to the ton? Marry her off?" She made a scornful sound. "As soon fling her into a pack of wolves!" Caressing the dog on her lap, she added, "Actually, wolves might be better. They are, after all, a kind of dog. Wolves might be fierce, but they are at least civilized."

Leo blinked. "Civilized?" In Russia last year, his sleigh had been chased by a pack of ravening wolves. Nothing civilized about that.

She made a dismissive gesture. "Perhaps 'rational' is a better word. Loyal. Devoted to their mates and cubs. *And* they hunt only for food." She bent and scooped up another little mutt, and said in a crooning tone—to Leo or the dog, he wasn't quite sure—"You know where you are with a wolf or a dog." She put the ratty little creature down and gave Leo a disparaging look. "Men are quite a different kind of beast." She snorted again. "Marry the gel off indeed! I want no part of it!"

"I appreciate that," Leo said with a smile. His aunt never changed, she just got more so. Nevertheless, he needed her. "The trouble is, Aunt Olive, the girls are on their way to London as we speak, and my London house is all at sixes and sevens. I am in the process of organizing tradesmen to effect repairs and renovations, but as yet, it is quite unfit for the housing of two young ladies."

"I should think not!" she exclaimed. "And you a bachelor—or have you married since last we met?"

"No, I'm still unmarried." And had every intention of staying that way for at least another ten years.

"Then they cannot possibly stay with you. It would be *quite* improper!"

"So you think I should send the girls to a hotel?" he said in his most clueless-male manner.

"A *hotel*?" she said, scandalized. "Hotbeds of vice, hotels. Filled with rakes on the prowl."

"Well, what else can I do?"

She snorted. "They must stay here, of course, with me. The dogs and I will protect them."

Leo looked at the shawl-swathed old lady and the misbegotten little mongrels that clustered around her. "Of course you will. What an excellent solution. Thank you, Aunt Olive. I'll bring the girls across when they arrive."

He took his leave of her and returned to his house, well pleased with his arrangements. The girls would be safely and respectably housed, and it would be a matter of moments to arrange an allowance for the er-relative, which would deal with that little problem. All that was left was to find a chaperone. Perfect.

And then back to his life.

It was late afternoon, and Leo sat in his bare, thoroughly cleaned library, going though papers and attending to matters that had been awaiting his attention until he returned to England. It would have been vastly more comfortable to do it at his club, where he was now staying—the unceasing chaos in the house was unbearable—but if the lawyer was correct, those wretched girls were likely to arrive at any time.

They would call at Melkin's office, and he would give them this address. Young women—women of any age— were not allowed in gentlemen's clubs.

He worked his way methodically through his papers, making a note of matters that needed his personal attention, and composing letters to his man of affairs, his bank manager and the estate manager at Salcott. Despite his long absence, everything had continued fairly smoothly; they were expecting a good harvest, most of his investments were continuing to pay healthy dividends, and those that weren't, he put aside for further consideration.

There were a few estate matters, however, that he would have to see to in person; he'd attend to them as soon as Studley's daughters were settled with his aunt.

The library was on the second floor at the front of the

house and, it being a warm day, he'd opened the windows. Thus, when he heard the sound of a carriage pulling up outside, he rose to take a look.

A shabby old-fashioned traveling carriage, piled high with luggage, covered with dust and pulled by four weary-looking horses, had stopped at his front entrance. This then was it. He sighed and for the thousandth time cursed Sir Bartleby Studley.

A footman let down the steps of the coach, and a young lady alighted. Slightly plump and dressed in pink, with a hat encrusted with roses, she stood on the footpath, gazing about her surroundings with interest. Which one was she, Leo wondered, the legitimate daughter or the other?

A second young woman stepped down from the coach. She was slender and dressed in an olive-green dress and a bronze-colored spencer. Her hat was plain straw and was simply finished with an olive-colored ribbon. A matter of taste or a lack of money?

He couldn't see their faces for their hats.

Matteo ran down the front steps, bowed to the young ladies, then turned with a sweeping gesture to halt the footman who was about to start unloading luggage. He spoke briefly to the coachman, who visibly bristled—large Englishmen apparently didn't take kindly to being ordered around by small Italians, but Leo had every faith in Matteo. His major-domo then escorted the young ladies into the house.

After allowing the young women to refresh themselves in an upstairs room he'd especially prepared for them, Matteo escorted them to the sitting room where Leo was waiting. "Miss Studley and Miss Studley, milor'," he said, presenting them with a flourish.

Miss Studley and Miss Burton, Leo corrected him mentally. Studley's illegitimate daughter had no right to his surname, but Matteo couldn't be expected to know that.

He introduced himself. Miss Flowery Hat turned out to

be Miss Clarissa Studley; the other one was, therefore, Isobel Burton. Leo took one look at her and his throat dried.

Oh. My. God. Why had no one warned him?

There could be no doubt of her paternity: she was the feminine embodiment of Sir Bartleby Studley—only beautiful. Stunningly beautiful. And not just in the common way. If beauty could ever be common.

Clad in a plainly cut dress of olive green and bronze, she should have looked drab, but instead the dull colors flattered her pure, satiny complexion and highlighted the color of her wide fern-green eyes, which, he couldn't help but notice, were framed with long dark lashes. Tiny dark curls danced around a face that was a perfect oval. His fingers itched to run through those curls, see if they were as soft and silky as they looked.

And her mouth, dear lord, her mouth . . . He swallowed. He had not bargained for this . . .

Matteo fussed around, getting the ladies seated and comfortable, which gave Leo a moment or two to gather his scattered wits.

He was jerked back to attention when Matteo cleared his throat ostentatiously. "I bring tea and cakes, milor', yes?" he suggested with a droll look that implied that he was repeating the question and was quite aware of the cause of Leo's distraction. And approved.

Leo nodded vaguely and tried to drag his gaze off Isobel Burton. She wasn't a conventional beauty, he told himself. She was arresting, rather than pretty, with a small straight nose, high cheekbones, a pointed chin, and a mouth that . . .

No. Leo swallowed again. He did *not* need to be thinking of her mouth. He was in some sense—at least for the moment—her guardian, not some irresponsible rake. His job was to get rid of her, not stare at her mouth as if it were . . . edible.

He tried to remember what he'd planned to say. He fastened his gaze, if not his whole attention, on Miss Studley. Who was much safer.

"Did you have a pleasant journey, Miss Studley?"

"Oh yes, most interesting," Miss Studley responded cheerfully. "Though it took a lot longer than we expected."

From the corner of his eye he watched as Isobel Burton pulled off her gloves, loosening one finger at a time. Removing gloves should not be erotic, Leo thought desperately. She draped them across her thigh, and smoothed them with long, elegant fingers.

Leo forced his attention back to the conversation. What had he asked about? Oh yes, the journey.

Oblivious of his inattention, Miss Studley continued, "We spent last night in an inn—the first time for either of us, and that was quite interesting. Nanny—my old nanny, you understand—wrote ahead and bespoke a bedchamber and a sitting room for us; otherwise, we would have had to share a bedchamber with strangers!"

She frowned and added breathlessly, "There will be provision made for the servants at Studley Park, won't there, Lord Salcott? Only, when we left, none of us knew whether Papa's cousin—the new owner—would be keeping everyone on, or staffing the house with his own people. It's very worrying. Nanny is quite old, and the others have worked at Studley Park as long as I can remember, haven't they, Izzy?"

Her half sister nodded. "Yes, we're very concerned about them. The lawyer's instructions were that we were only allowed to bring one maidservant to London—"

"And Nanny insisted she was too old to be racketing around London, so we brought Betty," Miss Studley added.

"So we had to leave Nanny and the others behind, not knowing what their future would be. Do you have any idea, Lord Salcott?" Isobel Burton's voice was low and melodious and velvety, a kind of audible honey.

Which was a ridiculous notion, Leo told himself sternly.

Honey was not audible. Besides, his job here was to free Miss Studley from her half sister's influence.

And not to drool over her.

"The staff at Studley Park Manor are nothing to do with me," he said. Damn Studley—yet another responsibility the man had dodged.

Isobel Burton leaned forward. "Perhaps not, but you can make inquiries on their behalf, can you not, Lord Salcott?" Her voice was soft and seductive, her eyes luminous and full of apparent sincerity.

Leo stiffened. Lavinia had used just such caressing tones. They'd meant nothing, except that she wanted something. Such tactics no longer had any effect on him, he vowed.

"Oh yes, please do," Miss Studley said.

"As I said, it is not my concern."

"But you could ask," Isobel Burton insisted. "We asked the lawyer, Mr. Melkin, about the situation with the servants, but he brushed our concerns aside, saying that such matters were nothing we should bother our pretty heads about." She snorted. "As if we had half a brain between us. But I'm sure if a man asked, especially a lord . . ."

Leo was not used to having his pronouncements questioned. He would investigate—elderly servants callously abandoned after a lifetime of loyal service? Studley should have been shot. But Leo did not want her—want these girls to get the impression that he'd jump through hoops at h—at *their* request.

He changed the subject. "So you found the journey interesting, Miss Studley. And are you looking forward to living in London?"

She hesitated, glanced at her half sister and said uncertainly, "I suppose so. The thing is, we have never been to London, and we found the sights quite strange, though fascinating of course. It took the coachman a while to find Mr. Melkin's address in the city, and then he had to find this place. The streets were so crowded and busy—especially in the city—and some were so narrow we weren't sure that the coach could fit through. And the houses are all so close together—I don't know how anyone manages to breathe."

Miss Studley was a chatty, soft cushion of a girl, Leo decided. A little shy, and not particularly pretty, but docile and due to inherit a fortune. She would not find it difficult to find a suitable husband. Miss Isobel Burton, however . . .

Lord, if she really did want to set up as a courtesan, she would have no trouble finding protectors. They would be lining up for her favors. The thought tasted sour in his mouth.

Though she did not act like a would-be courtesan. Her dress was quietly elegant and not at all provocative.

He glanced at her again and caught her looking around the room. She made no attempt to hide her curiosity. "Have you just bought this house, Lord Salcott?"

"No, but it has been leased out for the last ten years. As you can see, it's become shabby and is now in need of refurbishing. Which has only just begun."

"Oh, I see." She glanced at her half sister. "Clarissa and I did wonder when we saw that most of the rooms were empty." She finished on a note of faint inquiry, and he realized she was wondering where they would be expected to sleep.

"You will be staying with my aunt, Lady Scattergood," he said crisply.

Her face cleared. "Oh, so that is why your man—Matteo is it?—ordered Billy—he's the coachman—-not to unload our bags."

"Indeed," Leo said. So, she was the kind of girl who knew the names of servants. He turned back to Miss Studley. "You will enjoy exploring the more well-known sights of London, I am sure."

"Oh, yes," Miss Studley said. "We are looking forward to oh, so many things—the crown jewels, of course, and the wild beasts at the Royal Exchange, and Vauxhall Gardens and the fireworks, and plays—Izzy and I have never seen a play. And I suppose there will be balls and parties, and if we are lucky, someone will procure us vouchers for Almack's."

Us? Leo glanced at Isobel Burton sitting so demurely on the chaise longue. Did she imagine she would be entering society on her half sister's coattails? She did, he saw. They both did.

Damn. He would have to squash those expectations immediately. He'd been hoping to leave it to his aunt, but he supposed it would be better coming from him.

Miss Studley was burbling on about the delights in store. "Of course, we are so looking forward to shopping in the capital. We've heard so much about it. The Pantheon Bazaar, the Western Exchange in Bond Street—we passed Bond Street on the way here—"

"Hatchards bookshop," her half sister interjected.

"Oh yes, we are desperate for new books, and then of course we will want new dresses for our come-out—the village dressmaker is good, but she is not au courant with the latest fashions. Perhaps your aunt—"

Leo stopped the eager flow with a raised hand. "Spare me! I know nothing of feminine fashions." His aunt, as they would discover, knew even less, but that wasn't his concern. "Just have your bills sent to me and they will be taken care of."

He turned to the half sister. "And you, Miss Burton, what are your plans? Are you seeking employment? Perhaps I could help you find something suited to someone in your position."

"*Someone in her position?*" Miss Studley glanced at him, surprised. "Izzy will make her come-out with me, of course. And—"

"I'm afraid that's not possible," Leo said. "The circumstances of her birth—"

"Are not her fault." Miss Studley cut him off vehemently.

"Izzy and her mother were very badly treated by my father—*our* father—"

"Who ain't in heaven," her half sister interjected sotto voce. "Unhallowed be his name . . . because of course, he's in the other place."

Leo gave her a sharp look. She responded with a faint mischievous smile and raised one shoulder in an infinitesimal shrug. Nothing shy or demure about this one, Leo thought.

Miss Studley continued, "And Izzy does not deserve to be punished for their sins."

"Be that as it may," Leo responded, "society has very high standards and—"

"Nonsense," Miss Studley said crisply. Leo blinked. Not quite the docile cushion he'd thought her. She went on, "We might be from the country, Lord Salcott, and we might never have been to London, but we do read the newspapers and we're not completely ignorant. The royal princes have bastard children who move freely in society and—"

He cut her off. "The offspring of royalty have privileges that the illegitimate child of a mere baronet does not."

"But many of the leaders of society have children who it's widely known were not fathered by their mothers' husbands."

"They were, however, born in wedlock," he countered, "and as long as their putative fathers do not reject them, the law considers them legitimate. They are, therefore, acceptable in society."

"This very kingdom was founded by William the Conqueror, who was famously a bastard," she persisted.

"And the world has changed a great deal since then," Leo said firmly. "The truth is, Miss Studley, like it or not Miss Burton will not be accepted by society, and you will be making your come-out alone."

She drew herself up. "No, Lord Salcott, we will make it

together. And you will address my sister as Miss Studley, if you please."

Leo sighed. He did not please. The cushion was proving annoyingly argumentative. Oh, it was all said in a sweet, soft voice, but there was steel beneath that demure appearance. As for the half sister, if the glint in those extraordinary green eyes was anything to go by, she was sitting back and enjoying the show.

Again he averted his eyes. A man could drown in those eyes—if he weren't careful, of course. Leo had learned to be very careful.

Matteo entered then with a tray bearing the tea things, and a plate of small cakes filled with cream. He bustled around pouring the tea, adding milk, lemon or sugar as requested and handing around the cups.

The moment he left the room, Leo said, "Your half sister has no right to the Studley surname."

Miss Studley lifted her chin. "My *sister* was christened Isobel Burton Studley. You may address her as Miss Studley or, since she is slightly the younger, you may call her Miss Isobel when we are together. To avoid confusion." Her smile was sweet but implacable.

He glanced at the half sister. She was pretending to take no notice of the conversation—though that of course must be nonsense. She sipped her tea and perused the plate of cakes. Had she created this situation? Was she pulling her half sister's strings? Setting her legitimate sister up to defend her?

The witch has her claws in deep, their father had said in that letter.

Miss Burton selected a small cake filled with cream and topped with a dob of raspberry jam. She raised the cake to her mouth and slowly licked the jam away. Leo couldn't drag his eyes off her. She scooped up cream with a small pink tongue and, with a blissful expression, swallowed it.

Leo tensed, aware of every movement she made.

Slowly she devoured the little cake, lick by luscious lick, bite by tiny bite.

A groan threatened to rise in his throat. He forced it down.

She glanced up, saw him watching and blushed. "These cakes are delicious. My compliments to your cook."

"I don't have a cook yet." Leo's voice sounded hoarse. "My majordomo will have purchased them."

"Matteo?" She arched a silky dark brow. "I must ask him where he found them, then. He's a treasure, isn't he? He was *so* welcoming when we arrived."

Was that an indirect comment on the lack of welcome he'd given them? He muttered something innocuous. She leaned toward the plate of cakes, and Leo turned abruptly back to face her sister before the wench could demolish another cream cake—and his self-control.

Miss Studley, too, was in the process of eating a cream cake with every appearance of enjoyment, but she posed not the slightest threat to his composure. Leo glanced at the plate, sighed and took the last cake. It was gone in two bites. He drained his teacup and said, "Now, if you've finished your tea, I'll take you to meet my aunt."

Chapter Two

She couldn't make him out, Izzy decided as Lord Salcott ushered them out. Was he one of *those*—the sort of person who looked down on people whose birth was irregular? Or was he simply a bit awkward and stern and gruff with women?

If he was the former, he'd soon learn that she would have none of it. She'd had quite enough of that sort of treatment in her life, and things here in London were going to be different. She was determined on it.

Illegitimate people—illegitimate girls, especially— were supposed to be quiet, self-effacing and humble, grateful not to be openly scorned by their betters, who were superior by virtue of their parents having married.

She'd learned that lesson young. She'd run to help another little girl who'd fallen over. The girl's older brother had yanked Izzy backward, yelling at her, "Don't you dare touch my sister, you dirty little bastard!" And he'd shoved her in the mud and then spat on her, while some other children laughed.

That was the first time she'd heard the word *bastard*. She was four years old.

So, Lord Salcott, with his handsome face and his cold gray eyes, seemed to be the sort who prided himself on doing what he considered to be "the right thing," which in this case was squashing what he imagined to be Izzy's pretensions.

Like it or not Miss Burton will not be accepted by society, and you will be making your come-out alone.

So that was his plan. To freeze her out. Ignore her.

Izzy refused to be frozen out, by him or anyone. And Lord "I Dare You to Defy Me" Salcott would learn that Izzy was not someone to be ignored.

Much to her surprise, Lord Salcott directed them toward the back of his house. Did he keep his aunt in a shed in the back garden, then? She wouldn't be surprised. She almost asked him—she knew it would annoy him. But she resisted the temptation.

"Oh, look, Izzy, a garden!" Clarissa exclaimed as they passed through the gate at the back of the house. "And it's huge, almost a park. Hiding here behind all these houses! Oh, isn't it lovely?"

"The garden is shared by the residents of the houses that surround it," Lord Salcott began, but Clarissa wasn't listening. She wandered off, enchanted, exclaiming with delight over each discovery.

Izzy smiled. It was lovely to see Clarissa so pleased. She had been quite nervous about coming to London—not that they'd had any choice. She'd put on a good show in front of Lord Salcott, pretending she was looking forward to visiting famous places and exploring the shops, and Izzy knew she would end up enjoying them. Eventually. But her enthusiasm about the garden was spontaneous and genuine.

"I gather Miss Studley is fond of flowers," Lord Salcott said when it became clear that Clarissa wasn't returning anytime soon.

Was he being sardonic again? Izzy wasn't sure.

He cleared his throat. "Perhaps while your half sister is exploring the garden I could have a quiet word with you, Miss Burton."

Izzy didn't respond. He'd been asked to call her Miss Studley or Miss Isobel, and if he chose to ignore it, so be it. It was, perhaps, a little childish, but she would ignore him.

"Miss Burton?" he repeated.

As if he hadn't spoken at all, Izzy examined a dainty fuchsia bush with every sign of fascination.

"Miss Burton!"

She glanced around vaguely. He frowned at her. "You are not deaf, I presume."

"Oh no," she said blithely. "I didn't realize you were talking to me, that's all. I don't answer to that name, you see." She gave him a sweet smile.

His eyes narrowed. "Then you'd better get used to it."

She bent toward a rosebush and inhaled the fragrance of a blowsy yellow bloom.

"I have a proposition for you," he said.

Izzy stiffened, and slowly turned to face him.

"I am prepared to settle a handsome sum on you."

She arched an eyebrow and waited, her expression as bland as she could make it. Her pulse was racing. Her fingers had curled into fists. Not this, surely?

"Enough for you to purchase a home of your own, along with an annual allowance." He named a sum that would indeed support her in comfort, if not in luxury. "The allowance would, of course, cease if you married. The house would remain yours."

"I see. And what would you expect of me in exchange for such largesse?" She tried to keep the acid from her voice. It was not the first time a man had made her a dishonorable proposition, but she hadn't expected it from Clarissa's guardian. And certainly not within the first hour of meeting him.

"Leave. Disappear. Remove yourself entirely from Miss Studley's company. Have no further communication with her."

She narrowed her eyes. "None at all?"

He gave a curt nod. "Your association with Miss Studley must cease. Completely."

"And for abjuring the company of my sister you will give me a house and a handsome allowance? I don't have to do anything else?"

"No. As long as you stay away from her, you can do as you like."

She hadn't expected that. She'd been braced for quite another sort of offer. Which, to do him credit, he had not made. Still . . . "Why would you do such a thing?"

He said stiffly, "It is only what your father should have done in the first place."

Izzy glanced away, struggling with her emotions. Her father *should* have provided for her. He especially should have provided for her mother. After everything that Mama had done—and put up with—so that she and Izzy could survive . . .

An offer like this would have made all the difference in the world to their lives. Would still make a difference to hers.

A home of her own. Security. It had been a dream of hers for so long.

But to demand that she abandon her sister . . .

Izzy found she was shaking with anger.

She raised her chin and looked him square in the eye. "In a just world, my father would have made provision for my mother and me long ago. But to offer belated justice now, and with such a condition attached . . ." Her lip curled. "Keep your grubby little bribe, Lord Salcott. I'll keep my sister." She turned on her heel and marched down a random path.

She would show him. Abandon Clarissa? Better men

than he had tried to separate them. Well, no, not better men. Only Papa, really, and nobody could ever call Papa "better."

She marched on, brooding over Lord Salcott's offer, oblivious of the beauty of the garden, the fresh green foliage, the profusion of flowers. She could hear muffled little exclamations of pleasure from her sister and slowly made her way toward them. There were so many paths winding through the garden; it was a good place to get lost in.

She stopped and took several long deep breaths. It was tempting to storm off and tell Clarissa about his attempt to bribe her—her sister would be furious, too—but it would only upset her. And Lord Salcott was Clarissa's guardian, after all. She would have to work with him.

And it wasn't an ungenerous offer, just an unreasonable one. Totally unreasonable.

She noticed a clump of lamb's ears and bent to pick a leaf. It reminded her of the lambs they'd fed when she and Clarissa were small. She stood stroking its furry silvery leaf reflectively.

Those hard, gray, judgmental eyes. And what did he think he was playing at in that first interview, pretending he was talking to Clarissa all the time? He might not be talking to Izzy, but he wasn't ignoring her, either. Was that masculine speculation lurking in his gaze? It was hard to tell.

It was a shame he was such a closed-minded cold fish of a man. He was otherwise quite good-looking. She scowled. And didn't he know it?

Her father's male guests all considered themselves fine fashionable fellows—dandies even—but this man put them all to shame with his severely pruned-back elegance: snug-fitting buff breeches, an elegantly cut dark blue coat, a stylish neckcloth and gleaming top boots. No jangle of fobs and seals for him, either, just a plain gold watch chain.

But "handsome is as handsome does," as Nanny used to say. Izzy tossed the lamb's ear aside. Lord Salcott seemed intent on squashing Izzy and her imagined pretensions like a bug. Before he knew whether she even had any pretensions.

And you, Miss Burton, what are your plans?

She snorted.

He was a challenge Izzy couldn't resist. She was neither quiet nor humble, and she had not the slightest intention of currying favor with a man who looked down his long, aristocratic nose at her.

Lord Salcott would learn, if not to respect her, then at least not to underestimate her.

"There you are, Izzy," Clarissa exclaimed behind her. "Oh my goodness. A Spong!"

Izzy jumped backward, brushing her dress down and looking around. "What? Where?"

"Right in front of you, silly."

Izzy couldn't see anything that looked like a spong, whatever that was. "Where?"

"There." Clarissa pointed at the rose bush Izzy had been staring at without really noticing.

She peered closer. The flowers were small and pink. "I can't see any spongs. What do they look like?"

Clarissa gave a gurgle of laughter. "It's the name of that rose. I haven't seen one until now, but I've read about them, and they're small, but the fragrance is supposed to be . . ." She buried her nose in the rose and inhaled blissfully. "Oh, Izzy you have to smell this. It's glorious." She bent to smell it again.

Izzy didn't move. "Spong? Someone named this pretty little rose a *Spong*? Why would anyone do such a thing. It's practically an act of vandalism."

Clarissa laughed again. "I don't care. I'm just thrilled to find one growing here. Whoever designed this garden did a wonderful job. They have the most marvelous collection of roses, and each with a delicious fragrance. I've been smelling them all. There are several kinds of moss roses including a stunning Pink Moss, an Old Blush China that smells divine, a Marie Louise, a Celestial, a—"

"How delightful," Izzy interrupted her. Clarissa could go on forever about roses. To Izzy a rose was just a rose, but to her sister they were a whole world.

"I wonder who I'd have to ask to see if I can harvest them—" Clarissa began.

"Miss Studley," a grim voice grated through the shrubbery. And then a few seconds later, and a little bit louder: "Miss *Studley*! Are you there?"

Izzy giggled. "I'm guessing the Grumpy Guardian is getting sick of waiting."

Dismayed, Clarissa clapped her hand over her mouth. "Oh dear, I forgot all about him."

"The perfect way to handle him," Izzy said.

"No, it was dreadfully uncivil. He was taking us to meet his aunt. Come, Izzy, hurry." Clarissa hastened down a pathway toward the deep impatient voice.

Leo tapped his foot, waiting for the girls to reappear. Miss Burton had stormed off, magnificent—and infuriating—in her anger, hips swaying enticingly. Which he refused to notice.

Her reaction had surprised him. He'd been sure she would jump at the offer. It was generous—far more generous than she might have expected. *Grubby little bribe* indeed. It was more than her father had done for her.

So why the devil should she be angry? It was a perfectly respectable—and handsome—offer. Her ire would be more understandable if he'd made an offer of a less reputable kind. He frowned. Was that what she'd been expecting? A dishonorable proposition?

He thought about the accusations her father had made in his letter.

But even if she did plan to be a courtesan, why would his offer make her angry? He hadn't put any conditions on it, except to stay away from her half sister. She could live in the house he provided and still·be a courtesan.

No, it was the requirement that she not see her sister that had made her angry.

Keep your grubby little bribe . . . I'll keep my sister.

Was it loyalty or opportunism? Loyalty he could respect, though it was blasted inconvenient. But she could equally have meant that his offer was too small to interest her.

Damned if he could work her out.

Was she after marriage and respectability? Not an unreasonable desire for a baseborn woman, he supposed. With her looks she could easily find a husband, even without a dowry or any kind of fortune.

But surely she wasn't so naive as to imagine she could enter society along with her half sister? He obviously hadn't made that clear enough to her. To them.

He scanned the garden again. Where the hell had they gone? The garden was thickly planted and crisscrossed with pathways, and he knew if he went searching for them, it would end up as a wild-goose chase. Damned if he'd chase after them.

At his feet was a cleared patch of earth where a single weed was growing. He was no gardener, but he knew that once a weed got established, it could take over. He pulled it out and tossed it aside.

He straightened, hearing the murmur of feminine voices and a laugh or two. "Miss Studley?" he called. Silence. They'd heard him, then. He raised his voice and called again.

Just as he was about to give up and leave them to the fruits of their folly, they appeared.

"I'm so sorry to keep you waiting, Lord Salcott," Miss Studley exclaimed breathlessly. "First I lost track of time and then I was lost—so many paths winding around. But oh, this garden is so very beautiful. I will be so much happier living in London now I have this place to refresh myself in."

He glanced at Isobel Burton. Her creamy complexion glowed in the fresh air, a faint, wild-rose flush tinting her cheeks. She'd taken off her hat. Dark tendrils danced in the breeze.

Catching him staring, she lifted her chin, her expression otherwise unreadable. Had she told her half sister about their conversation? The *grubby little bribe*? He couldn't tell.

She moistened her lips with a sweep of her small pink tongue. He wrenched his gaze off her. "My aunt's house is over there. Come along. She will be expecting you." Matteo had directed the girls' carriage to her address, and their luggage would already be transferred to their bedchambers.

This time, since his aunt had already been warned, he entered through the back door. The moment they passed into the main part of the house, they were besieged by the usual host of yappy little dogs. Both girls fell to their knees, laughing as they embraced the excited little beasts.

He looked up to find his aunt standing in the hallway, watching with a benevolent smile. "I like these gels of yours," she told him. "They show a great deal of sense."

They weren't "his girls," nor did he think kneeling on a cold floor to allow a bunch of excitable little mongrels to jump all over them and dirty their dresses was particularly sensible, but since little Biddy had limped painfully out with the others and was now sitting at his feet gazing adoringly up at him, he could hardly argue.

He scooped up the pathetic little creature and followed his aunt and the girls into the sitting room—the other dogs frolicking around the girls' ankles.

Eyeing the little dog in his arms, Isobel Burton gave him an odd sideways look and quirked an eyebrow. Leo ignored her. If he wanted to carry around a battered little scrap of canine refuse, he would. It was nobody's business but his own.

His aunt called for tea and sandwiches. "They've already had tea and cakes," he told her. He didn't think he could stand the sight of Isobel Burton lavishing her attention on another cream cake.

Aunt Olive dismissed that with an airy wave. "Pooh, young gels are always hungry. Besides, whatever they don't eat, the dogs will." She produced her lorgnette and scrutinized the girls. "Well, missy, it's easy to tell who *your* father was," she said to Miss Burton. "Dreadful man. My commiserations."

"On his death?" Miss Burton asked.

"Good God, no—that's grounds for congratulations, I would have thought. I meant commiserations on having him for a father. I imagine he made an appalling parent. Always said he should have been drowned at birth. Same for this fellow's father." She jerked a thumb at Leo and added impatiently, "Well, don't dillydally, boy. Introduce us. Which gel is which? I can't keep calling them 'missy' or 'you there.'"

Leo introduced them, and then his aunt introduced each dog by name—not that Leo remembered which was which, apart from the one on his lap—and they all took their seats, the two girls sitting side by side on a chaise longue.

The females made chitchat. The butler and a maidservant brought in tea trays, one of which contained a plate of biscuits and a dish of dainty triangular sandwiches. The dogs, scenting the food, immediately assumed the saintly and pathetic mien of dogs on the verge of starvation.

Leo let the conversation wash over him. He was very aware of Isobel Burton's gaze touching on him from time to time. He was damnably aware of her. And how the hell could she unsettle him merely by being in the same room? It was . . . disturbing.

He watched as she leaned forward, selected a tiny sandwich, and bit off a small neat bite. She chewed meditatively, swallowed, then sipped her tea.

And why, wondered Leo furiously, should that be so compelling? It was a perfectly ordinary sandwich. He took one and ate it in two bites. Ham. Nothing special.

His aunt was on one of her usual rants. Apparently, Sir Bartleby had never allowed the girls any kind of pet, which she condemned as heartless and verging on the villainous.

Isobel Burton's vivid green eyes danced as she agreed solemnly that yes, it was quite unforgivable in a parent.

He dropped his gaze—she was too knowing, that one— and found himself watching in fascination as her long, slender fingers caressed the ears of one of the little dogs.

The girls told some sort of story about how they'd tried to tame one of the barn cats, but it was perfectly wild and would never allow them to get near enough. They told the tale together, finishing each other's sentences. Miss Studley's voice was light and breathy; Miss Burton's was mesmerizing, low and melodious.

"Oh well, cats," his aunt said, disgusted. "You should have had a puppy." And she went into another long rant about the glory of dogs.

Isobel Burton's fingers caressed the dog's silky ears. She glanced at him again, and caught him watching her. Her gaze briefly dropped to the small creature on his own lap, then returned to eye him thoughtfully.

Leo could stand it no more. Setting down the little dog, he lurched abruptly to his feet. Three feminine glances were directed at him, with varying expressions.

"Something bite you, nephew?" his aunt said caustically.

"My apologies, Aunt Olive, ladies. I've just recollected an urgent appointment and must hurry away." Inclining his head toward the sisters, he added, "I shall leave you ladies to get settled in. Miss Studley, I will call on you in a day or two to discuss what to do about your come-out."

"*Our* come-out," Miss Studley corrected him sweetly

and slipped an arm around her half sister's slender waist. The half sister smiled and batted her impossibly long eyelashes at him. Sheer, defiant mockery.

Gritting his teeth, Leo left. He marched across the garden, stepped through the open doorway of his house and stopped, appalled at the noise, dust and general chaos of dozens of workers.

Then recalling he no longer had any need to remain in the blasted house, he took himself off to the blissful peace and masculine sanity of his club.

Lady Scattergood's home was as eccentric as the lady herself, Izzy decided. It was filled with all kinds of exotic items from all corners of the globe. Fascinating Indian statues, one with many arms, another with an elephant head on a human body. There were fat little gold Buddhas, richly carved screens, embroidered fabric drapes studded with tiny glittering mirrors, furniture with animal heads and feet, and carpets, thick, rich carpets of exquisite design, layered every which way across the floor. There were also dozens of dog statues and paintings, from Chinese temple dogs to ordinary English china figurines. And not a cat to be seen.

Everything was cluttered together in a vivid multicolored explosion that had no rhyme or reason that Izzy could discern. It was vibrant and whimsical and eccentric, and Izzy loved it.

Lady Scattergood herself sat like some outlandish queen in a large, elaborately carved chair with a spreading peacock-tail-shaped back. Both she and the chair were draped with a multitude of vibrantly colored shawls in silk and cashmere.

"Eat up, gels, eat up," she urged. While they ate sandwiches—because Lord Salcott's cream cakes might have been delicious, but they had not appeased their hunger—she talked about her dogs and explained how she'd come across each. "It's disgraceful how some people treat animals. Abandoning innocent and loving creatures to somehow survive as best they can."

She fell silent for a moment, then leaned forward portentously. A silk shawl slithered unnoticed to the floor. "My nephew tells me he intends to find you gels husbands—is that true?"

Clarissa, caught with her mouth full of sandwich, simply nodded.

Lady Scattergood tsked loudly. "An appalling idea. I advise against it. The only reason for marriage is children, and you only need a man once for that, I believe. Having them hanging around afterward is just a nuisance."

Izzy and Clarissa blinked and carefully did not look at each other.

"Scattergood and I had the perfect marriage. He sailed off to India a few weeks after the wedding, saying he would send for me when he was settled, but of course he forgot, which suited me perfectly. He traveled extensively in Foreign Parts and made an enormous fortune, and then, just when he was set to return to England, he died most conveniently of a fever." She gestured to her cluttered surroundings. "All this came home in the ship bearing his ashes—that's him in that green cloisonné urn on the mantelpiece." She sighed reminiscently. "Ours was an ideal marriage. I was never so fond of him as when he left. Even fonder, of course, when he died and left me his fortune."

Izzy did not dare to look at Clarissa for fear she would give way to unseemly laughter. "How long was he gone for?" she asked once she had mastered herself.

"Twenty years? Thirty? I can't recall. A good long time, at any rate." She adjusted one of the shawls that kept sliding off her bony shoulders, and smiled at the girls. "So if you insist on taking the plunge into marriage, I recommend you choose a man who is set on going to live in Foreign Parts.

As long as he doesn't expect you to go with him of course. That would never do."

"But what about children?" Clarissa asked.

"Oh, dogs are just as good as children—better really. A good deal less trouble, too. The things some of my friends' children have put them through. Dreadful. And they often seem to grow up so ungrateful. No, dear, give me dogs any day."

She lifted her lorgnette and peered at the tea tray, which was now just a collection of crumbs. "Finished your sandwiches? Good. You can take the dogs out now. Not in the back garden, curse it—dogs are banned—blasted busybodies—nothing wrong with good honest dog poop, but no! My dogs are banned from my own backyard! Disgraceful. So you need to go to the other place—Jeremiah will show you. He'll do the necessary as well. There are busybodies everywhere."

"'The necessary'?" Izzy asked.

"Yes," Lady Scattergood said. "Jeremiah usually takes them out, but after being cooped up in that coach, it'll do you gels good to stretch your legs. It's all right, you'll be perfectly safe with Jeremiah. He's still a pup. Now, run along, gels, your bedchambers are on the second floor. And make sure you wear warm coats and rug up well—it's chilly outside."

The girls hurried away and ran upstairs to fetch their coats and hats, though it wasn't the slightest bit cold. At the top of the stairs they stopped, looked at each other and burst into giggles.

"What an extraordinary old lady," Clarissa said.

"She's wonderful," Izzy said. "I nearly burst trying to keep from laughing aloud. Her 'perfect marriage'—"

"And dogs are better than children?" Still chuckling, they turned to find their bedchambers. Betty had already unpacked their things, and it was the work of a moment to don coats and hats to go out.

"I don't mind walking her dogs," Clarissa said as they headed downstairs again. "But who is this Jeremiah, who is still a pup? And what is he supposed to protect us from?"

"I don't know but if 'the necessary' that he will take care of is what I think it is, I'm extremely grateful he's coming with us. Ah, I'm guessing that this must be he," Izzy added as a thin, spotty footman of about fourteen appeared in the hall below, leading the dogs on leashes. Though *leading* was a slight misnomer; the five little dogs were leaping excitedly about like fish on a line. The boy carried the sixth, the one with the injured leg. The one Lord Salcott had been so gentle with.

Such a difficult man to work out.

After distributing the dog leads between the three of them, Jeremiah led them out the front door and down the street. At the corner, Clarissa glanced back. "It's amazing. If you didn't know, you wouldn't have any idea that there's a beautiful garden behind all these houses."

Jeremiah took them to a nearby park, larger but not as pretty as the one behind Lady Scattergood's house. They strolled along, unable to walk very fast as the dogs insisted on sniffing everything and "christening" every second tree they passed. Jeremiah lagged behind, dealing with "the necessary."

"I can see why the dogs were banned from the garden," Clarissa murmured.

"Not exactly a glamorous job, poor boy," Izzy agreed.

"Oh, it's not so bad, miss," Jeremiah said, overhearing. "Better'n sleepin' in the streets, which is what I was doing when Lady Scatters found me."

"In the streets?" Clarissa asked. Entering a railed park, they unleashed the dogs to let them run freely.

He nodded. "Yeah, me mam was dead, I was just a nipper, and things was looking pretty grim. The old lady saw me from her carriage—she used to go out more in them days. She reckoned I fainted, but I never did. I just, um, fell down. Nothin' to eat for a few days. Made me dizzy it did. Anyway, she had her coachman pick me up outta the gutter and she took me home, give me a bath—just like the dogs. She reckoned I had fleas. I probably did, too—and told me I weren't never going back to the gutter." He grinned. "I know she seems a little bit cracked, but she's got a heart of gold, I reckon."

"And now you work for her," Izzy said.

"Yep, and I get as much food as I can eat, and these fine clothes"—he smoothed the sleeve of his smart olive and silver-gray livery—"and a bed of me own to sleep in. Wiv sheets and all. And all I got to do is walk the mutts twice a day and clean up after them, and run any errands people want. Old Treadwell—'e's the butler—is teaching me to read and write and figure—they're training me to be a footman or summat. *And* on top of all that, I get paid a bob a week." He glanced at one of the dogs. "Whoops, there goes Minnie." He darted off to do the necessary.

Izzy looked at Clarissa. "Now I like Lady Scattergood even more."

"Yes, she sounds very kind."

"Unlike her very annoying nephew."

"Yes, he's rather cold, isn't he? And he won't even try to help us with the situation with our Studley Park people." Clarissa wrinkled her nose. "'Not my concern,' he says, but Nanny and the others gave our family years of service. And now they might simply be turned off without even a pension. It's perfectly shaming."

"I know." Izzy knew she shouldn't feel guilty about it, but she did.

"If the cousin doesn't take them on, they'll never find another position. Who would employ an elderly nanny who falls asleep during the day?" Clarissa sighed. "I think we'll have to forgo the new dresses and other things we planned on. I couldn't possibly enjoy a shopping spree knowing that Nanny and some of the others could be left destitute."

"It's my fault," Izzy said.

"Of course it's not. It's Papa's fault. It was his responsibility."

"Yes, but it's because the servants never gave me up to him. He's punishing them for their disloyalty."

"Nonsense, they were completely loyal."

"To *you*, not to him," Izzy pointed out.

"No, they were loyal to *us*. Or, if you want to get pedantic, to me as the daughter of the house and later to you because they liked you. And because they know you are truly Papa's daughter."

Izzy pulled a skeptical face and Clarissa laughed. "Well, all right, they didn't *all* love you—especially when they didn't know you at first, but even though some of them really didn't approve, they still helped me to keep you."

Izzy nodded. "I know." It was true that some of the servants liked her, but some of them, well, the way they saw it, she was no better than they were—worse, even, because they at least had been born in wedlock. And to their way of thinking Izzy had no right to be there, living in the big house and hobnobbing with the master's daughter as if they were equals.

It was out of loyalty to Clarissa that they never betrayed Izzy's whereabouts to her father. Clarissa could have had them dismissed if they did, and they knew it. But fear and envy didn't make people kind. It was only when they found themselves alone with Izzy that they let her know it. Clarissa never knew about it. Izzy never let on. It would only have upset her.

Clarissa continued, "In any case, Papa has failed in his responsibilities yet again, and I cannot let it pass. I will write to his cousin and ask what he plans to do. I'm not sure how much is left of my quarterly allowance, but perhaps there will be enough to tide them over until we can sort things out."

"And if the cousin won't employ them?"

"Then I will write to my trustees and see if they will cover Papa's responsibilities."

Izzy gave her a skeptical look. "They won't." Clarissa's trustees were almost fanatical in ensuring not a penny of her money went to her father, and she was certain covering his responsibilities to his servants would come under the same heading, even though he was dead.

They walked on. Izzy glanced back to see where Jeremiah was and said in a low voice, "Lord Salcott tried to bribe me earlier."

Clarissa turned to her. "What?"

Izzy explained.

"That's outrageous!" Clarissa said, shocked. "I can't believe he would offer you money to abandon me."

Izzy linked her arm with her sister's. "He has no idea who he's dealing with. Don't worry, love, I won't abandon you."

"I know that, silly. But what makes him think he can separate us?"

"Ignorance," Izzy said. "And arrogance. He'll learn."

"Perhaps," Clarissa said darkly. "As for this nonsense about you not making a come-out with me—"

Izzy wrinkled her nose. "I suspect he might be right about that."

Clarissa turned her head sharply. "He is *not* right. He's a hypocritical bully and unreasonably prejudiced."

Izzy shook her head. She'd given it some thought. "He's definitely arrogant, but I think he thinks he's protecting you, 'Riss."

"Protecting me? From whom?"

"From me."

"Oh, that's ridiculous."

"It's not. It's one thing for most of the servants at Studley Park to accept me eventually, but society, particularly the ton, is a whole other thing. The ton prides itself on its exclusivity, and the kind of people they work to exclude is bastards like me."

Clarissa snorted. "That's so hypocritical. What about all those people—well-respected members of society at that—who are illegitimate in fact, if not law?"

"I know, but perhaps because they're only respectable by the skin of their teeth, it makes them more determined to keep out people like me who are illegitimate in fact *and* in law."

"Well, it's wrong."

Izzy shrugged. "It's life. But truly, I don't care about balls and routs and things. I'd be quite happy to miss all that fuss."

Clarissa gave her a skeptical look. "Hah! Don't expect me to swallow such nonsense—you would love all those parties and things. I'm the one who finds them nerve-racking, and I need you with me, Izzy. Without you I won't be able to stand it."

"You could, if only you tried. It might be hard at first but—"

"Hard? You know I have no conversation—I never know what to say to people. I especially never know what to say to men. And I can't flirt to save my life!"

"It's just a matter of practice I'm sure, like everything else," Izzy said hopefully.

"Besides, I need you to help me judge whether a man is sincere, or more interested in my inheritance than in me. My biggest dread is to fall for a man who is pretending to be nice but will turn out to be just like Papa. You are so good at seeing who people really are behind their false smiles."

There was some truth in that, Izzy acknowledged. When you were baseborn and penniless, you developed a sensitivity to people's true natures. Over the years she'd become quite good at detecting the attitudes beneath the surface, picking up the little telltale signs that the sentiments people expressed weren't those they truly felt. People often didn't consider her worth hiding their baser selves from.

She wondered about Lord Salcott's true nature. On the surface he seemed hard and even a bit ruthless, but then there was the way he'd treated that little dog. And he seemed very patient with the eccentricities of his aunt.

Jeremiah returned, and they collected the dogs and made their way back to Lady Scattergood's, walking in silence as if, like the dogs, they had expended their excess energy in the park.

The truth was, Izzy reflected, that while Clarissa had courage, she badly lacked confidence. A lifetime of being belittled and derided by her father had done untold damage. And her mother hadn't helped, either.

Izzy's own mother had loved her and had encouraged her to face the world with courage. Even though the world had been so harsh toward her.

But Clarissa's mother seemed to have accepted her husband's contemptuous attitude toward both her and her daughter. From everything Izzy had heard, Clarissa's mother made excuses for his behavior, implying that she and Clarissa didn't deserve any better, that they were plain and not of the aristocracy, and really, it was only the fortune that Great-Grandpapa Iverley had settled on them that had made them acceptable to Sir Bartleby. And they should be grateful for that.

Izzy didn't think much of Clarissa's mother. Giving in to bullies just encouraged them. Bullies needed to be stood up to.

It was only when Sir Bartleby tried to take Izzy away that Clarissa had found the courage to stand up to her father. And she'd become stronger as a result.

However, the poison Clarissa's mother and father had

fed into her ears over the years still festered. She had no faith in her own attractiveness. Or her worthiness to be loved. Except by Izzy.

Now Clarissa was faced with having to be launched into high society, knowing no one. And Lord Salcott wanted her to do it alone?

No, Izzy wouldn't abandon her sister, not for all the money in the world.

Chapter Three

Leo was just about to mount the stairs at the entrance to his club, when a tall, lanky figure emerged. It was one of his oldest friends. "Race!" he exclaimed.

Horatio, Lord Randall—Race to his friends—shook Leo's hand heartily. "Good lord, Leo, where did you spring from? I had no idea you were even back in England."

"Just got back last week," Leo explained, and then, noticing his friend was dressed in buckskin breeches and riding boots, he added, "Am I holding you up?"

Race shook his head. "Not at all. Just off for a ride. Blow away the cobwebs. Care to join me?"

"Just give me ten minutes to change," Leo said, and hurried up to his room. A short time later, dressed for riding, he joined Race at the front of the club. "I'll need to hire a—" He broke off, seeing a groom waiting with two saddled horses.

"Organized a mount for you while you were changing," Race said. "Where would you prefer, Hyde Park or Hampstead Heath?"

"The heath," Leo said. "I want a good long gallop." He glanced at his friend and added, "I *need* a good long gallop."

Race laughed. "Then let's go. You can tell me all about it once we've blown the cobwebs away."

Vigorous exercise in the fresh air did wonders for Leo's mood, and as he and Race threaded their way back through the London traffic, he reflected that of all the people he had run into, he couldn't have found any better confidant.

Race had a rakish reputation in society and was generally thought to be a frivolous kind of fellow, but Leo knew better. He'd known Race since school.

Leo's mother had died when he was seven, after which his grieving father couldn't stand to look at him, saying he looked too much like his mother. So, still grieving himself, Leo had been flung with no warning into boarding school, where the boys were big and loud and made a small boy nervous.

Desperately lonely and unhappy, he tried not to shame himself by crying into his pillow at night. Most of the time he succeeded.

But somehow, one of the boys found out something nasty about his mother, and he told the other boys, and they started teasing him about it. Of course Leo wasn't going to stand for having his beloved mother insulted, so he fought them—or tried to.

Small as he was, he always ended up the loser, and so his mother's reputation remained a plaything for other boys, a story to be bandied around and exaggerated and embellished. To his frustration and fury and distress.

He wasn't even sure what some of the stories meant. He adored his mother, but he didn't know her very well, though he wouldn't admit that to a soul. He'd lived in the country with Nanny and the servants, and his parents lived mostly in London.

But Mama was beautiful like an angel, and when she visited and he was called down to the sitting room to speak with her, she always embraced him, and she was so soft and pretty and smelled so good, he *knew* she was lovely and kind and everything a mother should be.

And he couldn't bear people spreading hateful lies about her.

So he fought and fought, defending her reputation, and the boys beat him and mocked him, and the masters caned him for fighting, and first term wasn't even finished before Leo understood that school was the worst place in the whole world.

He was in detention one day, kept in for getting into another fight. His face was bruised and sore from the fighting, and his backside ached from the caning he'd received. Caught between anger at the injustice of it all—why didn't anyone stop them spreading evil lies about his mother?—and utter misery and loneliness, he was copying out some tract that he'd been given, something stupid in Latin about the futility of violence, when another boy entered the room. It was clear that he'd just been caned, too, for the master who escorted him said sternly, "And let that be a lesson to you," or words to that effect.

The boy winked at Leo as he passed him and took a seat a few aisles across from him. Leo knew who he was: Randall, though some of the others called him Race, Leo didn't know why. Randall was a few years older than Leo, a tall, popular boy who made the other boys laugh. He was always getting caned, too, though not for fighting, but for playing pranks.

The master set Randall an assignment, ordered the boys to work in silence and left. After a few minutes, Randall said, "Why do you let them get to you?"

Leo looked up in surprise. Older boys rarely talked to

young ones, unless they were bullying them or ordering them about. But it didn't seem as though Randall planned anything mean, and in any case Leo decided he didn't care what Randall thought of him. "They say horrid things about my mother and I won't allow it."

"What does it matter what they say? Your mother is dead—she won't care."

Angered by his careless tone, Leo glared at Randall, but before he could say or do anything, Randall added quietly, "You think I don't know what it's like? My mother died three months ago."

"Oh," Leo said, shocked. "I'm sorry. I didn't know."

"No, because I haven't told a soul. And if it gets out now, I'll know who to blame."

"I would never—"

"No, but you see, if they don't know, they can't hurt you."

Leo frowned, turning it over in his mind.

Randall added, "Some of the fellows here look for vulnerability in others." Seeing that Leo didn't understand the word, he added, "Ways they can hurt or upset people. Like saying mean things about your mother. Or picking on someone because they're small or look funny or stutter or wet the bed or different in any way. They don't actually care what it is—they do it because they can."

Leo nodded. He knew he wasn't the only one who was bullied and picked on.

Randall continued, "So I pretend that nothing matters, that life is just a lark, and nobody bothers me—well, the masters do, but that's their job, I suppose. You, on the other hand, walk around with an expression on your face that might as well be a sign that reads *Kick Me*. And so they do, and you obligingly fight back, and so a boring day of dreary lessons is enlivened with a fight."

Leo could see his point, but still . . . "But I miss my mama, and I hate it when they say bad things about her."

"I know. I miss my mother, too. But do you think it

would make your mother happy to know that you're getting into fights every day, because of her?"

"No," Leo said in a small voice.

"And do you want those clods to keep winning?"

"No, but they're bigger than me."

"So be smarter."

"How?"

"Stop dancing to their tune."

"Dancing? But I'm not dan—"

"I mean reacting every time they taunt or tease you or say mean things about your mother. They only do it because they get a reaction."

"But—"

"Look, it's your choice. Keep fighting—I don't care—or learn to shrug it off. I play the clown, but you don't have to do it my way. Be a tortoise, develop a shell. You don't see a tortoise losing its temper, do you?"

"I don't know. I've never seen a tortoise."

Randall laughed. "Well, think about it anyway. Now hush, I need to get this Latin translation finished or I'll never get out of here."

Leo returned to his own exercise, but his mind was full of the ideas planted there by the older boy. The idea that you could think and *choose* how to be, instead of simply reacting. It was as if he'd been struggling grimly down a long, dark, hopeless tunnel, and suddenly there was a chink of light, showing a different path. It made all the difference in the world.

He'd watched Race Randall after that and learned that sometimes a sharp, funny comment could change the way people reacted, and that sometimes it was possible to defuse a situation without having to back down—because he refused to back down and be called a coward. Either way, it was a choice he could make.

Leo could never be the kind of witty, entertaining, popular boy that Randall was—he was too naturally serious for that—but he learned to deal with hurtful or upsetting comments designed to provoke, and to choose when to fight and when not to. And Randall had shown him another way of winning, to turn the tables on his tormenters by not reacting and appearing not to care.

After that, Leo started to make friends, and having friends, he found, made all the difference in the world at school. And despite the years between them, Race Randall remained a friend.

And years later they were still friends.

They returned to the club, bathed, changed and met again in the club dining room for dinner. After a hearty dinner of roast beef—Leo had missed good English food—a waiter brought them a very fine port, and they settled down in front of a cozy fire.

"Now, Leo," Race said, swirling his port and inhaling the aroma, "what—or should I say who—has got you all hot and bothered. A woman, is it?"

"No, not in the way you're thinking," he said, though that was a lie. "And there are two of them." He briefly explained the situation to his friend—the mistaken title in the will, the unwanted guardianship, and the problem of Studley's by-blow.

Race's brows rose. "And you've stuck them in that house with your crazy aunt?"

Leo shrugged. "No alternative."

"Tell me, does she still have those three little yappy mongrels?"

"No," Leo said, and after a moment added, "there are now six."

Race chuckled. "I almost feel sorry for these girls."

"Nonsense, they're perfectly happy there. If you're going to feel sorry for anyone, feel it for me. I'm the one who's going to be dragged into society." He pulled a face.

Race chuckled. "My heart bleeds for you." He sipped his port. "The legitimate one, the heiress—is she pretty?"

Leo thought for a moment. "Not really. More plain than otherwise. But a perfectly pleasant young woman all the same."

"Oh well, the fortune will make it easier to fire her off." He grinned and added meaningfully, "So, it's the other one, is it? Getting you all stirred up."

"What do you—no . . . of course not. Don't be ridiculous. I'm not stirred up." Aware of his oldest friend's scrutiny, he did his best to sound bored and indifferent.

Race gave a crack of laughter. "Don't tell me—Miss Whatever-her-name-is, the baseborn one, is pretty, isn't she?"

"Quite attractive," Leo said coolly. "But with no sense of her place."

"Pretty *and* spirited," Race said. "And you're wildly attracted to her and have no idea how to handle it. You try to talk to her, and your brain turns to mush and your body to steel, and you retreat, as usual, into your grumpy oyster shell."

"Oyster shell indeed," Leo said crossly. His friend was far too acute for his comfort. "What gave you such a ridiculous notion?"

Race laughed again. "How long have I known you?"

Leo mustered his dignity. "Well, you're wrong. I'm not 'all stirred up,' as you have it, I'm merely irritated."

"'Irritated'?" Is that what they're calling it now?" At Leo's snort Race leaned back with a grin. "Well, I'm delighted. About time you got over that ghastly Lascivia."

Leo scowled. "Nonsense! I haven't thought of Lavinia for years. The situation with Miss Isobel is nothing like that. It's just that as her half sister's guardian, I'm in a delicate position. Anyway, I made the girl an offer—no, get your mind out of the gutter and listen. It was a perfectly respectable—and generous—one that would have supported her in comfort, and the only condition was that she leave her half sister. Of course Studley should have done it years ago, but better late than never."

Race raised a brow. "And?"

"She didn't hesitate, flung it back in my teeth. Refuses to leave her half sister. And Clarissa—the legitimate one—is just as stubborn and insists she won't go about in society without Isobel."

Race frowned. "She can't do that. People won't stand for it. But I see your point—they're naive but stubborn. So what are you going to do?"

Leo leaned back in his chair, and contemplated the coals in the fire. "Nothing." He'd decided that when he was out riding. It was wonderful how fresh air and exercise helped clear one's mind.

Race quirked a brow. "Nothing?"

"Absolutely nothing. Leave them in the house with my aunt. They'll soon be bored to bits. They'll come to their senses eventually."

Race chuckled. "Excellent. Now, change of subject—I'm off to Tattersalls in the morning. Rumor has it that Jeavons lost a fortune at cards and has been forced to sell his grays. A matched pair, beautiful movers. Care to accompany me?"

Leo nodded. "I'll see if I can find a mount for myself at the same time. I've been envying you your gelding. A magnificent animal." Horses and masculine company would be a refreshing change from recalcitrant females and house renovations.

The following morning dawned sunny and bright, so after breakfast, since Lady Scattergood had nothing she wanted them to do, Clarissa and Izzy explored the garden. It was a magical place, with garden beds bursting with flowers, and several rose arbors that reminded Clarissa happily of her favorite spot at Studley Park. There were sunny stretches of lawn and hidden pockets of shady dells, places where one could be quite private even though the garden was surrounded by houses. Late-spring flowers were still in bloom, and Clarissa in particular was enchanted by the various fragrances.

"Oh, what a delicious combination these would make," she exclaimed as she sniffed flowers and rubbed leaves. "I must make some toilet waters from them. I brought the last batch of rose water that I made from the roses at Studley Park, but I want to keep that for special occasions. These will make a lovely light fragrance for everyday wear."

Izzy nodded. She occasionally helped Clarissa with her experiments with perfumes and fragrances, but it wasn't a passion with her as it was with Clarissa.

She tilted her head. "Did you hear that? It sounded like a child laughing."

At that instant there was another peal of laughter; obviously there were several children laughing. Izzy and Clarissa went to investigate. They hadn't met anyone in London yet, apart from Lady Scattergood and her household. And the Grumpy Guardian and his excellent Italian majordomo.

Rounding a corner, they came across a large spreading plane tree. A tall, slender lady and a small girl appeared to be talking to it. Giggles wafted down and, looking up, Izzy spied another two little girls up the tree. One of them wore a black-and-white cat draped around her neck. Its eyes glinted and its tail twitched, but it seemed quite content to be a living collar.

The tall lady turned, saw them and said with a smile, "How do you do? Isn't it a glorious morning?"

They exchanged pleasantries. The lady gave Izzy a searching look. "Forgive me, but have we met before? Your face seems oddly familiar." Then she laughed. "Oh, where are my manners? I'm sorry, I'm Alice, Lady Tarrant, and these are my stepdaughters. This is Miss Lina Tarrant, and the two in the tree are Judy and Debo Tarrant."

"And Mittens," said a voice from the tree.

"Yes, Mittens, a very important cat," Lady Tarrant agreed, her eyes twinkling.

Explaining they were newly arrived in London, they introduced themselves as Clarissa and Isobel Studley and added that they were staying with Lady Scattergood.

Lady Tarrant exclaimed, "Of course, that explains my notion that we'd met before. You must be Sir Bartleby Studley's daughter—the resemblance is really quite extraordinary."

"Did you know my father well?" Izzy asked.

"No, not well at all," Lady Tarrant said, rather abruptly. "He was a friend of my late husband." Then she added, "I have recently remarried, which is how I acquired these three delightful daughters."

"Anacat," came a voice from the tree.

"Yes, three delightful daughters and a cat. And, of course, a very handsome and wonderful husband," she added with a blush.

Izzy smiled. It was clear that Lady Tarrant was very much in love with her new husband.

"I'm delighted you're going to be one of our neighbors," Lady Tarrant said. "Have you met anyone else in Bellaire Gardens?"

"No, only Lady Scattergood."

"Well, she doesn't often go out, I gather. I've only met her a handful of times myself. But you two must come to tea. Lady Scattergood, too, of course."

"I doubt she'll come," Izzy said. "But we'd love to."

"Thank you, that would be wonderful," Clarissa agreed.

"Four o'clock this afternoon?"

"Perfect," Izzy said.

Lady Scattergood happily waved them off to tea, expressing no desire to visit her neighbor, but being otherwise quite complimentary about Lady Tarrant.

Clarissa and Izzy enjoyed themselves immensely. The tea was lavish, with cakes and fruit tarts and hot sausage rolls and all kinds of delicacies, Lady Tarrant was charming and hospitable, and the little girls—and cat—were most entertaining. As for tall, handsome Lord Tarrant, well, he was something special again.

Clarissa sighed happily as they walked back to Lady Scattergood's afterward.

"Did you see the way he looks at her, as if he completely adores her? So lovely. And he adores his children, too—and they're *daughters*."

"Yes, it gives you hope for what's possible, doesn't it?" Izzy agreed. Lord Tarrant's daughters seemed entirely confident of their father's love and approval, and he was openly affectionate toward them. None of the girls seemed at all in awe of him—they joked with him, and he teased them back—and yet it was clear he commanded their respect as well as their love.

How different would life have been for Clarissa and her if they'd had a father like Lord Tarrant?

Clarissa sighed again. "Oh, Izzy, do you think I'll ever find a man who looks at me like that?"

She sounded so wistful. "Of course you will," Izzy said stoutly. "You are completely lovable."

Clarissa wrinkled her nose. "People always say that when you're as plain as a stick. I'd much rather be pretty."

"Nonsense, you *are* pretty," Izzy insisted. "Your eyes are a lovely subtle color and you have perfect skin, and your hair—"

"Oh, stop it," Clarissa said, half laughing. "You're my sister. You're biased."

"I know, but you will find a man who will look at you the way Lord Tarrant looks at his wife, I promise."

"She's nice, isn't she? And so elegant."

"Oh," Izzy said, "I meant to tell you. I asked her whether she could recommend a dressmaker, and she told me she gets all her dresses from a Miss Chance at the House of Chance, off Piccadilly. She said Miss Chance is young, unconventional, and immensely talented. That she makes the best of each of her clients and is rapidly making a name for herself with society ladies."

Clarissa raised her brows. "How intriguing. Shall we call on her tomorr— Oh. I forgot. We can't buy anything new until we know what is happening with the servants. I wonder how long it will take for my letter to reach Papa's cousin."

"And whether he will even respond to it. Perhaps we can just walk past and look inside Miss Chance's shop," Izzy suggested. "We don't have to buy anything yet. I'm dying to explore London a little."

"But ought we go out at all tomorrow?" Clarissa said. "Didn't Lord Salcott say he'd call on us?"

"Pooh," Izzy said. "I'm not going to wait on his pleasure. If he doesn't have the decency to let us know when he's coming, he can hardly expect us to wait around indefinitely."

But when they returned to Lady Scattergood's, they found a curt note had been delivered informing them that Lord Salcott would call the following day at two o'clock and that the young ladies were to make themselves available.

Izzy glowered at the note. "He didn't even ask if it was convenient. Just issued an order. What if we had another engagement?"

"But we haven't," Clarissa said.

"We might have," Izzy insisted. "He's too high-handed for words."

I have spoken with the lawyer handling your father's affairs," Leo told Miss Studley. He and the young ladies were gathered in the front sitting room. Leo's aunt was, apparently, taking a nap. Leo waved away the butler's offer of tea. He wanted to get down to business and be gone.

Miss Burton was wearing a mulberry-colored dress that flattered her face and somehow drew his attention to her plum-satin lips. Not that he was looking.

"What about?" Miss Studley asked.

"About the servants?" Isobel Burton asked at the same time.

"Yes." He addressed Miss Studley. Much as he hated to acknowledge it, Race was right: when he looked at Miss Isobel Burton, all coherent thought vanished.

"But I thought you said it was none of your concern," Isobel Burton said.

Leo shrugged. True, it wasn't officially his area of responsibility, but he'd been disgusted by Sir Bartleby's lack of provision for Miss Burton, and for the servants who had served him and his family for most of their lives. A gentleman didn't behave in such a scaly way toward his dependents. But Leo had no intention of explaining himself.

He explained to Miss Studley, "Your father's cousin intends to keep most of the servants on. Of course, he may replace some of them if their work is not satisfactory—"

"It won't be," Isobel Burton interjected.

"But as the man is only recently married and there is no sign of children at this point, he will have no need of a nanny. In any case, I gather your former nanny is elderly, so even if his wife does conceive, he will no doubt want someone younger and more—"

"But what will happen to Nanny?" Miss Studley asked.

"There is no need to concern yourselves. She will be provided for." And that was all that Leo would say on the matter. They didn't need to know what he planned.

The two girls exchanged glances. "Does that mean we can go shopping?" Miss Studley asked.

Leo frowned. "Of course. Did I not tell you to have your bills sent to me?"

Miss Studley nodded. "Yes, but we thought we might

have to use my allowance to help Nanny and the other servants if they were dismissed."

Leo blinked. "You were planning to use your own personal allowance for that?"

"Clarissa is not like our father," Isobel Burton said. "She has a heart and a conscience."

"So I see." He still didn't look at her, though the effort was starting to give him a crick in the neck. "Well, there is no need to concern yourself, Miss Studley. You can shop to your heart's content."

"Excellent," Miss Studley said. "Thank you so much. So, have you made any arrangements yet for our come-out? We will need a lady to sponsor us. It's become quite clear that, kind as Lady Scattergood is, she does not move in society."

"Or indeed anywhere else," her half sister added.

"You mean *your* come-out, Miss Studley," he said.

Her face took on a mulish expression. "No, I mean *our* come-out. As I said the other day, Izzy and I will enter society together."

"And as I said, that will not be possible. Society will not accept someone of Miss Burton's—"

"Miss *Studley*!" Clarissa said sternly. "My sister was christened Isobel Burton Studley!"

Leo had checked into the legality of that. It seemed that though Miss Burton had no legal right to her natural father's surname, there was no law against naming someone whatever they wanted. "Nevertheless, society will not accept someone of such irregular birth."

Miss Studley snorted. "Hypocrites."

He inclined his head. "It is how the world operates. So, Miss Studley, it is *your* come-out we will discuss. And perhaps we can make other arrangements for your half sister."

"No." Miss Studley reached out and took her half sister's hand. "Either Izzy and I enter society together or not at all."

Leo eyed Isobel Burton narrowly. She looked back at him, her face expressionless.

"May I speak to you privately, Miss Burton?" he said.

"Miss *Studley*," she and her half sister said at the same time.

He inclined his head in noncommittal acknowledgment. "In the garden?" he suggested.

"Very well." She rose gracefully.

"But, Izzy—" her half sister began.

"Don't worry, 'Riss," she said. "I'll be perfectly all right." He gestured and she walked out into the garden ahead of him. Her hips swayed slightly as she walked. A light breeze caught the fabric of her dress, causing it to cling to her backside in a way that made his mouth dry, then billowed out again to wrap against her limbs in a flirtatious dance.

Leo averted his eyes. And walked into the gatepost.

O uch!" Lord Salcott grunted, and Izzy turned. "What is it?"

"Nothing," he growled. "A slight misstep, that's all." Scowling at Izzy as if she'd caused him to stumble, he waved her on ahead.

Izzy led him up the garden path—and oh, wouldn't that be fun, she thought, smiling to herself—to a pretty little wooden gazebo, covered with roses just coming into bloom.

She sat down and folded her hands, hoping she looked demure. She felt anything but demure. First, he'd all but ignored her, addressing all his comments to Clarissa—even when answering the questions Izzy asked, acting as if she weren't even in the room.

And now, he wanted to talk to her alone. It didn't bode well. "So, Lord Salcott, what did you wish to tell me without my sister hearing?"

He seated himself opposite and crossed one long, booted

leg over the other. "Have you reconsidered the offer I made the other day?"

"You mean your attempt to bribe me to abandon my sister? Of course not. My answer remains the same."

"It was not a bribe, it was—" He broke off, his mouth compressed in a hard line, his eyes boring into her like chips of ice. "I had the impression you cared about your half sister."

"I do."

"Then why are you trying to ruin her chance of making a good marriage?"

She frowned. "I'm not. It is my dearest wish that she find a husband who will love and care for her."

"She won't if you're with her all the time."

She shook her head. "Despite the impression you may have gained of her, Clarissa is very shy, particularly in large groups of people. Having me with her will—"

"Will distract all attention away from her onto you."

"Because of my irregular birth, you mean?"

"Yes, but as if that isn't enough of a disadvantage, there's also the way you look."

Izzy bristled and glanced down at her dress. "What's wrong with the way I look?"

His eyes turned to slits of steel. "There's nothing wrong," he grated. "Except that no man will look at Miss Studley if he sees you first. She's not precisely an anti-dote, but—"

"How dare you! Clarissa is *not* an antidote!"

"I never said she was, but she'll give the impression of one if you're standing next to her. Come, come," he said impatiently. "Enough of this false modesty. You must know that you outshine her in every way. And even without your irregular birth, if you appeared in public with her, Miss Studley wouldn't stand a chance of attracting an eligible connection."

Izzy frowned, racked with sudden doubt. Could that

possibly be true? No, she would not think so negatively. "You seem to forget that Clarissa is an heiress. Even apart from that, you might not think she has any beauty, but she has—and she also has a loyal and loving heart, which is worth more than physical beauty, which is only skin deep after all. And the right man will see that. The right man will not care about her fortune one way or the other."

"Don't pretend to be so naive. You know as well as I do that her fortune is her only real asset."

"Only to men like you, who cannot see past the nose on your face."

He snorted. Through the nose on his face.

She glared at him. "I intend to see that my sister marries a man who truly loves her, not some fellow who will marry her for her money and not appreciate her finer qualities."

"Oh, that's your purported reasoning, is it? And of course there is nothing in it for you," he said sardonically.

"Are you stupid? Of course there's something in it for me. I want my sister to be happy, but I also want that for myself. Why wouldn't I? Why *shouldn't* I?"

He simply looked at her, as expressionless as a rock. "What are you angling for?"

"Angling for?"

His voice was hard; his eyes were harder. "You know exactly what I mean; what is it you want to achieve by entering society? Access to rich men? To find a protector? You don't need to enter the ton for that."

Izzy was shocked and then furious, so furious that for a moment she couldn't speak. "'*A protector*'? You think I want to set myself up as a *courtesan*?"

She itched to slap him, but she wasn't going to let him goad her into it. She managed to draw a deep breath and say with some semblance of composure, though her voice shook with anger, "No, Lord Salcott, I am *not* looking for a protector."

There was a long silence. He watched her with narrowed eyes, then said, "I see I was mistaken."

"You most certainly were." She waited for an apology, but it didn't come.

"Nevertheless . . ." He rose abruptly. "I've made my position clear. I was warned about who pulls the strings in this relationship, so it's up to you now. If you care for your half sister at all, you will convince her to make the right decision. Think it over, Miss Burton. I will speak to you both again in an hour. My aunt should have finished her nap by then. I have an announcement to make that affects you all." And with that he marched away, his boots crunching on the crushed limestone pathway.

"Miss *Studley!*" she called after him. She'd been *christened* that, curse his stubbornness.

She glared after him, fuming. He was smug, self-satisfied, arrogant and wrong!

Imagining she wanted to set up as a courtesan! The nerve of the man!

What did the wretched man think she wanted out of life? He seemed to think she had only two choices—to sell her body and become a courtesan, or to hide in the shadows and not draw attention to herself. To be grateful for any crumbs people might toss her.

She wasn't built like that. She'd had a lifetime of hiding away, being invisible, being grateful, knowing she didn't really belong there—or anywhere. And now she had a chance to make a life for herself, she wasn't going to let Lord High-and-Mighty Salcott stop her.

Nor would she abandon her sister in exchange for a home and an allowance. For security. Which she'd never had in all her life.

The trouble was, he'd planted some doubts.

What did he mean by that comment about *pulling the strings*? He was wrong, of course—she and Clarissa always decided things together, but perhaps, if she really tried, she might be able to talk Clarissa out of making their come-out together.

Would it truly be better for her to withdraw from society and not be seen until after Clarissa was married? It went wholly against the grain, but she really didn't want to spoil Clarissa's chances.

Of course Izzy wanted her own chance at happiness. She wanted a home of her own where nobody could toss her out on a whim. She wanted to *belong*. And she wanted children, a family. Oh, she and Clarissa had made their own little family, but she'd always known that at any moment they could be torn apart—they'd faced that every time their father had visited Studley Park Manor.

Clarissa might have welcomed her with open arms, but Studley Park had never truly been Izzy's home—not by right. She'd had to hide every time her father visited, frightened that if he found her, she'd be dragged away and dumped in an orphan asylum.

Of course as the years passed, she was more confident of being able to stay with her sister, but those early years had left their scars.

And now here was Lord Salcott trying to do the same. Only a little more subtly.

In her early years with Mama, their various rented cottages had never been a secure home. Mama often struggled to pay the rent, and they'd been evicted several times with very little notice. Izzy had always been aware of it, though for the most part her memories were happy enough. Nevertheless, there were always secrets and evasions—things she was not allowed to talk about, questions that Mama wouldn't answer, things she wouldn't explain—like where her father was.

And there were whispers in the village. Undercurrents. Looks. Sly comments.

She'd learned to ignore them, to pretend she hadn't

noticed—but she had. And in recent years, as she'd come to adulthood, she'd wondered more and more about some of those secrets. She had an idea, too, about what they were, and it would certainly shame her if they ever came out. They would shame Clarissa, too, by association.

Could she even afford to hold out for love, as she'd once dreamed? With her background, and Mama's secrets . . .

But the only way to protect her own children was to have what Mama had never had—marriage. And while Izzy wanted to make a good marriage, she didn't want to make it at Clarissa's expense. Clarissa was the only person in the world who loved Izzy, and Izzy loved her dearly.

"Has he gone?" Startled, Izzy looked around and saw Clarissa peeping through the dainty hanging flowers of a nearby fuchsia bush.

"Yes."

Clarissa sat down beside her and inhaled blissfully. "Oh, don't all these roses smell divine? So, what did he want to say to you that he couldn't say in front of me?"

Feeling horribly awkward, Izzy tried to explain. "He's adamant that my appearing with you in public would seriously disadvantage you. Not just because of my illegitimacy, but also that"—she swallowed—"he thinks that I would distract attention away from you."

"Why? Because you're beautiful and I'm not? Pooh! What nonsense! Mama was plain and I look a lot like her, I'm told. But I love having a beautiful sister whom everyone admires. Anyway, it's not finding a husband that will be a problem; it's finding the right one. Plenty of men will want me for Great-Granddad's fortune alone, but I want a man who also values me for myself, and will come to care for me."

"No, a man who will *love* you," Izzy corrected her sternly. "Don't settle for half measures."

Clarissa smiled. "You're right. I don't want a marriage like Mama had but"—her smile faded—"I'm more like her than you realize. While he was courting her, Papa was so charming and attentive, she fell head over heels in love with him. I suppose rakes must know how to charm; otherwise, they wouldn't succeed at being rakes, if you know what I mean. And though her father didn't like Papa, Mama was determined to have him." She dimpled. "I guess we know where my stubborn streak comes from. Anyway, that's why her papa set up the trust, because he didn't trust Papa."

"And a good thing, too," Izzy said.

"Yes, but Papa never did bother with details, and he didn't read the terms of the settlement. Once he realized he couldn't get his hands on the bulk of her fortune, he was furious and treated Mama with utter contempt—well, you know how he treated me, but it must have been worse for Mama because she really did love him."

Izzy didn't say anything. Clarissa pretended she didn't care about her father's blatant indifference, but Izzy knew that deep down Clarissa had always ached for him to love her.

Clarissa sighed. "So he took it out on Mama, and even though he treated her badly—do you know he never once allowed her to go to London, he kept her immured at Studley Park? But she never stopped loving him. Even with her dying breath she sent him her love. Not that he was there, of course." She fell silent, remembering.

It wasn't the first time Izzy had heard this, how Clarissa mother's dying words were all directed to her faithless, undeserving, *absent* husband, and none at all for the loving young daughter sitting at her bedside.

Izzy's own mother's last words had been quite different. *Don't ever trust a man's promises, my darling.* And then after a few minutes she'd taken Izzy's hand and held it with feeble determination, saying, *Be good, my love, but above all be happy. Make the best life you possibly can. I love you, my darling girl. Don't let anyone make you feel ashamed of who you are. You're a wonderful girl and the best thing in my life*. And then she'd closed her eyes and slipped away.

Izzy's throat thickened with emotion. It had been a long time since she'd thought of Mama's last words. But the reminder was timely. *Don't let anyone make you feel ashamed of who you are.*

Clarissa sighed again. "I fear I'll be just as susceptible as my mother, Izzy. And that's another reason why I need you with me. To stop me falling for a man like Papa."

She squeezed Izzy's hand. "As for caring about your illegitimacy, I wouldn't *want* to marry a man who would look down on you, or who expected me to hide my sister away like a—like a thing to be ashamed of. And if some gentleman prefers your beauty to my plain looks, so be it. He won't be the man for me. So pooh to Lord Salcott and his gloomy prognostications. We *will* enter society—together!—and we will find ourselves a lovely husband."

"Two husbands might be better—one each," Izzy pointed out dryly.

Clarissa laughed merrily. "Yes, two lovely husbands!"

Izzy sobered. "We'd better go in. He said he was going to make an important announcement—he's waiting for Lady Scattergood to finish her nap."

"What do you think it will be?"

Izzy shrugged. "Something annoying, I'm sure."

Chapter Four

Leo assembled them in the drawing room, this time with his aunt present. Enough shilly-shallying around. It was time these young women learned who was in charge.

He stood by the mantelpiece, feet braced firmly apart. The stern impression he'd aimed for was marred slightly by three of the little dogs sniffing interestedly at his boots. Hoping they didn't decide to lift a leg, he tried to nudge them away; he was fond of these boots. So, apparently, were the dogs.

"Have you young ladies thought about what I said earlier? That Miss Studley must make her come-out in society alone."

They looked back at him with politely blank expressions. He glanced at his aunt, with a faint and probably misplaced hope that she might support what he was saying.

She was busy rearranging the three—or was it four?—elaborately embroidered shawls she wore.

"Aunt Olive?"

She looked up with a vague smile. "Yes, dear?"

"You would concur, would you not, that it is not possible for Miss Burton to make her come-out in society?"

"Miss Burton? Who is Miss Burton?"

He refused to grind his teeth. "I am referring to Miss Isobel and why she cannot make a come-out."

His aunt turned to Miss Burton. "Why, dear gel, are you ill?" She raised her lorgnette and scanned Miss Burton closely. "What nonsense, Leo. Ill? She's not ill. The gel is positively blooming with health and beauty."

"It's not her health I'm talking about," Leo said. He knew she was blooming, dammit. He didn't need to look at her to notice. He felt it clear to his bones.

"Then what other reason is there?" Aunt Olive said.

The two young ladies, hands folded demurely, the very picture of innocence, turned their heads to look inquiringly at him. As if they had no idea what he was talking about.

"I am referring to Miss Burton's irregular birth, Aunt Olive."

She made an exasperated noise. "Who is this Miss Burton you keep talking about, Leo? I told you, I don't know any Miss Burton, and I have even less interest in her birth, irregular or not."

"I am talking about Miss Isobel," he grated.

"Then why didn't you say so in the first place? Make up your mind, dear boy." She turned back to Miss Burton with a concerned expression and pointed her lorgnette at Miss Burton's middle. "Are you breeding, dear child?"

Miss Studley made a muffled noise and buried her face in a handkerchief. Miss Burton said calmly, "No, Lady Scattergood, I'm not breeding." She glanced at Leo, her green cat's eyes dancing with mischief. "I have no idea why Lord Salcott would think so."

"I did *not* say she was breeding!" Leo said.

"You did," his aunt said. "I distinctly recall you said—"

"I said her birth was *irregular*. She is Studley's *natural daughter*."

His aunt sniffed. "He could hardly have an unnatural one. Unless she really was delivered by a stork or found under a cabbage leaf, though why people persist in telling those ridiculous tales, I don't understand. It's not as if anyone could seriously believe—"

"Aunt Olive, Miss Isobel is a *bastard*," Leo said, goaded.

His aunt stared at him a moment. "Oh, what nonsense. She's a delightful gel, apart from her unfortunate resemblance to Sir Bartleby. And why should that prevent her from making her come-out with Clarissa? It's not as if she has her father's appalling personality. Not that I understand why any young gel would want to make her come-out. The Marriage Mart?" She shuddered. "Dreadful institution. But I suppose if the gels want it . . ." She looked at them. They nodded eagerly, and she made a helpless gesture. "See, lambs to the slaughter. I wash my hands of them."

Leo tried one more time. "Society would be outraged if we tried to introduce Miss Isobel into the ton."

"'We'? I'm not planning to introduce her anywhere, dear boy. You know I've given up on all that flimflam. I don't know why you wanted me to be present at this discussion anyway." She rose from her chair, releasing a small avalanche of shawls. "I cannot believe I cut short a lovely long hot bath for this—"

"I wanted you here because I wish to make an announcement."

She sat reluctantly. "Then for heaven's sake make it, dear boy, and stop wittering on about breeding gels and storks and cabbage leaves. Nasty stuff, cabbage. Never touch it myself."

Leo persisted. "I am going to the country for a short time. I need to visit my estate and—"

"Well, you don't need my permission for that," his aunt said.

"I am not asking anyone's permission," he ground out.

"Well then—"

Giving up on his aunt, he turned to Miss Studley with a stern look. "Miss Studley, you told me that if you could not make your come-out with your half sister, then you did not wish to make it at all. That either you would both come out together, or neither of you would. Is that correct?"

"Yes, and—"

"So be it." He cut her off crisply. "As long as you both continue to cling to that nonsense, it will be neither of you." He paused an instant to let that sink in, then continued. "As yet I have made no arrangements for your come-out, have found no suitable lady to sponsor you or to accompany you to appropriate *ton* events. While I am away you may reflect on your choice and reconsider its wisdom. In the meantime you will attend no society events; no balls, routs or ridottos; no—"

Miss Isobel leaned forward. "What *is* a ridotto, Lord Salcott?"

He stared blankly at her. *A ridotto?* How the hell would he know? He'd done his best to avoid that kind of society event. Except for his travels he'd spent most of his adult life on his estate. Suddenly noticing that his eyes were dwelling on how creamy and soft her bosom was and how enticingly it was exposed when she leaned forward, he immediately snapped his gaze to an amateurish portrait of a pug on the wall.

"I have never attended a ridotto," he told the pug. "And neither will you," he added to Miss Studley. "Not unless you reconsider your position."

"But that's not fa—" Miss Studley began. Her half sister grabbed her hand, and Miss Studley stopped in midsentence.

"Are you saying Lady Scattergood is not a suitable lady?" Miss Burton asked in a dulcet voice. Honey-dark and sweet as sin. He did not look at her. Or her bosom. Or her lips.

"Eh? What?" His aunt directed an indignant lorgnette in his direction.

"Of course I'm not saying that," Leo said. "My aunt is, of course, a perfect lady."

"So she can take us about?" Miss Burton almost purred.

"Naturally," Leo said with a sardonic smile in the direction of the pug. Apparently, Miss Burton had not yet noticed that his aunt went nowhere and socialized with nobody. He almost wished he could be there to see her face when she finally realized it.

Except he had resolved not to look at her. Race was right. She had a tendency to turn his brain to mush.

"What about shopping?" Miss Studley asked. "Can we go shopping?"

He shrugged. It made no difference to him. "I already said you could." He gently dislodged a small scruffy dog from his boot and moved toward the door.

"Wait," Miss Burton said.

Leo hid a smile. Second thoughts already. It was as he thought; once they realized he was serious, they would fall into line. He turned. "Yes?"

"What about horses?" Miss Burton said.

He blinked. "Horses? You girls ride?"

"No," Miss Burton said sweetly, "but it might be fun to fall off. We might even find a husband that way. Lady-in-distress kind of thing." She batted her eyelashes at him.

"Oh, Izzy," Clarissa said, laughing. "Of course we ride, Lord Salcott. Mr. Edwards, our father's estate manager, arranged for us to have lessons when we were ten. At home we used to ride daily."

"It's one thing for you to refuse to allow us to mix in society," Miss Burton added, "but would you really deny us the means of healthful exercise?"

It was on the tip of his tongue to point out that walking was healthful exercise requiring no expense, but before he could suggest it, she turned to her half sister and said, "Never mind, Clarissa, I'm sure Lord Tarrant will help us."

Leo frowned. "Lord Tarrant? Who is Lord Tarrant?"

And how the hell had she scraped acquaintance with a lord already? She'd been in London a bare few days.

"He's a very charming man who lives over there." She made a vague gesture. "I'm sure he'll help us acquire suitable mounts. He looks to be the kind of man who knows and appreciates good horseflesh when he sees it." She eyed Leo through her lashes.

He unclenched his jaw enough to say, "How did you meet this Lord Tarrant?"

"Ummm . . ." She twirled a lock of dark hair around her finger, as if considering how to answer him. Provocative. Her eyes danced with mischief; her finger twirled and twirled.

Her half sister chimed in, "Oh, we met his wife and daughters in the garden the other day, Lord Salcott, and she invited us for tea—Lady Scattergood, too, only she didn't want to come. We met Lord Tarrant there."

"Yes, that's how it was," Miss Burton agreed, quite as if she hadn't just tried to give him a completely different impression. "So, Lord Salcott, are you interested in mounting us, or must we ask Lord Tarrant?"

Despite her limpid gaze the minx knew perfectly well the suggestive double entendre she'd just made.

"I will hire something suitable," he said. "Expect me at ten tomorrow morning."

"You're giving us hired hacks?" Miss Burton said in open dismay.

"I am responsible for Miss Studley's welfare. Until I see how well she rides, I can have no idea of what kind of mounts will suit. Ten o'clock. Be ready."

After Lord Salcott left, Lady Scattergood went up to take her bath, and Izzy and Clarissa went out into the garden.

"Do you think he really means it?" Clarissa said. "About our not going to parties and balls and such."

"Oh yes. He's leaving us to stew and fret," Izzy said. "Trying to bore us into submission and hoping we'll change our minds."

"But we won't, will we?"

Izzy gave her sister a somber look. "That's up to you, love. I'm the fly in this ointment. If you agreed not to include me—"

"Never! And you're not a fly!" Clarissa declared. "We're sisters and nobody will divide us. Do you honestly think I care more about balls and parties and ridottos than you?" She glanced at Izzy. "Particularly ridottos. Oh, I nearly laughed aloud when you asked him that."

Izzy grinned. "Well, he was being so pompous and bossy, how could I resist?"

Clarissa laughed. "And *you* were being very naughty, getting his back up like that."

"*His* back? He gets *my* back up. He treats me like a brainless widgeon, and I can't help but react." He was so determined to put her in her place, and she was just as determined not to be put there, wherever it was he thought she belonged.

"Even when I ask him a question," she continued, "he invariably turns to *you* to answer it, as if I'm not even in the room. As if I'm invisible. He doesn't even look me in the eye."

"That's true. But when you're not looking—or glaring—at him, he watches you. I've noticed it."

Izzy gave a disbelieving snort.

"He is," Clarissa insisted. "He's always looking at you. It's as if he can't take his eyes off you."

Izzy dismissed it with a shake of her head. "If he is, it's for some nasty suspicious reason. Hoping to catch me out in some transgression."

"I'm sure that's not true," Clarissa said soothingly. "In any case, it was very clever of you to get him to agree to provide us with horses before he leaves. If we can't go to parties and things, we'll at least be able to ride. And otherwise it won't be much different from our lives at Studley Park. I can make my creams and lotions using plants from the garden—it should be easier to get the other ingredients in London—and we have books to read, and shops to visit."

Izzy gave her a sharp look. "Oh, we're going to balls and parties. No matter what the Grumpy Guardian says." He wasn't going to bore her into submission.

"We are?"

"We most definitely are."

"How?"

"I haven't worked it all out yet, but I will." She glanced at her sister. "Cinderella, you *will* go to the ridotto—whatever it is." They both laughed.

"Mind you"—Izzy's voice sobered—"it's a bit risky. It could all come crashing down around our ears, and if it does, you'll be ruined."

"Me? What about you?"

"Oh, I'm ruined anyway," Izzy said. "Thanks to my father, I was born ruined."

"Then we'll be ruined together," Clarissa declared. "High society doesn't matter to me anyway. I just want to find a nice, comfortable husband, and then I won't care if I never attend a ball or ridotto."

I'm taking my ward and her half sister riding with me tomorrow," Leo said to Race that evening over dinner at his club. "Would you care to join me?"

Race gave him a cynical glance. "For something that purports to be an invitation, why does it not sound particularly inviting?"

"Because it's a favor," Leo admitted with a wry chuckle. "Studley's daughters have asked me to get them horses, but I have no idea how well they ride. I would appreciate some support—you know how women generally overestimate their abilities on horseback."

"Lord, yes, I recall one young lady who shall remain nameless. She was determined to hook a friend of mine and attempted to cut a dash to impress him at a house party. Hobbs was the huntin', fishin', shootin' type and a bruising rider to hounds. The chit told him she hunted all the time— that she quite *lived* for a good chase—so the silly ass took her at her word and, on the day of the hunt, put her up on one of his hunters."

He snorted with remembered amusement. "She rode with all the grace of a sack of potatoes, and bounced and wobbled along until they got to the first fence, where she fell off—before the horse even jumped—and proceeded to shriek like a stuck pig."

"Ouch. What did your friend do?"

"Kept going without a backward look, of course. Nothing gets between Hobbs and a hunt. The young lady and her doting parents departed that same day in high dudgeon."

Leo chuckled.

"The irony is that Hobbs ended up marrying a woman who doesn't ride at all. She has no interest in horses or hunting, and yet they seem to suit each other perfectly. She sees him off at the start of a hunt with a stirrup cup, and welcomes him and his companions home at the end of the day with a good hot dinner, and that's it."

Leo laughed. "My guess is these girls can ride, but how well is another matter. They claim to have ridden regularly, but how far, how fast and on what kind of mount I am yet to ascertain. I might not have wanted the charge of the Studley girl, but I don't want her breaking her neck."

"Lord no. And the other girl?"

"She's another reason why I want you along. The girl is a minx."

Race's expression was ironic. "So you'll watch over your precious charge and I get to handle the minx."

"Miss Studley is not my precious charge," Leo said in a

repressive tone. "But she is my responsibility. As for her half sister, I fancy you might enjoy the task."

"Very well, I'll come, if only out of curiosity. But I'll want a slap-up dinner afterward. And some of that exotic liquor you brought back from your travels. I'm curious to try it."

"It'll blow your head off."

Race grinned. "Perfect. I expect that by then I'll need it."

W ill you look at that!" Izzy exclaimed in disgust. It was almost ten, and she and Clarissa, dressed in their riding habits, were watching from the window, waiting for Lord Salcott to arrive with their horses. "I knew it! He's brought us a pair of fat old rocking horses."

"They mightn't be that bad," Clarissa said, peering over her shoulder to where Lord Salcott and another gentleman were coming down the street mounted, with a third, who was obviously a groom, leading two plump mares who plodded along looking bored.

Izzy snorted. "I bet he asked for 'quiet, well-behaved ladies' mounts' and look at them, not an ounce of spirit between them. And yet look at the glorious creature *he's* riding!" She eyed his magnificent chestnut gelding balefully.

"He's brought a friend," Clarissa commented. "Very elegant and good-looking, too, don't you think? And he can certainly ride. What a beautiful creature."

"Who, the man or the horse?" Izzy said mischievously.

"The horse, of course," Clarissa said with dignity. The smoky gray gelding was clearly feeling his oats; he danced and fidgeted and even shied a couple of times, but Lord Salcott's friend sat his restless mount with casual ease.

Izzy was filled with envy. She wanted to ride that horse. Or Lord Salcott's.

As she and Clarissa came down the front steps, she heard Lord Salcott say, "Dammit, Race, you should have taken the edge off that fellow before you came—he's jumping out of his skin. I don't want to alarm the ladies."

"Alarm the ladies indeed," Izzy muttered.

Greetings were exchanged and introductions made—the handsome gentleman with the magnificent gray horse was called Lord Randall. Up until now, Lord Salcott had invariably addressed Izzy as Miss Burton, but to Izzy's surprise he introduced them to Lord Randall as Miss Studley and Miss, um, Isobel.

She was under no illusion that he'd changed his mind about her, so what was he up to?

"What a superb horse, Lord Randall," she said, walking closer.

"Be careful!" Lord Salcott snapped. "The animal is no tame pony."

Ignoring him, Izzy produced a chunk of apple and approached the horse, who stuck his nose out, sniffed curiously, then greedily lipped it from her palm. Smiling, she fed it another piece of apple, murmuring soft endearments as she did.

She glanced up at Lord Randall, who grinned down at her. "You have a way with horses, Miss Isobel."

"He's a beauty. What's his name?"

"Storm."

She laughed. "Because of his color or because he's full of mischief? And what glorious mischief he is, aren't you, beautiful?" She fed the horse a third piece of apple and then, aware everyone was waiting, turned reluctantly to the two hired hacks. "Which one of these creatures will you take, 'Riss? The bay armchair or the brown sofa?"

Her sister laughed. "Don't be mean; they're both very sweet. I'll take this one." She took the reins of the brown one.

Izzy sighed. "Very well, I'll take the bay." She checked

the fit of the saddle, fed the last of the apple to her mare, and glanced expectantly up at Lord Randall.

He dismounted, but Lord Salcott was before him. Linking his hands to receive Izzy's booted foot, he tossed her lightly into the sidesaddle. Lord Randall gave him a quizzical look, then helped Clarissa mount while Lord Salcott adjusted Izzy's stirrups.

They set off at a walk through the London streets. Lord Randall's horse took objection to all kinds of things—a dog, a scrap of paper blowing across the street, a man selling muffins. His owner didn't turn a hair, but rode slightly ahead to keep the horse from disturbing the others.

Izzy doubted an explosion would disturb her own mount. As she'd feared, the mare was a stodgy, unimaginative creature whose gait, if she'd been human, would have been called a trudge. So much for looking forward to a good ride. This was more like sitting in a rocking chair, only less comfortable.

They turned in to Hyde Park and, as expected, Lord Salcott led them to the Ladies' Bridle Path. There were very few other riders in evidence, but their pace barely altered. After a minute or two, Lord Randall veered off and took his horse to a deserted part of the park for a quick gallop. Izzy watched him enviously.

She and Clarissa urged their mounts to a trot. *If you could call it that*, Izzy thought in frustration. Her horse's was more like a shuffle, and after a few minutes it returned to trudging.

After a few minutes Lord Salcott dropped back to join Izzy. "You're unusually quiet, Miss Bur—" She shot him a narrow glance. "Miss Isobel," he amended smoothly.

"Shhh," she whispered.

He gave her a mildly puzzled look.

"I'm trying not to wake my horse," she explained.

A gleam of understanding appeared in his otherwise hard gray eyes. "I appear to have underestimated your abilities. You have an excellent seat, and your half sister also appears to ride well."

"'Appears to'?"

"She also rides well," he amended.

"How can you tell, mounted as we are on these slugs? We did tell you that we've ridden almost every day since we turned ten."

He raised a brow. "You're the same age?"

"I'm a few weeks younger."

"I see."

Izzy didn't know what he saw. But what she could see was Lord Randall in the distance, having a glorious ride. "What a superb animal," she exclaimed. "What I wouldn't give to ride a horse like that."

He gave her a thoughtful look, but said nothing.

Izzy's frustration with her own horse was growing. She tried to increase the pace. The mare wheezed into a lethargic trot, then after a dozen paces, it slowed again. Izzy gritted her teeth and was about to try a harder kick when she caught a glimpse of Lord Salcott's expression, a mix of rueful amusement and, surprisingly, fellow feeling.

"I expect you'll need a firecracker to move that one," he said.

It surprised a laugh out of her. "I was thinking a bomb." She glanced at him, and his flinty gray eyes glinted with amusement.

"Don't you dare laugh, you abominable man. You should be racked with guilt for saddling me with this appalling slug." As if it understood her insult, the horse came to a complete stop. She glanced at Lord Salcott's face and burst into peals of laughter.

"Could you have found any worse creature for me in the whole of London?" she said in mock despair when she'd recovered.

"My apologies. If I promise to get you and your sister

better mounts, will you come out with Randall and me again?"

She gave him a baleful look. "It depends on how much better."

He inclined his head. "I'll do my best." The amusement was still lurking in his eyes. It was disturbingly attractive. And good heavens! Was he actually *smiling*? He was! She was sure of it. A vertical groove had appeared in his cheek that in anyone less masculine and forbidding would be called a dimple. Surely not. Perhaps his face was cracking with the effort of smiling.

She edged a little closer. It *was* a dimple.

Lord Salcott—Lord Grumpy—had a dimple.

His brows drew together. "What are you staring at?"

"You have a dimple."

The smile vanished. "I do not." He wiped his cheek as if he could brush away the evidence. He knew exactly where to wipe, too.

Izzy laughed. It was the first time she'd ever seen him being anything other than serious and bossy. He looked quite different. It suddenly occurred to her that he was quite a young man, not yet thirty. The realization was a little unsettling.

"I would love to ride Lord Randall's Storm," Izzy said after a minute.

Lord Salcott frowned. "He's a handful."

Izzy gave him a demure look. "So am I."

He gave a choked-off laugh and said severely, "You, miss, are a minx."

Izzy blinked. Were they flirting? Surely not.

They walked on. "I heard you call your friend Race earlier," she said. "Is that because he likes to race?"

"He does, but that's not why he's called Race. He was christened Horatio, but at school it got shortened to Race." He glanced at her and added, "He probably came up with the name himself. He was dashing even at a young age."

"So you met at school?"

"Yes, I—oh, blast, excuse me." A dog was barking at the heels of Clarissa's horse, and he cantered away to deal with it. Not that he probably needed to: Clarissa's horse was almost as placid as Izzy's.

Izzy watched him go, bemused. She'd glimpsed a different side of him this morning and didn't quite know what to make of it. Not only could Lord Salcott smile, he had a dimple.

And he'd almost flirted. With her, the girl he seemed dedicated to getting rid of. What did it all mean?

Lord Randall returned and joined Izzy. "I see Leo has ridden to your sister's rescue. Are you enjoying the ride, Miss Isobel?"

Izzy gave him a droll look and made a snoring noise. He chuckled. "Yes, the stables didn't exactly provide the mounts you and your sister deserve."

"Lord Salcott has promised to bring us decent mounts next time. I trust you will hold him to it."

"Oh, I'm to be invited, am I?"

"Naturally." She shot him a mischievous glance. "I'm hoping for a ride on your beautiful Storm."

He shook his head. "Not possible, I'm afraid. He's not trained for sidesaddle."

"Neither am I."

He laughed. "I don't believe it."

"It's true." Clarissa joined them, leaving Lord Salcott speaking sternly to the dog owner. "Izzy taught herself to ride bareback when she was ten. It was only when I tried to imitate her and fell and broke my arm that Papa's estate manager decided we needed proper lessons."

"Only he insisted that we learn to ride sidesaddle like proper young ladies," Izzy said.

Lord Randall gave her a speculative look. "And were you obedient young ladies?"

"Of course we were," Izzy said.

"As long as Mr. Edwards was watching us," Clarissa added with a smile.

"And when he wasn't?" Lord Randall prompted.

"Oh, then Izzy would coax one of the grooms to saddle the horses with ordinary saddles."

He frowned. "And they obeyed? But you were only little girls then, weren't you?"

"Sidesaddles are dreary," Izzy said. "Ordinary saddles are easier and more convenient to use. And safer. And we don't need help to mount."

"But—" he began.

"If sidesaddles were as wonderful as men tell us they are, why is it that men never use them?" Izzy said.

Clarissa laughed at his expression and explained, "It wasn't so much that the stable lads obeyed us, as that they were afraid we'd ride bareback again, and they'd get into trouble if I were hurt. Besides, Izzy is quite good at persuading people."

Lord Randall gave her a searching look. "You said they'd be in trouble if you were hurt, Miss Studley. Miss Isobel, too, I presume?"

"Oh no," Izzy said blithely. "If I'd broken my neck, Papa would have probably rewarded them."

Lord Randall gave her a startled look, as if unsure whether she was joking or not.

"Oh, Izzy, he wouldn't," Clarissa exclaimed in distress.

"What does it matter?" she said lightly. "I never did fall off, did I? So, Lord Randall, when are you going to let me ride your horse?"

"Never," Lord Salcott said, coming up behind them. "It's an unsuitable mount for a lady." His eyes were all flinty again, and his mouth was flat and unsmiling. No hint of a dimple. Lord Grumpy was back. "It's time we returned. At the rate those mares move, it's going to take a while."

"And whose fault is that?" Izzy couldn't resist saying.

He gave her a hard-eyed look and moved off.

W ell, that went all right," Leo said that evening after the waiter had removed their empty plates.

"Yes, it was a fine dinner, and the pudding will be finer still, I expect," Race said. "I'm still waiting for a taste of that liquor you brought back from your travels."

"Later, when we've finished eating," Leo said. "As I warned you, it'll blow your head off."

Race chuckled. "We'll see about that."

"I wasn't talking about the meal, though. I meant the riding excursion went all right."

Race gave him an incredulous look. "You think so? Those young ladies are clearly experienced riders and yet you provided them with a pair of slugs."

Leo made a dismissive gesture. "Oh, that. No, I meant you and Miss Bur—Miss Isobel. What did you think of her?"

"Well, for a start you lied about her."

Leo frowned. "In what way?"

"You said she was 'quite attractive.'"

"She is."

"She is not—she's beautiful."

Leo shrugged. "Same thing." He felt uncomfortable revealing, even to his oldest friend, how powerfully attracted he was to her. Race knew too much about his disastrous past with women.

"She's also charming and lively and—"

"Yes, yes," Leo said impatiently. He didn't want to hear his friend listing Isobel Burton's finer points. He was all too well aware of them. "The point is, do you think you could seduce her?"

"*What?*" Race leaned forward but had to bite off whatever he'd been about to say because the waiter brought their puddings out and fussed around until Leo waved him off. "What the devil do you mean by that?" Race said across the table as soon as the waiter had gone.

"You're supposed to be the expert on women here. Do you think she might be looking for a protector?"

"No, I damn well don't! Why the devil should you imagine such a thing?"

Leo stirred his pudding thoughtfully, deciding what to say. "I didn't imagine anything," he said finally. "Her father claimed it in a deathbed letter to me."

"What? Her *father* did?"

Leo nodded. "Shocking, I know. But in the letter he was adamant. He was most explicit, describing Miss Isobel's immoral tendencies in detail, even giving examples. But"—he shook his head—"I know I haven't known her for long, but I just can't see it. She's a handful, no doubt about that—spirited, rebellious and with a strong mischievous streak—but I can see no sign of immorality in her."

But he was reluctant to trust his own impressions. With just a look or a smile—or even a scowl—Isobel Burton effortlessly sent his own mind spinning.

"Me neither." Race took a large mouthful of wine. "That's appalling. To malign his own daughter—baseborn or not—in such a way. Why do such a thing?"

Leo shook his head. "I don't know. I never really knew Sir Bartleby—he was an acquaintance of my father's, but his own reputation was unsavory—and yet he advised me, in the strongest terms, to get rid of Miss Isobel and remove her from Miss Studley's company."

"Because he thought she would lead Miss Studley astray? But if he believed that, why didn't he get rid of her himself?"

Leo inclined his head. "Exactly." And why leave Isobel without a penny so she was forced to depend on her half sister? "In any case, if it's influence we're talking, it seems to me that Miss Studley is equally as stubborn as her half sister."

Race pushed his bowl away, picked up his glass of wine and drained it. "So what are you going to do?"

"About the letter? I don't know." Leo drained his own glass. "But whether or not it's the tissue of lies it appears to be, the fact remains that Miss Isobel cannot enter society with her sister, and both girls are still insisting they can, so my plan remains unchanged."

"To leave them with your aunt to come to terms with their situation?"

Leo nodded. "I have estate matters to attend to, and I want to leave for my country property the day after tomorrow. In the meantime, will you come out riding with me and the girls again tomorrow? I'm trialing some horses for them."

"Happy to." Race rose from the table. "Now, where's that liquor you promised me? I think I need my head blown off."

Chapter Five

❧

The following day, Lord Salcott returned with two much more acceptable mounts. They were also hired horses, and while they were nowhere near the quality Izzy and Clarissa would have preferred, at least they were a big improvement on the stodgy mounts of the previous day.

He was accompanied by Lord Randall and a middle-aged groom whom he introduced as Addis. "Addis will accompany you whenever you ride out. Whenever you wish to ride, have a message sent to the stables and he will bring the horses." He added with a stern look, "He will also accompany you at all times."

Izzy and Clarissa exchanged glances. Izzy wrinkled her nose. Addis was to be some kind of keeper, then.

Addis held the horses while the two gentlemen tossed Izzy and Clarissa into their saddles and helped them adjust their stirrups.

Lord Salcott swung lithely up onto his own horse. "Now, Hyde Park?"

"Oh, not Hyde Park, Leo, not on such a glorious morning," Lord Randall said immediately. "Hyde Park will be crowded. Hampstead Heath would be much more the thing, don't you think? I'm guessing the ladies would rather stretch their mounts than walk or trot genteelly along."

"Yes indeed," Izzy said. "I'm dying for a good gallop."

"Besides," Clarissa added, "We've been to Hyde Park, but never to Hampstead Heath."

"It's quite a long way," Lord Salcott began, but then he relented, and for a reason that made Izzy want to hit him. "Still, we're most unlikely to come across anyone we know on the heath. Very well, Hampstead Heath it is."

Was he ashamed to be seen with them? With her? Izzy wondered, but she didn't brood for long. As they wove through the London streets making for Hampstead Heath, she delighted in the sheer variety of people and sights they came across. Street sellers peddling all kinds of things: ribbons and old clothes, hot pies and muffins. There were orange sellers and dancing dogs. There was even a hurdy-gurdy man with a little monkey in a red jacket.

For two girls who'd spent most of their lives at Studley Park Manor such sights were exotic and exciting, even if they did slow their progress.

Finally the green expanse of Hampstead Heath was spread out before them, and the horses moved restlessly, impatient to be off. Izzy gave a little crow of excitement and pointed to a clump of trees in the distance. "Race you to that copse over there, 'Riss." She set off immediately, Clarissa right on her heels, and after a startled pause, Lords Salcott and Randall and the groom, Addis, followed.

The fresh country air, free of the stink of the London streets; the breeze against her skin; the power of the horse beneath her; the fragrance of acres of green grass—Izzy reveled in it all.

Hoofbeats pounded behind her. She glanced back, expecting it to be Lord Randall on his glorious gelding, but to her surprise it was Lord Salcott. His expression was thunderous.

He drew level with her. "Slow down!"

"Pooh to that," she shouted back and urged her horse faster. She wanted to win the race. Besides, with every step her horse's hooves threw up the fresh scent of the dew-soaked grass and earth. It was intoxicating.

But a rental hack would never be able to outstrip a thoroughbred of the quality of Lord Salcott's gelding. He passed her and by the time she reached the copse, he'd flung himself off his horse, had tied the reins to a branch and was marching toward her. "What the devil did you think you were do—"

"Wasn't that simply glorious?" she exclaimed, laughing, too happy to allow his temper to affect her. "Though we should have given you and Lord Randall a handicap. It's simply not fair to pit your splendid thoroughbreds against our hired hacks." She turned to see where Clarissa was and saw that she and Lord Randall were cantering along in a leisurely manner, apparently uninterested in the race.

"I instructed Randall to prevent Miss Studley from racing," Lord Salcott said.

She pulled off her hat and shook out her hair, enjoying the breeze riffling through it. "Clarissa and I race all the time."

His eyes darkened. His mouth tightened. "Perhaps, but it's foolishly risky to race across unknown ground on a strange horse, and I am responsible—"

"For her safety, I know." It probably wouldn't matter to him if Izzy broke her neck. She told herself she didn't care. All her life she'd known that Clarissa's welfare was paramount, and she had no quarrel with that. She loved her sister and wanted only the best for her.

It was just, sometimes, when someone rubbed her nose

in the fact that she herself didn't matter . . . well, it left a kind of bruise on her spirit.

Not that she cared what he thought of her. And if he tried to wrap Clarissa in cotton wool, he'd soon learn that soft as she might look, Clarissa was no docile doll. She was almost as daring a rider as Izzy.

"Unfair, unfair," Clarissa called gaily as she and Lord Randall cantered up. "A thoroughbred against a hired mount?"

Izzy laughed. "Exactly what I said."

"Even so, you put up a very good show, Miss Isobel. You certainly can ride," Lord Randall said admiringly. "I wonder, have you ever visited Astley's Amphitheatre?"

"No, never," Izzy said. "What is Astley's Amphitheatre?"

"A kind of theater. I am persuaded you'd enjoy watching the lady equestriennes who perform there. Miss Studley told me you even perform tricks yourself on horseback."

"As long as she doesn't perform any here," growled Lord Grumpy.

Izzy ignored him. "We'd love to see these equestriennes, wouldn't we, Clarissa? I might even," she added with a sly glance at Lord Salcott, "look for employment there myself. It sounds like just the kind of thing suited to *someone in my position.*"

"Nonsense," he grated. To do him credit, he looked a little uncomfortable to have his words quoted back at him.

"Oh. You don't believe I'm good enough?" Before he could say anything, she cantered away. Spotting a spreading horse chestnut tree, she headed toward it, and as she'd hoped, she spotted some of last season's old horse-chestnuts lying among the leaves on the ground. They'd be soft and useless now, but they were perfect for Izzy's purpose.

Without slowing, she slipped sideways in her saddle. A masculine shout rang out. Izzy ignored it. Holding on with one hand, and keeping her body balanced with all her strength, she reached down until her other hand could touch the sparse grass beneath the tree, and scooped up a handful of nuts.

She pulled herself back upright and straightened in the saddle. Laughing, she turned her horse back toward her companions, only to find Lord Salcott thundering toward her again, his expression this time pale and tight. And clearly furious.

"What the devil do you think you're—"

"Here, have some conkers," she said, and tossed him the handful of soft, semi-decayed nuts. Nobody said conkers had to be hard to make a point.

He caught them reflexively and then, with a disgusted look, tossed them aside. "What kind of an insane—"

"Just proving a point."

His big leather-gloved hands opened and closed, as if itching to throttle her. "Do you have any idea how dangerous, how utterly stupid that kind of move is?"

She shrugged carelessly. "I've done it dozens of times. Clarissa fell the first time she tried it, but I never have."

"She fell? Good God, it's a wonder neither of you broke your neck if that's the kind of crazy stunt you tried."

"It's perfectly safe. I did adapt our old sidesaddles to make it easier, but we had to leave them at home when we came to London."

His hard gray eyes sliced into her. "Home?" he snapped. "You don't have a home. You never did."

There was a short, tense silence. Izzy's horse shifted restlessly. In the tree overhead a willy wagtail chittered.

"You're quite right," she said after a moment. "I never did have a home and I don't have one now. Foolish of me to forget. Thank you for reminding me."

"Dammit, I didn't mean—" he began, but Izzy had had enough of his disapproval. She cantered away, her emotions in a tangle.

* * *

Leo watched her leave and cursed his temper. That moment when she'd seemed to be about to be dashed to the ground had almost stopped his heart. In desperation he'd raced forward, hoping to snatch her up, hold her close. Keep her safe. All the time knowing he was too far away to save her.

And then she'd righted herself and tossed those blasted nuts at him, her vivid face alive with laughter and mischief. It was a stunt. A prank.

Relief and fury had mingled in an explosive mix, and he'd snapped at her with cruel, angry words. *You don't have a home. You never did.*

He hadn't actually meant it the way it sounded, but once the words were out, it was too late to try to take them back.

The laughter drained from her face, the light in her glorious emerald eyes died, and she'd responded stiffly. Hurt. But with dignity. She'd ridden away like a queen.

Again, he cursed his hasty temper.

But cruel as it was, what he'd said was true. Her blithe carelessness, her joyful recklessness simultaneously attracted and chafed at him. She acted as if she had not a worry in the world. And yet all that stood between her and absolute poverty was the goodwill of her half sister.

Not that Leo would let it come to that, but Isobel couldn't know it. And it frustrated him enormously.

Despite the life she had led, she still did not seem to realize that you could not depend on other people for security. Or happiness.

Defiance still sizzled through Izzy, but underlying that was hurt at his harsh reminder of her place in the world—her lack of one. True though it was. And beneath all of that she felt a little ashamed, a little embarrassed. She had, after all, been showing off. She'd meant to annoy him, so she could hardly complain when he reacted.

Oh, she liked performing tricks on horseback—she always had—but it was a little immature to have done what she did out here, in public. Just to irritate Lord Salcott.

But his constant attempts to squash her were infuriating. His responsibility was to Clarissa, not her: he'd repeatedly made that clear. So why didn't he just leave her alone?

The rest of the morning passed pleasantly enough. Izzy took care to avoid Lord Salcott. Clarissa and Lord Randall were much better company anyway than a brooding thundercloud on horseback.

They explored the heath, enjoying the quiet wooded sections and the open swaths of grass, the ponds and the pathways. And above all Izzy reveled in the openness of the country.

She hadn't realized it until she came up here, but she'd been feeling a little cramped in London, with its constant noise and dirt and smells, the close-set buildings and the endless push of humanity at every turn. Up here, looking out at the distant view of the city, she could breathe. She eyed the jumble of distant rooftops, picking out the spires and church towers, the dome of St. Paul's, wondering whether it was possible to see the treetops of Bellaire Gardens . . .

You don't have a home. You never did.

He was right. Studley Park Manor was never a proper home to her, not when every time her father visited she had to hide, but she would have a home of her own one day, she promised herself.

After an hour or so exploring the heath, they stopped for a short break. To her surprise, the groom, Addis, produced a rug from his saddlebags, followed by wrapped packets that turned out to contain ham and chicken sandwiches, grapes, apples and several bottles of cool, crisp cider and cups in which to drink it.

Lord Randall spread the rug on the ground, and they all sat down to an impromptu picnic.

"What a charming notion," Clarissa said. "Did you arrange this, Lord Randall?"

He shook his head. "Not I." He glanced at Lord Salcott. "You had every intention of coming here in the first place, didn't you, Leo? If we'd been going to Hyde Park, there would be no need to bring refreshments."

Lord Salcott made a dismissive gesture. "You can thank my man, Matteo. He seems to believe people will expire if they don't eat every few hours. It's a Neapolitan attitude."

But his disclaimer fooled nobody. Izzy ate a chicken sandwich thoughtfully. So Lord Salcott had intended all along to bring them to Hampstead Heath. Then why had he implied that he didn't want people in Hyde Park to see them? See her.

She glanced at him and found his gray gaze resting somberly on her. She put up her chin and stared back at him. He turned away, uncorked the cider and topped up everyone's drinks.

She ate another sandwich—ham and mustard this time—and then ate some grapes and sipped the cool cider. The food was simple but delicious, and she'd worked up an appetite.

She shot him a sideways glance. He'd been very quiet. Still brooding? Meantime, Lord Randall entertained them with tales of his own travels in Italy, so there were no awkward silences.

As his friend talked, Lord Salcott produced a knife, picked up an apple and began to peel it. She watched as his long fingers deftly peeled it in one unbroken coil. She'd never managed to do that. He quartered the apple, removed the core and then, to Izzy's astonishment, passed her a slice of apple.

Murmuring thanks, she took the slice and ate it. It was

crisp and sweet. He passed her another slice, then another, until she'd eaten the whole apple, straight from his hands. It felt oddly intimate. Was it a kind of wordless apology for his earlier bad temper, a peace offering?

But no, for then he peeled another apple—again in one continuous coil—and handed the pieces to Clarissa. Only he didn't feed Clarissa a slice at a time, but passed her the whole apple on a napkin, peeled and neatly sliced up.

Izzy finished her cider. The man was such a mix of bossiness, hostility and now this, feeding her carefully prepared pieces of apple as if it meant something. All in a kind of brooding silence. She didn't understand him at all.

He rose and fed the apple cores and peels to the horses. They packed up and mounted, ready to return to Bellaire Gardens. This time they rode two by two. Izzy rode with Lord Randall. Clarissa and Lord Salcott were some distance ahead, well out of earshot, when Lord Randall moved closer. "Don't be too hard on Leo, Miss Isobel."

She looked at him in surprise. "I beg your pardon?"

"About him losing his temper like that at your clever riding."

She raised an eyebrow.

"He was worried about your safety, that's all."

Izzy sniffed. "I doubt that."

"Believe me, he was. He can't help it. He's very protective of those in his care."

"But I'm not in his care, am I? Clarissa is his ward, not I."

Lord Randall smiled but said nothing. They rode on.

Leo returned the young women to his aunt's house and accompanied them inside.

"I shall be leaving for my country estate shortly. I'm not sure how long I will be absent—several weeks, I expect. In the meantime, you will be in the care of my aunt." He glanced at his aunt, who was busy scratching the stomach of a small scruffy beast that lay blissfully across her lap. He raised his voice. "Isn't that right, Aunt Olive?"

She looked up vaguely. "Eh, what's that?"

"You will be in charge of the young ladies."

"Yes, yes, whatever you say. And yes, my darling, I will scratch your dear little tummy next, don't you worry."

Leo reminded himself that she was talking to the dog waiting hopefully at her feet, and that his own stomach was in no danger of being scratched. He said to the young ladies, who were trying to suppress giggles at his aunt's antics, "I trust in the interim, you two young ladies will respect Lady Scattergood's authority." Such as it was—her "authority" was a joke. But he had no choice. There was no one else he could leave them with.

"You may use my absence to consider your position," he continued. "You know my conditions, and should you agree to them, I shall make all the necessary arrangements for you to make your come-out in society, Miss Studley—alone." He glanced at her sister. "Should you decide what your own arrangements will be, Miss Burton, I am willing to assist with them, too, depending, of course, on what they are."

They stared stonily back at him, all amusement wiped from their faces. At least they were taking him seriously. Several weeks of the unrelieved company of his aunt and her dogs should bring the girls to their senses. It was hard, he knew, to exclude Miss Burton from her half sister's activities, but society had its rules.

And better she learn that now than be publicly humiliated later on.

He bowed curtly and turned on his heel to leave. Halfway to the door he paused. Yes, he needed to say it. He turned back and looked straight at Miss Burton. She lifted her chin and stared back at him, defiance glittering from those glorious green eyes.

"Miss Burton, I ap—"

"Miss *Studley*," she and her half sister said in unison.

He clenched his jaw. "Miss Isobel, I must apologize for what I said to you on the heath earlier. About your home. I overreacted to your . . . stunt and I spoke hastily and without thought. It was unfair of me."

He didn't wait for her response, but turned and marched from the room, the dignity of his exit slightly marred by the flock of scruffy little beasts cavorting around his boots.

W hat did he say to you on the heath?" Clarissa asked after Lord Salcott had left. They'd taken themselves outside to the garden.

Izzy shook her head. "I don't remember."

"But—"

"He was his usual annoying self, that's all. I have no idea why he thought an apology was in order." But she did know, and it had thrown her completely. He was referring to that gibe he'd made about her having no home. It had hurt, but it was the truth, after all. People didn't need to apologize for telling the truth.

I overreacted to your stunt.

It seemed Lord Randall was right, that Lord Salcott had been worried about her safety.

"But he apologized," Clarissa persisted. "Men never apologize."

Izzy shrugged. "It's a mystery to me. Anyway, he's gone for who knows how long."

Clarissa nodded. "I know. I've spoken to Lady Scattergood, and she's given me the use of a small room off the scullery to make my lotions and creams."

"That's nice."

"You don't sound very interested," Clarissa said reproachfully. "But with several weeks of not going out except for rides and walking the dogs, we're going to have to find something to occupy ourselves or else we'll die of boredom."

"'Several weeks of not going out'?" Izzy echoed. "I have no intention of sitting here rotting with boredom on the say-so of Lord High-and-Mighty."

"But that's why I thought of my little room—"

"You can make all the creams and lotions you like, my love, but we *are* going out. What's more, we're going to start meeting and mixing with the ton—both of us together."

"But he said—"

"I know what he said. But I have a plan. As long as you're *sure*, that is—very sure about me coming, too. Because I don't want to drag you down, 'Riss."

"Nonsense, there's no question of you dragging me anywhere," Clarissa said firmly. "I need you with me, and I won't let my stubborn guardian or any ill-natured society gossip stop us. Anyway, how would anyone in London even know you were Papa's natural daughter?"

"I'm lucky he didn't have *B* for *bastard* branded on my forehead," Izzy said cynically.

"Oh, don't—that's horrid. Anyway, if we continue to introduce ourselves as sisters—the Misses Studley—why would anyone have reason to doubt us?"

"I suppose."

"Almost nobody knew Mama," Clarissa pointed out. "She wasn't from the ton, and after her marriage Papa kept her shut away at Studley Park, as he did with us—so who is to know how many children she had?"

"There are birth records," Izzy began doubtfully.

"Pooh, an entry in a small church in some obscure village somewhere in the country? I don't even know where you were baptized. Who is going to bother going to the trouble of searching for that? No, as long as I claim you as my sister, people will accept it."

It made sense, Izzy had to agree. "What if my father told people about me?"

Clarissa wrinkled her nose, considering it. "He might have mentioned an illegitimate child—though I don't see why he would—but for all we know we could have other half siblings, so why should it be you?"

That was true.

"What about his guests, the men who came to Studley Park for the hunting?"

Clarissa shook her head decisively. "Apart from that awful man that time, they hardly even saw us. And you know how Papa hated that we bested him. He'd hardly want that known."

Izzy nodded. "And for all we know his friends are probably dead anyway. All right then, you've convinced me that my presence won't necessarily shame you—though it is a risk."

"A risk I'm more than happy to take." Clarissa reached out and squeezed Izzy's hands affectionately. "I want you with me when we brave the Marriage Mart." Then her smile faded. "But without Lord Salcott's support, how can we enter it? Lady Scattergood won't be any help, that's obvious."

Izzy smiled. "I have a plan."

At dinner that night, Izzy raised the topic of books to read. Lady Scattergood had a well-stocked library containing a good many novels as well as weightier texts and, what was most telling, the pages of the novels had all been cut, unlike those of the duller titles.

"You have a wonderful collection of novels, Lady Scattergood. Clarissa and I were delighted to see the range you have."

"Yes, all the newest titles, too," Clarissa added.

They talked then about several of the books they'd read, and it soon became clear that the old lady didn't simply purchase books for the look of it, as some people did, but actually read them with pleasure—the novels, at any rate, as well as some of the poetry.

"Lady Tarrant mentioned the other day that you belong to a book club," Izzy said.

"Book club? Book club? Oh, you mean Bea Davenham's literary society? No, I haven't been to that in an age." She served herself a large helping of quaking pudding and poured a lavish amount of cream over it.

"But you used to enjoy it, didn't you?" Izzy persisted.

"Mmm, yes. Good stories those gels used to read to us."

"Read to you?" Clarissa echoed, puzzled.

Lady Scattergood nodded. "It's not the usual sort of literary society—those gels of Bea's read stories aloud and the rest of us listened. And later we talked. A godsend to those of us whose eyesight is fading. And no pretentious talk afterward, where people spout off, trying to sound learned." She snorted. "Bea won't stand for that kind of nonsense. But I don't go anymore. Have you tried this pudding? Cook has used lemons instead of rose water, and it's very good."

"You didn't fall out with Lady Davenham, did you?" Izzy asked anxiously. The literary society was key to her plan.

Lady Scattergood shook her head. "Not at all. I just . . ." Her gaze dropped. "Oh, I'm not in the mood for going out these days."

"Oh," Izzy said in a dejected voice.

The old lady gave her a narrow look. "What do you mean 'oh'?"

"It's just that Lord Salcott refuses to let Izzy appear in society with me," Clarissa explained. "So far we haven't met anyone in London except for Lord and Lady Tarrant and their daughters."

"And we only met them because of the garden," Izzy added,

"But I want to meet people and I want Izzy with me. I need her. She gives me confidence."

Lady Scattergood frowned. "Is this because of that illegitimacy nonsense?"

Izzy nodded. She didn't think it was "nonsense"—her whole life had been blighted because of it. But she wasn't going to give up.

Lady Scattergood snorted. "Don't know what maggot the boy's got in his brain. Punishing the child for the sins of the father." She dug into her pudding, glanced up at Izzy and added, "And a perfectly nice child at that!"

Izzy felt a warm glow at her words. "Thank you, Lady Scattergood," she said softly.

"Breeding counts, yes indeed," the old lady continued. "As does blood, but your mother was from a good enough family, wasn't she? Before that villain seduced her. Your grandparents threw her out, I gather, the moment they learned she was breeding!" She shook her head. "Respectable, undoubtedly, though not what I call the behavior of a good family, mind. She should have been protected from the likes of your father. It was their disgrace, not hers—or yours."

Izzy was deeply touched by the old lady's understanding and sympathy. It was rare, and precious.

Lady Scattergood stirred more cream into her pudding and added meditatively, "I expect you weren't the first child he got on a young innocent, either, the rutting swine."

"Lord Salcott said no balls or routs or ridottos," Izzy said, "but we thought perhaps we could attend the literary society with you and meet some people that way." Lady Tarrant was her second choice to ask, but Lady Scattergood was her first. It would establish who they were and that they were living with a respectable—if eccentric—lady.

Izzy leaned forward. "So, will you take us, dear Lady Scattergood?"

Lady Scattergood glanced at her but said nothing. She scowled at her pudding and poked at it with her spoon. The girls waited. Finally, the old lady said in a voice of extreme reluctance, "I suppose we could go in the carriage."

"Oh, but it's—ow!" Clarissa broke off as Izzy kicked her on the ankle.

"Thank you, Lady Scattergood, that would be wonderful," Izzy said. "I really appreciate it—*we* really appreciate it."

"*Hmph.* We'll see."

For the next few minutes there was no conversation, only the clinking of cutlery and crockery. Luckily the old lady was concentrating on her pudding and didn't see the silent conversation going on between Izzy and Clarissa, a conversation of gestures and looks and eyebrows.

"Lady Scattergood," Clarissa said, having lost the silent debate.

The old lady looked up with a baleful look. "What is it now?"

"We need new clothes." Lady Scattergood picked up her lorgnette again and Clarissa hurried on. "The few dresses we have were made by the village dressmaker when we ended our period of mourning. Before that all our clothes were, of course, black, but knowing we were going to London, we didn't have many new dresses made."

"The village dressmaker being rather old fashioned and not up with the latest modes," Izzy added.

"I find shawls and scarves fill the purpose nicely." Lady Scattergood adjusted the shawl that was currently sliding off her narrow shoulders. "Doesn't matter what you wear underneath."

Clarissa gave Izzy a look of silent appeal.

"Your shawls are very beautiful," Izzy said, "but we really do need to order a whole new wardrobe and—"

"Lord Salcott gave us permission, and told me to have the bills sent to him," Clarissa said.

"And Lady Tarrant recommended her own dressmaker to us. A Miss Chance, near Piccadilly Circus," Izzy finished.

Lady Scattergood nodded. "Oh yes, Daisy. Very well, I'll have Treadwell order the carriage for tomorrow. You won't need me—I have no interest at all in being à la mode," she said unnecessarily. "Take your maid and Jeremiah." She wiped her mouth, burped genteelly into her napkin and tossed it aside. "Now if that's all, I'm for my bed. Good night, gels." She toddled off, accompanied by her herd of little dogs, leaving Izzy and Clarissa gazing at each other in bemusement.

"Well, that was easier than I thought it would be," Izzy said.

Clarissa clapped her hands. "I know. New clothes! I can't wait. *And* she's going to take us to that literary society. Whatever made you think of asking her?"

Izzy grinned. "While we were gallivanting around on horseback this morning, I was hatching out a plan."

"Really? I thought you were hatching out yet another quarrel with Lord Salcott. It certainly looked that way to me. Was that what his apology was about?"

Izzy pulled a face. She still had very mixed feelings about the Grumpy Guardian, and wasn't proud of her behavior. And his apology had quite unsettled her. "I don't want to talk about it."

Clarissa sighed. "Why do you always antagonize him? You'll catch more flies with honey than vinegar."

"Are you calling your noble guardian a *fly*, Clarissa? For shame." Izzy laughed at Clarissa's expression. "Besides, when he talks down to me in that bossy, irritating way he has, I *feel* vinegary. Now, do you want to hear the rest of my plan or not?" She glanced at the servants who were waiting to clear the table. "Let's go outside."

It was a fine, dry evening, but a brisk breeze had sprung up and they decided to sit in the summerhouse, a fascinating octagonal structure of vaguely oriental design, built almost entirely of glass. Lady Tarrant had told them where the summerhouse key was kept hidden, but the weather had been so good, they'd only glanced through the windows and hadn't been inside.

Entering the pretty little building they found a daybed and several comfy bamboo chairs piled with big squashy cushions. Clarissa threw herself into one. "Oh, isn't this lovely? What a perfect place this would be for reading. And we must have a picnic in here one rainy day."

"A picnic," Izzy repeated thoughtfully. "Yes." She made a note on the pad she'd brought with her.

"So, why did you kick me under the table?" Clarissa asked, wriggling back among the cushions. "I was only going to point out that Lady Davenham's house was but a short walk away and we wouldn't need the carriage. It's not as if Lady Scattergood is infirm or anything. A walk would probably do her good."

The twilight was turning from deep cobalt to navy blue; it would be dark soon.

"I know." A dozen or so candles in holders sat on a shelf. Izzy lit them and placed them at intervals around the summerhouse. "But Lady Scattergood doesn't go out in the open air, haven't you noticed?"

"Yes, but what does that signify?"

"There was a woman like that in the village I lived in with Mama. She never, ever left her house—Mama said she was frightened to go out, I don't know why. But if you visited her in her home, she was perfectly normal and hospitable. I think Lady Scattergood is a bit like that. So she won't walk out in the garden, or in the street, or go shopping with us, but maybe in a closed carriage, going from one house to another, she feels safer."

"Oh. Well, at least she agreed to take us. Now, tell me about this plan of yours."

Izzy began, "It's a bit outrageous—he's going to be furious—but I thought we might—"

"What are you doing in here? This place is private!" A sharp voice interrupted them. The summerhouse door opened, and a young woman of about their own age stepped in. Plump and pretty with glossy dark hair clustered around her face in fat sausage curls, she was fussily dressed in a lavishly trimmed pink-and-white dress covered in frills and tucks.

She eyed them suspiciously. "This place is for residents only. How did you get in?"

"We are staying with Lady Scattergood," Clarissa explained.

"Is it any concern of yours?" Izzy said at the same time. The girl's accusatory tone annoyed her.

"That peculiar old lady? *Hmph!* Mama and I thought she was dead." The girl narrowed her eyes at Izzy. "And of course it is my business. We don't want riffraff getting in."

"And yet here you are," Izzy said with a smile.

The girl stiffened. "How dare—"

"Oh, please don't let's quarrel." Clarissa floundered her way out of the squashy cushions and approached the girl, smiling. "How do you do? I'm Clarissa Studley and this is my sister Isobel, but we call her Izzy. And you are . . . ?"

The girl pouted, slanted a frosty glance at Izzy, then said with an air of consequence, "I am Miss Millicent Harrington."

"It's so nice to meet you, Miss Harrington," Clarissa said. "We've only recently arrived in London, and so far we've only met Lord and Lady Tarrant and their daughters."

Miss Harrington sniffed. "They're not her daughters. She only married him recently. Her nephew, Lord Thornton, is a diplomat, you know. He married her goddaughter. They are living in Vienna at the moment."

"Yes, we know. Won't you sit down?" Clarissa gestured to one of the comfy chairs. "It's so nice to meet someone of our own age."

Miss Harrington gave Izzy another cold look and then, as if conferring a favor on Clarissa, consented to sit. "I am making my come-out this season," she announced. "We have vouchers for Almack's."

"How delightful," Clarissa said. "We hope to visit Almack's, but nothing is yet organized."

"The vouchers are extremely difficult to obtain. You have to know the right people," Miss Harrington said. She smoothed her ruffles complacently. "Mama is second cousin to a duke, you know. Naturally, she knows all the right people."

Izzy instantly vowed that by hook or by crook they would somehow obtain vouchers for Almack's.

"Who is sponsoring you?" Miss Harrington asked. "Your mother?"

"No, Mama is dead," Clarissa said.

"And Papa died a year ago," Izzy added.

"So who is sponsoring you? Not that crazy old lady, I hope."

"If you mean Lady Scattergood—our hostess—she's not in the least bit crazy, and I won't have her spoken of so disrespectfully," Izzy said.

Miss Harrington pouted, then said pettishly, "I'm sure I didn't mean anything by it. I'm only repeating what everybody says."

"Well, don't, because 'everybody' is wrong," Izzy said.

Miss Harrington pouted again. She glanced from Izzy

to Clarissa and back again. "You don't look much like sisters to me."

"No," Clarissa said pleasantly. "I take after my mother and Izzy looks like our father. Do you have any brothers and sisters, Miss Harrington?"

"No, I am an only child."

"What a pity," Clarissa said. "It must be so lonely."

Miss Harrington looked surprised. "Not at all. I prefer it that way."

"Really? I don't know what I'd do without Izzy."

"Milly, Milly darling, where are you?" a fretful voice called from the garden.

Miss Harrington stood up. "That's Mama. I must be off. She dotes on me, you know, and worries if I'm gone too long." She glanced at Izzy again. "But you shouldn't be burning candles in here. They're dangerous."

"Nonsense," Izzy retorted. She'd placed the candles carefully.

"And the gentle glow they make is so pretty, much prettier than a lantern," Clarissa said.

"Well, just make sure you put them out before you leave," Miss Harrington said and flounced out.

"Bossy cow," Izzy said. "As if we don't know better than to leave candles burning unattended."

"Perhaps she's just a bit awkward meeting new people," Clarissa suggested.

Izzy laughed. "Yes, as awkward as a rhinoceros. Ah well, you wanted to meet more of our neighbors. At least so far they're balanced."

"Balanced?"

"Two delightful and two abominable. I say two, because I can't imagine Mama Harrington is any better than her toplofty daughter. We have to get vouchers for Almack's, 'Riss, we just have to."

Clarissa sighed. "I know. But how?"

"I'll think of something."

* * *

The following morning they were washing their hands and tidying their hair after walking the dogs with Jeremiah, when their maid, Betty, knocked at the door. "Beggin' your pardon, misses, but the carriage to take you to the dressmaker's is at the front door. And Lady Scattergood says Jeremiah and me are to go with you." She bounced up and down on her toes. "I ain't never been to any dressmaker's shop, let alone a proper posh London one."

Izzy and Clarissa hurried to don hats and pelisses. They were as excited as Betty.

They gave the coachman the address of the dressmaker Lady Tarrant had told them about: Miss Chance, off Piccadilly.

More than two hours later they piled back into the carriage, a little dazed. "Well, what did you think of that?" Clarissa said as she collapsed onto the seat.

"I know," Izzy agreed. "Whatever I expected, Miss Chance wasn't it." The dressmaker was small, elegant, outspoken, Cockney and had a decided limp. Izzy had had doubts at first, but by the end of the session she'd decided Miss Chance was a marvel.

First she'd told Betty to go into the back room and ask someone called Polly to give her a cup of tea and a seat because the ladies would be a while. A dressmaker who was considerate of a maidservant—that was a surprise.

Then she'd turned to Izzy, her gaze raking her from top to toe. She'd given a brusque nod, then she examined Clarissa with just as close a scrutiny.

"Sisters, eh? I 'ope you're not plannin' to wear matching dresses."

"No, not at all," Izzy said.

"Good, because it wouldn't suit you, and in any case, I wouldn't do it." She grinned. "You each 'ave a very different kind of beauty, and you each need different styles to bring out your beauty."

"Beauty? *Me?*" Clarissa blurted.

The little dressmaker directed a stern look at her. "Yes, you, Miss Studley. Every woman is beautiful in her own way and it's me purpose in life to bring it out. Now, will you trust me to know my business?"

Clarissa hesitated. "Yes," Izzy said firmly.

Cups of tea and a dish of almond biscuits were brought in while they perused fashion magazines—mostly English, but some also from Paris and even one from Germany. "I make up me own designs," Miss Chance assured them. "These are just for you to look at and let me know the kind of thing you like and don't like."

Izzy had decided tastes and she didn't hesitate to approve some styles and condemn others. Miss Chance nodded. "You know what suits you, I reckon, miss. That's good." She turned to Clarissa. "What about you, miss? Anything here take your fancy?"

Clarissa looked at the drawings doubtfully. "All these ladies look six foot tall, and are as thin as a lath."

Miss Chance laughed. "I know. Nutty, ain't it? Don't worry, I'll design your dresses special just for you, and you'll look and feel stunning." She added, "That's the key to bein' beautiful, Miss Studley—first you gotta *feel* beautiful and then people will start to notice that you *are* beautiful. It's all in your attitude."

Izzy could have hugged the little lady. Izzy had been telling Clarissa that kind of thing for years, and now that a fashionable London dressmaker was saying it, maybe Clarissa might even believe it.

They were then ushered behind the velvet curtains, where embarrassingly detailed measurements were taken by Polly, assisted by Betty.

Next there was a discussion between Miss Chance and

her assistant, Polly, about the colors and fabrics and styles that would suit each young lady. One room contained rolls and rolls of sumptuous fabrics; it was an Aladdin's cave of gorgeousness.

Izzy and Clarissa, who up to now had only ever worn clothes made by maidservants or the village dressmaker, were dazzled by the rich range of fabrics and the detail Miss Chance and Polly went into, trying this and that, with Polly making notes all the time.

They ordered lavishly—morning dresses, walking dresses, half dresses, evening dresses and ball gowns—along with sets of the prettiest underclothes they'd ever seen. They ordered spencers and pelisses and even an opera cloak, though they'd never been to the opera. Miss Chance also recommended a couple of milliners, a glover, and a shoemaker who could be relied on to make elegant new shoes to match their pretty new outfits.

In the carriage going back to Lady Scattergood's a thoughtful silence fell. Izzy guessed that Clarissa was thinking much the same as she was: What was the point of getting so many lovely new clothes if they didn't have a chance to wear them for something more exciting than walking the dogs and attending a literary society?

But they would. Izzy was determined on it.

"Lord Salcott is going to hit the roof when he sees the bill," Clarissa said.

Izzy waved that idea away. "Nonsense, if he's going to be miserly, he shouldn't have told you to go ahead and order what you needed. He must know London is expensive."

But he'd approved the spending for Clarissa, not Izzy. She felt a little bit guilty about that. But, she reminded herself, he'd been prepared to make her a handsome allowance and more if she'd agreed to disappear. This way he'd still be spending money on her while retaining the privilege of her company. Her much more elegantly dressed company.

A spurt of laughter escaped her as she imagined his expression if she presented him with that point of view. He wanted her gone, gone, gone. But she wasn't going anywhere.

"What's so funny?" Clarissa asked.

"Nothing," she said. "Just something amusing I saw in the street. We've passed it now."

Chapter Six

❧

Leo's traveling chaise passed between the gateposts of Studley Park Manor. He hadn't mentioned to the young ladies that he planned to visit their former home; he wanted to learn for himself what their life had been.

As it happened, the cousin who had inherited the estate was away from home at some kind of family gathering, which turned out to be a good thing. The servants, once they realized Leo was Miss Clarissa's guardian, were eager to talk to him and get news of the girls.

Both girls, he noted, not just Miss Clarissa. The cook gave him tea and dainty biscuits and someone summoned Edwards, the estate manager. He quickly joined Leo and helped himself to the refreshments.

"I'm inquiring about the arrangements made for Sir Bartleby's former servants," Leo told him.

"Oh aye?" The man quirked an eyebrow in a manner indicating he thought it none of Leo's business.

"Miss Studley is concerned about their welfare," Leo

explained. "Fearing her father might not have made sufficient provision."

The man relaxed. "She was right there. But you can tell Miss Clarissa that we're all in good hands with the new master."

"Everyone is employed?"

"All but a groom I would have sacked anyway, and old Nanny Best." He grimaced. "The young master is only just wed and has no need for a nanny yet. Even so, she's really too old to take charge of a young child—she's past seventy. The master has been sympathetic, but she's been given until the end of the month to make other arrangements." His expression was grim. "I don't know what will become of her."

"Nanny Best will be taken care of," Leo said briskly. "Arrangements have been made for her."

"Oh aye?" Edwards said cynically. "What sort of arrangements and by whom? Not Sir Bartleby, I'm thinking."

Leo gave him a mind-your-own-business kind of look that normally quelled questioners, but Edwards just laughed. "I didn't think so. That man never spent a penny except on himself. So you or the girls are taking responsibility?"

Leo gave a curt nod. "There is a cottage vacant on my estate. She will live there, and be given a pension to live on. And be cared for in her old age."

Edwards's eyes warmed. "Thank you, my lord, it's very good of you. Nanny Best was Miss Clarissa's mother's nanny, too, and it was a disgrace that after decades of service she was left with nothing."

Leo hadn't realized that.

Edwards glanced at the cooling pot of tea and sent for ale and sandwiches, which arrived quickly. Leo took advantage of the relaxed atmosphere to ask him about the young ladies' histories. He told himself it was part of his duty as a guardian, but really, he was just curious.

"Miss Izzy was the best thing that ever happened to Miss Clarissa," Edwards said. "Before she came, little Miss Clarissa wouldn't say boo to a goose. She used to drift around the house, a shy and lonely little sprout. The master never let her play with the village children, see, and look around you"—he gestured—"have you seen anyone under the age of fifty here? As I said, Nanny Best is past seventy now, and what kind of company was that for a young girl?" He tasted his ale, gave an approving nod and took a deeper draft. "Miss Clarissa and Miss Izzy took to each other from the very first day, and from that moment on they were inseparable."

"Sir Bartleby expressed concern that his natural daughter was exerting undue influence over Miss Studely."

Edwards gave a scornful snort. "As if he would know. He barely came near this place while the girls were growing up, and when he did—" He broke off. "Well, no use in speaking ill of the dead . . ." He picked up a sandwich and ate it in two bites.

"If Sir Bartleby was so unhappy with his natural daughter living here, why did he allow it?"

Edwards snorted again. "Miss Clarissa wouldn't let him take her away. You should have seen her standing up to her father—her that used to be as soft as a newborn kitten. Grew a backbone, she did, once her sister came to live with her. Told her father to his face, more than once, 'She's my sister, Papa, and I'm keeping her.' And whenever Sir Bartleby was in residence—which wasn't often—the girls hid themselves away." Edwards chuckled reminiscently. "They reckoned he couldn't toss Miss Izzy out if he couldn't find her."

Leo drank his ale. It was very good. Edwards, and indeed all the servants, must have cooperated to conceal Isobel from her father. How interesting.

Leo looked up to find Edwards watching him. "Any influence Miss Izzy had over Miss Clarissa was all to the good," the man said firmly. "She's a handful, Miss Izzy, full of mischief—and didn't she lead us all a merry dance at times?—but she's a good-hearted little lass and there's not a mean bone in her body. She'd do anything for her sister. And after she came to live here, Miss Clarissa blossomed."

Edwards set down his tankard, leaned forward and gave Leo a stern look. "You don't want to take too much notice of whatever Sir Bartleby told you, my lord. He had it in for that child from the moment he knew of her. It's as if he blamed her for her own birth." He shook his head. "And he punished Miss Clarissa for siding with her sister."

"How?" Leo asked.

Edwards made a disgusted gesture. "Made them both homeless didn't he? Sir Bartleby should have left Miss Clarissa the house and estate, but instead he left it to some distant cousin he'd never even met. He thrust his own daughter—both his daughters—out into the cold, made them homeless." If they'd been outdoors, Leo thought, the man would have spat.

Leo blinked. "I assumed there was an entail."

"'An entail'?" Edwards repeated scornfully. "No, Lord Salcott, there was no entail. Sir Bartleby could have left the estate to whoever he wanted. And so he did. That man never did forgive the girls for defying him, and he made that will out of pure spite."

How shocking, that a man could make both his daughters homeless for such a petty reason. And leave a damning letter behind to make things worse for Isobel.

Even as a young girl, she was attempting to work her wiles on my guests.

"Sir Bartleby implied Miss Isobel showed a . . . an untoward interest in his male guests."

Edwards made a scornful noise. "More like the boot was on the other foot."

"I beg your pardon?"

For a short time Leo didn't think Edwards was going to answer. He just picked at some invisible irregularity in the fabric of his breeches. Leo was about to ask him again what he meant, when he started speaking. "Look, I don't know the full story—you'd best ask the women about all that, but I'll warn you now, they keep it between themselves. I knew there was something nasty afoot—it blew up when young Isobel was fifteen or sixteen—even then she was budding fair to become a rare little beauty. And the kind of guests Sir Bartleby invited, well, they weren't the sort who were encumbered by morals or even common decency." His mouth twisted. "To that kind of man, a lovely young girl is temptation."

Leo must have made some kind of sound, because Edwards looked up, his face grim. "As I said, the girls tended to disappear when their father was visiting. I don't rightly know what happened—I was out on the day—but it was clear something untoward had taken place. When I got back, Sir Bartleby was in a rage and his guests were all stirred up—some were laughing and jeering, and the one they were laughing at was in a white-hot fury. And the women of the house—" He met Leo's gaze, his eyes glittering with anger. "I'm talking about the women servants, not the doxies Sir Bartleby's guests brought with them—the women of the house clammed up like you wouldn't believe. Could not get a word out of them about what had happened, but after that they made sure neither of the girls was ever alone again while their father and his guests were visiting."

"I see." There was a sour taste in Leo's mouth, and it wasn't the ale. "Thank you for letting me know. Now, I'd like to leave within the hour. Would you have Nanny Best step in here, please?"

When he informed Nanny Best that she was to be housed in a cottage of her own on his estate, and given a generous pension to support her, the old woman burst into tears. Leo shifted uncomfortably. Women's tears unmanned him.

He hurried her off with instructions to pack what she needed—anything she forgot could be sent on afterward.

While he was waiting for her to pack her belongings, Leo questioned the cook and several of the women servants about the tale Edwards had told him, but as the man had said, they were vague and evasive, and he came away none the wiser about the details. But it was clear whom they supported, and it wasn't Sir Bartleby.

He drove away from Studley Park Manor with more questions than answers, and in the company of an elderly nanny who was embarrassingly grateful. The only way he could stop the endless flow of thanks was to ask her about the girls, and so the trip between Studley Park and his own estate—thankfully not a very long one—was filled with stories about the doings of Miss Clarissa and Miss Isobel. She, too, was fond of both girls, though Clarissa was clearly her darling. Understandable if she'd been nanny to Clarissa's mother as well.

None of what he'd learned about Isobel Burton in this visit fitted with any of the accusations Sir Bartleby had made in his letter. The letter, like the will he'd left, was an act of spite.

The Isobel the servants talked about—bright, lively, mischievous and a little rebellious—was the Isobel he'd seen from the start.

And yet from the day he first met her, he'd let himself be influenced by the calumnies in Sir Bartleby's letter. Of course, he was bound by the weight of it being a deathbed communication—and at that time he hadn't known the girls at all. But he'd believed it at first—or at least tried to—though why he had was a mystery, even to him.

Now, his visit to Studley Park Manor had extinguished

any lingering doubts, and all he had to wonder about was the kind of man who would leave his daughters without a home simply because they'd defied him—successfully.

The prospect of separating the two girls was looking even more impossible now. But somehow he had to do it.

"Well, wasn't that fun?" Clarissa said. She and Izzy were on the front steps of Lady Davenham's house, waiting for the carriage to collect them. "I never thought a literary society would be like that."

Izzy nodded. "Lady Scattergood enjoyed herself, too, don't you think? From the reaction of some of the people there, she's been greatly missed." Lady Scattergood was awaiting the carriage from inside the house. She had entered and exited the carriage in a rush, clinging to the girls, her eyes closed, as if trying to block out all awareness of the outside world. Izzy was enormously grateful to her for making the effort of coming out. Because it clearly was an effort.

"Did you see her with Lady Davenham's cats?" Clarissa murmured.

Izzy chuckled. "I did. The more she narrowed her eyes at them, pulling her best cat-repelling face, the more the cats were intrigued and approached her."

Their carriage arrived, and for the next few minutes they concentrated on getting the old lady into it. The girls took one arm each and led her—eyes scrunched closed—to the carriage. She was tense and shaking, though not as much as she had been when they'd left her house earlier in the evening.

A few minutes later they pulled up outside her house and repeated the exercise in reverse.

Once inside, Lady Scattergood shook off their hands, heaved a huge sigh and looked around her, as if reassuring herself that nothing had changed. "Well," she said. "Well."

The little dogs yapped and frolicked around her feet, and she picked one of them up and hugged it to her bosom.

"I did it," she said. "Didn't I?"

"You did," Izzy said. "And it wasn't easy, I know. You were very brave."

"Pshaw!" she said, but she looked pleased. "It wasn't as hard as I thought. Yes, my precious ones, it *is* beastly cats you can smell," she added to the interestedly sniffing dogs. "Bea's house is infested with the creatures."

"Everyone was very happy to see you," Clarissa said. "Lady Davenham thanked us for bringing you along."

"Bea did?"

Clarissa nodded. "She said she'd missed you."

"Did she?" Lady Scattergood said vaguely.

Izzy hid a smile. Lady Davenham, who'd told the girls to call her Lady Beatrice, had made no bones about it. She'd informed her old friend that she wasn't going to be allowed to rot in solitude any longer, that she knew what that was like from personal experience, and it was dashed unhealthy!

Her parting words to Lady Scattergood were an order to come to the next meeting. "And if you don't, I'll come and roust you out myself, Olive Scattergood, don't think I won't! And you needn't bother instructing your butler to tell me you're not at home. I won't fall for that nonsense again!" She was a redoubtable old lady, and Izzy didn't doubt her for a minute.

"So we'll go to the next literary society meeting?" Izzy prompted.

"We'll see," Lady Scattergood said. "I'm exhausted. Tell Cook I'll take my supper on a tray tonight. Good night, gels." She tottered upstairs, accompanied by her little pack of dogs.

Izzy turned to Clarissa. "I hadn't expected to see quite so many society people in attendance. There were titles galore. To be honest, it was a little intimidating."

"I know. And I certainly didn't expect to see Miss Chance the dressmaker there, but she seemed quite at home, didn't she?"

"I think she *is* at home," Izzy said. "I gather she lives there, in Lady Davenham's house, with her husband and young daughter."

"How unusual. Come, let's talk upstairs." Clarissa led the way to the small cozy sitting room between their bedchambers. It had become their own special place.

Izzy kicked off her shoes and curled up on the sofa. "I can't believe how everyone was so friendly. I don't know about you, but several people promised to send us invitations—"

"Yes, some ladies told me that, too," Clarissa said, snuggling into the overstuffed chair that was her favorite. "We'll have to compare."

"Not to balls or anything because we're not officially out—"

"And we probably won't ever be if Lord Salcott has his way," Clarissa said gloomily.

"No. *You* could make your come-out," Izzy reminded her. "*I'm* the problem."

"As if I'd want to do it without you. Not that it matters now." Clarissa gave her sister a look of triumph and bounced up and down in her seat. "We have our first ton invitation. Old Lady Gastonbury invited us to her *soirée musicale* tomorrow evening."

"That's wonderful." Izzy couldn't recall which old lady Lady Gastonbury was, and had only the vaguest idea of what a *soirée musicale* might involve, but it was a start. "It's exactly the kind of thing we need—invitations to small family parties and informal evenings."

"Yes, and quite a few ladies said they would call on us in the morning," Clarissa added.

Izzy sat up. "Morning calls? Oh dear, should we make

them, too? I'm not quite sure what the process is. We leave cards or something, don't we?"

Clarissa shook her head. "I'm not sure, either. But we can't make any morning calls, not without Lady Scattergood, and she won't be going out to make them. But I'm sure people will understand."

It started to rain, the drops pattering softly against the windows. Treadwell arrived and lit the gas lamps.

"Do you think all those people who said they'd send us invitations will actually do it?" Izzy said when he'd left.

Clarissa shrugged. "Who knows? People often say things they don't mean. We'll just have to wait and see. Now, I want to read the rest of that story they were reading today. Do you think Lady Scattergood will have it in her library?"

Izzy jumped up. "I'll go and see."

"No, I will," Clarissa said.

"First one to find it gets to read it," Izzy said. Laughing, they raced each other to the library.

Leo settled Nanny Best in her new home, introduced her to the neighbors, made sure she had enough supplies and presented her with an advance on her pension, which in future would be paid through his estate manager. He'd told her it was being paid via Clarissa's trust, and was a bequest from Clarissa's mother, which was the easiest way to stop the flow of thanks.

Next he turned his attention to the state of his estate. Despite the efficiency of his estate manager, after almost a year away, he had much to catch up on. And having traveled widely and observed how things were done in other countries, Leo had returned with ideas and techniques that he was planning to implement.

He was almost entirely focused on the agricultural aspects of the estate—new farming techniques, new crops and livestock breeding programs, and with his estate manager he visited his tenant farmers, talking about what he'd learned and finding out which farmers might be interested in implementing some of these new ideas.

But each day as he returned home, he became more and more aware of the faded, out-of-date interior of his house. Oh, his servants had kept it clean, well-scrubbed and polished, but cleaning could only go so far.

Much of the furniture was worn as well as heavy and old-fashioned; the curtains had faded and some rugs were quite threadbare. It hadn't occurred to him until he'd gone away, but apart from general maintenance, very little of the house had been updated since he was a small boy. His mother hadn't spent enough time there to care about the interior of the house, as long as the public rooms where she received guests, and her own suite of rooms, were up to the mark and to her taste. The rest she'd ignored, and Leo's father, like Leo, had been oblivious.

The change Matteo had wrought on the London house made Leo very aware that this house—his true home—was also in dire need of refurbishment. But he had no idea where to start. He'd never been much interested in design; all he knew was that his house looked shabby and he didn't like it. He would have to get Matteo onto it.

By the end of the first week, he'd made good progress and, planning a visit to one of the more distant of his tenants, the name of a village popped out at him from the map. It was the village where, he'd learned from Edwards, the manager of Studley Park Manor, Isobel Burton had spent the early years of her life with her mother.

Leo stared at the map. It wasn't far out of his way. He could . . .

No, he didn't need to go there. Any remaining doubts he'd had about Isobel had been thoroughly eradicated by his visit to Studley Park Manor. He thrust all thought of visiting the village firmly from his mind.

But his eyes kept returning to the map.

He was curious, that was all, curious about her early childhood before she'd arrived at Studley Park, curious to see how she and her mother had lived. He wanted to know everything about her, and not because he mistrusted her. The truth was, he was becoming all too fascinated by that young lady.

But no, he wasn't going there. He had quite enough to do without visiting obscure villages for no reason but simple curiosity.

A nother invitation, for Thursday." Izzy fished it out of her pocket and handed it to Clarissa. "That's six for this week alone."

"Not counting Lord Randall's invitation to Astley's Amphitheatre tomorrow night," Clarissa reminded her.

"Oh, I haven't forgotten that one. I'm really looking forward to it. Unlike this 'musical evening'—I hope it's not like Lady Gastonbury's soirée was." She pulled a face. "That granddaughter of hers—lord, she can't hit a note to save her life!"

"Oh, but she's so nice. And so enthusiastic."

Izzy laughed. "You're so much nicer than I am. I like Cicely, too, but the moment she opens her mouth to sing, I'd happily smother her."

Clarissa arranged the invitations in a fan on the table in front of her. They'd fallen into the habit of spending their free evenings in the summerhouse after Lady Scattergood, who kept very early hours, went to bed. "It's working well, isn't it, our plan?"

Izzy nodded. The Studley sisters were gradually being absorbed into the ton, as she'd hoped. But it wasn't without mixed feelings on her part.

They sat quietly, watching the night slowly darkening around them. The sky was cobalt blue, the candles inside glowing golden, setting shadows dancing with every faint air current.

"Isn't it beautiful here?" Clarissa said. "It's like the fairy houses we used to imagine when we were children."

Izzy's thoughts were elsewhere. "Clarissa, have you noticed how we've been introducing ourselves to other people?"

"What do you mean? We do it as we always have."

"Yes, but until we came to London, we rarely had to introduce ourselves to anyone—everyone at Studley Park knew who we were."

Clarissa's brow furrowed slightly. "What are you're getting at?"

"We tell people our names, and we say we're sisters, and then when they comment on our lack of resemblance, we explain that you take after your mama and I take after our father."

"Which is all perfectly true."

"Yes, but we never so much as hint that we had different mothers. Or that I'm not legitimate."

Clarissa shrugged. "Well, why should we? It's nobody's business but ours."

"It's not very honest."

"No, it's not, but I don't think we have any choice. If people are so stupidly prejudiced . . ."

Izzy gave her a troubled look. "You realize once the truth gets out—and it will—you will bear the brunt of the blame."

"Nonsense. They'll all blame you, as everyone always has in the past. You know they will, Izzy. For some ridiculous reason I'm held to be the naive, easily led one, and you're the bad one who leads poor, pure, innocent me into temptation of all the wickedest sorts."

Izzy grimaced. "Baaaad blood will out," she said in a very fair imitation of one of the servants at Studley Park.

Clarissa snorted. "It's not fair and it never has been, but you deserve to make your come-out and make a future for yourself just as much as I do. And I need you with me if I'm to manage. Anyway, it's not a lie, not really—just not the complete truth. And nobody ever tells the complete truth anyway, do they?"

That was true enough, Izzy conceded.

"So whatever happens, we'll deal with it together—agreed?"

Izzy sighed. "Agreed." But she still wasn't comfortable with the deception, even though it had been her own idea to enter society this way, via the back door. It was all very well for Clarissa to insist that she needed Izzy with her, but what would happen when the axe finally fell and their mendacity was exposed—as it was bound to be eventually? It could get very nasty—people *hated* being tricked—and Clarissa wouldn't be able to handle that at all. She was the softest-hearted creature in the world. And it would all be Izzy's fault.

W ell, it's very good of you to visit, melord," Leo's tenant farmer said, "but I don't take to them foreign newfangled notions. My father farmed this land and his father before him and his father before that, and what was good enough for them is good enough for me."

Leo knew there was no point in pushing his suggestions. Change happened slowly in the country, and once this fellow saw how other farmers on the estate were increasing their harvest and their profits from those same "newfangled notions," he'd change his mind. Profit was a great innovator.

He took his leave, climbed into his carriage and drove

away. And stopped at a crossroad. The right-hand turn would take him home. The left-hand one led to the village where Isobel Burton had spent the early years of her childhood.

After a brief wrestle with his conscience, Leo took the left turn.

It was a neat little village, with a low-beamed half-timbered inn opposite the village green. He pulled up there, handed his horses over to an ostler and went inside.

A tankard of home-brewed ale and a tasty meat pie later, he ventured a few questions to the landlord about a Miss or Mrs. Burton who used to live here ten years or so ago.

"*Mrs.* Burton?" A nosy oldster sitting nearby scoffed. "Weren't no Mrs. about that one. A miss she was when she came here and a miss when she died, child or no."

"I see," Leo said. "And the child?"

The landlord shrugged. "Was took away when her ma died. Don't know what became of her."

"Wages of sin," the old fellow muttered. "Mother and daughter both."

"Now, Abel, they did no harm to anyone," the innkeeper said pacifically.

"'No harm'?" the ancient repeated. "'No harm'? She were a whore, and no doubt the child will follow her down that same sinful path."

"'A whore'?" Leo repeated. He was shocked. It was one thing to be a fallen woman with an illegitimate child, but quite another to be known as a whore.

"Just village gossip, your honor," the innkeeper said apologetically.

"Gossip my aunt Fanny! And din't the squire come callin' every week after dark and stay there half the night, leavin' in the small hours after takin' his fill of her?"

"You don't know that for sure, Abel," the innkeeper said.

The old man made a derisive noise. "I do! The whole

village knowed it, George, and it's no use you tryin' to pretty it up for the gentleman." He turned to Leo. "If you want to know more, sir, you ask Agnes Purdey in the white cottage at the end of the lane, the one half-smothered wi' roses. Ask her about the little visitor who stayed with her every Thursday night, and why the little visitor's mother could pay all her bills of a Friday mornin'." He snorted and took a deep draft of his pint of best bitter. "Whorin' she was, ain't no doubt about it."

Leo was of two minds whether to speak to Agnes Purdey or not. It felt . . . grubby.

He wished now he'd never come.

But he had, and now . . . He was torn. None of Sir Bartleby's former servants had spoken ill of Isobel, just that she was mischievous and adventurous and bold—none of which were criticisms, more like descriptions of a lively and intelligent child. And their continuing concern for the welfare of both girls spoke volumes. Servants might be paid to take care of children, but they weren't paid to care about them, or be fond.

His friend, Race, also liked her and saw nothing disreputable in her behavior. His aunt also liked her, and though Aunt Olive was eccentric, she wasn't stupid or easily deceived.

As for his own feelings about Isobel Burton, they weren't . . . simple. He was strongly attracted to her, and that was unsettling enough, given his position as her sister's guardian. And there were times when her mischief and defiance found him torn between itching to throttle her and wanting to kiss her senseless. His feelings? They were a tangle of contradictions.

As for her feelings about him, he had no idea. And it drove him crazy.

But before Leo could sort out his feelings, let alone act on them, he needed to know the truth about her past. It would help him clarify . . . what? He wasn't sure. It was just that having heard this about her mother . . .

It was probably just spiteful gossip. He should just walk away and forget what he'd heard.

But he couldn't. The thought made him sick, but he had to know. He found the rose-covered white cottage at the end of the lane, and knocked on the door.

Chapter Seven

❧

The excursion to Astley's Amphitheatre was one Izzy would never forget. She was still talking about it the next day. "Can you imagine how much training it must have taken to teach those horses to move all together like that, moving as one, so that man could ride three horses at once?"

"While standing upright on their backs and performing acrobatic tricks," Clarissa added. "I was breathless with anxiety the whole time. I also enjoyed the mock battle, and didn't you love those funny clownish acts?"

"Yes, it was all marvelous. But the horses were the best."

"I liked Lord Randall's cousin and her husband, too, didn't you?"

"Yes, they were very nice," Izzy agreed.

"And with the cousin to play chaperone, Lady Scattergood could rest easy about letting us go with only Betty to accompany us," Clarissa said.

Izzy flopped back in her chair. "Oh, I could happily go again tonight and watch it all over again." The whole evening had been enthralling. They'd gasped, marveled, laughed and gasped again, and then, once the show was over, Lord Randall took them all out to a place he knew where they sat outside in the open air—for the pleasure and novelty of it as much as for propriety—and ate a delicious supper.

Clarissa laughed. "It would be exhausting. I'd rather wait and then have it all happen again as something of a surprise. Perhaps Lord Salcott would take us. It is very good of Lord Randall to escort us, standing in for his friend. Not to mention taking us riding so often."

Izzy lifted her head and gave Clarissa a direct look. "He isn't just standing in for the Grumpy Guardian, 'Riss. He likes you, you know. *Likes* likes."

"Who? Lord Randall?" Clarissa's cheeks pinkened, but she dismissed the comment with a decisive shake of her head. "He's very charming, of course, but he's like that with everyone—every female."

"Perhaps, but I also think he is quite interested in you."

"I can't imagine why you'd think so. He's famous for escorting—and that, I presume is a euphemism—stunning beauties. In addition, he's reputed to be very rich, so he doesn't need my fortune. And as for the rest, well, what sort of a rake would he be if he didn't try to have every woman eating out of his hand?"

Izzy could see that Clarissa had given the matter some thought. And that faint blush had to mean something. "That's rather harsh isn't it?" she said. "He might actually just like you—as in enjoy your company."

Lord Randall flirted lightheartedly with Izzy, but she knew it meant nothing. He didn't flirt at all with Clarissa— obviously he'd noted she wasn't comfortable with flirting— but there was a kind of quiet solicitude in his attitude toward her. Which Izzy thoroughly approved of. Too many men ignored Clarissa because they considered her not worth noticing.

Clarissa shrugged. "He could have any woman he wanted. Why would he even look at me?"

"Why wouldn't he?" Izzy said. "Don't belittle yourself, 'Riss. You're—"

She broke off as Lady Scattergood's butler, Treadwell, entered the room. "Letter for you, Miss Studley." He presented Clarissa with a letter on a silver salver.

"Thank you, Treadwell." The minute the butler closed the door behind him, Clarissa continued, "Lord Randall is not interested in me, Izzy, he's just being polite. Besides, you know I could never be interested in a rake—have you forgotten so quickly the damage Papa's rakish ways caused? So get that thought right out of your mind. Now, let's see who this is from. Oh, it's from Nanny Best."

She broke the seal and carefully read through the letter, which was crossed and recrossed with Nanny's small spidery writing, and looked up at Izzy with a puzzled expression. "She's writing to thank me."

"What for?"

"The cottage and the pension."

"What cottage and pension?"

"The one my mother and I supposedly gave her." She handed Izzy the letter. "See for yourself."

Izzy read it. "A cottage on Lord Salcott's estate? He took her there himself in his carriage? And made sure she was settled comfortably and had everything she needed? It doesn't sound like the Grumpy Guardian at all."

Clarissa gave her a troubled look. "We'd better stop calling him that, if he's gone to all that trouble for Nanny Best. He didn't even know her. And it was Papa's responsibility to look after her after all her years of service, not his."

"Might he have arranged it with your trustees?"

Clarissa raised a skeptical brow. "A cottage on his own estate? Settling her in himself? My trustees might approve a pension, though I doubt it, but the rest is pure kindness."

Izzy had to concede her sister's point. For no reason she

could think of, Lord Salcott had given Nanny Best a home and security for the rest of her life. And not only had he seen to the old woman's comfort personally rather than assigning a servant, reading between the lines, it sounded like he'd done it in a very sensitive manner, respecting Nanny's dignity. And ascribing the kindness to Nanny's beloved Clarissa and her mother, rather than making the old woman feel like a charity case.

It was very good of him. It was also a little irritating. Just when she'd decided he was an annoying, bossy, arrogant, interfering nuisance, he did something kind and thoughtful, like this.

What would make him do such a thing? Izzy wondered. Did Lord Salcott perhaps have a tendre for Clarissa and do this to gain her approval? The idea disturbed her a little. Lord Salcott wouldn't be right for Clarissa at all. Besides, it would be unethical, surely, for a guardian to make advances to his ward, at least while she was under his legal control. No, he wouldn't do that. He was the sort who prided himself on doing the correct thing.

She glanced at her sister, who'd found paper, pen and ink and was writing back to Nanny. "Perhaps Lord Salcott did it to please you."

Clarissa snorted and didn't even look up. "Me? I'm not the one Lord Salcott never takes his eyes off. Face it, Izzy, he was just being kind."

Izzy sniffed at that. The man was a mass of contradictions. She refused to think about him anymore. She glanced at the clock on the overmantel. "Let's finalize our plans in the summerhouse after supper. I don't want old busybody Treadwell seeing what we're doing."

Clarissa looked up from her letter with an expression that was part excited and part apprehensive. "I can't believe we're really going to do it."

"We most definitely are, and it's going to be utterly

splendid." Izzy grinned to herself. And Lord Salcott was going to be absolutely furious.

The cottage door opened, and a small, tidy, white-haired woman peeked curiously out at Leo. She looked him up and down and the air of puzzlement on her face deepened. "Can I help you?"

He bowed slightly. "Good afternoon. Mrs. Purdey, I presume. My name is Leo Thorne." He'd decided not to use his title. It tended to have a strange effect on some people. When the woman didn't respond, he continued, "I'm here enquiring about a woman and her daughter who used to live in this village—a Miss or Mrs. Burton and her daughter Isobel."

The old woman's eyes narrowed suspiciously. "Oh aye?"

"I was told at the village inn that you might be able to help me."

She sniffed, unimpressed. "Is that so? By old Abel Miller, I'll be bound. And they say women gossip." She gave him another searching look, glanced beyond him at the carriage waiting in the road and the groom tending his horses, and pursed her lips.

For a moment Leo thought she was about to refuse to talk to him. And for a fleeting moment he hoped she would. He wasn't sure he wanted to hear the sordid details of Isobel Burton's childhood. But he had to know.

Then the old woman sighed and gestured for him to enter. "You might as well come in then, sir." It was a grudging invitation. Country people were usually very hospitable.

Leo had to bend his head to avoid knocking it on the lintel. She ushered him into her front parlor, a small, cramped, scrupulously neat room. It smelled of beeswax. There were fussy little china ornaments arranged on every highly polished surface. She waved him to a chair and bade him sit himself down. Her manner was businesslike, rather than friendly. Perhaps he should have used his title after all. She offered him tea, which he refused.

"What is it you want to know, sir?" She sat stiffly, twisting her apron between gnarled fingers.

"What can you tell me about Miss or Mrs. Burton and her daughter?"

"Louisa Burton, the mother, is dead. She died some ten or eleven years ago. As for young Isobel, I have no idea where she is now. A gentleman took her away on the day of her mother's funeral, never even gave the child a chance to say goodbye—her uncle I was told."

"Her uncle?" He'd had no idea she had an uncle. Nobody had ever mentioned it.

"Her mother's brother, I understand. He didn't exactly introduce himself to the likes of me—though I was one of the few people who attended the funeral. Now if that's all . . ." She made to rise.

Leo didn't move. "Could you tell me about how they lived?"

"It was in the cottage over yonder." She gestured.

"I didn't say where, I said how."

She sat back, her eyes narrowed. "Why do you want to know? It's all in the past."

Leo waited. Two could play at the waiting game.

Her lips compressed. "Abe filled your ears with nasty gossip, I suppose."

"He suggested a reason why young Isobel stayed with you every Thursday night when her mother had a visitor. And why she was able to pay her bills on a Friday."

"I wouldn't believe a thing Abel Miller said," she declared hotly. "He's a nasty old hypocrite. It's all sour grapes, sir. Louisa Burton was a lovely young woman, and half the village men were panting after her, including Abe Miller hisself!" She snorted. "But she wouldn't have a bar of any of them. She were a lady. And if her little daughter stayed with me on Thursday nights, what of it?" Her jaw jutted belligerently.

Leo waited.

"She were a decent, gently-raised lady fallen on hard times," Mrs. Purdey continued, her tone defensive. "When she first came here, she didn't know how to light a fire, how to cook, how to plant a garden to feed her and the babe. But she worked at learning it, oh yes, how she worked. No hoity-toity airs and graces there, no fussing about her soft little hands getting rough from hard work, for all she was as beautiful as a sunrise—and she was. Never seen a lovelier woman in all my life."

Leo nodded. He could believe it.

The old woman went on, "And *if* she'd chosen to whore herself, she could have made a *lot* more money and not been so short all the time—but she didn't!"

Leo raised a skeptical brow.

"And if the squire chose to befriend her and help her out from time to time, what business was it of anyone else's?" She glared at him, daring him to contradict her.

Leo could read between the lines. A gently bred woman with an illegitimate child, struggling to support herself and the babe, apparently without any assistance from her family or the father of the child. And if she sold her body to the squire in exchange for help? It was immoral, but the responsibility lay equally with Sir Bartleby.

"So Isobel stayed with you on Thursday nights?"

"If she did, what of it? Nothing wrong with visiting a neighbor, is there? Louisa adored that child, looked after her the very best she could. And I liked having her—good company the little lass was, even as a toddler. A bright, happy little soul, for all that her life weren't easy." Her expression grew bleak. "I wish I knew what had become of her."

She smoothed her apron thoughtfully, then gave Leo a

shrewd glance. "You know where she is, don't you, sir? 'Tis why you're askin' about young Izzy's ma."

Leo nodded. "She's living in London now."

"And that's all you're going to tell me?" she said indignantly. "London is a wicked place, full of sin and danger. Is my Izzy all right? Is she with people who love her? How is she getting along?"

Her concern for Isobel was touching. "She's in good hands—she's living with my aunt and her half sister."

She clapped a hand to her bosom. "She has a half sister?"

He nodded. "One who loves her very much, so you need have no fears for her."

"Then why are you here, asking about her and her ma? Coming all this way to dig up dirt. If you mean her ill . . ."

"I mean her no ill. I just . . . needed to know." Even to his own ears it sounded feeble. He rose. "I'll take my leave now. Thank you for your time."

"Wait."

He turned.

"You'll be seeing Izzy? You said she was living with your aunt."

He nodded.

"Then wait a moment, I've something for her." She hurried out and returned a few minutes later with a wrapped brown-paper bundle tied with string. "Would you give this to her, sir, please? It's just a few bits and pieces I took from her mother's cottage after her uncle took the child away. I thought one day she might come back and want them."

Leo tucked the parcel under his arm and turned to leave, when the woman spoke again. "Young Isobel, sir—has she turned out beautiful like her mother?" She looked at him expectantly.

"She looks like her father, but yes, she's beautiful." It came out a little husky. And then, for some unknown reason, he found himself adding, "Very."

Her face softened and she nodded. "You be good to my Izzy, then."

Feeling absurdly self-conscious—why on earth had he said that?—Leo bowed curtly and left the cottage. He'd be glad to leave the wretched village behind him.

He wished he'd never come here, never learned those sordid details about her mother. Isobel was not like her mother, no matter what Sir Bartleby had claimed. Even her mother was not the whore that Sir Bartleby had claimed. Her actions, immoral as they might be, were no doubt unavoidable, given her vulnerable position, and Leo couldn't find it in his heart to blame her.

Ohhh, I'm getting cramps." Clarissa flexed the fingers of her right hand. "I'm so glad you had the idea to get them printed. It's bad enough having to write out all the addresses."

Izzy addressed her last invitation and sat back with a sigh of relief. "There, that's my lot done. How are you doing?"

"Three more to go. How many is that now?"

Izzy grinned. "More than a hundred."

Clarissa groaned. "Lord Salcott is going to kill us."

Izzy gathered up the stack of invitations and packed them into a box. "Perhaps, but by then it'll be too late. Matteo said he'll get these delivered for us."

"Isn't he wonderful?" Clarissa shot her a troubled glance. "Don't you think we ought to warn him that Lord Salcott doesn't know a thing about it?"

"No," Izzy said. "We might as well be hanged for a sheep as for a lamb, and besides, if Matteo doesn't know the truth, Lord Salcott can hardly blame him for being tricked. He will have been tricked, too."

"What are you girls up to?" A voice came from the doorway of the summerhouse. Izzy suppressed a sigh. Miss

Millicent Harrington, local busybody and general irritation, entered and surveyed the room in a proprietorial manner. She spied the box of letters. "What are those?"

"A secret," Izzy said, closing the lid of the box. "You'll find out in a day or two." She and Clarissa had discussed it and reluctantly agreed that Milly and her mother would have to be asked.

Milly pouted and flounced into one of the comfortable chairs. "I heard you went to Astley's Amphitheatre."

"Yes, we did." Clarissa said.

"Mama says it's nothing but vulgar spectacle. Not a place for a lady." But she sounded envious.

"Really?" Izzy said. "We enjoyed it very much, didn't we, Clarissa?"

Milly continued, "I heard you were escorted by Lord Randall."

"Indeed?" Izzy said in a bored voice. "You hear a lot, don't you?"

"Yes! I don't know how you dared—he's a terrible rake, you know." She sounded both scandalized and thrilled by the notion.

"Mama says so, does she?" Izzy said.

Milly completely missed the ironic tone. "Yes, Mama warned me to stay well away from him, to give him no encouragement whatsoever." She glanced from Izzy to Clarissa and added, "Mama knows these things, being second cousin to a duke."

Clarissa compressed her lips and said nothing. Izzy yawned in an ostentatious manner.

"I've seen Lord Randall at a distance and he's terribly good-looking," Milly said after a moment. "So what was he like? Did he tell you any warm stories? Make improper suggestions?"

Izzy was about to give the silly creature a sharp setdown when she had a better idea. "He did tell one very warm story, didn't he, Clarissa?"

Clarissa gave her a puzzled look. Lord Randall hadn't told any scandalous tales. Izzy winked at her.

Milly leaned forward avidly. "Oooh, do tell."

"It was about his travels in Italy," Izzy said.

Milly's eyes brightened. "Mama says foreigners are frightfully immoral. So what happened?"

"Well," Izzy said, "he told us a story about when he visited Naples. He climbed up this mountain that overlooks the city and the bay. It's an amazing spectacle, apparently."

"Yes, but what *happened*?" Milly repeated.

"Well"—Izzy leaned forward and lowered her voice in a conspiratorial manner—"this mountain was a volcano, and it smoked constantly, and he went right to the edge of the crater and looked into the red-hot, violently bubbling core. Sparks and spurts of flame, smoke and frightful smells boiled up, and it was so hot and terrifying and glorious that several spectators fainted!" Izzy finished and sat back with a smile.

Milly stared at her. "Is that it? I thought you said he told you a warm story."

"But it was," Izzy said seriously. "That volcano is more than just warm—it was frightfully, fearfully hot."

Milly regarded her doubtfully, not quite sure what to think.

"Milly, Lord Randall has been a perfect gentleman at all times," Clarissa said firmly. "And you and your mother have no business spreading gossip about him. Now please leave. Izzy and I have much to talk about and we wish to be private."

Milly blinked. "Well!" she said. "Well! If that's how you feel!"

"We do," Izzy said. "Good evening."

Milly struggled out of the chair and stomped to the door. "And don't pretend you don't go riding with him nearly every day. I've *seen* you! I shouldn't even be *talking* to people who associate with rakes! Mama warned me!"

"Take her advice then," Clarissa said. "We won't mind."

"Regards to Mama," Izzy called after her. "Anytime she wants a warm story . . ."

Milly flounced off, and Izzy turned to Clarissa. "You talk to the gardeners here, don't you, 'Riss?"

Clarissa blinked, surprised by the abrupt change of subject. "Yes."

"Good. See if you can get them to plant a big tree—better still several trees, no, a hedge—blocking the view from the Harrington house. I'm fed up with that ghastly girl spying on us."

Clarissa giggled. "I'll see what I can do."

The sun was riding low in the sky, glinting off the dome of St. Paul's as London came into view. Leo felt oddly glad to be back. Three weeks since he was here last. In the past he'd always been glad to escape London. Now . . .

How had the young ladies found life in his absence? Flat, dull and uneventful, he hoped. He smiled to himself. After three weeks of the unalloyed company of Aunt Olive and her little mutts, they'd be willing to listen to reason.

His carriage pulled up in front of his house. It wasn't quite dark yet, but the front entry hall was lit up. Leo hadn't told Matteo exactly when to expect him, but the man was a miracle of efficiency. How close to completion was the refurbishment of the house, he wondered as he climbed the front steps. He reached for the doorbell, but to his surprise the front door opened and a complete stranger faced him.

"I'm sorry, sir, this is not the correct entrance. You need to go around the block to number 17."

"What the devil do you mean, 'not the correct entrance'? And who the devil are you?"

The footman stiffened. "I am Lord Salcott's footman, Grose, sir. And who might you be?"

"I am Lord Salcott," Leo said pushing past him. "And this is my house."

The man, horrified by his introduction to his new employer, gabbled apologies.

"Yes, yes, enough of that." Leo handed the man his hat and coat. "Understandable mistake. I suppose Matteo hired you. But what the devil did you mean by sending me to my aunt's address?"

"For the party, my lord."

"My aunt having a party, eh?" One of her little card parties no doubt. They were all she had, these days. She never went out.

"Er, yes, my lord." The man collected Leo's bag and followed him upstairs. Leo was glad to see no remaining evidence of workmen or workwomen—just a pristine, elegant house. Matteo had done a superb job.

"Where is Matteo, by the way?" he asked his new footman.

"Assisting your aunt, my lord." Passing Leo in the hallway, he hurried ahead and threw open the door to Leo's bedchamber. "Your rooms, my lord," he said proudly. "They are to your liking?"

They were. The walls were papered with a simple design of bamboo on a soft blue background, the architraves and ornamental plasterwork were crisp white, and the bedcover was of some richly textured stuff in dark reds and blues. There were no bed hangings. Leo was pleased. He'd always found bed hangings stifling.

"Italian silk, my lord," the footman said, reverently smoothing his hand over the bedspread as he set the valise on the floor beside it. He hurried across and drew the curtains, which were a plain dark blue with a delicate pattern like a watermark woven through them. "Shall I unpack for you now, my lord?"

Leo waved him away. "Later. And, Grose, you don't need to call me 'my lord' every second sentence."

"Very good, my lord. Will you want dinner sent up, my lord?"

Leo sighed. "No." He rather thought he'd dine at his club. With any luck he'd run into Race or some other friend. He was in the mood for congenial and undemanding company—male company.

He glanced around the room again. Matteo had done a very good job. It was pleasingly masculine, rich without being fussy or ornate. A strip of light showing between the folds of the curtains made him frown. Light? At this time of evening? His windows looked out to the gardens at the rear of the house, not the front, where gas lamps lit the streets.

He strolled to the window and drew one of the curtains aside. And blinked.

Instead of the shadowed serenity of the gardens at night, the place was brightly lit with dozens of globes of light strung between the trees—Chinese paper lanterns, if he wasn't mistaken.

And there were people moving around, lots of people, elegantly dressed ladies and gentlemen, drinking and chatting and laughing for all the world as if they were at Vauxhall instead of the much smaller and very private Bellaire Gardens. What on earth?

Curious as to the occasion, he went downstairs and entered the garden through his back gate. It looked beautiful, he had to admit, with the glowing lanterns lighting up the evening, throwing shadows, patterning the leaves. What was the occasion? Hearing music playing, he made his way toward it.

"Oho, cheeky aren't you, sneaking in that way?" a feminine voice called. "We were told to enter through Lady Scattergood's." Leo turned. It was a lady of his acquaintance whose name he could not immediately recollect. He smiled and bowed, murmured something inconsequential and moved on.

"Delightful party, Salcott," said a portly gentleman who was a member of his club. Alder? Aldridge? Some name like that. "Didn't think you were going to make it."

"Been on the road." Leo gestured to his traveling clothes, though why he should be expected to attend a party when he had no idea who was holding—

A thought struck him. No. They wouldn't. They couldn't.

"Charmin' gels, your wards," another gentleman said.

Leo smiled, trying not to grit his teeth, and moved on.

"Congratulations on holding such a bold and unusual event," a Roman-nosed matron wearing an enormous feathered turban told him. "The hostesses of the ton will be gnashing their collective teeth in envy. A twilight *soirée au jardin*—such a clever conceit and so refreshingly unusual."

Leo moved through the crowd, smiling, inclining his head in greeting, and uttering meaningless politenesses. Where the devil were those blasted girls? And how on earth had they managed to collect such a distinguished and fashionable crowd of guests?

"You were uncommonly lucky with the weather, Salcott," someone said. "Rain would have ruined everything."

"Yes, wouldn't it?" Leo agreed grimly, wishing for a downpour at this very instant. But the sky remained cloudless and the air almost balmy, curse it. And where were all the blasted biting insects when you needed them?

"A delightful event, Lord Salcott," an elegant lady of the ton greeted him. She'd been one of Race's flirts, he recalled.

"Have you seen Lord Randall?" he asked. Because surely they would have invited Race. And if he'd known about it and not told Leo . . .

Her smile froze. "Lord Randall?" she said as if she'd never heard of him. "Why on earth would I know? Or care?" She drifted languidly away, and he recalled that she'd been mightily displeased when Race had declined to take it further than flirting.

He prowled through the crowds, searching.

"I hadn't realized you'd become the guardian of Sir Bartleby's gels, Leo, m'boy," a friend of his father's told him. "Could have knocked me over with a feather."

"I think Studley originally intended the role for my father," Leo said.

"Wouldn't have minded taking on the dark-haired one for him. What a little beauty, eh?" He nudged Leo and gave a sly chuckle.

Leo wanted to punch him but had to content himself with "It is a responsibility I take very seriously," delivered with a hard look in a freezing voice.

"Yes, yes, of course," the old lecher said hastily. "Delightful party. Thank you for the invitation."

So *Leo* had invited all these people had he? Hah!

The summerhouse was ablaze with light. He looked in and to his surprise there was his aunt, seated on her peacock throne, holding court, surrounded by a group of older ladies and a few gentlemen, her little dogs seated at her feet. How on earth had the girls persuaded her out of the house?

She saw him and waved regally. "Leo, dear boy, you're late. Whatever kept you? Matteo, a drink for my nephew."

Beaming, Matteo hurried forward with a glass of wine. "Welcome 'ome, milor'."

Leo glowered. *Et tu, Matteo?*

Matteo beamed at him. "Is all going superbly, milor'. Everybody we invite has come. Is a grand success!" He didn't seem the least bit self-conscious. No shadow of guilt crossed his open face. No, Matteo wasn't responsible for this betrayal of trust.

Leo frowned. How had they done it? Somehow those two girls had roped his aunt and Matteo into this completely unauthorized, ridiculously fashionable, surprisingly well-organized party. Held in *his* name! Without a word to him from anyone. He didn't even know half the people here.

He glanced at the group surrounding his aunt. From his aunt's generation, he recognized among them a duchess, two countesses, an Austrian princess, a Polish baroness and a smattering of other distinguished-looking ladies.

"Your dear aunt brought your delightful Studley sisters to my literary society meetings," an elderly lady with improbably bright red hair told him. "They were, of course, an instant success. We all adore the dear gels." She beamed at him.

His Studley sisters? They weren't his at all. Nor were they "the Studley sisters."

He wasn't responsible for this—this travesty. He opened his mouth, ready to denounce them, to repudiate all responsibility for the party. And closed it again.

He looked for Isobel Burton among the crowd outside, but could see only Clarissa Studley, smiling and laughing, as happy as he'd ever seen her, standing with several ladies and a couple of gentlemen he didn't recognize. Leo's friend, Race, lurked on the edge of the group. The traitor. Why the devil hadn't he warned Leo?

His gaze returned to Clarissa. She was his ward, his responsibility. If he disclaimed all responsibility for the party, she would be the one disgraced. As would his aunt. And it was his duty to protect Clarissa Studley. And his aunt.

He knew who was really responsible for this flagrant piece of audacity, and it galled him that he couldn't punish her as she deserved without also humiliating the innocents involved.

Ah, there she was at last, Isobel Burton, at the center of a lively group of fashionably dressed young bloods all vying for her attention. And quite a few older ones, he observed grimly. She caught his eye and stepped away from them, deliberately placing herself between him and her half sister, cutting Clarissa off from his sight.

Elegant and lovely in a gown of the palest apricot, she

lifted her chin and smiled slowly across at him, triumph in every line of her body.

Across the crowd he raised his wineglass to her in an ironic salute.

Her eyes narrowed. Her smile faltered and a line appeared between her delicate brows. Good. She was under no illusion that he was congratulating her. Still less that he was conceding victory.

No, it was a promise of things to come.

He turned away and started talking to the nearest woman. He had no idea who she was, but he didn't care. She was both young and pretty and would provide sufficient distraction. From the corner of his eye he watched as Isobel Burton turned back to her circle of admirers, saying something that made them all laugh.

He gritted his teeth.

"D id you see?" Clarissa murmured to Izzy. "Lord Salcott is here."

Izzy nodded. "I know, I saw him."

"What bad luck. I was sure he wasn't going to return to town in time. How do you think he found out?"

Izzy shrugged, and shook her head.

"Maybe it will be all right," Clarissa said hopefully. "He hasn't said anything to you, has he? He saw me, but made no attempt to speak to me. And he didn't look angry to me."

"Oh, believe me, he was angry," Izzy said. Furious, in fact.

"You think so?"

"I know so. But don't let it worry you. It's a lovely party and almost everyone came, and I, for one, have no intention of letting Lord Grumpy spoil one minute of it for me."

Clarissa brightened. "It is a lovely party, isn't it? Everyone is saying so. The garden looks quite magical—the Chinese lanterns were the perfect touch. They look so pretty.

And hasn't Matteo done a wonderful job organizing the food and drink? I wouldn't have known what to do. Even Lady Scattergood is having a lovely time. I never thought we could get her out here, but Matteo's suggestion worked a treat."

"Matteo is a gem. Lord Salcott doesn't deserve him." Izzy had been observing Lord Salcott's interactions with Matteo. He didn't seem to be angry with him, but then he was also pretending he wasn't angry with her, and she knew that was a lie. She would have to make it clear to him that Matteo wasn't responsible.

But not tonight. This was her first ever party—Clarissa's, too—and Izzy was determined that nothing and no one were going to spoil it.

The string quartet began another tune. She swayed in time with the music. Oh, how she wanted to dance, but grass and gravel paths did not lend themselves to dancing— not the proper kind of dancing they did in London. Next time she would make sure they found some way to include dancing. Perhaps they could construct a low platform over the top of the grass.

Izzy laughed at her foolish thoughts. Next time? If Lord Salcott had his way, there would be no next time. Not for her. All the more reason to enjoy herself tonight. She reached out and snagged a glass of champagne from a passing waiter. Another first—champagne.

Aware of Lord Salcott's gaze boring into her from a distance, she turned to the nearest man and smiled.

Chapter Eight

❧

Leo circulated through the party, smiling through gritted teeth as compliments were showered on him: how charming the Studley sisters were, how lucky he was to have the guardianship of two such sweet gels, what a delightful party it was, how ever did he come up with such an original concept—surely it was the young ladies' idea? Such clever gels. And those Chinese lanterns, creating such an enchanting atmosphere, did he bring them back from his travels?

His jaw ached from smiling and pretending to feel pleasantly host-like and hospitable when he actually felt like punching someone, preferably one of those callow young idiots clustering around Isobel Burton, or better still those older jaded roués who edged too damned close, eyeing her with speculative interest.

And where had Race disappeared to? His supposedly good friend, who'd allowed this party to go ahead knowing full well Leo had forbidden the girls to attend any society entertainments, and yet had failed to inform Leo of what was happening. Race certainly deserved a punch on the nose. He knew his crime, too, for he'd managed to avoid Leo all evening.

"Lord Salcott?"

He turned to find a plump, dark-haired, fussily dressed matron beaming familiarly. A younger version of herself stood by her side, smiling coquettishly up at him. He sighed and tried to plaster a polite expression on his face.

"Mrs. Gertrude Harrington, Lord Salcott, and this is my daughter Millicent," the woman prompted him, adding with delicate emphasis, "*Miss* Millicent Harrington. We're your neighbors." She waved in the direction of one of the other houses that bordered the garden.

Leo bowed and murmured a greeting.

"Delightful to meet you at long last, your lordship, isn't it, Milly dear?"

The girl simpered. "Yes, Mama. How do you do, your lordship?"

"Such an oddity of life in the city that one may live a stone's throw from a dear neighbor and yet never see each other," the woman said.

An advantage of city living that had only just occurred to Leo.

"And such a delightfully unusual party. I wonder how you gained permission to hold it here in our gardens—there has never been anything like this held before, and as far as I know, none of the other residents were consulted," she said, sour beneath her smiles.

Ah. Leo would no doubt receive a raft of complaints from the neighbors in the morning. Delightful.

Her smile widened. "But what does that matter when you have such a distinguished collection of guests gathered here? Her grace and I were chatting with the countess earlier. They were both very complimentary about Milly's new hairstyle—weren't they, Milly darling?—but I'm not so sure." She laid a hand on Leo's arm. "What do you think, your lordship? You gentlemen are so much better than we ladies at knowing what suits us." The woman eyed him expectantly; the daughter preened and tried to manufacture a blush. Leo edged away. The woman's grasp of his arm tightened.

"I'm afraid I never notice such things," he said bluntly.

The woman and her daughter laughed delightedly as if he'd uttered some brilliant witticism. "Oh, indeed, your lordship, so true. How delightfully masculine. And shall we see you at Almack's in the near future? We have vouchers, you know. As I was saying to the princess just now, it is such a relief knowing that the patronesses insist on absolute exclusivity, and we are protected from the importunities of—"

Leo fixed his gaze on a bush over her shoulder. "Excuse me, madam, Miss um, I must speak to Mr.—oh, there he is." He bowed curtly and strode away looking decisive.

He'd invented the fellow he was supposedly looking for, but as luck would have it, he came upon Race. He pounced on him and drew him into a secluded corner. "What the devil are you doing here, Judas?"

Race delicately detached Leo's grip from his coat and smoothed the crumpled fabric. "Hands off, barbarian, this coat is new. What was the question again? Oh yes, why am I here? Because you invited me."

"You know perfectly well I did no such blasted thing. I knew nothing about this affair. Why didn't you warn me what the girls were up to?"

Race shrugged. "None of my business, is it, old chap? I'm not their guardian, am I?"

"I'm no*t their* guardian at all, only Clarissa's."

Race gave a knowing smile.

"What?" Leo snapped.

Race gave him an innocent look. "Nothing. Just that Miss Isobel is the first young woman in which you've shown an interest since Lavinia What's-her-name."

His words caused a curl of irritation in Leo's belly. "Nonsense," he said brusquely. "I have no interest in that young woman." It was a lie: she was rapidly becoming an obsession. But he didn't *want* to have an interest in her. That way madness—or at least danger—lay.

All the way back to London he'd been thinking kind thoughts of her, unjustly condemned by her father, loved by those who truly knew her. But now, here in this fragrant evening garden, luminous by lamplight, and in her element among the distinguished guests—it wasn't just her flagrant disregard of his instructions, but her lighthearted, mischievous, *triumphant* response to his anger. It drove him wild.

And the knowledge that he wanted her regardless drove him even wilder.

"I'm merely doing my duty—my unasked-for and unwelcome duty—by her half sister."

Race smirked. "Of course you are."

Ignoring the annoying smirk, Leo returned to the issue at hand. "Which is why I asked you to keep an eye on them while I was away."

"No, you asked me to take them riding from time to time. Which I did—and before you say another thing, think, hothead. How the devil do you imagine I could have stopped this affair if the first thing I knew about it was when I—along with half of London—received my invitation? It was far too late."

"Not too late to inform me."

"No, not too late for that," Race agreed. "And what would you have done if I had managed to get a message to you, buried as you were in your rural wilds?"

Leo opened his mouth, then shut it, realizing that he would probably have done exactly what he was doing now—nothing. To rush back to London and cancel it at the last minute would have caused a great deal of unwelcome speculation. And the kind of attention he was hoping to avoid.

"Besides, you give a most delightful party." It was deliberate provocation. Leo glowered at him, and Race laughed. "Oh, cut line, Leo. You're not angry because I didn't warn you; you're angry because the girls tricked you. And because the party is a splendid success. You laid down the rules and they broke them in splendid fashion, and now they're out in the world and you don't know what to do."

"Damn you, Race." His friend knew him too well.

His friend laughed again. "You know I'm right."

"Smugness is most unattractive in a man."

"And in a woman?" Race's eyes wandered to where Isobel was standing. Leo followed his gaze.

She turned, saw Leo watching, and again stepped deliberately in between him and her sister, shielding Clarissa from his gaze. Her message was clear. She was taking responsibility for this event, shouldering the blame, protecting Clarissa from his wrath.

It was infuriating. And, a small, reluctant part of him had to admit, admirable.

Race laughed softly, patted him on the arm and drifted off to join another group. For a moment Leo watched Isobel, laughing and chatting, a dozen gentlemen admirers hanging off her every word. And looking more beautiful in the lamplight than any woman had a right to be.

The urge to confront her chafed at him. But he didn't trust himself to do it in public.

A large matron trailing a wispy-looking daughter eyed him acquisitively and altered course, bearing down on him like a gunship in full sail towing a muslin-clad jolly boat. That decided him. He would speak to the girls in the morning. It was too late to do anything about this wretched party, and he didn't trust himself to hang on to his temper.

Leo turned and marched purposefully in the opposite direction—almost into the arms of a third woman with another unmarried daughter. She brightened, drew her daughter forward and gave him a welcoming smile. He scowled and veered off along a narrow pathway and lurked in the shadows behind a bush, waiting for them to pass.

The indignity of it only added to his temper.

This, *this* was why he wanted nothing to do with society. All these females hunting for a wedding ring with a title attached. Regardless of what *he* wanted.

And where were all the other unmarried gentlemen, dammit? Hanging around Isobel Burton, no doubt, like bees round a honeypot. Curse them!

Well, he wasn't going to add to her vanity by joining them, particularly knowing he would be forced to play the gracious host when actually he itched to shake the little minx until she rattled. Or kiss her until—no, he wouldn't even think of that!

As for staying here to be hunted by matchmaking mamas—in his own blasted back garden! He slipped quietly away and took himself back to his house, where he collected the brandy decanter and took it up to his bedchamber. He poured himself a large brandy and stood at the window in the dark, glowering down at the moving figures lit so romantically by the glowing lanterns.

It was his duty, he told himself, to keep a protective eye on Clarissa, his ward. And to see what mischief her half sister was up to.

Dammit, what was he going to do now that society believed the two girls to be Studley's legitimate daughters? Too late now to try to separate Isobel from her sister. Too late to hide Studley's baseborn daughter from the ton.

What a fool he'd been to believe they'd obey his instructions about not mixing in society. An even bigger fool to leave them to it. And to assume his aunt would continue to live in the isolation he thought she preferred.

How had they done it? Half of society was here tonight.

He watched as Matteo wove through the crowd, distributing refreshments and managing the footmen. The girls had even managed to suborn his own blasted majordomo, curse them.

Several hours later, Leo jerked awake, startled by the sound of a book hitting the floor beside him. He'd been reading and must have dozed off. He rose from the armchair, stretched and removed his coat and neckcloth. He was about to pull off his shirt and boots when he noticed there was no sound coming from the garden below. The clock on the overmantel chimed softly. Two in the morning.

He looked out of the window. The garden was deserted, not a soul remained—no, wait, a moving shadow caught his eye. A slender feminine figure was moving from lantern to lantern, using a long pole to lift each one down, then extinguishing it.

It was a job for a servant, but that was no servant. She was just a shadowy silhouette flitting about the garden, but Leo would know her anywhere: Isobel Burton. What the devil was she doing down there? Alone?

It was the opportunity he'd been waiting for, the chance to tell her exactly what he thought of her deception and duplicity. And her barefaced disobedience. The anger that had been simmering inside him all evening came boiling back up again.

He didn't hesitate. Dressed only in shirt, breeches and boots—what did it matter? It was a warm night and there was nobody to offend with his state of undress—he marched downstairs and let himself into the garden.

He made his way through the shadowy labyrinth of the garden, heading toward the light of the last few Chinese lanterns, drawn by the sound of humming.

Humming?

He paused in the shadows and watched, entranced, as she twirled and hummed, dancing alone in the darkness. At each hanging lantern she stopped, unhooked it with a long pole, lifted it down, and twirled a few more times with the lantern in her arms, like a partner. The light from each lantern cast her in gold, her delicate features limned in soft radiance. Then she snuffed out the candle inside, put it down and danced on to deal with the next lantern, all the time humming to herself, low and melodic.

Leo swallowed. His anger slowly drained away. She was utterly . . . bewitching.

She extinguished another lantern and danced on to the next, still humming. He must have made some kind of sound—his boots crunching on the gravel pathway perhaps—because she turned and said, "Oh, it's you. I thought you left the party early."

"I did." He moved closer.

"Wasn't it a lovvvvely party?" she said dreamily. "The garden looked sooo pretty and everyone said they had a simply wonnnderful time."

He didn't respond.

"Everyone we invited came, you know. Clarissa was worried a lot of people wouldn't—a twilight garden party—but they did. And of course the weather was perrrfect." She gestured to the sky. "Even the darling old moon came to our party, see? Not quite full, but still so beautiful." She blew it a kiss. "Even the stars were twinkling, though they're harder to see in London. Did you know in the country the sky has a lot more stars? Isn't that amazing?"

He did know, but he said nothing. He just stood there like a stump, as she burbled happily on, dancing to unheard music.

She must have noticed his expression, for she laughed. "Don't mind me, I'm still in alt. It was our first ever party—Clarissa's and mine—and it was glorrrrious!" She twirled happily, and then laughed. "I drank champagne, too—several glasses. I didn't much like it at first but then . . . all those little fizzy bubbles. Just delightful."

"I can tell you've been drinking." He sounded like a bear.

She laughed again. "But I'm not drunk, just happy. Are you happy, Lord Salcott?" She peered at him and pulled a face. "No, you're not happy are you? You're never happy. Why not?"

He didn't answer.

She took down the last of the Chinese paper lanterns. "Weren't these an inspiration? Clarissa's idea. She's very creative, you know. We could only find six, but then your wonderful Matteo found the rest for us. Do you know"—she faced him earnestly, the lantern still alight and glowing in her arms—"that man is an absolute treasure. I hope you appreciate him."

"I am aware of Matteo's qualities," he said. Even to his own ears he sounded stuffy.

A cleft appeared between her brows. "You mustn't blame him. He had no idea we were disobeying your horrid instructions. He thought he was helping us and pleasing you. And he's so clever. It was his idea to bring Lady Scattergood out to the summerhouse in a closed sedan chair—it kept her feeling safe, you see. How brilliant was that?"

"Very clever." He knew Matteo was enormously capable; he didn't need her to tell him so.

"So you mustn't blame him for anything."

"I don't blame Matteo."

"You promise? I wouldn't want him to get into trouble. None of it was his fault," she said earnestly.

"I know. I promise."

She gave him a doubtful look, then her face cleared. "Good," she said, and gave him a brilliant smile. It took his breath away.

He clamped down on the feeling. He was here to reprimand her for her blatant disobedience, not to let himself be enticed. She was charming, he had to admit it. But he refused to be charmed.

He would not be so susceptible to a woman again.

She headed toward the summerhouse, in which dozens

of candles were still burning. He followed. She picked up a candle and blew it out.

"Why are you doing this?" he asked. "Dealing with the lights like this."

"It's dangerous to leave candles burning unattended." The glass windows of the summerhouse reflected a dozen images of her, glowing by candlelight against the darkness of the night. She was perfect from every angle.

"I meant why aren't the servants doing it?"

"Oh, they've all worked so hard, I sent them to bed. Besides"—she picked up a candle and twirled around, holding it high—"I'm too happy and excited to sleep. I don't want this lovely, lovely night to end."

He could see that.

She cupped her hand behind the candle flame and blew, snuffing it out. She put it down and gave him a curious look. "You're very quiet. I thought you'd be angry with us."

"I am." He took a step toward her

"Yes, but I expected you to be furious."

"I am furious," he said softly, and moved a little closer.

She laughed. "You're not furious. I know how you look when you're furious."

A light breeze sprang up outside, bringing through the open door the scent of moist spring-damp earth and dewy flowers, stirring the air in the summerhouse, which was tinged with the smell of stale alcohol and recently snuffed candles. The remaining candle flames flickered, sending their shadows dancing. Leo raised a brow. "Oh? How do I look when I'm furious?"

She tilted her head, considering. "Well, your eyes go all hard and slaty. And when you're really angry they practically throw sparks."

"Sparks?"

"Sparks," she affirmed. "And sometimes you get a little tic just here." She reached up and touched a spot on his jaw. He jumped.

"But only when you're trying to hide how angry you are," she continued. "Sometimes you get these little white lines here"—a soft finger stroked a line out from the side of his nose—"and here." She stroked the other side.

He couldn't move. He could barely think.

Her gaze dropped to his mouth. "And then there's your lips," she murmured.

"What about my lips?" he managed to say. His voice sounded hoarse.

"When you're cross, they almost disappear. You squish them together sooo hard." She shook her head sadly. "You shouldn't treat them like that. They're quite nice lips, when they're not being squished into hard lines."

Leo swallowed convulsively. She had been drinking champagne, he reminded himself. For the first time. She was unused to its effect.

"But the biggest giveaway . . ." Her eyes danced with mischief.

They were talking about his anger, he recalled with an effort. He waited.

"The biggest giveaway, Lord Salcott, is that when you're angry, your dimple totally disappears. But a few minutes ago your dimple"—she stroked a line down his cheek—"the one you claim doesn't exist, came out to play."

"Did it?" he breathed. Her hand now rested lightly on his chest. She was so close he could smell her: roses and vanilla and warm, enticing woman. He moved one step closer and now their bodies were touching, only just brushing, but he was achingly aware of every breath that she took. As for himself, he wasn't sure whether he was breathing or not. Nor did he care.

She made no attempt to move away from him, made no attempt to remove her hand from his chest. It was barely a touch, yet he felt it clear to his bones. The mischief had vanished from her eyes. In the soft candlelight they were no longer emerald but luminous pools of darkness.

He cupped her chin in one hand. Her skin was like silk; her gaze didn't waver. Slowly he stroked his thumb over her full lower lip, warm and satin soft. Her breath hitched and she swayed toward him.

Leo couldn't help himself. He bent and kissed her, softly at first, a bare brush of skin against skin, a delicate invitation that took all his self-control to keep light. He felt a tremor pass through her, but she made no move to step away.

He kissed her again, still keeping it soft and light, though his body was shaking with the effort of restraint. She leaned into him, slipping her hands up over his chest. She found the opening of his shirt—he'd forgotten he'd come out here without coat or neckcloth—and slipped two fingers inside to touch his skin. Hot shivers ripped through him. His body hardened.

He deepened the kiss. Her lips quivered, then parted to receive him. She wrapped her hands around his neck and pulled him closer, melting against him, angling her mouth to fit him as she kissed him back. She was all heat and softness and sweet, luscious acceptance. Fire licked through him.

He wrapped her hard against him, deepening the kiss, lost to the moment, inflamed by the taste of her, her soft responsive body signaling a welcome and sparking a craving deep within him that he'd never before experienced. Or even dreamed was possible.

She pressed herself against him, arching her body like a sinuous little cat, moving restlessly as she slid her fingers into his hair and pulled him closer. Small hums of pleasure escaped her from time to time. They made him feel ten feet tall.

She ran her palms down his body, returning to the opening of his shirt, over the hard muscles of his chest and then up the column of his throat, caressing, exploring, making him harder with every touch. And all the time kissing him, her mouth warm, sweet and generous.

Her fingers stroked along his jawline. They were cool against his suddenly heated skin. He hadn't shaved since morning, but she didn't seem to mind the roughness. Quite the contrary. She stroked her thumbs back and forth along his jaw, as if enjoying the friction.

"Oh my goodness!" The voice broke them apart.

Leo turned, breathing hard as if he'd run a mile, and blinked at the speaker who stood in the doorway, a young female wrapped in a pink satin garment that was all frills, staring with eyes that popped. "What on earth is going on here?" the female said. Her avid gaze dropped to his crotch and stayed there. Leo, realizing that his body was heavy and aroused, stepped behind a chair.

"Who the devil are you?" he snapped. She looked vaguely familiar, but at the moment he couldn't think straight. All he knew was that he wanted to strangle her. What the hell was she doing out here at this hour of the night? Bursting in on something that was clearly private.

Izzy gathered her scattered wits about her. It was as though someone had thrown a bucket of icy water over her, shocking her back to reality. Except that her body was still hot and pliant and breathless and . . . and hungry. She felt, rather than saw, Lord Salcott step away from her.

She stared in disbelief at the unwelcome intruder, and the glorious bubble burst, the fragments falling around her feet, well and truly shattered. "*Milly?* What on earth are you doing out here at this time of night?" It must be two, or even three in the morning. Milly wore a ridiculous frilly dressing gown over what was clearly a nightgown.

The girl gave an indignant huff. "You have the gall to ask me that, Isobel Studley, when *you're* so clearly Up To No Good! What are *you* doing out at this time of night, as if I didn't know. *Alone!* With *a Man*! *Kissing* and—and *worse?*"

Izzy gave a low, unsteady laugh. "I don't think there was any 'worse' about it. It was all utterly blissful." She glanced at Lord Salcott, who stood silent and unmoving as a stone statue.

Milly gasped. "You are totally shameless. Mama was right!"

"Isn't she always?" Izzy said sardonically.

Milly's gaze darted back and forth between Izzy and Lord Salcott. "I am shocked! Shocked by this Appalling Impropriety. You're well and truly Compromised now, you know, Izzy." She was trying to sound scandalized, but her voice oozed salacious glee.

The pretense of righteous moral outrage when Milly was so clearly delighted to have a scandal to nourish sparked Izzy's temper. She stepped forward. "You keep your pointy little nose out of my affairs, Millicent Harrington, or I'll—"

Milly skittered back. "Don't you dare touch me, Izzy Studley or, or—I'll call Mama!"

"Your mama will be snoring her head off, judging by the amount she drank at the party tonight."

"How dare you! Mama doesn't snore. And my nose is not pointy." She covered her nose protectively.

Izzy rolled her eyes. "Just leave, Milly. Get out of here, and if you dare to breathe a word of this to anyone—and I include your precious mama in that—I guarantee I'll make you regret it."

Milly hesitated.

"Get. Out!" Izzy said, and lifting a hand, took a threatening step toward her.

Milly gave a little squeak. "Just make sure you put all those candles out," she said in a parting shot, and then flounced away. The desperately frilly dressing gown, like all Milly's clothes, was made for flouncing.

Izzy turned to Lord Salcott. "I'm sorry about Milly—"

"I'm sure you are," he said crisply. "Good night, Miss

Burton." And with a curt bow he departed, leaving Izzy staring after him.

What had just happened? One minute she was experiencing the most glorious bliss in his arms, the next it was as if he barely knew her. And she was Miss Burton again, not even the Miss Isobel he'd been calling her lately.

Was he angry about being interrupted? Of course he must be, but then so was she. And she could hardly be blamed for Milly's unexpected arrival. She could gladly have throttled the girl.

But the way he'd acted, his abrupt departure, was very strange. And rather disappointing. This evening she'd discovered a very different Lord Salcott beneath the coldly autocratic man she'd met before. Until tonight she'd only had an occasional sense that he could be different—in his interactions with his friend Lord Randall he was much more relaxed and quite . . . appealing.

And their brief exchange when they'd been riding that day, revealing a man on the brink of flirting, quite charmingly. It was just enough to make her curious, and to want to know him better.

Tonight she'd learned he could be far more than just appealing.

She swallowed. The heat he'd sent spiraling through her still lingered. Her body was aching for . . . for she didn't know what. But it was all to do with him. And his kisses. Those heated, luscious kisses.

She'd had no idea kissing could be like that.

The only other experience she'd had was when a horrid friend of her father's had forced a kiss on her when she was a young girl. It had felt like a warm snail slithering over her skin. And when he'd tried to shove his disgusting slimy tongue between her lips—she shuddered, remembering.

By contrast Lord Salcott's kisses were . . . she couldn't think of a word. Sublime. Blissful. Enchanting.

And now that wretched Milly had broken in on the most

glorious kiss—kisses!—of Izzy's life, and she wanted to strangle her.

One day, Izzy vowed, she would have the chance to discover where kissing like that could lead to. Because she knew it had been building toward *something* . . . but what?

He'd taken himself off. She looked around and sighed. There was nothing else to do but put out the last few candles and go to bed.

Leo dragged off his shirt and flung it on the floor. He'd walked right into that one. He pulled off his boots and hurled them at the wall, leaving a mark on the new Chinese wallpaper that Matteo was so proud of. The wretched female's voice rang in his ears.

You're well and truly compromised now, you know, Izzy.

The glee in her voice, the delight. The triumph.

And dammit, she was right. What the hell had he been thinking?

He hadn't been thinking at all, that was the problem. The little witch had well and truly caught him in her spell. Talking about his eyes and his lips and his dimple—when he didn't even have a blasted dimple!

He poured himself a brandy and looked out of the window again. All was in darkness below. As it should have been when he'd looked out earlier.

It was a setup. It had been from the start. Why else would she be extinguishing lanterns alone, and at a ridiculous time of night? Servants did that kind of thing, not young ladies.

Young ladies—hah!

It was obvious to him now. She'd arranged for that harpy with the frills to accost them at the exact right moment. How long had she been lurking outside, waiting and watching while Isobel blasted Burton seduced a gullible blasted fool?

And if that ghastly frill creature had waited longer, where might it have ended?

Against all his intentions he'd let himself get totally carried away. He dragged off his breeches, glanced down at himself—desire unfulfilled—and swallowed his brandy in one gulp.

So much for her pose of being an innocent like her sister. She might not be the woman her father's letter had described, but she had more of her mother in her than he'd realized. Those soft kisses, the tender caresses—all calculated to drive a man to the edge of madness. An innocent? Hah!

He sloshed more brandy into his glass.

You're well and truly compromised now, you know, Izzy . . . well and truly compromised . . .

He'd always considered himself a man of honor, but he refused to be trapped into marriage. It was just a few kisses, dammit!

Ones that *she* had instigated.

Honesty forced him to retract that thought. He'd wanted it as much as she had. But had she wanted his kisses, or had she been, like all the others, angling for a ring on her finger, a fortune and a title?

As he stared, brooding, into his glass, swirling the dregs of his brandy, the cold realization hardened: that female arriving when she did was too much of a coincidence to swallow.

Chapter Nine

❧

The following morning Izzy lazily drifted to consciousness, reluctant to face the day, luxuriating in the dreamy recollection of the previous night in the summerhouse.

She smiled as she recalled his reactions as she'd pointed out the various signs of his anger: he'd been struggling not to smile. She found it so endearing, the battle between the serious face he usually showed to the world—well, to her and Clarissa, at least—and the man he tried to hide from everyone. She wanted to know more of that man.

And then there was the kiss . . . kisses.

She shivered deliciously as she recalled each dreamy little sensation. His big hands cupping her face, cradling her as if she were something precious. The way his thumbs caressed her skin, slowly, sending tiny, exquisite ripples through her body.

The controlled power of his body, so close they were touching, but only just. Tantalizing. She'd wanted to move closer, to wrap herself around him.

She stretched langorously, recalling the feel of his mouth over hers, questing lightly. And gentle, so gentle it almost brought tears to her eyes; she felt cherished in a way that she'd never felt before in her life.

Underneath those light, soft kisses she could feel the leashed desire quivering through his big hard body. His restraint both thrilled and frustrated her. She wanted . . . she didn't know quite what she wanted. But he did, she could tell. She could feel it in his body, in the way he touched her and the way her body responded to him, like a harp to music.

She sighed, curling up in her bed and snuggling her bed-clothes around her as she relived the moment when those light, tender kisses had turned hungry, demanding, passionate, as if someone had lit a torch within him, and in her. Setting her alight like touch paper to fireworks. Hot, shivery, thrilling sensations.

And then Milly. Wretched, nosy, infuriating creature. No wonder Lord Salcott—no, she was going to think of him as Leo now—no wonder Leo had been angry.

His curt farewell doubtless came of frustration. And embarrassment at being caught kissing her. He was a very private, rather proper man.

Izzy wasn't embarrassed. On the contrary she wanted to sing it to the rooftops. But of course she couldn't.

Would Milly blab? Izzy thought about it. Apart from the threats she herself had made, if Milly's mother ever discovered her precious daughter was in the habit of wandering the garden in her nightgown in the middle of the night, Milly would be in such big trouble.

No, there was no danger of Milly telling. Even if she did, who would believe her? It would be Izzy's word against Milly's. There were no other witnesses, apart from Lord Salcott and he wouldn't be telling.

If it got out, Izzy's reputation would be ruined, but Lord Salcott would be held to be acting as any man would—

taking advantage of what was offered. In any case, nobody would dream of trying to force an earl to marry the illegitimate daughter of a baronet.

Gray morning light slipped through the cracks in the curtains. She didn't want to get up: she wanted to stay here in bed, reliving the glorious sensations of the night before.

On the other hand she was bound to see him again this morning. What would he say? What would she say?

Last night had revealed a whole new Lord Salcott to her—one she'd only caught glimpses of before—and she couldn't wait to see more of him, to get to know him as a man, not just as the Grumpy Guardian.

Would he kiss her again? A delectable shiver ran through her as she considered the possibilities. Smiling to herself, she stretched again and threw back the bedclothes.

L eo slept badly that night, tossing and turning. He drifted in dreams where he was lost in magical kisses, then woke up sharply with the gut-wrenching awareness that she'd sprung a trap on him—or tried to.

Sleepily he relived the sweetness of her expression as she teased him about his anger. The touch of her soft fingertip as she traced invisible lines on his face. The scent of her that wrapped itself around his awareness so that never again would he mistake that fragrance for anyone else. The warmth, the soft sensual giving of her.

Her kisses had felt real. Sincere. Heartfelt.

He ran a hand through his hair. He'd been fooled before by a woman's so-called sincerity . . .

Words echoed in his brain. *You're well and truly compromised now . . . well and truly compromised . . . well and truly compromised.*

He sat up in bed, the chill of the predawn air bringing him to full wakefulness.

He refused to be trapped into marriage by anyone, let alone a pair of manipulative females. What did they think he was? Some kind of weak, gentlemanly fool? An easy mark?

Manipulative. Sir Bartleby had warned him, and Leo had dismissed the letter as spite. More fool him.

He rose and, after seeing to his needs, dashed water on his face. He glanced at his reflection in the looking glass and clenched his jaw.

They're quite nice lips, when they're not being squished into hard lines.

Dammit, she was haunting him. He tried to relax his face, to banish the signs of his anger—anger that *she'd* put there. But the more he tried, the more his frustration grew.

Exercise, that's what he needed, exercise to drive out the demons. He pulled on riding breeches and a coat and dragged on his riding boots. He yanked the curtains back and saw it had started raining. The paper lanterns from the party lay limp and soggy on the grass below. The sight gave him a perverse satisfaction.

He went downstairs, dashed off a note to Race, inviting him to a late breakfast, then took himself off for a dawn ride in Hyde Park.

The rain intensified. Cold pellets stung his skin. Leo relished it. It spoke to his mood. The scent of wet grass and muddy earth, the vital heat and smell of the horse beneath him, and the faint tang of smoke from a thousand chimneys were refreshing, he told himself, ridding him of the scent of woman and roses and vanilla. The scent of betrayal.

You're well and truly compromised now . . .

There were very few others in the park—the rain and the hour of the morning—and Leo rode hard and fast in the pouring rain until he was soaked to the skin and his horse was tired. He turned for home.

His demons were subdued, at least, if not entirely vanquished.

Matteo exclaimed in horror as he dripped on the floor, and rushed to fetch him a towel. "Stop fussing, man," Leo told him, and rubbed the towel roughly over his face. "A spot of rain never hurt anyone. I'm English."

He marched upstairs and was about to strip off his wet clothes when he noticed Matteo watching him dejectedly, and felt a pang of conscience.

"The young ladies told you the party last night was my idea, didn't they?"

Matteo, who was collecting the clothes Leo had dropped on the floor the previous night, turned with an anxious expression. "*Sì*, milor'. Were you satisfied with it all?"

His expression was so guileless and so eager that, sour as he felt, Leo couldn't bring himself to disabuse him. "Your organization, as always, was superb, Matteo. Now, Lord Randall will be coming for a late breakfast. You may order me a bath." Matteo hurried off smiling.

Leo turned to strip, but glancing out of the window, he saw Isobel in his aunt's small yard, feeding one of the little dogs, looking as innocent as a milkmaid.

His anger returned in a rush. Giving no thought to his appearance, he stormed back downstairs, crossed the garden and entered his aunt's house by the back door. There was no sign of either girl.

"Lord Salcott!" the butler exclaimed, faint shock breaking through his usual impassivity.

"I wish to speak to the young ladies," Leo said brusquely. "Have them attend me in the blue saloon."

"But, my lord—"

"Did you not hear me?"

"Yes, m'lord, but perhaps I could have a maid bring you a tow—"

"Just fetch those girls." He stomped into the blue saloon and waited.

* * *

L ord Salcott wishes to speak to the young ladies," Lady Scattergood's butler informed them. "He awaits you in the blue saloon."

Izzy and Clarissa exchanged glances. "He's going to read us a lecture about the party," Clarissa said gloomily. "We knew it was coming. I managed to avoid speaking to him last night. What about you? Did you speak to him at all?"

Izzy nodded, but was unable to keep the smile off her face.

"What?" Clarissa said. "Did something happen that you're not telling me?"

"Later." Izzy tidied her hair in the mirror. She hadn't yet found a suitable moment to tell Clarissa about her meeting with Lord Salcott in the summerhouse last night.

Besides, it still felt so private, so special and wonderful, she wasn't quite ready yet to share it with anyone, not even her sister. She didn't blame him for his abrupt departure. He was angry at Milly's interruption. So was she.

But oh, what a shame it had to end like that. She'd spent half the night dreaming of those kisses and where they might have led.

"And while I'm thinking about it," she told Clarissa, "you need to speak to those gardeners immediately and tell them that the hedge needs to be at least twelve or fifteen feet tall. Taller if possible. And prickly, very prickly."

Clarissa looked at her in surprise. "What hedge?"

"The one you're going to get planted in front of Milly Harrington's house. That girl spies on us, and I want it stopped."

Clarissa gave her a bemused glance. "I'll speak to them, though I can't promise anything. But what on earth made you think of that now? Lord Salcott is waiting downstairs. Aren't you worried about what he's going to say to us?"

Izzy felt her cheeks warm. "No, not really. He can't do anything too terrible to us now. The party was a brilliant success, and flowers and notes and more invitations have been flooding in this morning. We're launched now, 'Riss, and he can't do anything about it." Not that she thought he would try to stop them. It was too late, and besides, he would hardly kiss her practically senseless in the wee small hours of the morning and then arrive only hours later to tear strips off her.

The girls hurried down the stairs. Izzy was torn between anticipation of seeing him again—the sensations he'd roused in her still lingered and tingled—and the worry that he'd feel obliged to punish them for their disobedience, which she had to concede was not unfair. Though if he did, she would oppose him. Surely the success of last night's party showed that he was wrong about society's willingness to accept her. Even if they didn't know about her irregular birth. Did they need to know?

Entering the blue saloon, they found Lord Salcott standing before the fire, looking grim and handsome, and . . . damp? His dark hair clung to his forehead in clumps. His breeches molded to his long, hard thighs. Steam rose gently from them.

"Be seated," he said curtly.

"Would you like me to fetch you a towel?" Izzy asked him.

"No," he said, as if he had no idea why anyone would offer him such a thing. "Sit down."

They sat side by side on the chaise longue. There was a long silence. Clarissa slipped a cold hand into Izzy's. Izzy squeezed it in reassurance, but the expression on his face, the ice in his gaze were making her wary.

"Do you care to explain why half of London is under the impression that I gave that party last night? A party I knew nothing about?"

Izzy said nothing. There was nothing to explain. It was

obvious. And why would he be so angry about it now, when it was all over? He hadn't been angry last night when he'd spoken to her in the summerhouse—only at first, but it hasn't lasted. So why now?

And why was he wet?

"I'm sorry," Clarissa began. "I will, of course, cover the cost."

"Damn the cost!"

Clarissa flinched.

"And you're not sorry, are you?" he snapped. Izzy stiffened. Nobody spoke to Clarissa like that, not if she could help it.

"I'm not sorry," Izzy said boldly. "You told us we could not mix in society, you—"

"No, I said that *you* could not mix in society."

She tossed her head at that. "And we disagreed. You wanted us to stay at home with your aunt, twiddling our thumbs. Well, we weren't prepared to do that. And so, when people invited us places, we went."

"Invitations you no doubt wangled out of them—and don't try to deny it. My aunt hasn't set foot out of this house in several years, and yet within days of my departure, she's out attending that literary society and holding court in the summerhouse."

"And isn't that something to celebrate?" She gave him a defiant look.

He clenched his jaw a moment, then said in a more moderate voice. "Yes, I was pleased to see it. But you don't seem to understand the consequences of what you've done."

"We held a lovely party—"

He cut her off. "Apparently *I* held it!"

She lifted a careless shoulder. "Nevertheless, it was very successful."

"So successful in fact, that when it comes out—and believe me it will come out sooner than later—that you are Sir Bartleby's baseborn daughter, moving in society under false pretensions, society will be scandalized, and I don't mean the delicious kind of *on-dits* that pass for scandal in ladylike circles. People will be *angry*." He took a few paces around the room. "Nobody likes being deceived, and you have tricked them all. And they won't like it."

"But—"

"You think it's only about you, don't you, Miss Burton?" He sounded savagely, coldly angry.

The harshness of his tone, his icy demeanor shook her. What had happened to the man who had kissed her so tenderly last night? The man who'd been amused when she'd pointed out the ways she could read his anger on his face— they were all there now, all those telltale features. And there was nothing amusing at all about it.

Now he looked as if he despised her. What could possibly have changed since last night?

He continued the tirade. "But you won't be the only one who is shunned. Clarissa will also be blamed—"

"As I should. Izzy and I acted together in this," Clarissa said bravely, though her voice shook a little. He really was quite formidable in his anger.

Lord Salcott ignored her. "Lady Scattergood will also come into her fair share of blame, as she has appeared as your sponsor." He paused, his gray eyes hard, boring into Izzy. "So congratulate yourselves all you like for getting her to leave the house. Once this comes out, she won't ever want to go out again—this time because she will not be welcomed anywhere."

Clarissa bit her lip and looked down.

"And," he finished coldly, "since the party was held in my name, I will be held responsible. And probably shunned as well."

"But nobody knows," Izzy began.

"They will. This kind of thing always comes out."

A tear trickled down Clarissa's cheek. Izzy put an arm around her and glared up at Lord Salcott. Her sister hated arguments; they brought back all those horrid scenes with her father.

Lord Salcott added in a quieter, but no less implacable tone, "Think about it. Did your father make a secret of Isobel's existence? No, he did not. Did his friends and cronies know? Yes, they did. Are his cronies part of the ton? Yes, they are." He paused to let his words sink in, then repeated, "It *will* come out. It's just a matter of time."

"So what are you going to do?" Izzy asked. She was shocked, seeing this hostile side of him. Especially after last night.

"Nothing," he said.

"'Nothing'?" Izzy repeated, puzzled.

"You two have made your bed, and now you must lie in it. The scandal will break, and you must manage as best you can. I wash my hands of you."

There was a short silence. Izzy thought about what he had said. "Is that it?" she said.

Leo blinked. What the hell did she mean, was that it? Weren't scandal and disgrace enough?

Isobel rose slowly to her feet. "Do you imagine we are some kind of naive ninnies?" Her green eyes glinted with fire. "We *know* there will eventually be unpleasant consequences. We *know* it will all fall apart eventually, that there are people in the ton who know about my birth and who will happily spread the gossip. Nastily."

If they knew, then why the hell had they done what they did? Leo wondered.

Clarissa nodded. "But being shunned by society will be nothing new for us."

Leo frowned. "What do you mean?"

"Until we came to London," Clarissa said, "we had never visited anyone in their home, had never been invited for tea or dinner, or to any kind of party. We'd never been to a dance or a ball."

Leo glanced at Isobel. She'd said something of the sort the previous night, but he hadn't really taken it in. "You never visited people in the country?"

She shook her head. "We were not allowed outside the boundaries of the estate. Nor did we have any visitors ourselves."

"Papa wouldn't allow it," Clarissa said. "Even the vicar and his wife were forbidden to call. Only Papa's own visitors—and those we avoided as much as possible." Both girls screwed up their noses in distaste at the memory. "So we decided to experience as much of London society as we could, while we had the opportunity."

"But Miss Studley," Leo began, exasperated. "*You* could have—"

"Do you imagine I could enjoy myself knowing the same pleasures were forbidden to my sister?" she said hotly. "Besides, I know now that I don't much enjoy big ton social occasions as much as I thought I would. I don't like crowds. I prefer smaller, more intimate gatherings, though I did enjoy our twilight party," she added to her sister. "Perhaps because the garden is the place I love the best, and so I felt at home there and could breathe. And because Izzy was with me." She glanced back at Leo. "But just so you know, when the axe, as you put it, falls, being shunned won't be too much of a hardship for us to bear."

"And when the news of my irregular birth breaks," Isobel said, seeming quite unperturbed by the prospect, "there will no doubt be a bit of a scandal, but everyone will soon realize that you and Lady Scattergood were not at fault, that you were deceived—"

"By us." Clarissa stepped forward and took her sister's hand in a show of solidarity. Leo had to admit he was impressed by her loyalty. Misguided as it was.

Not that he relished the thought of appearing to the ton as the dupe of two young women.

"No, by me. I will wear most of the blame," Isobel said matter-of-factly, as if it were a foregone conclusion. "It's what invariably happens."

"It's true," Clarissa agreed. "It's not fair, but it's what happens. People always blame Izzy, even for things I did. Even if I admit responsibility, they still blame her."

Isobel nodded. "Because of my illegitimacy, my so-called bad blood. It will be decided that I exerted my unwholesome influence over poor Clarissa. She will be forgiven. Eventually."

"Only I don't want to be forgiven if Izzy is being shunned. As we said when we first spoke to you, it must be both of us or neither." Clarissa smiled tranquilly up at him.

"And in the meantime," Isobel said, "we are going to experience as much of London society as we can. And when the axe falls"—she shrugged—"so be it."

Leo was stunned. He'd assumed the girls had gone ahead with their arrangements in a spirit of naivety, not giving a thought to possible consequences, assuming in the way of spoiled and pampered young ladies that it would all work out well in the end.

Instead, they'd calculated the risks and gone ahead, more like soldiers going into battle. Accepting the consequences they knew would result.

He didn't think they were lying, either. What he'd learned about their lives when he visited Studley Park Hall fitted with what Clarissa had just described. He just hadn't quite envisaged it.

No visitors—ever. Except for Sir Bartleby's cronies, whom they avoided as much as possible. Never having visited anyone in their home. Nineteen years with only the company of servants. It was almost inconceivable. And it was a disgrace.

Aware they were awaiting his response, Leo dragged his

thoughts back to the issue at hand. "But are you young ladies not looking for husbands?"

"Oh, yes indeed," Clarissa said brightly. "And we've met quite a few gentlemen, haven't we, Izzy?"

Isobel smiled a siren's smile. "We have."

"But when your half sister's secret is discovered—" Leo began.

To his amazement, Clarissa laughed. "Don't you see? That will make a fine husbandly test."

"Test?" He frowned.

"Do you think I would marry any man who looked down his nose at Izzy? Who would try to separate us? Who would not welcome her into his family?" Clarissa gave a delicate snort.

"And if you get no offers at all? If all your suitors evaporate overnight?"

Clarissa's smile was sad, and a little cynical. "I think you're forgetting my inheritance, Lord Salcott." There was a short silence, then she added, "If that is all?"

Leo nodded. "You may go," he said, but when both girls turned to leave, he added, "Not you, Miss Burton. I wish to have private speech with you."

She raised an imperious eyebrow at him, and he found himself adding, "Please." Something had changed in the last half hour, and he could no longer regard the two young women as flighty, irresponsible creatures that he could— and should—order around, as befitted a guardian.

He might disagree with what they'd done, but he found himself unwillingly respecting their acceptance of the inevitable consequences.

Clarissa immediately took Isobel's hand again and faced Leo, her chin raised. "Whatever you say to Izzy you can say to me."

"It's all right, 'Riss," Isobel told her quietly. "Go. I'll explain later."

Reluctantly, Clarissa left.

*   *   *

Once Clarissa had left the room, silence fell. Izzy seated herself in an armchair this time. She had no idea what Lord Salcott wanted to talk about. From the grim expression on his face, it wasn't to pick up where they'd left off last night in the summerhouse.

Shame about that.

So what was it? Surely he'd said all he could on the subject of her going about in society.

Stern and forbidding looking, he stood glowering down at her for the longest moment. His damp buckskin breeches clung like a second skin to his long, hard thighs. His jaw was unshaven—she longed to feel its roughness against her skin. His hair was damp, tousled and unkempt. His boots were mud spattered, and a thin smear of mud lay unnoticed on his cheekbone.

Every other time she'd seen him, he'd been dressed immaculately. Now he loomed over her, rugged, rumpled—and magnificent.

He cleared his throat, and she looked up expectantly. "About last night," he began, and stopped. He went to straighten his neckcloth, and then frowned, seeming to realize only now that it was wet, and that he was, in fact, quite wet himself.

"Are you sure this can't wait until after you've changed?" she said.

"No. Better to get it out in the open now," he said curtly.

Get what out in the open? she wondered.

"The thing is . . . the thing is—" He cleared his throat again. "It will not work."

Just as she was about to ask him what would not work, he said in a rush, "I don't know what game you and that female thought you were playing last night, but I must make it clear once and for all that I will not be jockeyed into marriage, no matter how loudly you claim you've been compromised."

Izzy gasped. "*What?*"

He glanced at her and gave a nod of grim satisfaction.

"I don't know how the two of you contrived to arrange for us to be caught like that, but I find it despicable in the extreme, and I refuse to fall for such a shabby little scheme."

Izzy rose to her feet. She was shaking. "You—you think *I* contrived with that . . . that vile Milly Harrington to compromise you?"

"Did you not?" he said, but it wasn't a question. A hard knot lodged in Izzy's chest. He'd already decided her guilt. Without even giving her the benefit of the doubt.

"I had no idea she was there, no idea she would come bursting in on us like that."

"Really?" His voice oozed flat disbelief. "So it was pure coincidence that a sheltered young woman would come outside into a shared garden—in her dressing gown and slippers, after two in the morning—just in time to see you kissing me? And to then burst in loudly exclaiming that I had compromised you."

"Coincidence?" Izzy's voice was shaking with anger and indignation. "Yes, it was exactly that. Milly Harrington is a stupid, nosy, grubby-minded busybody, and she pops up uninvited at all kinds of inopportune moments." She broke off and took a deep breath, but it wasn't in the least calming. "Didn't you hear me threaten her? Warning her not to breathe a word to a soul—not even to her mother—on pain of dire consequences?"

He shrugged. "Pretty playacting. But it didn't fool me."

"'Pretty playacting'?" She clenched her fists. She stared at him, unable to believe her ears. Could this hard-faced, arrogant, judgmental man be the same man who'd reduced her to a puddle of bliss the previous night?

"Really! Really?" She was almost dancing with rage.

"So that's what you think, is it? Then how do you account for the fact that *you* chose to come down when you did, after two in the morning, when the party was over and everyone had left? I arranged that, did I? And did I tell Milly Harrington to wait and be ready for you when you came down? Because I must have, mustn't I? Naturally I knew you'd appear, and obviously we would kiss, because what else does one do when a man arrives unexpectedly in the summerhouse at two in the morning after a party?"

She glared at him. He had a frozen look on his face, as if he'd just swallowed a live toad. She only wished he had.

"*You* approached me, Lord Salcott. *You* kissed me. Nobody forced you—and nobody was trying to compromise you."

He didn't say a word. His face was still stupidly blank. She wanted to hit him. She took a few paces around the room. "You called it 'despicable in the extreme,' but I find it despicable of *you* to even *suspect* I could stoop to such a vile and shabby scheme. I would *never* play such a nasty underhanded trick—not on any man, and especially not on you! Not even now I know what a conceited, self-important, pompous ass you are."

She stalked to the door. "I don't need to trap men into marriage, Lord Salcott. In case you didn't notice, there were a dozen or more fine gentlemen vying for my attention last night. And there will be others interested, I'm sure. So take your self-importance and your arrogance and your stupid suspicious mind and . . . and . . . bottle it!"

Izzy slammed the door behind her, ran up the stairs, flung herself on the bed and burst into tears.

Leo took himself back to his house in something of a daze.

What had he done? It hadn't been a trap after all. He'd jumped to a wholly unreasonable conclusion. And now he'd insulted and offended her. Badly.

He stripped off his wet clothes, realizing as he did that he was chilled right through. Matteo had a hot bath waiting, and he sank into it

His damnable temper. He thought about those kisses in the summerhouse, and groaned. He'd ruined everything.

"Milor'?" Matteo asked anxiously. "The water too hot? Not hot enough?"

"No, it's fine."

"I shave you now?"

Leo nodded, closed his eyes as Matteo laid a hot towel across his face, and gave himself up to the man's skillful ministrations with the razor. A good shave could be wonderfully soothing, but this time it did little to ease the turmoil of his mind.

He forced his thoughts away from the conundrum that was Isobel and his own disastrous misapprehension, and turned his mind to the girls' stated intention of bluffing as long as they could, expecting that once their deception was discovered, they would be shunned. It was crazy, but he had to respect their courage, if courage it was and not reckless foolhardiness.

What would it be like to be shunned? He pondered the notion. In his earliest weeks at school he'd felt alone and friendless. Was that the same as being shunned? He didn't think so.

The effect would probably depend on what kind of person was being shunned, how sociable they were and how much they would miss being able to mix in society. And how much they needed other people's approval.

Leo wasn't terribly sociable. As long as he had one or two good loyal friends, that was enough. But he had a feeling that Studley's daughters were the sociable type—especially Isobel. Not that he was thinking about her at the moment.

He lay back and focused on the agreeable scrape of the razor over his skin, the sensation of heat and the scent of the shaving soap.

For years after his father's seizure had taken place, Leo lived quite an isolated life. He hadn't had much of a social life at all—there was so much to do, and his worries were such that he was rarely in the mood for frivolous pastimes and pointless entertainments. But he had friends who visited, and a few locals he saw regularly, so his restricted life hadn't bothered him much at all.

And of course, having his friend, Mabel, had helped. Leo smiled to himself, thinking of her. He'd never known how to think of her place in his life—she would laugh to hear herself called his mistress, though in truth that was what she was. But Mabel was no kept woman and would have smacked anyone who suggested as much, Leo included.

A blunt speaker herself, Mabel would probably approve of a young woman who could blister his ears as Isobel had. *Take your self-importance and your arrogance and your stupid suspicious mind and . . . and . . . bottle it!*

The first storm of Izzy's angry tears eventually slowed, and what was left was . . . desolation. And shame. Last night she'd practically thrown herself at him—he was right in that. Though it hadn't been in the slightest premeditated. How could it be when she hadn't expected to see him?

She'd been floating on air after the success of their party. The garden had looked magical, beautiful, like something out of *A Midsummer Night's Dream.* And then he'd appeared, standing silently in the shadows, watching her with such a look in his eyes it took her breath away.

And she'd thought . . . she'd imagined . . .

But instead he turned out to be a complete ass, only without the big donkey ears. *Midsummer Night's Dream* indeed.

A soft knock sounded on her bedroom door. "Izzy?" It was Clarissa.

Izzy sat up, hastily rubbing at the evidence of tears.
"Come in."

"Izzy? What is it? You've been crying." Clarissa hurried
over and put her arms around Izzy. "He made you cry? Oh,
I should never have left you alone with him. The man is a
monster! I'm going to give him a piece of my mind. How
dare he make you cry!"

Izzy gave a shaky laugh. Her sister was normally so soft
and gentle, but when roused in the defense of someone she
loved, Clarissa became a tigress.

"It's all right. I'm all right, love."

"If he—"

"No, he's annoying and stupid and arrogant and block-
headed, but he's not a monster."

"But—"

"If I'm upset, it's my own fault. No, truly it is. I deceived
myself, and if I'm disappointed . . ." She tried to put on a
positive face. "I must wear the blame."

Clarissa sat back and gave her a searching look. "Something happened at the party, didn't it? I didn't even talk to
Lord Salcott, and I thought you hadn't, either, but I can see
now that something happened between you." She settled
herself more comfortably on the bed facing Izzy. "So,
tell me."

Izzy slipped off the bed, walked to the washstand and
washed her face in the cool water in the jug. Part gathering
her composure, part putting off the moment.

All her life she and Clarissa had told each other everything, sharing their hopes and dreams, their worries and
their problems. Now, for the first time ever, Izzy was reluctant to share. Her feelings were too new, too raw to be exposed, even to her sister.

But she couldn't say nothing. That would hurt Clarissa
terribly.

She returned to the bed and climbed onto it. She and her
sister faced each other, cross-legged on the bed, as they'd

sat a thousand times before. It made her smile, remembering.

"That's better," Clarissa said, relaxing a little. "Now, tell me what happened."

"It was long after the party had finished. You'd gone to bed—everyone had, or so I thought. But I was wide awake, still floating on air, and not in any mood to sleep."

Clarissa leaned forward and squeezed her hands. "It was a lovely party wasn't it? The loveliest ever."

Izzy smiled mistily. "The best."

"So what did you do?"

Izzy wanted to laugh; her gentle sister was like a dog with a bone. "I remembered that the lanterns in the garden were still lit, and the candles in the summerhouse were still burning."

"But wouldn't the servants—?"

"I'd sent them all to bed. So I went out to do it myself and . . . and Lord Salcott appeared out of nowhere."

Clarissa made a surprised exclamation. "At that hour of the night?"

Izzy nodded. "We . . . talked in the summerhouse."

"Was he angry?"

"N . . . no. Well, he might have been at first, but that soon passed."

Clarissa gave her a searching look. "So you just talked?"

"Yes." Izzy felt her cheeks warming under her sister's intent gaze.

For a long moment Clarissa remained silent, then she gave a little crow of excitement. "Isobel Burton Studley, Lord Salcott kissed you, didn't he? Oh, don't bother to deny it! I can tell." She snorted. "'Talked' indeed." She leaned forward excitedly. "So tell me, what was it like? Was it horrid, like Lord Pomphret's warm snails, or was it wonderful?"

"Wonderful." Izzy sighed. "No, better than wonderful."

"Oh my. Your first proper kiss. I'm so envious."

Izzy pulled a rueful face.

Clarissa's excitement dimmed. "So what went wrong?"

"Milly interrupted us."

"*Milly* did? That wretched girl. What on earth was she doing outside at—what time was this?"

"After two. But it wasn't the interruption so much, it was what she said and the horridly salacious way she said it." She told Clarissa what Milly had said, and how Lord Salcott had interpreted it, and what he'd accused her of this morning. And what she'd told him in response.

By the time she'd finished, Clarissa's eyes were sparkling with indignation. "The horrid suspicious beast! How dare he imagine you'd be a party to such a nasty trap! I've a good mind to go over to his place right this minute and blister his ears good and proper!"

Izzy laughed and put a calming hand on her sister's knee. "No, don't, love. I've said enough to him already that I suspect his ears are still burning. Now, how about we go for a nice long ride, put Lord Salcott right out of our minds."

Clarissa gave her an odd look. "What? Now?"

"Yes, of course now. Why not?"

Clarissa gave a gurgle of laughter and pointed at the window against which rain was pelting. "He has put you in a state, hasn't he? It's been raining like that all morning."

"Oh." Izzy was a little embarrassed, but joined in the laughter. "Well then, let us send a note over to Lady Tarrant and see if she'd like some help entertaining the children. They won't like being cooped up inside, either."

"Oh yes, lovely idea," Clarissa agreed. "I'll write that note this very minute." She slipped off the bed and hurried to the door, then paused and looked back. "And don't think I've forgotten about that kiss, sister dear. You haven't told me nearly enough. We never-been-kissed spinsters need detail. Between 'not like warm snails' and 'better than wonderful' there's an enormous gulf of possibilities. I'm willing to wait until you're ready to share, but not for long."

Chapter Ten

❧

Race arrived just as Leo was coming downstairs to breakfast. Race wore all the appearance of a man who had slept badly. Or was, perhaps, still the worse for drink. Leo's mood lightened.

"Matteo has hired a new cook—Neapolitan, so lord knows what we'll get for breakfast," he told his friend. When he'd visited Naples, breakfast was usually just coffee and pastries, which, although tasty, didn't fill a man up.

"As long as there is good Italian coffee, hot and strong and plentiful, I don't care," Race said.

"Feeling a touch delicate, are we?" Leo said with spurious sympathy.

For answer Race gave him a baleful look.

Leo laughed.

Breakfast started with ale—"hair of the dog"—followed by an endless supply of truly excellent coffee, hot and strong. Then came bacon and eggs. The eggs were scrambled and contained some kind of foreign cheese, but they were delicious. And to follow there were pancakes, hot and sweet and stuffed, some with a sweetish soft cheese and some with jam. There was little conversation, only the sound of eating and drinking.

When they were finished, Race sat back in his chair with a satisfied sigh. "Now, that's what I call a breakfast. Hang on to that cook, or I'll steal him myself."

"Mm."

Race eyed Leo thoughtfully. "A breakfast like that should have put paid to that mood you've been brewing, but it hasn't. It's not just the party is it? What's got you in a stew?"

"I spoke to the girls this morning."

"Read them the riot act, did you?"

Leo nodded. "And warned them what would happen when their deception—Isobel's birth—came out, as it inevitably will."

"And?"

"It didn't bother them at all. They know it will happen—they actually expect it."

Race's brows rose. "So what's the plan? Bundle them out of town? Banish Miss Isobel to the country somewhere?"

Leo shook his head. "Can't be done—they refuse to be separated and, short of kidnapping, there's not a lot I can do. They're determined to continue as they've started."

"Bold words. So what will you do?"

"Wait and see what happens and then manage the situation as best I can."

Race whistled. "No wonder you're frustrated."

Leo sighed. "That's not the only reason." He called for a fresh pot of coffee to be brought to the library, where a fire was burning, and when they'd settled themselves—Matteo having also brought a plate of what he called biscotti in case they perished of hunger in the meantime—Leo told Race what had happened the previous night, concentrating on the stupid chit who'd interrupted them, not so much on what had taken place before that. Then he explained how he'd interpreted the interruption, and what he'd said to Isobel this morning. And how she'd reacted.

When he finished, there was a long silence.

"What the devil were you thinking of?"

"I wasn't thinking at all," Leo said gloomily.

"Clearly not."

"I know. I couldn't understand why she. . ?"

"Kissed you?" Race poured himself another cup of coffee and crunched through a biscuit. "Possibly for some unknown, completely inconceivable reason, she was attracted to you. You're not completely hideous, you know. It is possible for a female—misguided or not—to fancy you. Though I can't see it myself."

Leo groaned. "She's never going to talk to me again."

There was another long silence broken only by the sound of the crackling fire and the crunching of biscotti. Then Race said, "You know, you really need to get over your mistrust of women."

"I don't mistrust women," Leo growled.

His friend made a scornful sound. "Yes, you do. Oh, I know you have reason, what with the way your mother behaved, and then Lavinia What's-her-name—that female you were almost betrothed to?

"Ledbetter," Leo said heavily.

"You made a lucky escape there. The number of grooms and footmen her husband has had to sack." Race shook his head. "And I hear his firstborn is looking more and more like the family coachman each day."

Leo didn't reply. He'd been utterly besotted with the beauteous Lavinia until he'd discovered her in the stables that time, bare as an egg, writhing happily between two equally naked grooms.

"Not all women are like your mother and Lavinia the Lustful," Race said.

"I know that."

"Yes, but do you? Your mother didn't just betray your father—she betrayed you as well."

"Me?" His mother had made no vows to him.

"Yes, you," Race said. "I haven't forgotten the way you used to defend her reputation at school, all those bloody noses and bruises, not to mention the canings afterward for fighting. And all in a lost cause. I wanted to tell you then that the rumors were true, and that her behavior was even worse than our schoolfellows claimed. But would you have believed me?"

Leo scowled. He didn't want to think about his mother. All those years he'd believed she was an angel—his own pure and lovely angel mother. Instead she'd been rutting with anyone and everyone. Her immorality had been a by-word among the ton, but Leo hadn't discovered the truth until he was sixteen and abruptly summoned home.

His mother hadn't died when he was seven as he'd been told. She'd run off with an Italian painter hired to paint her portrait. In Italy, she'd left the painter for a Hungarian count. Then left him for a French sculptor. And moved on to a Polish baron, and after him . . . who knew?

His father had been driven mad trying to trace her movements until eventually he learned she'd drowned in the Mediterranean, along with her lover, when their yacht had sunk. It was the news of her death that had brought on the apoplexy. Yet it was clear to Leo that despite her infidelities, his father still loved her. Or at least was obsessed with her.

Leo's biggest fear was that, like his father, he'd love not wisely but too well.

"Your disillusionment with your mother almost destroyed you. And then you fell into the toils of the beauteous but ghastly Lavinia. But you can't judge all women by the example of your mother or the Ledbetter chit."

"I know that," Leo said.

"Really?" Race persisted. "And yet you condemned Miss Isobel out of hand simply because her nosy neighbor appeared out of nowhere while you were kissing her. It's my guess that you enjoyed that kiss far too much for your own comfort. Which made you feel vulnerable. And so you reacted badly."

Leo gritted his teeth. That was the trouble with old friends; they thought they knew you so well. But they weren't always right.

Vulnerable? He hadn't felt the slightest bit vulnerable. What nonsense.

He was perfectly entitled to be annoyed about that wretched female interrupting them in the summerhouse. And if he'd jumped to the wrong conclusion, well, it was understandable, given the way women stalked him.

Understandable, but unfortunate.

Anyway, Race was one to talk about trusting women— he was notorious for flitting from female to female like a buzzing bee. Race would never settle down with just one woman. At least Leo had tried once, even if it was a failure. Race had never even approached the idea of a betrothal.

"When I marry, it will be because I must, for the sake of an heir. And I decided long ago to choose with my head, not my heart. A girl with no particular beauty—someone ordinary but pleasant looking, a girl who won't be a temptation to other men. A respectable girl, one that I can trust."

"I've never heard anything so depressing."

Leo rolled his eyes. "Says the deeply cynical rake. But you'll marry eventually, won't you?"

Race lifted a weary shoulder. "One must for the sake of the succession, but . . . I haven't yet met the right woman."

Leo frowned. "You're not . . . not holding out for love, are you? You, the famous rake?"

Race gave him a dry look and sipped his coffee. "Don't be ridiculous. And don't change the subject. We're not talking about me. In any case, you and I are different. And it's clear to me that you haven't yet understood."

"Understood what?"

"That love is the prize. The ultimate prize."

Leo stared at him a moment, then snorted. It was rich, his famously rakish friend lecturing him about love. "You're mistaken. Love doesn't last. And worse, it's dangerous. Look at my father—he was besotted with my mother and thought she felt the same about him. And how well did that turn out?" He swirled the coffee in his cup and added quietly, "Love destroyed him."

Race inclined his head, conceding the truth of that. "It does have the power to destroy, but that only makes true love all the more precious." He glanced toward the window and said reminiscently, "I remember my mother saying once that love is like a garden. If you neglect it, the bloom will wither on the vine, and love will die of starvation. That's when the weeds creep in and take over." He added with faint, sardonic amusement, "Naturally, having been one of those weeds, I understand how it works."

Leo stared. His oldest friend and he'd never seen this side of him. "Good God, don't tell me—you can't be— you're not a *romantic*, are you?"

Arching a cynical eyebrow, Race snorted. "What do you think?"

Leo nodded and sat back. Race, a romantic? It was a ridiculous notion.

Race added, "But you are."

"What rot. I am not."

Race shook his head. "Beneath that cynical shell you affect, there's the beating heart of a romantic."

"What rubbish! I'm as romantic as"—Leo looked around for inspiration—"as that coal scuttle over there."

"Ah, but dust that coal scuttle off, polish it up—it's brass and copper, I think—and it will shine. And set a light to its contents and the coal will glow with passion."

Leo snorted. "You're drunk. Or infected with poetry, and I don't know which is worse."

Race laughed again. "We're drinking coffee. You forget that I knew the little boy who gallantly fought every schoolboy—no matter how much bigger—in defense of his sainted mother's reputation."

And much good it did him, Leo thought bitterly.

Race continued. "That boy's romantic little heart is still beating in the chest of the man—"

"Nonsense!"

"Bruised, bloodied but still beating," Race insisted. "And waiting for the right woman."

"To crush it beneath her heel? Not bloody likely."

Race waved a knowing finger at him. "You'll see. In fact, if you ask me, you've already met her."

"I have not," Leo denied it hotly. Possibly too hotly, he realized.

Race smirked. "Methinks the gentleman doth protest too much."

A gain? He wants to speak to me in private again?" Izzy looked up from her book.

Treadwell, Lady Scattergood's butler, inclined his head graciously. "As I said, miss."

"Do you want me to come with you?" Clarissa asked.

"No, I'll be fine," Izzy assured her. If Lord Salcott thought he was going to rake her over the coals again, she'd happily give him another piece of her mind. Since she'd stormed out the day before, she'd been brooding up a whole list of things to say to him to put him in his place. To utterly *shrivel* him.

She glanced at her reflection in the cheval mirror and tidied her hair, then ran lightly downstairs. He awaited her in the blue saloon, standing in front of the fireplace, looking elegant, serious and annoyingly handsome. His thick dark hair was freshly trimmed and brushed à la Brutus. Buff doeskin breeches hugged his narrow hips and hard muscular thighs. His boots were elegant and highly polished; his neckcloth was tied in a no-nonsense style that wasn't fashionable, but somehow suited him. His slate-blue coat exactly matched his eyes.

He'd dressed for the occasion, then. She couldn't decide whether that was good or bad.

He cleared his throat. "Good morning, Miss Isobel."

Miss Isobel, not Miss Burton. A small concession. She returned the greeting and waited. He waved her to a chair, then seated himself opposite. He looked at her a moment, then cleared his throat again.

Obviously, he had something unpleasant to say to her. As if he hadn't already said enough. Izzy braced herself.

He cleared his throat a third time, then said, "I owe you an apology."

She looked at him in surprise. He did, of course, but it was the last thing she'd expected. She waited. Was that it? How did he expect her to react?

He ran a finger around his collar as if it was too tight, and continued. "I was wrong to accuse you of trying to trick me the other night."

Izzy raised a brow. "'Trick'?"

"Entrap. I was wrong and I was offensive. I apologize. Unreservedly."

It was a handsome apology, Izzy had to admit. Men in general were not prone to apologizing for anything. Nevertheless . . . She still smarted that he'd taken one of the most moving experiences of her life—her first real kiss, and it had been magic—and decided it was a grubby little plot.

"So, will you accept my apology?"

His prompt annoyed her. Was she just supposed to roll

over like a grateful puppy, accept it and make everything better—for him? So that he could feel better about himself? While she still smarted with hurt and disillusionment?

"I'm not sure," she began. He frowned, and she continued, "It's been my experience that when people expect the worst of others, it is a reflection of the kind of person they are."

His frown deepened.

"When we first met," she reminded him, "your first act was to offer me a bribe to abandon my sister." He opened his mouth, but she swept on. "And then the other night, your instant reaction to Milly Harrington's interruption was to decide I was trying to entrap you into marriage."

He didn't say anything. He looked a little pale.

Not surprising, she thought. He could hardly deny it. "I've always thought that the kind of person who expects someone to take a bribe, or entrap another person, is the kind of person who will accept a bribe or lay a trap themselves."

His jaw tightened.

She wasn't trying to punish him, just make him understand. "It's not very flattering, is it, your opinion of me?" He'd kissed her as if she were a dream come to life. And she'd kissed him back with everything in her. She couldn't shake that off easily.

And then he'd decided she was a contemptible schemer.

She wasn't going to risk that again.

"So while I suppose I can forgive you, I don't think I would be able to forget it, and really, isn't it part of the forgiveness process to put the insult behind one?" She shook her head. "I'm not sure I can."

It wasn't only that she didn't think she could trust him again, it was that this episode had shown her that she couldn't trust herself. Clarissa feared she'd be too susceptible to charming but unworthy men and was relying on

Izzy to protect her from making a huge mistake—but look at how easily Izzy had fallen into Lord Salcott's arms.

On the basis of a little flirting and some kisses—that admittedly had been magical—she'd been on the verge of opening her heart to him.

She was just as vulnerable as Clarissa—maybe even more so—and wasn't that a shock? She'd always considered herself a good judge of character, even a bit of a cynic when it came to men—and yet . . .

He stood abruptly, and she blinked, half expecting him to yell or storm furiously out. Instead he said, "Will you wait here a moment? Please? There is something I need to show you."

She hesitated, then nodded, and he was gone.

He returned in a few minutes with a folded paper and a brown-paper bundle tied with string. He placed the parcel on the seat next to him and held up the paper. "This letter was my initial introduction to you. Before we had even met. To my shame, I fear I allowed it to influence me unduly." He passed her the letter.

Bemused, and more than a little curious, Izzy unfolded it. She read, and as she read, bile rose in her throat. Her father, her thrice-damned father. Even from the grave . . .

She read it though twice—not that she needed to; the vicious phrases had burned into her memory. But it gave her time to gather her thoughts and work out what she wanted to say to Lord Salcott.

One sentence stood out as particularly offensive and vindictive: *Isobel has shown every sign of being as immoral and manipulative as her whore of a mother.*

How dare Sir Bartleby describe her mother so.

She wanted to rip the letter up and hurl the pieces into the fireplace. Instead, without a word, she refolded it carefully and handed it back to Lord Salcott. Her hands were shaking. He noticed it, too.

There was a long silence.

"So," she said finally, "you believed what he said."

His shoulders rose infinitesimally. "At the time I had no reason to doubt it." She didn't respond and he added, "I had nothing else to go on. It was a deathbed request. And he *was* your father."

Izzy wanted to spit. "He was no kind of a father, not to me, not even to Clarissa. He was a selfish, spiteful, conscienceless, self-indulgent, heartless pig. As for what he said about my mother, it's utterly false, a complete calumny of a wonderful woman."

He raised a brow, but said nothing.

It annoyed her. "What? What does that look mean?"

"I visited the village in which you spent your childhood years."

Her eyes narrowed. "Spying, were you?"

"Endeavoring to discover the truth," he said stiffly.

"Whose truth? My father's? Yours?" Her lip curled scornfully. "Or were you looking for more reasons to despise me?"

L eo had to admit there was some justice to her accusations, although reasons to despise her had been the very last thing on his mind. He had no desire to despise her at all. But he'd wanted to *know*. Needed to know.

And what he'd learned was that Isobel's mother was hardly "a wonderful woman." She might not have been a whore who sold her body on street corners, or slept with a variety of men, but she had effectively sold herself to the local squire. And not just once, but repeatedly over a number of years. And even though he had to admit she had her reasons, it still . . . bothered him.

Dammit, this conversation was not going the way he'd planned it. He'd apologized, and shown her the letter as a justification for his early hostility. She was supposed to accept his explanation and apology so they could then move on. To what, he wasn't yet sure, but he didn't want to be at daggers drawn with her.

Instead she was bristling like a drenched cat, those gorgeous green eyes narrowed and spitting with anger, her hands bunched into tight little fists.

Forced to defend himself, he said awkwardly, "I met your former neighbor, Mrs. Purdey, with whom you spent every Thursday."

"So, I'm sure your nasty, suspicious mind has worked it all out. The squire's visits, my stays with Mrs. Purdey are exactly what you think—in part. But you don't know the whole story." She glared at him. "And before you say another word, my mother wasn't a whore as my father claimed: she was a desperate young woman doing what she could to keep a roof over our heads and food on the table."

"That's all very well but—"

"My mother lay with two men in her entire life—two! One was my father when she was too young and innocent to know what she was doing. And the other was the squire."

She shot Leo a dagger look; his skepticism must have shown. But honestly, didn't all fallen women claim they didn't know what they were doing?

She continued, her voice shaking with anger. "My father seduced a sixteen-year-old schoolgirl, too innocent and unworldly to know what he was about. He was almost forty, worldly and sophisticated. Mama was young, naive—and very beautiful. But she didn't even know how babies were made—her mother had never explained it."

He frowned. "Did her parents not attempt to protect her?"

She snorted. "They were too impressed by him—his sophistication, his urbane air and address, and his title, so no, they trusted him as a gentleman, and assumed his intentions were honorable. Whether they were greedy and ambitious or as unworldly and naive as their daughter, you

must decide. As it turned out, he was already married, but
they didn't know that, then."

"I see." The parents were no doubt hoping for a good
match for their daughter. The greedy fools.

"My father was a notorious rake, the squire a well-
known womanizer who used his position to coerce village
women—and yet my mother was the one branded as a
whore!" She gestured furiously. "How is that in any way
just? Why is there no similar word for men, eh? Because for
sure my father was a male whore and so was the squire."

"I suppose—"

She swept on. "Libertine, rake, philanderer, Romeo, Ca-
sanova, Lothario—none of them carry even a sliver of the
depth of condemnation of 'whore.' Some even carry a suggestion of glamour. Call a man a rake or a Romeo, and
more likely than not he'll be flattered."

Leo inclined his head. True enough.

"But to return to my mother, there she was, sixteen years
old, discovering she was with child—she didn't even realize it until she started to show—she was a true innocent,
you see. And what did her parents do? They gave her two
choices—have the baby in secret and get rid of it, or be
banished from the family."

Leo frowned. Wasn't that what most respectable parents
would do? It seemed like a reasonable solution to him.
Though he could see how Isobel might see it differently.

"She did give birth to me in secret, and their plan was to
place me in Captain Coram's home for foundlings. But
once I was born, she realized she loved me and refused to
give me up."

The foundling hospital? Leo was shocked. Treated as a
foundling, and trained up to be a servant? He couldn't
imagine it.

"So Mama's loving family threw her out. Gave her no
support, no money, made no arrangements to provide her

with a place to live. She sold the few trinkets she'd inherited from her grandmother, and after a few false starts, she found a mean little house on the edge of a small village, and there—alone and unsupported—she set out to raise me." Her voice hardened. "Seventeen years old and all alone in the world except for a baby."

"Sir Bartleby—"

"Gave her not a penny, though she wrote to him a number of times. Nobody gave her a penny—until the squire came along, just when she was at her most desperate. He made her an offer she couldn't refuse; the cottage rent and a small allowance—enough for us both to live on—in exchange for those Thursday nights. Oh, and in case you're wondering, he was past fifty and a charmless, ugly brute. She was, as I said, seventeen and very beautiful."

Leo swallowed. No wonder Isobel was bitter. He thought about how Sir Bartleby had described her mother in his letter: *Isobel has shown every sign of being as immoral and manipulative as her whore of a mother.* But it was Sir Bartleby who was immoral and manipulative, and her mother, the innocent victim of his lust.

Any halfway-decent man would have, at the very least, supported the child and the child's mother with an allowance. Leaving them both to starve was unconscionable. Isobel Burton's mother had not been fortunate in her choice of lover, or in her family. Her daughter, now—her daughter was magnificent, a daughter any mother would be proud of.

"The squire wanted to set Mama up as his permanent mistress—move her to a much bigger, nicer house in town, give her pretty clothes and jewelry—on the condition that she give me up, put me in an orphan asylum or leave me with one of his farming tenants. Mama refused. My mother loved me."

Tears glittered like diamonds on the tips of her long dark lashes as she finished, her voice shaking with passion. "My mother gave up *everything* for me—her good name, her family, a happy life, social acceptance, and the chance of a husband and family of her own." Her voice broke slightly as she added, "So don't you *dare* call her a whore to me! And she *was* a truly wonderful woman."

Leo handed her a handkerchief. "I can see that," he said quietly. "I cannot imagine what it must have been like for her—for you both. How is it then that you were raised by Sir Bartleby?"

She made a scornful sound. "'Raised by Sir Bartleby'? Hardly. When my mother died, her brother, my uncle, appeared at the funeral, swept me away and tried to dump me on Sir Bartleby's doorstep. He, of course, refused and said I should be dumped in the nearest orphan asylum—I heard him with my own ears." Her voice softened. "But Clarissa found me, and we hid from the adults. And by the time they discovered us, she refused to let us be parted."

"*She* did?"

She smiled. "Clarissa only seems meek and mild. When it's something that matters to her, she's a tigress. My father never did manage to get rid of me, though he tried many times." Her eyes hardened. "And neither will you."

Leo held up his hands. "That's all in the past. I accept that now. Your father's letter misled me."

She arched a cynical brow. "So you don't think I'm— what was it?—'immoral and manipulative'? A witch with my claws in my innocent sister? A would-be courtesan?" She snorted. "You haven't even asked me yet about my so-called attempts to 'work my wiles' on his friends."

"Nor will I," Leo said firmly. "I'm quite convinced now that your father's letter was nothing but malice. Even Edwards, the estate manager at Studley Park Manor, called the leaving of the estate to a distant relative instead of your half sister an act of spite."

Her expression softened. "Mr. Edwards is a good man. He was the closest thing to a father Clarissa and I had."

"I only produced the letter so you would understand my earlier attitude. Bribing people, as you called it, is not a habit of mine."

She gave a reluctant nod. "Very well, I accept your apology. Is that all?" She rose to leave.

"Not quite." He picked up the brown-paper parcel and handed it to her. "Mrs. Purdey gave me this to give to you."

She took it hesitantly. "Mrs. Purdey did?"

He nodded. "You might want to know that she refused to say anything to your mother's detriment. You have a loyal friend there."

She raised her chin and gave him a challenging look. "Loyalty is a quality Mama and I learned to prize. In this world, it's very rare and precious." Her grip tightened on the parcel. "Thank you for passing this on," she added, and left.

Izzy ran upstairs, clutching the parcel to her bosom. Something from Mrs. Purdey. What could it be? She felt it carefully. It didn't feel like rhubarb or potatoes or turnips or a pie, which was the kind of thing Mrs. Purdey used to send her home with when she was a child. This parcel was soft and squashy.

She hurried to her bedroom to open it.

Clarissa was waiting. "How did it go? Did he make you cry again?"

Izzy laughed. "You won't believe it, but he wanted to apologize."

Clarissa's jaw dropped. "Really? Again? That's the second time."

It was actually the third, but Izzy didn't want to explain. "I know." She still had mixed thoughts about it. About him.

"A man who can apologize? Better snap him up at once," Clarissa said with a laugh.

"Or have him stuffed and put on display in a museum of rarities," Izzy said dryly. "He gave me this parcel." As she unpicked the knots, she explained Mrs. Purdey as a neighbor she often used to visit. She opened the wrapping, and her eyes filled with tears.

"Oh, how pretty," Clarissa exclaimed as Izzy picked up a small pale yellow dress, embroidered with blue forget-me-nots around the neck, sleeves and hem.

"Mama was making me this before she died," Izzy said in a choked voice. "I never got to wear it—it's not quite finished, see?" The last few forget-me-nots around the hem were missing. Mama had embroidered forget-me-nots on all of Izzy's clothes—they used to be Izzy's favorite flowers. Now they carried a poignant message. *Forget me not.* And she never would, Izzy promised silently.

"She made this for you?"

Izzy nodded. "Sewing was her one skill. She used to make and sell things." Though she never made enough for them to live on. "When she was a girl, she even embroidered several ecclesiastical stoles that their vicar wore—of course she never charged for that. It was an honor for her work to be accepted."

There were more things in the parcel, mostly clothing that Izzy had worn as a baby or a toddler, all things her mother had made for her. A delicate shawl she'd knitted, a patchwork quilt she'd made from leftover fabric scraps she'd collected. Every piece sparked a memory, and as Izzy lifted each piece, a faint floral scent was released that reminded her of her mother. She inhaled it deeply. *Oh, Mama.*

Then, underneath the pile of lovingly made, carefully preserved clothing she found a shabby, beloved, handmade doll with curly black hair and green embroidered eyes. "Oh, look, it's my Gwendolyn." Izzy picked up the doll and cradled her lovingly. She gave a shaky little laugh. "Poor

Gwendolyn, look how faded and worn she is, but oh, how I loved her. I still do." She hugged the doll again.

"I used to take her everywhere—she was my only friend back then—but she did get quite grubby. Getting loved to pieces, Mama called it, but luckily Gwendolyn was washable. And she had adventures. See, here's where one of the village children ripped her arm off and threw her in the mud."

She showed Clarissa the arm. "Mama offered to make a new doll for me, but I would have none of it. Gwendolyn was a person, and you can't replace people. So Mama washed the mud off her and sewed her arm back on, and my Gwendolyn was as good as new." She glanced at Clarissa and added, "I used to pretend she was my secret sister."

Clarissa hugged her. "And then your horrid uncle took you away and made you leave Gwendolyn behind, but luckily you found your real sister. And so did I. I used to have a pretend sister, too, until you came along."

Izzy looked at all the items spread out on the bed—her childhood in a brown-paper parcel. "Wasn't it wonderful that Mrs. Purdey saved these for me? I'm going to write to her. And send her a gift. She cannot know how much these things mean to me."

"Oh, I think she must," Clarissa said softly. "Why else would she have saved them all this time?"

Izzy nodded, unable to speak. Tears prickled at the back of her eyes again. Mrs. Purdey had been thinking of her, saving these things for her, knowing how precious they were to her and keeping them all these years.

"And wasn't it kind of Lord Salcott to bring them to you?" Clarissa added.

Again, Izzy only nodded. He couldn't know how much these things would mean to her. He probably didn't even know what the parcel contained. But Clarissa was right—it was kind of him to bring her a gift from a poor old country-woman so far below him in rank.

Except that he had gone there in the first place to dig for dirt.

And found it.

Leo warmed his hands at the fire before thrusting them into his pockets. He left his aunt's place via the back door, as usual. The sky had cleared and a watery-looking sun was out.

What did that parcel contain? Isobel certainly seemed to value it. He was glad now he'd brought it, even though in a sense even knowing about the neighbor damned him.

He walked in a leisurely manner along one of the curved paths, enjoying the scent of moist earth and rain-dampened herbs and flowers drying in the sun. His boots crunched on the crushed limestone pathway. Birds chattered noisily in the trees and the bees were out already, buzzing from flower to flower. Where did they live, so deep in the city?

He'd apologized. It hadn't been easy, but he was glad he'd done it.

And she'd accepted it, in a manner of speaking.

While I suppose I can forgive you, I don't think I would be able to forget it.

Was it a mistake, showing her Studley's damning letter? It had certainly upset her—understandably. But he'd wanted—no, needed—to explain why he'd had such a prejudice against her at the start. To get everything out in the open.

Again he wondered about the man who could treat his own daughter so. And the daughter's mother.

Sixteen when he'd seduced her. And not a penny to support her and the babe. His own child. Unconscionable.

Reluctant to go inside just yet and feeling embraced by the peace in the garden surrounds—you'd never believe this was in the heart of the biggest city in the world—Leo found his way to the rose arbor and sat down.

The scent of roses, released by rain and sun, surrounded him.

Despite her angry reaction, he was glad he'd shown Isobel the letter; he'd never have learned the truth about her
mother otherwise.

The truth? One of them.

For any one story there were several truths, depending
on the source and what they believed. He thought about the
mother Isobel had portrayed, and the varied portraits
painted by Sir Bartleby's letter, the old codger in the village
inn, the grateful nanny and old Mrs. Purdey, each of them
telling a different story, showing the same woman in a very
different light.

He thought about Isobel's passionate defense of her
young mother, and a line from Shakespeare came to him:
"In thy face I see the map of honor, truth, and loyalty."

Honor, truth and loyalty . . .

*Loyalty is a quality Mama and I learned to prize. In this
world, it's very rare and precious.*

It was a quality Leo prized as well. He might not have
hordes of friends, as some fellows he knew claimed to have,
but he could rely absolutely on those few he had. He hoped
they felt the same about him.

Isobel had said she'd forgiven him, but had she really?
Only time would tell.

Not that Leo could talk. He'd never forgotten a
betrayal . . .

He watched a small spider traversing an intricate web,
the delicate threads hung with crystal drops of dew. They
quivered and some fell with the spider's movement.

You really need to get over your mistrust of women.

He'd been annoyed with Race at the time, but Race had
only spoken the truth as he saw it. He'd been right about
Leo's mother and Lavinia Ledbetter, and the effect they'd
had on him, but he wasn't right about everything.

Lavinia's behavior had been a ghastly shock, but seeing

the evidence of her blatant faithlessness with his own eyes had radically changed his view of her. Lavinia had been relatively easy to get over. His mother was another matter.

All those years defending her so-called honor. The bitter scald of betrayal he'd felt when he'd learned the truth. And every time he thought about what she'd done.

And yet to his shame, he still loved her.

The spider finished repairing his web—her web?—and scuttled off to hide under a leaf and wait for prey. A rose petal fell, drifting down to land on Leo's thigh. He picked it up, inhaled its faint scent and fingered its texture, as soft as Isobel's skin.

Race was wrong, claiming Leo couldn't trust any woman. There had been one woman in Leo's life that he'd trusted completely, and who'd never let him down: Mabel, his first serious lover.

He'd been nineteen when he met her, and was feeling beleaguered on all sides. Hauled abruptly out of school, he'd been struggling to come to terms with a difficult invalid father and the shattered image of a mother who was the opposite of the angel he'd believed her to be. And at the same time he was trying to learn how to rebuild a badly neglected estate for which he was now solely responsible.

Almost ten years older than he, Mabel was a childless widow who ran the farm her late husband had owned, though it had been in her family for generations. She ran it much better than he ever had, and declared she had no intention of marrying again and having her farm ruined by another husband—not after all the good work she'd done to bring it back into productivity.

Her outspoken words had struck a chord in Leo, who had been working hard to bring his family estate back from the state his father's wastefulness and neglect had created. And so their friendship had begun, at first just an exchange of views about new farming methods. In Mabel he found an intelligent conversationalist, and a farmer who was inter-

ested in some of the new scientific practices. Her insight
and farming successes gave him the confidence to push his
own tenant farmers to adopt some of the new practices he
was advocating.

Comfortably rounded and as wholesome as fresh-baked
bread, Mabel was also earthy and frankly bawdy. After several weeks of friendly conversation, she'd told him bluntly
that the only place she missed a man in her life was in the
bedchamber. She'd led Leo, still a callow youth, up the stairs
to her bed and proceeded to teach him how to please a
woman, as well as himself.

He took to dropping in on her several times a week,
where they'd pass an evening of good conversation inter-
spersed with vigorous and extremely satisfying bed sports.
It was fondness and friendship, rather than love, and the
arrangement suited them both.

But when Leo turned twenty-five, Mabel had put an end
to their affair, saying that it wasn't fitting any longer for
him to be dallying with a farm woman, and that it was high
time Leo went out into the world, found himself a pretty
young lady and made her his bride.

Hence Lavinia. And what a mistake that had been. He'd
thought her as innocent as she'd appeared—and acted.

His experience with Lavinia had made Leo cynical
about the much-vaunted innocence of society misses. And
being stalked for the sake of his title by many a fawning
society miss had only deepened the cynicism.

Though not all young ladies cared about his wealth and
his title. Isobel had not a penny to her name, and yet . . .

*Take your self-importance and your arrogance and
your stupid suspicious mind and . . . and . . . bottle it!*

He smiled to himself. He could think of no other woman
who would dare to scold him so roundly. And she'd done it
twice. Isobel's straightforward anger was refreshing. Each
time she'd told him exactly what she'd thought of him. She
hadn't held back for fear of angering him. She hadn't sulked

and sighed and pouted, forcing him to try to guess what the matter was. No, she'd given him a right royal trimming, not caring in the least what he thought.

She'd forced him to reconsider. And she'd been right and so he'd apologized, and though it had been risky, producing the letter and digging up her mother's past like that, at least it was all out in the open now. And she'd accepted his apology and they'd cleared the air.

He rose to his feet and took a deep breath.

At least he hoped so.

Chapter Eleven

For the next few days, Izzy's and Clarissa's lives, though very busy and entertaining, continued more or less undisturbed. Invitations kept arriving addressed to Lady Scattergood, who simply passed them on. She enjoyed a wide correspondence, she informed them, but had no interest in society invitations, so Clarissa, as the eldest Studley sister, could respond on her behalf. Which Clarissa happily did, writing acceptances to almost every one.

And contrary to their expectations, Lord Salcott didn't interfere. It was probably too good to be true, Izzy thought, but she was determined to enjoy herself while she could.

They attended the next literary afternoon at Lady Beatrice's, and to their great pleasure, Lady Scattergood came in Matteo's closed sedan chair. It worked even better for her than the carriage, as it transported her from inside her own entry hall to indoors at Lady Beatrice's. It wasn't company that Lady Scattergood couldn't tolerate, it was the outside world.

"I think she secretly enjoys being transported like some kind of grand potentate," Clarissa had commented quietly as they set off for the literary society meeting, the two girls walking behind the sedan chair.

Izzy grinned. "She's certainly dressing the part." Lady Scattergood's maid had fashioned some of her numerous colorful Indian shawls into magnificent turbans.

Lady Scattergood even held an occasional card party at her home—she was a demon card player, they soon learned. Her guests, all older women who also attended the literary society, were likewise utterly cutthroat and competitive. Izzy and Clarissa, not being skilled in the games the ladies preferred, quickly learned to stay in the background. "It's nerve-racking, playing with them," Clarissa whispered, and Izzy could only agree.

Lady Tarrant and her husband had invited them out to the theater, and several times, when she was attending the same party, she'd acted as their chaperone.

And each time they attended an event, the web of their acquaintances widened, and the number of invitations increased.

"Are you finding mixing in society easier now?" Izzy asked her sister as they cut through the garden to Lady Tarrant's house. They were all going to Lady Benton's rout together.

Clarissa nodded. "I do find the very crowded parties a bit of a trial, but the smaller ones, now that I know so many people, are quite tolerable."

Izzy laughed. "'Quite tolerable'? I'm sure our grand hostesses would be utterly thrilled by such a glowing encomium."

Clarissa dimpled. "You know what I mean."

Izzy laughed again. "I do, love, but please don't use the phrase 'quite tolerable' in any of your thank-you letters, or that lovely pile of invitations will dry up overnight."

* * *

There was no point in trying to lock the stable door now that the horses had bolted, Leo decided. The girls were already mixing in society. Now it was up to him to make the kind of arrangements the lawyer had advised him back—was it only a matter of a few weeks ago? It felt much longer. He'd said Leo should escort Clarissa to events like balls, routs, and the opera. And Almack's. He shuddered. The kind of activities he least enjoyed.

The sisters' time in society wouldn't last long, he was sure, so they might as well enjoy themselves while they could. The knowledge that their father had denied them any kind of society as they were growing up had shocked him. No wonder they'd defied Leo's orders.

In the spirit of biting the bullet, he sent a note over to his aunt's inviting Clarissa and her sister to join him in promenading in Hyde Park at the fashionable hour. They accepted, and at the appropriate hour he collected them and, since it was a lovely afternoon, they decided to walk to Hyde Park.

"Where do you think you're taking those gels?" his aunt demanded as they were about to leave.

Leo blinked. "Walking in Hyde Park."

"On their own?"

"No, with me."

She made a rudely disparaging noise, rang the bell and told the butler to fetch Betty, the maid. "The gels must be *properly* escorted," Aunt Olive told Leo. "You," she added with a beady look, "are *a man*."

Behind him he heard a muffled choke of laughter. He turned and saw two young ladies standing with unnaturally blank expressions. One pair of vivid green eyes danced, inviting him to join in the joke.

He winked at her, and her eyes widened in surprise. And appreciation.

He was a man, was he? Indeed he was.

As a young maid hurried down to join them, pulling on a dark red wool pelisse and a gray hat, the lawyer's words came back to Leo: *A maidservant would give Miss Studley neither the respectability nor the consequence required.*

His aunt was nominally the young ladies' sponsor, but since she rarely left the house, she could hardly act as chaperone. He sighed. He'd have to find a proper, well-connected chaperone to give them the respectable appearance and consequence they required. He'd speak to Aunt Olive about it later.

Leo strolled along with a young lady on each arm, more or less in silence: Clarissa was no chatterbox, and Isobel seemed unusually thoughtful. And he was no easy charmer like his friend Race, able to spin witty conversation out of thin air.

He slid a sidelong glance at Isobel. Was she still angry with him? He couldn't tell.

As they entered Hyde Park, he noted gloomily that the sunshine had brought out the crowds. The place was crammed with elegantly dressed people promenading, or inching, along a congested Rotten Row in carriages and on horseback.

Given his preference, he would about-face and head in the opposite direction. Instead he gritted his teeth, plastered what he hoped was a pleasant expression on his face and moved toward the crowd.

A smothered sound came from Isobel. He glanced at her, and she smiled up at him, her eyes sparkling with mischief. "You love the fashionable crush, don't you, Lord Martyr?"

"Simply adore it," he grumped, and she laughed aloud. The sound unraveled a tight band around his chest that he hadn't realized was even there.

"Oh, good, for a moment there I was worried you were going to hate every minute of it. But since you love it sooooo much, we'll stay right to the very end, won't we, Clarissa?"

He gave her a mock glower and she laughed again.

Her sister smiled. "She's teasing you, Lord Salcott. She knows I also find the press of crowds a little uncomfortable. We rarely stay a full hour."

The girls were frequently hailed, and as Leo listened to the discussion of events they'd mutually attended or were planning to attend, it was borne in on him how many society people they'd met while he was away and just how busy and social his life was going to become.

Oh, the joy.

Sometimes he walked with Clarissa on his arm, sometimes Isobel, and sometimes they walked ahead of him with Betty their maid.

Clarissa, he found, was hard work to talk to: she was shy and rarely initiated conversation. Isobel had called her a tigress: he saw no sign of that. But at least she was sweet and compliant, and there were enough distractions in the sights before them to offer up topics of conversation, bland as they were.

Izzy was neither sweet nor compliant, but he had to admit to a silent sigh of relief when she swapped places with her sister and took his arm. There was no shortage of conversation with Isobel—and no boredom, either.

The first time she'd walked with him on their own, she said, "Thank you for bringing that parcel from Mrs. Purdey." Another tight band around his chest loosened.

"Was it something important?"

"Only to me," she said softly. "Just some things from my childhood, things my mother made me. Not important, as such," she added after a minute, "but precious to me. So thank you."

"It was my pleasure."

They walked on in silence.

"Oh, there's Mrs. Gastonbury—have you met her?" she

asked in a bright, chatty voice. She nodded to an elegantly dressed old lady with a cane, walking with a young woman. "That's her granddaughter with her, Cicely, whom she dotes on."

Leo gave her a cautious look. Was she matchmaking? "We've never met."

"Well, if you ever get invited to one of Mrs. Gastonbury's *soirées musicale*—and you will, she's famous for them—make sure you take a large lump of malleable wax."

He gave her a bemused look. "Wax?"

Her eyes were dancing with mischief. "Mrs. Gastonbury is a darling and Cicely is very sweet and just adores performing, but try as she will, the poor girl cannot quite hit the note—any note. So take wax and your ears will thank you."

He choked on a laugh.

A few moments later he noticed a plump fellow in tight yellow breeches making a determined beeline toward them. He was beaming at Miss Isobel.

"An admirer?" he said jokingly.

She looked. "Oh, drat, it's Lord Giddings. Shall we walk this way?" Without waiting for an answer, she practically dragged him in the opposite direction, plunging them into a tight knot of people.

"Avoiding Lord Giddings, Miss Isobel?" he asked silkily.

"If you knew Lord Giddings, you'd avoid him, too."

Leo did know Giddings, or at least he was acquainted with him. A member of one of Leo's clubs, Giddings was a shocking bore, pompous and self-righteous. So he was an admirer of Miss Isobel, was he? Leo was amused. He couldn't imagine a more unlikely match. Quicksilver and clay.

They lost Giddings in the crowd, and she continued to point out people to him. Helping Leo get acquainted with

London society, she claimed. Rubbing his nose in how well she and her sister had infiltrated society, more like.

"That's Lady Entwhistle," she said, indicating a large Roman-nosed matron wearing a hat encrusted with flowers and a stuffed bird. "Also a very sweet old lady, she is an expert on her husband's family history. They go back before the Conquest, you know. If you ever get stuck in a corner with her, I promise you, you'll end up knowing every detail of the intervening seven centuries. Soooo thrilling."

He smothered a laugh and bowed to Lady Entwhistle, who was nodding and smiling and beckoning him to approach. She had an unmarried granddaughter, he suddenly recalled. Pretending not to see her invitation, he hurried them away.

Isobel gave a gurgle of laughter. "Lord Salcott, I never dreamed you were a coward."

"I'm not."

"Look at you, running from a big bad dowager. You never know, her sweet little granddaughter might be the very one for you."

"She isn't," he grated. "Now, speaking of running away, where is that charming fellow, Lord Giddings? Perhaps you'd prefer to walk with him."

She laughed again, that gurgle of laughter that so entranced him, then skipped ahead to join her sister.

Leo strolled and nodded and bowed and smiled until his jaw was aching. Everywhere he looked he saw young females being escorted by their mothers or aunts or grandmothers, occasionally by some gentleman and, in some cases, a female who looked like a governess. Even the very young girls strolling in pairs were accompanied by some respectable-looking female.

And everywhere he looked there were gentlemen—and less-than-gentlemen—on the prowl. Both Clarissa and Isobel attracted a great deal of masculine interest. Leo made a note of those he recognized and resolved to learn about those he didn't. Several gazetted fortune hunters clustered around Clarissa; obviously news of her inheritance was out, blast it. Thankfully Clarissa made no effort to encourage any of them; in fact she looked a little uncomfortable.

Leo's role here was to stand close by and look grim and forbidding, which exactly suited his mood.

By far the largest group made for Isobel, mostly elegant young bucks, callow boys whom he decided were harmless. But there were a number of older men—men in their thirties and forties—some titled, most wealthy, some married and some widowed. And a good many jaded older rakes. Leo didn't like the look of any of them.

Isobel laughed and flirted and chatted happily with them all. Even Lord Giddings, who had tracked her down again.

Leo scowled and broke up the little clusters, keeping both girls on the move.

Guardian? More like a blasted sheepdog!

"You look rather grim," Isobel said, rejoining him after stopping to chat with a small group of ladies and gentlemen. "Why? Can it be that you're not enjoying yourself?" Her eyes twinkled up at him.

"On the contrary, I'm finding it delightful. Social chitchat with relative strangers—how could anyone fail to enjoy never-ending meaningless exchanges?" He bared his teeth in a mirthless smile and she laughed.

"But all the ladies have been soooo delighted to see you here," she pointed out. "Aren't you flattered by all the attention you've been getting?"

He gave her a mock-baleful look. "Emptying the butter boat, Miss Isobel?" Again she laughed, and again he got that warm feeling in his chest.

As for the toad-eating he'd been subjected to, he loathed the unsubtle attentions of some of the ladies with marriageable daughters. Flattery always caused him to poker up. He had no way of dealing with it.

What was he to do? Agree that yes, he was indeed the handsomest man in London? Or point out that actually he was quite ordinary—which was the truth, but would only cause the flatterers to laugh gaily and proceed to smother him with more outrageous compliments. Ghastly stuff.

He glanced at Clarissa and Betty walking ahead, their arms linked. It attracted several disapproving glances, he noticed. None of the other young ladies here linked arms with their maid or governess. "You and your sister should not link arms with your maid."

Isobel immediately stiffened. "Why not? We like Betty. We've known her since we were children together."

"Yes, I noticed you gave her your new red pelisse—and no, I have no objection to your giving her clothes," he added as she opened her mouth to argue. "But it's not appropriate to treat her like a friend in public." Leo knew he sounded stuffy. For himself he couldn't care less, but it was his responsibility to care for them, and part of that responsibility was to ensure that they did not attract censure from society. At least for now.

"But she's our friend as well as our maid."

"Then keep your displays of friendship private. Unless you wish to attract public disapproval."

She scowled, dropped his arm and stalked off to join Clarissa and the maid. She glanced back and pointedly linked arms with the maid. He wanted to laugh—she was nothing if not predictable. Loyalty was bred into her through and through. As was defiance.

Lord, but he loathed being in this position that forced his interactions with Isobel to be more like a stern schoolmaster with a pupil than a man with a woman. A woman he found fascinating, though as her purported guardian, he should not.

But she and Clarissa, whether they acknowledged it or not, were in a delicate situation and could not afford to attract unwelcome interest.

When they returned to Bellaire Gardens, Leo entered his aunt's house with the young ladies and told Treadwell that he wished to speak with his aunt, that he had something of importance to discuss with her.

Isobel eyed him suspiciously. "What do you want to speak to her about?"

"Izzy," her sister murmured repressively.

"No, I want to know."

Shaking her head, Clarissa went upstairs.

Leo went into the blue saloon to await his aunt. Isobel followed him in. "Well? Is this about Betty? You're not going to dismiss her, are you?"

"It's not about Betty, at least not directly—and no, I'm not going to dismiss her. I'm going to hire a proper chaperone for you and your sister."

"A proper chaperone?" Isobel's green eyes narrowed to cat slits. "Who?"

"I haven't yet decided. I'm thinking an older woman might be suitable, someone with experience of society—perhaps a widow in her fourth or fifth decade, a woman with no other charges on her time. That's what I'm going to talk to my aunt about."

She folded her arms tightly beneath her bosom, her expression mutinous. "Why do we need some old lady to watch over us? Don't you trust us?"

Leo wasn't going near that one. "It's convention," he said mildly. "As Clarissa's guardian, I am responsible for ensuring that not a breath of scandal attaches to her name." He gave her a meaningful look, and she had the grace to flush slightly. She knew what he meant.

"There's no danger of that—Clarissa is always perfectly behaved," she said. "So this is about me, then. About"—she flushed—"the other night." When they'd kissed.

Her blush was enchanting. His whole body tightened.

"No," he said. "It's not about either of you in particular. It's simply a societal convention that must be respected."

"I don't believe you. I don't think you trust us."

"Why ever would you imagine such a thing?" he said dryly.

For a moment she stood, glaring down her imperious little nose at him, then a gurgle of reluctant laughter escaped her. "All right, so behind your back we organized a tiny little party in your name."

He snorted at the word *tiny*.

"*And*"—she added as if goaded—"we did enter society against your specific instructions. But it all worked out in the end, didn't it?"

He didn't respond, and the mischief slowly faded from her eyes. "Even if we did disobey you, that's no reason to saddle us with a—a gaoler. Clarissa and I have been virtually locked up all our lives, and now, when we're finally free, you hire a gaoler?" There was a plea as well as defiance in her voice.

Again he cursed Studley for forcing this guardianship on him. For her to see him as her gaoler was agony. She was young, spirited and passionate—and he hated to crush that in her. But once he accepted a responsibility, he carried it out to the best of his ability, and this was no different. Much as she hated the idea of a chaperone, it was for her own and her sister's good.

"Don't be so melodramatic. She won't be a gaoler, just a respectable lady who will help steer you and your sister through the shoals and reefs of London society."

"But we don't need anyone to tell us how to go on. We have friends willing to chaperone us, and we've been managing just fine on our own."

"You've hardly begun. Growing up as isolated as you were, you have no idea how intricate and rigid the unspoken rules of society can be. A respectable chaperone will ensure that society will note that all proper arrangements have been made." He was also hoping the presence of a chaperone would underline the girls' respectability. "Now, I don't propose to argue, Isobel. I intend to make the arrangement and that's the end to it."

"Oh, you just don't want us to have any fun at all." She turned on her heel and marched to the door.

"That's not it at all," he began. "I just don't want you to be"—the door slammed behind her—"hurt," he finished.

He understood, more than she realized. He knew she and her sister had been shut away from the world for most of their lives. It was much how he'd felt in the ten years he'd been stuck on his family estate, desperately working to get it back into shape, while his former school friends traveled the world, having adventures.

However, he'd had the choice, he reflected. He could make short visits to London when everything got too much for him. And after his father's death, once the estate was profitable again, he'd taken a year to go adventuring.

Isobel and her sister were poised on the brink of their own little adventure, their first taste of freedom. And he was clipping their wings.

But he couldn't see any other way around it. Society was rigid in its expectations of young unmarried girls. And unforgiving of those who transgressed.

It will be some horrid old battle-axe," Izzy told her sister. They were in the small room near the scullery that Clarissa had turned into her workroom. "She'll watch us like a hawk and we won't be able to have any fun."

"Mmm." Clarissa stirred three drops of rose oil into one of her concoctions.

Izzy picked up a small phial from the collection on the shelf and stared at it with unseeing eyes. "She's bound to be ghastly—he said he was looking for an elderly widow."

Clarissa gently removed the phial from her grasp and replaced it. "I thought you said he was looking for someone in their fourth or fifth decade. That's hardly elderly."

"No, but she'll act elderly and stuffy, I'm sure," Izzy said darkly. She paced back and forth in the small room.

Clarissa sniffed at her mix, frowned, added another drop of rose oil and kept stirring.

Izzy watched, brooding. "I hate that he doesn't trust us. Doesn't it bother you?"

"Not really. And I don't think it's a lack of trust that bothers you—it's being told what to do. You've always hated that."

"I know," Izzy admitted with a rueful grin.

"And you must admit he has good reason not to trust us. We've disobeyed him so often. And quite blatantly."

Izzy smirked. "True."

Clarissa continued. "And Milly has said numerous times that her mother considers it a scandal that we often go about with only a maidservant or young Jeremiah in attendance. Or no one at all."

Izzy rolled her eyes. "Oh, Milly and her never-ending bleats of what Mama says! That girl has raised irritation to an art form."

Clarissa gave a huff of laughter. "Yes, but I suspect she's right. Chaperoning each other is sufficient for some occasions, but not for grand balls and things like that." She returned to the fragrant cream she was working on.

"But Lady Tarrant has often chaperoned us."

"Yes, when she's also attending the same event. But we cannot expect Lady Tarrant to accompany us everywhere," Clarissa reminded her. "She's newly married to that lovely man, and has her own life to lead."

"I know," Izzy admitted glumly. "And I suppose, having recently finished sponsoring her goddaughter's come-out, she must be fed up with having to play the chaperone. I would be." She picked up a bowl of some herbal mix, sniffed and put it down with a snap. "Oh, it's all so stupid—we've been doing fine up 'til now without a permanent chaperone interfering with everything we do."

"Well, there's nothing we can do about it now," Clarissa said placidly. "Lord Salcott has made the decision and we'll just have to hope this woman works out. Now, pass me the third little bottle from the end—yes, that one. It's essence of orange blossom. I'm trying something new."

Chapter Twelve

❦

Over the next few days, it became clear to Izzy that Lord Salcott was very serious about ensuring they—she—didn't step out of line. He turned up at every event—and how he always seemed to know where they were going was a source of endless speculation.

The first time she saw him turn up, Izzy had been quite pleased. She'd enjoyed their walk in the park, and thought he was softening toward them. She was gradually coming to terms with the notion of a chaperone, but was reserving judgment on the actual person he hired, whom they hadn't met yet.

But though he'd greeted them on arrival at the first party, he made no further move to speak to either of them, not even to invite them to dance, which had surprised her.

The second party they attended that week, it was the same. He occasionally chatted to this person or that, but he didn't dance with anyone. Mostly what he did was stand and watch her and Clarissa in a way that Izzy found increasingly irritating. It was clear he wasn't attending these events for his own enjoyment. Then why come at all?

The answer, to Izzy, was becoming clear.

Now they were at their third party and, "There he is again," Izzy muttered. They'd been at Lady Benton's for a bare half hour. "What does he think we're going to do that he needs to spy on us?"

Tall and elegant in immaculate evening wear, Lord Salcott leaned against a decorative column, gazing across the crowded room with those mesmerizing flinty gray eyes.

Clarissa laughed. "He's not spying. He explained to me that, as my guardian, it's his duty to protect me, and you know what? I quite like it. He doesn't interfere in what we're doing, and he makes me feel safe."

"'Safe'?" Izzy echoed incredulously. "How can you feel safe with those icy gray eyes boring into you all the time?"

Clarissa laughed again. "They're not boring into *me*," she said meaningfully.

Izzy flushed and tossed her head. "If you mean he's watching me all the time, I don't believe it. Or if he is, it's because he doesn't trust me."

Clarissa shook her head and, smiling, strolled away to join another group. Lord Salcott's gaze didn't shift away from Izzy. He was definitely watching her.

But Izzy didn't think it was the sort of interest that Clarissa was imagining—Clarissa was a romantic. Lord Salcott didn't feel that way about Izzy—his reaction that night when Milly had appeared and claimed he'd compromised Izzy had proved that. He'd run like a rabbit.

Izzy had been utterly beguiled by the magic of his kisses that night, but she'd realized since that it had been the magic of the party and the evening . . . And the champagne.

Her own foolish and unconsidered actions had instigated the whole thing. No wonder he'd reacted the way he had. He was only responding to her thoughtless flirting.

In retrospect his cold reaction when they were discovered

had left her cringing inwardly at her own naivety. Even his eventual apology had been from a position of acknowledging his own mistake—keeping to the high moral standards he set for himself, rather than showing concern for her feelings.

No, Izzy had her own theory, one she wasn't going to explain to Clarissa. All Izzy's life—well, since she was fourteen or fifteen—men had looked at her in a certain way.

Lord Salcott knew about her mother now, and he knew better than anyone that Izzy had not a penny to her name. It was only through marriage—or some less respectable arrangement—that Izzy's future would be secured.

He was keeping a watchful eye on her, making sure she didn't disgrace Clarissa—as if she would. But she refused to allow him to spoil her enjoyment of the party. Let him prop up that column and brood. She was going to have fun.

However, as the night wore on, it became clear to Izzy that he had no intention of remaining on the sidelines. Over the past few days she'd been enjoying a lighthearted flirtation with Sir Jasper Vibart, a sophisticated rake whose dry, cynical observations she found quite entertaining. There was nothing in the slightest bit serious about it, and when he'd learned the other day that she would be attending Lady Benton's rout party, he'd engaged Izzy for a couple of dances.

But tonight Sir Jasper had approached her, saying in his languid manner, "So entertaining, my dear. I've actually been warned off by your guardian, or should I say your guard dog?"

"*What?*"

His hard eyes glittered with appreciation. "I know— ridiculous, is it not? But fear not, dear lady, you shall not lack for a partner. My dances, Lord Salcott informs me, have now been granted to Lord Giddings."

Lord Giddings? Izzy was furious. And she wasn't going to stand for it. She marched across the room to confront Lord Salcott. "What do you think you're doing?"

"Good evening, Miss Isobel," he said smoothly. "You look lovely tonight. That color suits you very well."

Izzy felt herself flushing. There was an undertone in his voice that she didn't trust at all. A slight ironic note? Aware of the interested ears close by, she muttered a passably polite greeting. Amusement glinted in his eyes.

She bristled. She opened her mouth to blast him, then recalled the listeners avidly swaying closer, ears subtly pricked. Curse it, how could she possibly confront him here? There was a reason they called it "polite society"— people might be at daggers drawn, but they would never show it openly. Instead they exchanged remarks that seemed polite and unexceptional on the surface but were tremendously cutting underneath.

She tried to think of something polite but tremendously cutting to say to him. But couldn't think of a thing. Those ice-gray eyes were too distracting.

"How dare you decide who I dance with," she said in a low voice.

"Of course, it's time for our dance, is it not?" he said loudly as if she'd come to remind him. Without waiting for a response, he tucked her hand into the crook of his arm and led her onto the dance floor.

"But—" She bit her lip. If she resisted, it would only cause the kind of gossip she wanted to avoid.

It was a country-dance, so there was very little chance of conversation. Her jaw tight with resentment, she danced, meeting his gaze as infrequently as possible. But she was aware the whole time of his eyes on her.

When the dance finished and everyone was leaving the floor, she hung back a little, waiting for a chance at private speech. When it occurred, she said to him in a vehement undertone, "What I do and with whom I do it is none of your business. You are Clarissa's guardian, not mine—"

"Thank God for that."

She glared at him. "So concern yourself with her, not

me. I will dance with whomever I choose, and I will thank you to stay out of my affairs."

"Sir Jasper Vibart is an inveterate gambler and a ruthless rake."

"I care nothing for that. He is good-looking, entertaining company and an excellent dancer. Which is all that matters to me at the moment."

"He has ruined several young women. You can't trust him."

"I was simply going to *dance* with him! In public at a crowded party," she snapped. "Besides, whatever I choose to do with him or any other man is my business, Lord Salcott. Yours is to protect Clarissa. She doesn't mind your bossy ways. I do. I will take care of my own future, thank you, so stop interfering."

"I did it for your own good," he said stiffly.

"Well, stop it. My good—or my bad—is for me to decide." She marched off the dance floor, only to find Lord Giddings, in knee breeches and a tight coat of purple satin, waiting for her, his plump face wreathed in smiles.

"Miss Isobel, how very delightful you look this evening. Our dance, I believe."

Trapped, Izzy pasted a polite smile over gritted teeth and allowed him to lead her out for the next set. If that dratted chaperone didn't arrive soon, she would probably murder Lord Salcott.

The following day, Leo, having learned Clarissa and Isobel were attending Lord and Lady Clendon's rout that evening, announced that he would escort them to it.

"But it's already arranged," Isobel said, bristling visibly. "Lord and Lady Tarrant are going and Lady Tarrant offered to chaperone us."

"Very generous of her. Nevertheless, I will escort you. As Clarissa's guardian, it is my duty," Leo said, aware he sounded like an antediluvian old fossil. "I have notified Lord and Lady Tarrant. And," he added, as his aunt opened her mouth to enter the fray, "I have arranged for Betty to accompany us in the carriage. She will await the young ladies' pleasure in the servants' quarters."

As he spoke, the maid emerged from belowstairs, her eyes shining. "Thank you, melord, I never been to a proper lord's party," she confided. "Not indoors, I mean. I'm ever so excited."

And that, more than anything Leo could say, put an end to any argument from Isobel. So much for Leo being in charge.

The carriage pulled up at the front of the house, the young ladies donned their evening cloaks, and Leo helped them into the carriage. Isobel was looking enchanting in a dress of mulberry silk trimmed with lace. Her hair was up, bound in place by a thin mulberry ribbon. Tiny dark curls clustered around her temples and nape. He longed to trail his fingers through them.

Clarissa, too, looked very smart in a gauzy peach-colored dress. The maid was wearing a blue dress he'd seen on Isobel once, and wore the red pelisse over it. Isobel noticed him observing it and with a challenging look raised her chin. The maid's fine clothing was a statement.

A temporary truce might have been arranged, but hostilities still simmered underneath. But Leo had plans for that.

They entered Lady Clendon's home. Clarissa looked ahead and gave a little sigh of pleasure. The carpets had been rolled back, chairs were arranged around the edge of the room, and musicians were tuning up. "Oh good, there's going to be dancing," she exclaimed. "So much more pleasant than *conversazione*."

Leo immediately reserved two dances with Clarissa and two with Isobel.

The house filled quickly, and the party was soon held to

be "a sad crush"—no small encomium. As Leo had hoped, Lady Clendon, known for her gregarious nature and her vibrant personality, had scheduled a number of waltzes, even though the party wasn't a ball, as such.

He danced a country-dance with Clarissa, which made conversation between them unnecessary. She ended it, looking a little flushed. The dance had been rather long. Her partner for the next dance hovered, holding a drink out in anticipation. Clarissa accepted it gratefully, and allowed the man to escort her to a seat.

Isobel, too, was coming off the floor. Leo seized the opportunity. "Would you care to step outside for a little fresh air?" he asked her, and offered her his arm. He'd removed his gloves, and his hands were bare.

She hesitated, then laid her hand on his arm.

Outside in the small courtyard, the breeze was soft and balmy, but her arms and neck were bare. "Should I fetch your shawl?" he asked.

She shook her head. "No, it's cool, but not cold."

They strolled between the potted shrubs and flowers. She stopped at a large blue ceramic pot spilling over with fragrant lilies in bloom, turned and said abruptly, "I have a temper and I don't always control it as I should." She took a deep breath and met his gaze frankly. "But I really hate the idea of someone watching over me, monitoring everything I do and say." Turning away, she pulled off one of her long evening gloves and stroked her fingers up the stem of a lavender flower spike.

"You mean the chaperone?"

"I mean, as you very well know, your practice of overruling my choice of dance partners. I'm not exactly delighted about the chaperone, but I should add that Clarissa doesn't at all mind the idea. As usual, I'm the difficult one." She raised her hand to smell the lavender fragrance on her fingers.

Leo swallowed. He opened his mouth to explain, but she

got in first. "I've never taken well to being told what to do. It's one of my abiding faults."

It was the kind of not quite an apology that Leo was sometimes guilty of himself—but he appreciated her honesty. "And perhaps ten years of running my estates and telling everyone what to do has caused me to become a little . . . autocratic."

"Only a little?" she queried, but there was a smile in her eyes.

He shrugged. "My only excuse is that Sir Jasper Vibart is the kind of man all young women should be warned against." Seeing her eyes kindling for battle, he held his hand up. "But I take your point. In future if I think you need some background on any of the gentlemen you meet in society, I will inform you privately."

"And?" she prompted.

He rolled his eyes. "And allow you to make the final decision."

She nodded. "Thank you. We can agree on that." She narrowed her eyes at him. "But if you *ever* cancel one of my dance partners and replace him with Lord Giddings or anyone else, I will . . . I don't know what I will do, but I guarantee you won't like it!"

He nodded. "Yes, that was ill done of me."

"It was."

He couldn't help but smile. "I have a temper, too, and I'm afraid I couldn't resist. And it made the poor fellow so very happy."

She gave him a baleful look.

They turned down a little pathway bordered by a low hedge of clipped rosemary.

"I understand that you're worried this chaperone might act like a gaoler, but I assure you she won't. Or if she does, I'll dismiss her." After a minute, he added, "Like you and your sister, I know what it's like to be confined."

She quirked a skeptical brow at him.

"I was unable to leave my father's estate for years. He was an invalid—fretful and demanding of my presence day and night—and I, just out of school, was suddenly solely responsible for . . . for everything and everyone."

They strolled on and he tried to explain what it had been like for him, pitchforked into responsibilities—economic and emotional—that he'd had no preparation for. Without any real support. "And before that I was at school," he finished, "and that *was* like being in gaol."

He glanced at her. "I wasn't free to do what I wanted until my father died. So last year I escaped, left the country, put the estate in the hands of my manager and traveled. I started to discover who I was. And it was glorious. Until I came home to learn . . ."

She turned to look at him. "Learn what?" she prompted after a minute.

"That without my knowledge or agreement, I'd become your sister's legal guardian." He explained the mistake her father had made in his will.

She stared at him a moment, then burst out laughing. "You mean you came home from your glorious adventure only to be landed with us? And we were soooo grateful for your interference. And so obedient. What a homecoming."

He couldn't help but smile. "Exactly."

She pulled a slender branch of lime blossom toward her and bent to inhale its fragrance. The lanterns arranged around the courtyard threw her face into shadow. Her silhouette was pure and perfect. Tiny curls clustered around her face. He itched to run his fingers through them, to bend and kiss the soft skin of her nape.

She straightened, misinterpreted his expression and smiled. "Clarissa has taught me to appreciate the fragrance of flowers. I don't know the names of them all, but I do recognize lime trees, at least when they're in flower. They have the sweetest scent."

He plucked a leaf and crushed it between his fingers, but

it wasn't the lime trees he could smell, it was her own distinctive perfume that filled his senses.

She released the lime and pulled her long white glove back on, smoothing it along her arm with long strokes. "Thank you for sharing your story with me, Lord Salcott. I would almost feel sorry for you, but since you keep trying to control us—"

"It's not for my own pleasure, believe me," he said bitterly. If she only knew how the role of guardian chafed at him. "And while I might understand—and sympathize—with your position and your delight in the freedom you and your sister have just begun to taste, you have little experience of London society and how it can condemn people—especially unmarried young ladies—for the slightest infraction."

A crease appeared between her smooth brows. "But—"

"You are spirited and unconventional, bold and vivacious," he told her, and she blushed. His voice hardened: he had to make her understand. "A duke's daughter who is spirited and unconventional will be forgiven, and indulgently regarded as 'an original.' An ordinary girl, even the legitimate daughter of a baronet, who behaves the same way?" He shook his head.

Her furrowed brow and thoughtful expression showed she had filled in the gaps.

"Which is why I've hired this chaperone. I don't want you or Clarissa to make some unknowing mistake and be punished for it. You're on thin enough ice as it is." She swallowed, and he continued quietly, "Try to think of this woman as your and Clarissa's guide and protector. You never know, she might even become a friend."

She made a faint skeptical sound at that, but he could see she'd understood his message. "Very well, I'll try," she said finally. "But if she's horrid . . ."

A faint breeze stirred the tiny curls that danced around

her nape. The scent of roses teased his senses, but there were no roses in this garden. Only Isobel. Belle.

The silence stretched. He wanted nothing more than to kiss her out here in the darkness, to wrap her slender body against him and breathe in her scent and kiss her. And kiss her. And kiss her.

But he couldn't. He could hardly give in to his instincts after preaching propriety at her. Being alone with her out here was unconventional enough. People kept wandering through, though nobody was around at the moment. Kissing her here and now could ruin her in an instant. He stared down at her, battling with his desires.

With one finger he stroked lightly down her cheek, the faintest of caresses, her skin soft and warm.

She gazed up at him, her eyes wide and dark in the faint moonlight. He fancied he could see a silent question in them. A faint blush colored her cheeks, as if she could read his mind. She swallowed, met his gaze full on and moistened her wine-dark mouth, full and bold and oh so tempting. He closed his eyes, remembering the taste of her, the shape and feeling and texture of her skin under his hand, under his mouth. He ached to touch her again. Taste her again.

But he could not. Not here. Not now.

Inside the musicians started up again. A waltz.

Leo held out his hand to her. "Dance with me."

L ord Salcott stood back to let Izzy go before him through the French doors. She thought about what he'd just told her, how he'd been trapped on his family estate, how he'd considered her position and tried to understand.

It was the rules he tried to impose that she so disliked. Could she separate the rules from the man? She understood that he was trying to do his best by Clarissa. But he had no obligation to concern himself with her.

The waltz began. She hadn't danced it very often. She and Clarissa had tried to teach themselves when they were younger, and since coming to London had taken several lessons. But this . . .

It wasn't quite what she'd expected. He took her hand and swept her onto the dance floor, his hand firm at her waist. Thoughts about their recent conversation scattered. He was wearing gloves but somehow she could feel the heat of his touch through the layers of her dress. It felt scandalously close, but nobody batted an eyelid. The other dancers were just as close.

There was no need to mind her steps: he was wholly in control, and after a few circuits she stopped trying to order her feet and just let herself float and twirl in his arms.

It was glorious. She felt weightless. Breathless.

For a man who didn't move much in society, who'd been shut up on his family estate for years, he waltzed superbly. "I'm surprised," she told him.

"In what way?"

"You waltz so well."

"It was all the rage when I was in Vienna." He twirled her masterfully around.

The rest of the company blurred, and it was as if there were only the two of them in the room, moving as one to music intended just for them. Izzy's entire awareness was filled with him and the smooth control of his powerful, graceful body—in this she was happy to let him take the lead. To command.

His eyes devoured her. At first she felt oddly shy, his gaze was so intense, so demanding. She resisted its pull, instead letting her gaze drift over his other features: the fine grain of his skin, freshly shaven with an elusive tang of masculine cologne, or perhaps the fragrant leaves he'd crushed earlier; the bold nose, the firm chin, the hard unsmiling mouth, its sternness so appealing and yet such a challenge. No sign of that fugitive dimple tonight.

But it was not anger she saw in him tonight. It was desire. Leashed, to be sure, but simmering under his skin. Unmistakable. Her blood leapt in response. She wanted to move closer, to press her body against him, to twine around him.

Such feelings . . . she didn't know how to handle them in this company. She couldn't see them, but she knew eyes were all around them.

She closed her eyes in a vain attempt to block out the intensity in his smoke-gray eyes. She felt it with every movement. She tried to concentrate on the music and the dance, to disguise her aching awareness of his every movement, every touch.

But it was impossible.

They danced and their bodies touched, a fleeting brush of thigh against thigh, the brief graze of breast against chest. His big warm hands held her, spinning her around and around in his orbit. Each touch shimmered through her.

Like those kisses in the summerhouse that she'd tried so hard to forget. And couldn't. And craved more of.

She stopped fighting him—and herself—and surrendered to the magic and the moment. And, for this little while at least, to the man.

The dance finished. Leo bowed and Isobel curtsied—no, he was going to think of her as Belle from now on. Her eyes were dazed, and the way she looked up at him . . . He just wanted to sweep her away, out of sight of all these people and—

A dowager gripped his elbow. "You dance divinely, Lord Salcott. My granddaughter is all admiration." Smiling meaningfully, she indicated a blushing young miss standing by.

Dammit, they'd barely left the dance floor and the vultures were circling already. Leo inclined his head. "Thank you, Lady um—

Her smile hardened. "Lady Billston. I am an old friend of your father's. I knew you when you were in short coats. My granddaughter is Miss Fenella Falway." She nudged the girl forward. She bobbed a curtsy and gave him a nervous smile.

"Indeed? How do you do, Lady Billston, Miss Falway. Please excuse me, my partner is parched and I promised her refreshment." He hurried Isobel away.

She looked up at him, her eyes dancing with laughter. "Fleeing again, Lord Salcott?"

He gave her a mock-threatening look. "Do you want refreshment, wench, or shall I hand you over to your fond admirer over there?" He indicated Lord Giddings, portly in puce, who waved, beaming hopefully at Isobel.

"No, no, not Lord Giddings," she exclaimed like the heroine in a melodrama, but softly so that only he could hear. "I take it all back. You don't cravenly flee from dowagers and debutantes: you're amazingly brave—brave as a lion, courageous as a cougar, fearless as a"—she paused to think—"a ferret?"

"Baggage," he growled, and handed her a glass of lemonade.

She gave him a provocative wide-eyed look. "Are baggages brave, then?"

"No, reckless. And begging for a spanking."

She let out a huff of laughter. "Ooh, fighting words, Lord Salcott, but your dimple is showing."

"I don't have a dimple," Leo began, but sets were forming for the next dance, and a cluster of eager men approached her. A Mr. Greelish claimed victory and led her away.

Leo frowned, watching them take the floor. Greelish was thirty-five or so, a rich widower, perfectly respectable, if not top drawer. But he wasn't a suitable partner for her. It was like pairing an Italian greyhound with a spaniel.

Oh, what the hell was he doing, watching over her like a guard dog, brooding about the men she attracted? Of course

she attracted men. She was beautiful and charming and . . .
damn near irresistible.

It wasn't her fault. She couldn't help it that she attracted
men like bees to a honeypot. And he was just one more sad
drone who couldn't keep away.

Was this how it had been for his father, fruitlessly pining
after his mother?

What was he doing, dancing and flirting with her—with
the whole of society looking on? He had to stop this, stop
yearning after what it was too dangerous to want.

Noticing a hopeful matron bringing her daughter toward
him, he slipped behind a knot of people and vanished into
the crowd. He needed a drink.

D og in the manger, I call it."
       "Salcott doesn't even need the fortune."
Hearing his name, Leo froze. There were several potted
palms and a column between him and the two speakers. He
leaned closer.

"Studley was a fool to have left his girls to Salcott's care
in the first place."

"Naturally, Salcott would nab the beautiful one. Are you
sure they're both due to inherit a fortune?"

"I believe so. The girls' mother was a cit—granddaughter
of some northern manufacturer—sausages or woolen mills
or pickles, something like that. She inherited a fortune, but
her father didn't take much to Studley—"

"Can't blame him."

"So the old man tied it all up so Studley couldn't touch
it. I remember Studley ranting about it to m'father."

"So now the mother's fortune goes to her heirs—those
girls."

"Exactly. Outrageous of Salcott to be annexing the
pretty one, though. He's supposed to be her guardian, not a
blasted suitor."

"Taking advantage of his privileged position. It's a dashed disgrace. He doesn't even need a fortune!"

"There's still the other one."

"Yes, the plain one. I'd better go and ask her to dance."

Leo frowned. So people were imagining Isobel was also an heiress. And that he was courting her—which, if he truly were her guardian, would be quite unethical.

And dammit, he did not like Clarissa being referred to as "the plain one." Even if she was.

He leaned out to see who the two men were. Frencham and Taunton. Right. Frencham was young and elegant—no doubt women thought him charming—but his estates were a shambles, and as far as Leo knew, he was making no effort to repair the damage but relying on his so-called charm with women to get him out of the mess. Leo had no patience for that.

Taunton was another useless waster—tall, good-looking, a rake and a gambler. Neither man would see a penny of Clarissa's money, he vowed.

He watched as the two men crossed the floor. Frencham bowed gracefully over Clarissa's hand and a moment later led her, blushing, out to dance.

Damn and blast. But it wasn't the two fortune hunters' intentions toward his ward that disturbed him most—he'd see them both off easily enough. It was their earlier conversation that bothered him.

He sought out Race and asked him straight out, "Have you heard any gossip about Miss Isobel and me?"

Race gave him a thoughtful look, as if considering whether to answer, then he shrugged. "People have noticed."

"Noticed what?"

Race gave a huff of laughter. "If you don't want people to talk, you'll have to stop gazing at the girl as if she's a long cool drink and you're a man dying of thirst in the desert."

Leo frowned. "I don't."

Race laughed. "No, of course you don't, that's why people are speculating."

"About what?"

"What your game is. You're supposedly her guardian, and yet it looks very much like a courtship."

Leo scowled. "Damn."

"Well, what did you expect? You've made it obvious that you have no interest in any of the eligible young ladies people have been pushing at you since you came to town, and yet you apparently can't stay away from Isobel Studley." He glanced at Leo and added in a lower voice, "It's also widely believed that both girls are heiresses, not just Clarissa. I don't know how you'll handle that one when the time comes."

Neither did Leo. He swore under his breath.

To make the true situation clear would be their ruin. A guardian had no business even flirting with his ward; it was entirely unethical. And for all their sakes he could not be seen to be forming an attachment.

He didn't even know if he was forming an attachment. Certainly, he was powerfully drawn to Isobel, but whether it was lust or something more, he wasn't yet sure. But one thing was certain: he had to change his ways, withdraw his attentions and behave in a much more formal and circumspect manner toward her. Dammit.

To that end he sought her out in the next interval between dances and said in a low voice, "It has come to my attention that people in society have the wrong idea about us."

A faint furrow appeared between her brows. "Wrong idea?"

"Yes, they are imagining that I'm courting you."

The furrow deepened, but she said nothing.

"So I think it best if we distance ourselves from each other in future, starting with our planned waltz."

She narrowed her eyes. "You're canceling our waltz?"

"I think it's best. You will have no difficulty finding another partner, I'm sure."

Her expression was unreadable. He could see she wanted to discuss it further, but he couldn't explain it here, in public, and draw even more attention to them, so he gave her a curt nod and walked away. He felt her gaze following him but did not turn back until he reached the door.

Turning for one last look at her, he saw Sir Jasper Vibart leading her out for the waltz. For Leo's waltz, damn his cheek. She saw him looking, raised her chin and gave a defiant little smile. He swore silently and left.

Chapter Thirteen

Izzy slept badly that night. His words kept circling round and round in her brain.

People in society have the wrong idea about us . . .

People had all sorts of ideas, often quite erroneous. Was she to conduct herself according to what other people *might* think?

She grimaced. She supposed she should. It went against the grain, though.

They are imagining that I'm courting you.

She'd started to suspect the same thing, fool that she was. She knew—*knew*—that she was not the kind of girl a man of his rank would take seriously. Especially knowing what he did about her.

I think it best if we distance ourselves from each other in future.

What exactly did that mean? Clearly, he meant not to dance with her, but as Clarissa's guardian, he was obliged to have some minimal degree of interaction.

You will have no difficulty finding another partner, I'm sure.

The words at least were clear enough, but his tone of voice? Was there an underlying criticism there? Or was she being oversensitive?

By dawn she was utterly fed up with the questions clamoring at her brain. She rose, found Jeremiah and accompanied him for an early morning walk with the dogs. When she returned, she found Clarissa preparing to take a bath, so Izzy took herself out to the rose-covered arbor to read.

She opened her book. The morning sun was beautifully warm, and the scent of the roses filled her senses, but she realized after a while that she'd been staring at the same page for the last ten minutes and hadn't taken in a word. Her mind kept drifting to the events of the previous night.

The way he'd looked at her. The silent intensity. The way he'd danced with her. It wasn't simply a dance, it had felt like something . . . more.

He'd reserved country-dances with Clarissa, and waltzes with Izzy. Which seemed to be significant—at least at the time she'd thought so. Now she wasn't sure.

First, a magical interlude in the courtyard, followed by a heavenly dance, and then a short time later he'd approached her, all grim and serious and reneged on their second waltz. Saying they should distance themselves in future

Why had he changed his mind? Was it something she'd done? Broken one of those arcane society rules? She tried to think what it could be, but nothing came to mind.

The man blew hot and cold. She couldn't make him out.

One minute she was sure he was interested in her—seriously interested, and that something special was growing between them—and the next minute he was all bossy and grim and guardian-y and distant.

Had she imagined that intensity between them?

She hadn't set out to fall in love with him—or any man.

Not that she was in love with him, she told herself firmly. Especially when he seemed so changeable. She knew her situation. All she had going for her was her face. To many men, Izzy's birth and background, and her lack of fortune, would outweigh everything.

Her time in society would be limited, and she needed to make the most of it and get herself settled before the axe fell.

It was different for Clarissa. With her inheritance, she had all the time in the world to fall in love. Izzy didn't. She'd resolved from the start to make a good, solid, practical marriage, and she'd let herself forget that.

She hadn't wanted to fall for Lord Salcott—in fact she'd actively disliked him at the start. But then . . . Oh, why had she kissed him in the summerhouse that night? That magical, beautiful night . . .

How many times had she told herself that it was just a kiss? It meant nothing—to him at least. Earls didn't court bastards, she knew that. *Knew* it.

But despite all her determination to be practical, to stop dreaming foolish, impossible dreams, all it took was a look, a touch—a kiss—and her common sense scattered to the four winds.

She stared at the pages of her book, trying to force herself to think of something else.

A squeaking gate behind her distracted her. Footsteps approached. "You've been seeing rather a lot of Lord Salcott, haven't you?" a waspish feminine voice accused.

"Have I?" Izzy didn't even bother to look around.

"Mama and I saw the way you were dancing with him last night. Mama said it was disgracefully unladylike. As for the way you were looking at him . . ." Milly Harrington plonked herself down on the seat opposite Izzy. "It won't do you any good, you know."

"Won't it?" Izzy raised her glance from the book she hadn't been reading and eyed her narrowly. "Have you been gossiping about me, Milly? Because you know what I told you . . ."

The girl flushed and tossed her head. "I don't gossip."

Izzy didn't bother pointing out the obvious.

"I learned something about Lord Salcott last night," Milly went on. She glanced around the garden with ostentatious caution.

Izzy sighed. What did the tedious creature want now? There was nobody around. A gardener was working on the other side of the gardens, and in the distance, Izzy could hear the sound of Lady Tarrant's little girls playing.

Milly leaned forward and said in a hushed voice, "Mama explained to me about Lord Salcott and what he would require in a bride."

"Did she indeed?" Izzy said in a bored voice. "And has she explained it to Lord Salcott?"

Milly frowned. "No," she said, puzzled. "Only to me."

"Good, then keep it to yourself." Izzy returned to her book.

Milly sat there staring at her. "Don't you want to know?"

"No. It's none of my business."

"It is if you have hopes."

Izzy arched a sardonic eyebrow. "Hopes?"

"Of Lord Salcott."

"I have no hopes—whatever you mean by that—of Lord Salcott, or any other man," Izzy said firmly. And it was true. Last night had established that.

The girl stared at her a minute. "I don't believe you. Mama and I saw the way you were with him at Lady Clendon's. Mama said your behavior was quite ill-bred. And she doesn't even know about the other night when you let him kiss you in the summerhouse."

Izzy put down her book. "I thought I made it clear that was none of your business, Milly."

The girl pouted. "Well, you obviously do have hopes,

but I'm here to tell you that there's no point. He has very particular requirements in a wife."

"Good for him." Izzy picked up her book.

"It's because of his mother."

Izzy turned a page.

"She was a whore." Milly sounded part shocked, part gleeful.

Izzy gave her a hard look. She hated it when women were called whores, no matter what the reason.

"Well, it's true, Mama told me," Milly retorted defensively. "Lady Salcott was notorious, utterly shameless—the scandal of the ton. Mama said she took lover after lover, even running off to Italy with an Italian portrait painter—and worse. Half the nobility of Europe were said to have known her—and you know what I mean by 'know' don't you? It's in the Bible."

Izzy didn't respond.

"Naturally her poor husband was utterly mortified—he became a recluse, Mama said. The poor man was devastated, destroyed by a whor—" Catching Izzy's eye she broke off, then said, "Destroyed by an immoral woman. And of course so was her son." She waited for Izzy to react.

Izzy turned a page, pretending to be engrossed in her book, but her mind was spinning. Was that why he'd been so quick to condemn her mother? No, any respectable gentleman would, she knew, whether his mother had been a pillar of virtue or the opposite. It was the way of the world: the woman was always to blame.

Milly waited a moment, then went on, as if Izzy had begged her to continue. "So of course, now that Lord Salcott is looking for the next Lady Salcott, he will only consider a woman of the highest morality, a girl without a stain on her character." She gave a smug smile, preening herself. "A girl whom no breath of scandal has ever touched."

Izzy turned another page. It didn't surprise her. It was

what most men of the ton expected: regardless of their own morality, their brides must be pure and innocent. Hypocrites.

"And naturally he has his position as an earl to consider, so he won't be looking at a *nobody,* no matter how pretty she might be. Only a girl of noble heritage will do for him." Milly curled one of her ringlets around her finger and added coyly, "Have I mentioned that Mama is second cousin to a duke?"

Izzy's mouth tasted of ashes. "Sorry, did you say something, Milly? Only this book is so entertaining I quite forgot you were here." She turned her head. "Oh. Isn't that your mama calling? You'd better run along now."

"I didn't hear anything," Milly said sulkily. Not surprising, since Izzy had made it up.

Izzy shrugged indifferently and returned to her book. "Suit yourself. I thought your mama fretted whenever you were off the leash." Milly glared at her, made a frustrated noise and hurried away.

Izzy tried to return to her book, to no avail. It all made sense now. If his mother had been a byword for scandal and infidelity, of course Lord Salcott would wish to distance himself from someone of Izzy's background. The minute he realized she was attracted to him.

You obviously do have hopes . . .

It was mortifying to reflect that she had, for a short while at least. Despite all common sense.

Had she been obvious and ill-bred? Normally she would ignore anything Milly and her mama said, but . . . obviously she'd revealed . . . something.

Mama Harrington had certainly thought so.

A few kisses, the slow stroke of a finger down her cheek and a waltz. What a fool she'd been. A nobody who built castles in the air deserved all the disillusionment she would get.

And one who made her feelings plain was setting herself up to be an object of gossip and spite. Even a laughingstock.

A cold lump lodged in Izzy's throat. What had she been thinking? He was an earl. An *earl*! And she was a nobody. An illegitimate nobody to boot. A hopeless case who apparently couldn't even disguise her hopes.

She knew now why he'd canceled their second waltz so abruptly. He'd seen that she'd been more affected by the dance than he was comfortable with. Of course he'd walked away.

Izzy gazed out at the garden, watching as the breeze set the leaves dancing. A tiny jenny wren hopped about in the freshly turned earth, trilling happily as she hunted for worms. Ensuring her survival, feeding her babies . . .

Before they came to London, before they'd even met Lord Salcott, Izzy had resolved to make a practical marriage. A girl with nothing to her name had to be practical, she knew. And act quickly because it would be her only chance to make a respectable marriage.

The minute society gentlemen discovered her background, Izzy knew the kind of offers she'd get: she'd be following in her mother's footsteps. And she refused to let that happen.

She couldn't afford the luxury of hanging out for a love match.

She'd never owned anything, never had a home where she truly belonged, a place where nobody could toss her out on her ear. She wanted that, so much. And she wanted a family of her own, children who would grow up knowing they were loved. And that they belonged.

She'd jeopardized that dream, reading more into Lord Salcott's behavior than he'd intended. She'd let herself be distracted. Lord Salcott wasn't seriously interested in her. He was just flirting. As society gentlemen were wont to do. And she'd been . . . foolish.

The warning had come in time.

She might be "a nobody" as far as the ton was concerned but, bastard or not, she wasn't going to let it stop her from

having the best life she could. She refused to be branded by
her mother's misfortunes. She didn't need a man with a title; she didn't even need him to be rich—just not poor. She
wanted to be a wife and a mother, and she was going to find
a kind man to love and live a happy life with—no matter
what.

She was sure she would find such a man. And soon, she
hoped, before it all came crashing down around them.

And naturally before she agreed to marry him, she
would explain all about her background. She had no intention of entering a marriage based on deception.

She picked up her book again, but turned her head as
hurried footsteps sounded on the path.

"Izzy?" It was Clarissa. "A lady has just arrived. I think
it's the chaperone."

The two girls hurried back into the house, where they
found a plump, well-preserved woman in the hall, di-
recting the servants to carry up a neat valise and two band-
boxes that a coachman had carried in from a dusty traveling
carriage.

She was dressed from head to toe in unrelieved black—
black dress, a voluminous black cloak, and black kidskin
gloves. Her hat was . . . strange—black straw decorated
with black cherries, black leaves, and what looked like a
stuffed black . . . canary? Her earrings and necklace were
made of jet, and even her eyes were so dark as to look
black. She seemed to absorb all the light in the hall.

The girls exchanged glances. This was their new
chaperone? It didn't look promising.

She can't be planning a long stay, Izzy thought hopefully, not with only one medium-size valise and two band-
boxes.

"Such a journey, I'm utterly shattered," the woman said
to nobody in particular. She shrugged off her cloak.

Treadwell caught it before it hit the floor. "Ah, Treadwell," she said briskly as if she knew him very well, "in twenty minutes I'll want a large pot of strong tea in the sitting room, and a plate of whatever cakes or biscuits your cook can provide."

She turned, saw the girls and smiled. "You must be Miss Clarissa and Miss Isobel. Delightful to meet you. I'm Mrs. Price-Jones."

They greeted her cautiously and she laughed. "I look like the Black Crow of Doom, don't I, but I assure you I had not a thing to wear. The minute my poor husband breathed his last, my wretched stepson had the servants dye every last thing I owned black—even my favorite hat!" She pulled a face. "They're all very grim and serious up there. So for a whole year and two weeks it's been nothing but black, black, black for me. So dreadfully gloomy! And if my stepson had his way, I'd be draped in widow's weeds for the rest of my days. Luckily Olive's letter has enabled me to escape."

"'Olive's letter'?" Izzy repeated.

"Didn't she mention me?"

"No."

Mrs. Price-Jones chuckled. "Typical. She wrote to me, saying I was urgently needed, and once she'd sealed the letter and given it to Treadwell to post, she no doubt forgot all about it."

It was very like Lady Scattergood, Izzy had to admit.

The woman beamed at them. "Althea Price-Jones, widowed one year and two weeks ago, and until now, stuck in the wilds of north Wales."

She unpinned her hat and handed it to Treadwell, who received it with a dubious expression. "Olive wrote that she didn't go about much these days, but that she had two delightful young ladies making their come-out who were in need of a chaperone. Naturally I seized the opportunity—sheep and mountains and daffodil meadows are all very well, but they don't compare with London! So here I am. I'll just pop upstairs and make myself comfortable"—she winked—"and then I'll be down for a cup of tea and a little something to eat. Cannot wait to get to know you gels."

Without further ado, she bustled up the stairs, seeming to know exactly where she was going.

"I'm not at all sure about this," Izzy murmured to Clarissa as Mrs. Price-Jones disappeared up the stairs. "She seems quite bossy. She's even got Treadwell hopping to it."

Clarissa nodded. "Though I did like the way she called herself the Black Crow of Doom."

"Let's hope it's not prophetic," Izzy said.

Twenty minutes later, their new chaperone sat presiding over the tea tray, firing questions at the girls, drinking tea and eating cake.

"Finding husbands, is it?" she asked them, and they explained that yes, they wished to marry, that Clarissa was an heiress and Izzy needed a practical marriage. By mutual agreement they'd decided not to mention Izzy's illegitimacy. The fewer people who knew about that the better.

Her finely plucked brows rose. "Only the eldest girl inherits? How peculiar. Still, we'll have no trouble firing you both off. Oh, the London season, how I've missed it."

"This is not your first visit to London then, Mrs. Price-Jones?" Clarissa asked.

"Heavens no, I grew up and made my come-out here—how do you think I know Olive and everyone?" She sighed. "Had I not fallen madly in love with my beloved Price-Jones, I would never have gone to dwell in far-flung obscurity." She brightened. "Still, I'm here now and cannot wait to dive back into society with you gels. Such fun. Who made your clothes?"

Izzy blinked at the sudden change of topic. "Miss Chance off Piccadilly."

Mrs. Price-Jones nodded. "I like her style. We'll go there after lunch." She laughed at their expressions. "Well, you don't think I'm going to escort you to parties dressed like this, do you?"

"You don't wish to rest after your long journey, ma'am?" Clarissa asked.

"Good gad, no. Clothes are far more important than rest," their new chaperone declared, setting down her empty cup and rising. "Now, I'll go and see if Olive is ready for company. We have so much to catch up on." She turned back to the girls. "She still doesn't leave the house?"

"Mostly not, but we've persuaded her to attend a literary society," Izzy said. "Traveling in a closed sedan chair."

"Clever notion. I gather you mean Bea Davenham's literary society. Excellent. I'm looking forward to renewing my acquaintances there. Many men attend?"

Clarissa shook her head. "Not many."

"Oh well, you can't have everything." She sailed off, leaving Izzy and Clarissa looking at each other, bemused.

"She's not at all what I expected," Clarissa said.

"No indeed," Izzy said with a chuckle. "I wonder what the Grumpy Guardian will make of her. Did he have any idea of the kind of woman he was hiring?"

Clarissa gave her a troubled look. "Are you still calling him that? I thought you two were getting on much better these days."

Izzy had thought so, too, but . . . *I think it best if we distance ourselves from each other in future.*

"No, he's still impossible," she said lightly. She'd decided not to tell Clarissa what had happened. Her sister had such a soft heart she didn't want to upset her. Besides, Izzy was still trying to sort out her own feelings.

On being informed that the girls' chaperone had finally arrived, Leo went to call on her immediately. Aunt Olive had assured him her old friend would make a perfect chaperone, being widowed and wellborn, and that, despite her years in Wales, Mrs. Price-Jones had kept in touch with all her old London friends and would know exactly how girls making their come-out should go on.

He had to admit he was relieved. Having a chaperone in charge of the girls would define his role more clearly to society and lessen any gossip about him and Isobel. And with a chaperone taking care of things, he could keep his distance more easily—until the gossip died down at least.

He also needed to have a private word with Isobel. He had the feeling she'd quite misinterpreted his suggestion about distancing themselves from each other in public.

He found all the ladies in the sitting room, drinking tea. Treadwell fetched another cup for him. Isobel was sitting on the sofa with her sister. She didn't even look at him when he entered, just murmured a polite greeting in his general direction.

Yes, he'd offended her. Or upset her. Or something. Blast.

"So, dear boy, you're in charge of these delightful gels," Mrs. Price-Jones said after they'd been introduced. "My, my, how time does fly."

Noticing his expression at her calling him "dear boy" so familiarly, she laughed. "You won't remember me, but I knew you before you were breeched, young man. I was acquainted with both your parents. My condolences on their passing. Now, what eligible young men have you found for these gels so far?"

Leo blinked. "'Eligible young men'?" he repeated. He was still adjusting to the spectacle of the entirely black-clad woman sitting among Aunt Olive's bright possessions like a large chunk of coal.

And Isobel's unsettling demeanor.

He'd known Aunt Olive's friend was a widow, but this woman was not at all what he'd imagined. Or hoped for. He wanted someone strict enough to control the more outrageous impulses of the girls—well, Isobel—but also to befriend and guide them. This woman looked as though for two pins she'd pull out a whip.

"The gels are in search of husbands," she reminded him bluntly. "And as an eligible young man yourself, you must know plenty of others to present to them."

Playing for time, because he couldn't think of anyone suitable, Leo picked up the teapot to top up his aunt's cup. As he did, the chaperone woman leaned across to the young ladies and said in what she must have believed was a whisper, "He's very handsome. Why haven't one of you set your cap for him?"

Leo almost dropped the teapot. He plonked it down and glared at the woman and the young ladies sitting demurely side by side on the sofa. "I am their guardian," he said repressively. "It would not be appropriate."

Miss Clarissa's eyes danced. Isobel set her jaw and looked away. Something was definitely wrong.

Mrs. Price-Jones, quite unembarrassed at being caught in her indiscretion, laughed. "Oh piffle, you men and your notions of honor. As if love doesn't trump everything. Still, if we can't match you up with one of these charming young ladies, one of your friends might do. Who have they met so far?" She looked at Leo expectantly, her eyes twinkling like boot buttons.

"My friend, Lord Randall, has taken the young ladies riding several times," he said stiffly. This woman was outrageous. Mocking his honor and discussing him with the girls like that in his presence. Talking of his friends as if they were shopping at the market.

And Isobel still hadn't met his eyes once.

"Quite inappropriate," Aunt Olive said scathingly from her peacock chair. "Randall is a *rake*!"

Mrs. Price-Jones considered that, then shook her head. "I won't rule him out until I've met him. Rakes can be delightful company, yet it must be admitted that many are unreliable and often untrustworthy. Some, however, are redeemable, I believe. Who else?"

Leo looked at her blankly. Apart from Race, he hadn't made any attempt to introduce the girls to his friends.

"Sir Jasper Vibart seems both eligible and charming," Isobel said. She glanced briefly at Leo—the first time that day—and batted her eyelashes. Mocking him.

His temper flared. "Completely unacceptable," he snapped. "And dangerous. Apart from being a notorious rake, Sir Jasper also gambles recklessly and to excess." He'd warned her about Vibart. Why the devil didn't she listen?

"I wonder if Sir Jasper is as handsome and charming as his father was?" Mrs. Price-Jones said, adding reluctantly, "But the Vibarts have always been ruinous gamblers. Flirt with him if you wish, dear gel, but do not let it go any further. Next?"

Leo clenched his jaw. The woman irritated him. She might dress like a grim gorgon, but she wasn't behaving like any chaperone he'd ever heard of. Chaperones were supposed to keep their charges away from rakes and unworthy men and to ensure their behavior was demure and circumspect. Instead, this wretched woman was openly encouraging Isobel to flirt with the blasted man. Despite Leo's warning.

He was stuck with her now. Why had he ever thought his aunt's recommendation was a good idea? He could hardly sack her dear old friend.

Mrs. Price-Jones peered at him, then shook her head. "Is that all then? Tsk tsk, I can see I have my work cut out for me. Still, thank you for dropping by, Lord Salcott. The gels and I are going shopping now."

It was a clear dismissal. Leo could hardly believe his ears. He was this woman's employer, and yet she'd as good as told him to run along as if he were the little boy she claimed to remember. He could hardly argue, however, and besides he had nothing else to say.

And Isobel was freezing him out, acting as if he didn't

exist, and while he'd told her they needed to put some distance between them, he'd meant *in public*.

But he couldn't explain that here with this woman watching him with her bright beady eyes.

"Would you care to come driving in the park this afternoon?" he asked the girls. He'd find an opportunity then to explain to Isobel about what had happened the previous night. And remove that unsettling expression from her eyes.

Mrs. Price-Jones answered for them. "Charming of you to invite us, dear boy, but as I said, we are going shopping. Two gels making their come-out—you men have no understanding of how much there is to be done. Good day." She beamed an even more pointed dismissal at him.

Leo bowed curtly, wished them all a good day and stalked from the room.

As the door closed behind him, he heard a burst of feminine laughter and gritted his teeth. A chaperone was supposed to solve his problems, not add to them.

O n that first day in London, Mrs. Price-Jones embarked on an orgy of shopping, starting with Miss Chance's dress shop. After a brief exchange with Miss Chance, she sent the girls off to entertain themselves at Hatchards bookshop or wherever took their fancy, saying that she'd be at least two hours.

Izzy and Clarissa happily obliged, amused that the first action of the dreaded chaperone was to send them off by themselves.

Returning to Miss Chance's two hours later, they couldn't believe the transformation. "The Black Crow of Doom is no more, eh, gels?" she said, beaming as she twirled delightedly. "I am myself again!"

Izzy and Clarissa blinked. Mrs. Price-Jones's dress was bright yellow, worn under a vivid red-and-blue-patterned spencer. Around her shoulders she'd draped a multicolored shawl of which green, orange and purple were the main colors. It was one of Lady Scattergood's, Izzy thought. She must have brought it with her.

With one accord the two girls looked at Miss Chance, whose taste was usually impeccable.

Miss Chance simply laughed. "We've let out her inner butterfly. Mrs. Price-Jones fell in love with that yeller dress and so we got all my girls working like fury to get the alterations done so she could wear it. Wait 'til you see what else is coming."

Inner butterfly? More like a multicolored parrot, Izzy thought. But she had to admit the vivid clash of colors suited Mrs. Price-Jones much better than unrelieved black.

"I've had the most divine time," Mrs. Price-Jones declared happily. "And look what else I bought." She brought out two items of nightwear—just wisps of satin, net and lace in red and black—and draped them suggestively against her body. "Bea Davenham told me about these—a speciality of Daisy's. Aren't they wonderfully improper?"

Izzy laughed. The garments looked rather too dashing for a widow in her sixth decade, but the woman's clear delight in her new possessions was irresistible.

After that they went to a milliner that Miss Chance had recommended, where Mrs. Price-Jones gleefully purchased several large, colorful, splashy hats. "Here you are, my dear," she said, handing the milliner's assistant the strange black hat with the black canary and black cherries. "Burn the horrid thing!"

She plopped the biggest hat on her head and turned to Izzy and Clarissa with a grin. "Now I feel much more myself again. Let's go to Gunter's for ices."

Leo needed to talk to Isobel alone. He was certain now that she'd taken his advice about keeping their distance in public completely the wrong way. And that expression when she looked at him—correction, avoided looking at him—was . . . disturbing.

He sent a message to Treadwell asking him to inform Leo the moment the young ladies returned from their shopping expedition. His aunt's young footman brought the news the following afternoon. Apparently the shopping had taken almost two full days. He confided that he'd carried more than twenty-six parcels upstairs, and the ladies were expecting more to be delivered.

Leo shuddered to think of the bills he was going to receive. His aunt had convinced him that Mrs. Price-Jones would need appropriate clothing for her role, and having seen her in her widow's weeds, he had to concur.

He hurried over to his aunt's house and sent Treadwell off with a message that he wished to speak privately with Miss Isobel. He would await her in the front sitting room.

A short time later the door opened and Isobel entered. Leo rose to his feet. "Miss Isobel, thank you for—" he began, and then broke off as a large female clad in bright, clashing colors followed her into the room. It took a moment to recognize her. "Mrs. Price-Jones?"

"Indeed, Lord Salcott. As you see, I have left my widow's weeds behind me." She plumped herself down on the sofa, pulled out some knitting and eyed him brightly. "Now, what did you wish to talk about?"

"I wished to speak with *Miss Isobel*," he said with delicate emphasis.

She nodded. "Go ahead."

"Privately."

"Yes, yes. Private as you like. I am the soul of discretion." The knitting needles clacked busily.

Frustrated, Leo glanced at Isobel, hoping she would explain to this fool of a woman that they needed private conversation. Instead she stood gazing serenely out of the window, acting as if the discussion had nothing to do with her. Though he thought she was secretly amused.

He turned back to the chaperone. "Mrs. Price-Jones, I don't think you understand. I wish to speak with Miss Isobel. *Alone. In private*."

"Oh heavens no, dear boy, we can't allow that. What sort of a chaperone would you take me for if I left one of my charges alone with an unmarried man, eh?" She finished one row, turned her knitting around and started another.

"I am her guardian, and your employer," he grated. "It's perfectly proper."

"You're not my guardian," Isobel pointed out. "You're Clarissa's but not mine."

Leo gritted his teeth.

The chaperone nodded complacently. "Even so, I wouldn't leave Miss Studley alone with you, either. Mooosssst improper." She beamed at him and kept knitting. "So talk away, I won't mind."

"But I mind," Leo said savagely. "Good day to you, ladies." He left.

That went well, don't you agree?" Mrs. Price-Jones said as the back door slammed.

Izzy looked at her. "'Well'? He's furious."

"Yes, dear, furious and beautifully frustrated. It's a very good sign." Mrs. Price-Jones kept knitting.

Puzzled, Izzy sat down opposite her. "I did think it was quite amusing, but in what way is infuriating Lord Salcott a good sign?"

The woman stopped knitting. "The man is obviously enamored of you, dear gel. And so, when I denied him his private conversation, he was practically foaming at the mouth with frustration." She chuckled. "I do like to see that in a man."

"'Enamored'? He's not. He can't be."

Mrs. Price-Jones laughed. "Oh, my dear, of course he is. I saw it at once the day I arrived. He barely took his eyes off you. He's dotty about you, though, like most men, he's having trouble admitting it."

Izzy shook her head. "I don't think so."

"Trust me, my dear, of course he is. Now, the question is, do you want him?"

Izzy gave her a troubled look. Did she want Lord Salcott? Well, of course she did, but that didn't signify. The fact was, she couldn't have him. Earls simply didn't marry penniless bastards. But she couldn't explain that to Mrs. Price-Jones. They'd agreed to keep Izzy's illegitimacy from her. It was one thing to deceive society themselves, but another to implicate their chaperone. When the truth came out, she could be as shocked as everyone else.

Slowly she shook her head. "No, I don't want Lord Salcott."

Mrs. Price-Jones gave her a shrewd look. "Really? If you say so, my dear." She turned her knitting around and started a new row. "So, tell me, what do you want in a husband?"

"I'm not looking for a love match," Izzy told her, squashing the pang she felt as she said it. "I need to make a practical marriage. Having no fortune, I want security more than anything."

The chaperone nodded. "Very sensible. Security is important. What else? Age? Looks? A title?"

"I don't want a title, and don't really care about looks, though pleasant looking would be nice, I suppose. As for age, I wouldn't want to be married to a very old gentleman."

"Heavens no, you need a man with plenty of masculine vigor. You want children, too, yes?"

Izzy felt herself blushing. *Masculine vigor?* "Yes."

"Then no widowers with a flock of children."

"I wouldn't mind it if there were children," Izzy began, thinking of Lady Tarrant and her adorable stepdaughters.

Mrs. Price-Jones shook her head decisively. "Too risky. What if the children resent you? Nothing like a sainted dead mother to make a new bride feel like an unwanted interloper, and believe me, I know all about how that feels. Now, is there anything else? The more I know about what you want the more I can help you."

Izzy thought about it. "I would like to make a match quite quickly." Before the truth about her came out. Of course she would tell the gentleman concerned the truth about herself before she accepted an offer, but it would make things a lot easier on Clarissa and everyone if Izzy were married and far away when the scandal finally broke.

Mrs. Price-Jones's well-plucked brows rose. "I see. Get the business out of the way quickly, is it?" She leaned forward. "There's no particular *need* for a hasty wedding, is there, my dear?"

Izzy was puzzled for a moment and then she realized what the lady meant. "Oh no, there's nothing like that."

"You're still a virgin?"

Izzy's face heated. She nodded. "Yes, I just want to be married quickly, that's all." And start building a solid future instead of castles in the air.

"Good." Mrs. Price-Jones sat back and resumed her knitting. "In that case I'll do my best to point out some likely prospects for you, and you can let me know how you feel about each of them."

Chapter Fourteen

Despite her age, Mrs. Price-Jones seemed inexhaustible. From the very first day she threw herself into ton activities. There were daily walks in the park, weather permitting, where they greeted people practically nonstop. Clearly her correspondence over the years had kept her up with all the latest on-dits, and people seemed to greet her return to London with pleasure.

With Izzy and Clarissa's new chaperone firmly in charge, their social activities exploded. There were morning calls to make and receive; afternoon teas to attend; evening soirées, musical and otherwise; and all kinds of parties. There were balls and routs and even a ridotto, which turned out to be a musical evening with dancing, sometimes with masks and costumes, though many people came for the gambling and card games in private rooms. Izzy and Clarissa preferred the dancing.

For two young women raised in relative isolation in the country, it felt like a positive whirlwind of activity.

They were meeting men galore. Mrs. Price-Jones made

sure of it, reminding them that as well as chaperoning, it was her duty to help them find a suitable husband. She introduced them to young men, older men, rich men, handsome ones and ugly ones—adding that ugly men often made the best lovers. Which was not generally the kind of advice given to young unmarried girls.

She had one clear criterion for husbandly suitability: wealth. "I married for love, my dears, and though Mr. Price-Jones was a dear man and we were very happy, when he died, all his wealth went to the children of his first marriage—I'm barren, you see—and the stepson who was supposed to support me in my old age is a miserly creature who made me the stingiest of allowances. So, don't trust to love to take care of you—marry money, my dears, and make sure your settlement is a good one. Lord Salcott will take care of that aspect of things, I'm sure."

Izzy wasn't so sure of that. He would no doubt take care of Clarissa's settlements, but as he'd pointed out before, Izzy was no responsibility of his. For her, Mrs. Price-Jones's advice was most pertinent. Though not always the most conventional.

One night she took them to the theater, even arranging gentlemen to escort them. "A gel is judged by the quality of masculine company she keeps," she declared.

"Her choice of male escorts is quite eccentric, don't you think?" Izzy murmured to Clarissa as they waited for the play to start. Their male escorts were charming, wealthy, wellborn, well dressed and in all ways a desirable catch—but not one of them was under fifty, and at least one of them had to be seventy or more.

Clarissa gave her an amused glance. "Haven't you realized yet?"

"Realized what?"

"As well as helping us find husbands, Mrs. Price-Jones is looking for one for herself."

"Ohhh." Izzy could see it now. It was quite entertaining

to watch, and rather educational. A widow had a great deal more leeway in her behavior than an unmarried miss.

Tonight they were attending the Gainsborough ball. Mrs. Price-Jones, having ensured they were engaged for every dance, had wafted away on the arm of a silver-haired gentleman, leaving them to their own devices. "Enjoy yourselves, gels," she'd said. "And remember, you need to kiss a lot of frogs to find your prince."

Clarissa was a little shocked. "Is she actually suggesting that we should be kissing men?"

Izzy giggled. "Apparently so."

Clarissa looked doubtful. "It's not very chaperone-y, is it?"

"Not at all," Izzy agreed. "Which makes her the perfect chaperone."

Clarissa's jaw dropped. "Izzy! How can you say such a thing? Apart from throwing us at men and telling us to kiss any we fancy, she seems to have no interest in watching over us at all."

"She's made sure we have partners for every dance," Izzy pointed out.

"Yes, while she's off dancing and flirting madly herself, instead of watching us."

Izzy grinned. "As I said, she's perfect."

Clarissa laughed. "Well, I suppose she doesn't interfere with us too much."

"Exactly. And her frankness is refreshing. Imagine if we had someone like Milly's mother chaperoning us, bleating on endlessly about what we must and mustn't do." Izzy shuddered. "We wouldn't have a moment of peace."

"Oh, but"—Clarissa twirled an imaginary curl—"she is second cousin to a duke, you know."

Izzy laughed. "Yes, it's lovely to be able to enjoy ourselves without having someone breathing down our necks."

"You mean because Lord Salcott isn't here?"

"Oh, isn't he?" Izzy said innocently. "I hadn't noticed."

Clarissa laughed.

I suppose you're feeling quite relieved," Race said. The two friends had met for dinner at their club.

Leo looked up. He'd been miles away, brooding into his glass. The Studley sisters and their chaperone had gone to the Gainsborough ball. He'd decided instead to seek the comfort of an evening in purely masculine company. Peaceful. Congenial. Away from the social whirl.

But it wasn't having quite the soothing effect he'd hoped for. He kept wondering what Isobel was doing, with whom she was dancing—and flirting. That swine Vibart, for instance. That wretched chaperone—the same one who refused to let him speak to Isobel in private—had told her she might flirt all she liked with Vibart. Talk about inconsistency.

"'Relieved'? What do you mean?"

"To be free at last."

Leo frowned. "'Free'?" he repeated stupidly. Free to do what? He still hadn't been able to talk to Isobel in private and it was driving him mad. Every time he got near her, that blasted chaperone had stuck her nose in. Even when he'd managed to walk with her in Hyde Park—which was hardly private, but he needed to speak to her—the wretched chaperone blithely thrust herself between them and hooked her arm through his.

Isobel had laughed—actually laughed. And then drifted off to join another group, leaving him stuck with the chaperone.

It was one thing to suggest to Isobel that they needed to be more discreet in public—which seemed to him to be an entirely logical move—but she seemed to take it as an order to treat him as if he were a stranger.

"Free of the more tedious of your guardian responsibilities," Race continued. "Having that chaperone must make your life a lot easier now you don't have to play the eternal guard dog."

Leo grunted. *Easier? Hah!* But all he said was "I do have to keep playing the guard dog. I'm getting requests for the girls' hands already." And that was driving him mad, too.

Race stilled. "Anyone we know?" he asked after a minute, his tone casual.

"Wasters, mostly." And a couple of quite respectable offers from men who nevertheless weren't nearly good enough for Isobel.

"'Wasters'?" Race repeated. "You mean for Miss Studley?"

"Mmm, yes, her, too." Leo nodded. "The usual fortune hunters."

"And you said . . . what?"

Leo gave his friend a surprised look. "I refused the lot of them of course. It's early days yet. There's plenty of time."

"But is there? Their secret could come out any day. All it takes is one person who knows Sir Bartleby's natural daughter—"

"We'll deal with that when it happens. At the moment the girls are enjoying themselves." And he had to admit the chaperone had helped with that—she seemed to know everyone.

"Well then." Race drained his glass and stood.

Leo looked up, surprised. "Going out?" He'd expected to spend a long lazy evening in. Perhaps a game of billiards or two. Or a round of cards.

"Thought I might drop in to the Gainsborough ball."

"The Gainsborough ball? I thought you weren't going to that."

"Changed my mind."

Leo drained his glass and set it aside. "Wait a minute, I'll come with you."

Race frowned. "I thought you wanted a break from your social duties."

"Changed my mind."

Are you enjoying yourself, Mr. Harvey?" Izzy asked her current partner. The Gainsborough ball was not one of the grandest social occasions, but she was enjoying herself immensely.

"To tell the truth, Miss Isobel, I'm feeling rather melancholy," Mr. Harvey said heavily, which was strange, because he was usually quite amiable. He had sought her out at every social occasion since she and Clarissa had first made an appearance in society, and was about to lead her out for a country-dance.

In fact Mr. Harvey was on the list Izzy and Mrs. Price-Jones were compiling of men suitable for Izzy's practical marriage intentions. Though not very high on the list, Izzy had to admit.

Not that Izzy could rouse much enthusiasm for any of them, but that would come, she told herself. She just had to put her mind to it, instead of letting it drift off in the direction of a certain irritating man. Who was, thankfully, not here tonight, so she could relax.

"I'm sorry to hear that, Mr. Harvey. Is there anything I can do to help cheer you up?"

He gave her a strange look. "But, Miss Isobel, you are the cause of my melancholy."

"I am?" she said brightly, thinking he was attempting some kind of flirty badinage. Which he never had before—he was a rather earnest fellow—but you never knew. "Pray, what have I done?"

He gave her a wounded look. "You refused me." He sounded quite serious.

Izzy was puzzled. "Refused you what? I am about to dance with you now, am I not?"

"Refused your hand."

She glanced at her hand involuntarily. "My hand in what sense, Mr. Harvey? No, please don't look at me like that. I promise I am not toying with you. I truly don't understand what you are saying."

"Your hand in marriage, Miss Isobel."

She stared at him blankly. "But you haven't asked for my hand in marriage."

"I did. I applied to your guardian for permission to court you with a view to marriage. He refused me without a second's hesitation."

She narrowed her eyes. "You mean you asked Lord Salcott?"

"Your guardian, yes." He pointed. "That man over there."

Izzy whirled around. There he was indeed, the interfering, impossible, infuriating man, standing in the entrance with Lord Randall as if they'd just arrived. He wasn't supposed to have come tonight, but now she was glad he had. She glared across the room at him. "So that man over there refused you permission to court me?"

"Yes. He made it absolutely clear that I had no hope. Hence my dejection."

"Oh, he did, did he?" Fury choked her. "He had no right."

"But he's your guardian," Harvey pointed out. "Of course he has the right."

"We'll see about that," Izzy said, and stormed off the dance floor.

Leo saw her coming. In a fine temper by the look of it. Dazzling in a dress of the palest straw-yellow silk that caressed her limbs as she strode across the floor, drawing all eyes. She marched straight up to him and poked him in the chest. "How dare—"

She broke off as Leo glanced pointedly to the people surrounding them, realizing that whatever she was going to say was bound to be indiscreet. That ears were everywhere, and her march across the room had drawn quite a bit of attention.

She glared at him, breathing heavily, fulminating in frustrated silence.

Leo smiled. It was quite satisfying to observe her frustration, after the failure of all his recent attempts to talk to her in private.

For the sake of those watching, she forced an unconvincing smile onto her face and said, "How dare you tell Mr. Harvey that I won't marry him." Her voice was low and vehement.

"Oh, did you want to marry Harvey? Bit of a dull dog for you, I would have thought. Still, if you're desperate to marry him . . ."

"No, I'm not desperate to marry him," she flashed in an undertone. "But you had no right to refuse him."

He frowned. "Because you do want to marry him? Make up your mind."

She stamped her foot. "I do *not* want to marry Mr. Harvey."

Leo nodded. "Good, because that's what I told him. And by the way, he's standing right behind you."

She whirled and faced Harvey, who stood gazing at her with all the effervescence of a plucked hen. "Mr. Harvey. I'm sorry—"

Harvey drooped visibly. "So you don't want to marry me."

She flushed and bit her lip. "No, I'm sorry you had to hear that."

Harvey jerked his chin at Leo. "So he was right, then. I did say so."

"Y—n—oh this is impossible. I'm sorry, Mr. Harvey. Lord Salcott, can we discuss this—"

"While we're dancing? Yes, of course," Leo said, and

cupping her elbow in his hand he steered her toward the dance floor, where sets were forming.

She glared at him but allowed herself to be led onto the dance floor. Better to dance with the enemy than endure the misery of the doleful swain, he supposed.

"I'm not finished with you yet," she hissed.

"No, but we can't talk here," he murmured soothingly. "I'll call on you tomorrow morning." Though how he was going to get her alone without that blasted chaperone . . . At least this time she wanted to talk to him, even if it was just to give him a good wigging. But it would be an opportunity to clear things up.

"Can't. Shopping." The dance began. He bowed, she curtsied, and they moved into the first figure. "Lunchtime tomorrow?" he said when they came together again.

She shook her head. "We're lunching with Lady Tarrant." The "we" would be her sister and the chaperone. "After that?"

She grimaced. "Morning calls."

Leo swore silently. From the sound of things she had not a moment free—and in any case that wretched chaperone would no doubt push her way in.

They danced on. She danced impersonally, as if dancing with a stranger, and the hard look in her eyes told him she was still angry with him. But she also looked thoughtful. She gave a speculative glance at him, bit her lip and opened her mouth as if to say something, but didn't.

They went through several more figures of the dance before she made up her mind. The next time they came together, she murmured, "The summerhouse tonight, after the ball."

Leo blinked. Given what had happened last time they'd met there at night, her suggestion shocked him. But she was right—it was the one place and time where they could be sure to be private.

"Very well," he said when they came together in a twirl, "the summerhouse tonight."

* * *

What was all that about?" Clarissa asked Izzy shortly after the dance had finished. Lord Salcott had taken himself off somewhere, Izzy didn't care where. "It looked like you poked him, actually poked him in the chest."

Izzy sniffed. "He's lucky I didn't give him a smack on the nose."

"Izzy!" Clarissa exclaimed, half-amused, half-shocked. She glanced around to see if they had an audience and lowered her voice. "What prompted that?"

Izzy was glad to be able to unburden herself to a sympathetic listener. "Can you believe it, Mr. Harvey called on him this morning and asked for permission to court me with a view to marriage, and Lord Salcott refused! He actually told Mr. Harvey he had no hope of marrying me. Isn't that outrageous?"

Clarissa stared at her. "Did you want to marry Mr. Harvey? I had no idea."

"No, of course I don't want to marry Mr. Harvey. That's not the point."

"Then what is?"

Izzy regarded her sister in frustration. "He had no right."

"Who, Mr. Harvey? But—"

"No, Lord Salcott. How dare he refuse my hand in marriage without consulting me."

Clarissa considered it, then shook her head. "I actually don't mind it."

"You don't?" Izzy blinked. "Do you mean he's done it to you as well?"

Clarissa smiled. "Oh yes."

"I had no idea you had a serious suitor," Izzy exclaimed. Clarissa had never mentioned it. "Who was it?"

"Lord Frencham."

Izzy tried to recall who Lord Frencham was. "He's not the bandy-legged old fellow, is he? The one with snuff stains all around his nose?"

Clarissa shook her head. "I think that's Lord Blandford, and anyway he's more interested in you than me. No, I danced with Lord Frencham at the rout the other night—twice. He's quite young—twenty-five or so—and is quite nice looking and very elegantly dressed."

"And he proposed after what—a couple of dances? He sounds smitten."

"Yes, with my fortune." Clarissa wrinkled her nose. "According to Lord Salcott his estates are heavily encumbered and he's hanging out for a rich wife. Hence the speedy proposal."

"So what did you tell him?"

"Oh, I didn't need to tell him anything. Lord Salcott had already refused on my behalf."

Izzy bristled in her sister's defense. "Without even consulting you? See, that's what I mean—how dare he make decisions like that without even asking us!"

Clarissa shrugged. "I don't mind, I wasn't interested in Lord Frencham anyway. And I'd rather Lord Salcott deal with the fortune hunters and save me the trouble."

Izzy could appreciate that. Clarissa was so softhearted, she would hate to disappoint even the most hardened fortune hunter.

Still, it was outrageous of Lord Salcott to think he could refuse their suitors without consulting them. And so Izzy would tell him in the summerhouse tonight. She would make it very clear to him that she was not as compliant as her sister, that she wouldn't be told what to do. And that she would choose her own husband. Whatever he thought.

When Izzy and Clarissa got home from the ball, they found Betty waiting up for them. They'd told her before not to wait up, that they could help each other undress, but Betty had learned from the other servants at Lady Scattergood's that a proper lady's maid would wait up to help her mistress disrobe, no matter how late the hour. And Betty was determined to be a proper lady's maid.

Izzy let Betty help her out of her ball dress, but as soon as she'd been stripped down to her underclothes, she gently pushed Betty out the door, saying, "I can do the rest thank you, Betty dear. Go and help Clarissa. "

The minute Betty was gone, Izzy threw an old dress on over her chemise and put on some sturdy shoes. She didn't want to go out into the garden and get dew all over the hem of her ball dress and dancing slippers anyway.

Besides, she had preparations to make. Precautions to take.

Half an hour later she made her way to the summer-house, carrying a small lantern. The night was dark, with a blanket of clouds concealing the moon and stars. She unlocked the summerhouse and used the lantern to light a couple of candles, then placed it in the window as a signal to Lord Salcott.

She lit a few more candles. It was late, after two. Maybe he'd fallen asleep. He'd left the ball shortly after their dance.

Lord Salcott appeared so silently he startled her.

"Thank you for coming," he said. "I have wanted to speak to you privately for some time." He glanced around. "Thank God that chaperone didn't come. The woman has been driving me mad."

Izzy would have laughed if she hadn't been mentally preparing for a quarrel. "You hired her," she pointed out. "You can hardly blame her for doing her job."

"I can and I do," he said. "But let's not argue about her. What I wanted to say—"

Izzy cut him off. "What *I* wanted to say was how dare you dismiss my suitors without consulting me."

He rolled his eyes. "Is this about Harvey again? Have you decided you want him after all? Make up your mind."

"No, it's *not* about Mr. Harvey," she said, exasperated.

He knew perfectly well she didn't want to marry Mr. Harvey. He was just saying it to annoy her. "It's about you, deciding who is or isn't allowed to court me! It's not your decision to make—it's mine."

"He came to my house and asked me straight out."

"You should have sent him away."

"I did."

"Without telling him yea or nay, I mean."

"He came to me as your guardian. What was I to do?"

"But you're *not* my guardian. You're Clarissa's."

"And you want me to explain that to every man who comes calling? Expecting an answer from *your guardian*."

"Oh." She saw his point now. Curses. "Well, I see that it would be awkward to explain that, but why not just tell him to speak to me? Explain that it's my choice."

"I could I suppose, but isn't it better if—" He broke off as the sound of jangling bells shattered the peace of the night outside. "What the—"

"Quick, lock the door." Izzy pushed him toward the door. "Hurry!" She extinguished the little lantern and ran around blowing out candles.

"Now, lie down on the day bed." Thankfully he didn't argue.

"What the devil is going on?"

"Shhuush!" she hissed. "It's Milly."

"Who?"

"The neighbor who spies on us—remember? Now hush or she'll catch us again." Izzy had wound a string of Lady Scattergood's Indian brass bells around the Harringtons' garden gate. It had served beautifully as a warning.

"Lie down flat on the daybed; she won't be able to see you there," she told him.

She blew out the last candle and felt her way toward the big squashy chair but tripped over something in the dark.

"Oof!" Lord Salcott exclaimed as she landed half on him. Before she could scramble to her feet, he pulled the

rest of her up so she was lying full length on top of him. She
started to clamber off him, but froze when the door handle
rattled.

Milly was carrying a small lantern. It threw a dim light,
enough to see that Milly's hair was in rag curlers and that
she was wearing a nightgown with a dressing gown over it.
Didn't the girl ever sleep?

And what on earth did she think she was doing coming
out here in the middle of the night, dressed as she was? Her
mother would have kittens if she knew her precious daughter was a night prowler.

"Don't move or make a sound," Izzy breathed.

Strong arms wrapped around her, and he settled down
as if getting comfortable. *Comfortable?* In this situation?

Milly shone the lantern in at the window. Izzy tensed,
and pressed herself down against Lord Salcott, hoping that
from the outside they would look like cushions on the
daybed.

His body was big and firm and warm.

Milly shone the lantern this way and that. Luckily the
beam was too weak to illuminate the scene inside. Mainly
it lit up Milly's face. She rattled the door handle again.
"Izzy? Is that you in there, Izzy Studley?" Thank goodness
the door was locked.

She bent down and scrabbled around in the stone lantern
by the door. "The key's gone. You're not supposed to remove the key."

Izzy grinned to herself. She'd placed the key on the inside of the lock, just in case.

Milly knocked on the window. "I know you're in there,
Isobel Studley. What are you doing sitting in the dark? I
saw the lights before I came down, so I know you're hiding.
Do you have a man in there with you?" She pressed her face
up close to the window, desperately trying to peer inside.
The night was gray and gloomy, but inside the summerhouse all was dark and still.

"You do have a man there, I'm sure of it. Why else hide in the dark?" She rattled the door handle again. "Locked in with a man! You're a disgrace, that's what you are. I'll tell Mama, I will."

Izzy wanted to say, "And what will Mama say when she learns you wander around the garden in the wee small hours in your nightgown?" But the situation was so ridiculous she wanted to laugh. Instead she pressed her face against Lord Salcott's chest.

Big mistake. The man smelled . . . enticing. A combination of clean linen, soap, his spicy cologne water and, underneath it all, the tantalizing scent of a deeply masculine man.

She ought to pull away. She really should. At least turn her face away so she wasn't breathing in that compelling male essence. That addictive male essence.

She buried her nose in the smooth linen of his shirt and inhaled deeply. How was it that a man could smell so . . . irresistible?

She lay plastered against him, covering his body with hers, connecting so intimately that were she not wearing this very thin dress, and he those supple breeches . . .

Best not to think about that. It was a shocking position to be in. Instead it felt right, so very right.

Milly thumped a frustrated fist on the window. "You are so bad, Izzy Studley. Oh, let me in, do."

She was being bad, Izzy reflected. And enjoying every delicious moment.

Beneath Izzy, Lord Salcott's body started to shake. "Stop that," Izzy whispered.

The shaking continued. The wretched man—how could he laugh at a time like this? She poked him. "Hush, it's not funny."

The shaking increased. "It's hilarious. That female is deranged." He pulled her tighter against him, his big warm hands bracing her hips. He moved his legs slightly apart and gave a kind of wriggle, and Izzy's body slipped into the space he'd made, as if she belonged there. She lay cradled against him, her breasts pressing against his chest, her legs bracketed between his.

He felt very warm and firm beneath her. His hands rested lightly on her hips, barely a touch, but she felt them clear through to her core. The heat of his body soaked into her. And there was a growing hardness against her stomach that she ought not be able to feel. She really should pull away. Roll off him. Separate herself from him.

She couldn't bring herself to move.

His hands slipped from her hips to cup her bottom, and he did that little wriggle again that somehow brought them even closer. Her body was melting around him.

She closed her eyes, willing herself not to respond, not to feel. But every sense she possessed—including common sense—was scrambled by his proximity. The scent of him, the touch, the feel . . .

He moved his hand in slow lazy circles, caressing her through the fabric of her dress. Warm shivers rippled through her.

She swallowed. Her mouth was dry.

"I *know* you're in there." Milly rapped on the window, jerking Izzy back to awareness. Turning her head, she watched as Milly cupped her hands around her eyes and pressed her face against the glass, trying again to peer into the dark interior. "The windows are steaming up. What are you doing in there to make the windows steam up?"

Lord Salcott's big body jerked with silent laughter. Izzy bit her lip, but she couldn't help it, she started laughing, too. She stuffed her fist in her mouth to keep from making a noise.

A large hand came up and gently removed her fist. "What are you—*mmff.*"

His mouth covered hers. There was no hesitation, no warning, just a hard, hot, possessive kiss that drove all thoughts of laughter from her mind. She stilled in surprise at first, then as his heat and the familiar, intoxicating taste of him spiraled through her, she softened against him.

Without conscious volition she parted her lips, opening to him, and he deepened the kiss, each sweep of his tongue sending ripples of pleasure through her.

She pressed herself against him, seeking more. She wanted to touch him, but wasn't sure where or how. He was wearing only a shirt and breeches—and boots, of course.

Cupping her head in his hands, he lavished attention on her mouth, and when she was left gasping and helpless and wanting, he pulled back, raining tiny kisses over her closed eyelids, so tender they almost brought her to tears.

How she wished she could see him, see his eyes, his face, but it was too dark. He was just a shadow—a very hard, solid, warm one—and all she could do was close her eyes and feel. And oh . . . how she felt . . .

She smoothed her palms along his jawline, reveling in the friction of his bristles against her soft skin. He rubbed against her palms like a big cat and made a thrilling sound deep in his throat. He liked her touching him.

She slid her fingers into his thick dark hair and found it cool and slightly crispy—some kind of hair product, no doubt, to maintain that tousled appearance that was so fashionable.

She smiled to herself. Even his spontaneous-looking, careless-seeming hairstyle was strictly controlled. She didn't know why she should find that endearing, but she did.

Exploring further, she discovered the open neck of his shirt and slipped her fingers in, finding warm skin and a light dusting of hair.

She could feel his heart thudding. Hers was, too.

He stroked along her jawline with his thumbs and followed with his mouth, nuzzling and nibbling his way down her neck. He found a sensitive place just beneath her ear and bit gently, and she gasped as a hot spear of pleasure arced through her.

Biting? Really? She tried to commit it to mind, but his hands and his mouth kept dissolving all coherent thought.

He cupped her breasts, and with thumb and fingers teased the already aching nipples.

She thrust hungrily against him and heard someone moan aloud. She started. Her eyes flew open. Was that really her?

"It's all right, she gave up and left." His breath was hot on her skin.

"Who?"

He laughed softly. "That ridiculous female."

"Oh." Izzy had completely forgotten about Milly.

There was a short silence. "Are you all right with this? We can stop if you want." His voice was deep and sounded a little strained.

Izzy didn't even have to think. "No." She didn't want to stop. She knew where this was leading and she didn't care—no, not didn't care—she wanted it. Fiercely.

He returned to caressing her breasts, and she shuddered and quivered as he teased and aroused. Through the fabric of her dress his mouth closed over a nipple, hot and moist. He sucked hard and she arched against him. Then he bit gently and she almost screamed as a hot wire of pleasure-pain spiked through her. She grabbed handfuls of his hair.

"Too much?" he asked.

"No," she gasped. And guided his head to her other breast.

Moments—or an eternity—later she was left panting and gasping, and he lay back, smoothing his hands possessively down over her spine and backside. The friction was delicious.

A cool draft whispered over her legs, her bare legs. He was sliding her skirts up. A big warm hand closed over her thigh and she jumped.

"All right?" he asked.

She nodded then, remembering that he couldn't see, said, "Yes. Just surprised."

And as her dress climbed higher, she decided, "Fair's fair." And pulled his shirt out from his breeches and pushed it up so she could feel his lovely firm torso.

He sat up and dragged it over his head. "This what you wanted?"

"Mmmmm." She rubbed her palms over him. So warm, so firm, so deliciously muscular. But oh, how she wished she could see him.

"Sauce for the gander," he muttered, and drew her dress up over her head and tossed it aside.

"Damn that wretched female."

Izzy jumped. "Why? Is she back?"

"No, she's long gone, but I want to see you, and it's too dark."

"Me, too. But we daren't light a candle."

"I know."

"We'll just have to use our imaginations."

He snorted. "I've been imagining this ever since I met you."

He had? The knowledge thrilled her.

He cupped her bare breasts, kissing, licking and nibbling until she was a puddle of ecstasy. He slid his hands down her sides, sending shivers through her. "Not cold are you?"

"Not at all." He grasped her bottom, her bare bottom, and with a murmur of appreciation he stroked it and then eased her over him. She hadn't planned it this way. She and Clarissa had grown up never wearing drawers—like most older people, Nanny didn't approve of them. *Drawers are made for gentlemen, and little girls don't wear gentlemen's clothing.*

Izzy wasn't a little girl anymore.

She rocked against him, rubbing herself against his hardness. "Slow down," he gasped. "Better for you."

But she could feel the tension throbbing through him. He was taking things slowly for her sake, letting her dictate the pace.

She was the impatient one.

She reached down and pressed her hand over the front of his breeches, feeling the hard rod that was there.

He grabbed her hand and moved it away. "Not yet," he rasped.

He slipped his hands between her thighs and cupped her. Then stroked with one long finger. She could hear the sound of wetness. She grimaced in embarrassment and tried to close her legs.

"Don't. You're perfect," he murmured. "Just perfect." He kept stroking. Her legs quivered and fell apart. She was panting, her entire being focused on where his fingers were creating magic. Her legs trembled uncontrollably. The heat between them built. She writhed, aching, grinding her body against his hand.

He eased her away and rolled to one side, and she was about to complain, when she realized he was unbuttoning his breeches. She reached out to touch him, but he caught her hand. "No." She froze, but then he ground out, "I'm on a knife-edge of control as it is, Belle. If you touch me I'll shatter."

A surge of purely female satisfaction filled her.

He moved over her, and she could feel him poised at her entrance. "Sure about this?" His voice was hoarse.

In answer she lifted her bottom and pushed. He gripped her hips, and with one long slow thrust entered her.

She stiffened, flinching a little, but then her body adjusted around him.

"Belle?"

"Keep going." She pushed against him and he groaned and started moving, slowly at first, then finding his rhythm. At first for Izzy it was a mix of pleasure and pain, but then he slid a finger between them and did something. A streak of fire shot through her and she shrieked and almost jack-knifed. And then found herself moving to his rhythm, her body no longer in her control, as if it knew exactly what to do and was impelled to do it.

The pressure built and built. She was striving—for what, she didn't know—but then he did that thing again, and she arched and . . . shattered around him.

Distantly she felt him stiffen and give a long shudder, and with a moan he collapsed on top of her.

Chapter Fifteen

Slowly, drowsily, Izzy came back to herself, lying beneath Lord Salcott—Leo—feeling his warm, heavy weight on her—deliciously so. She ran her hands over him. His skin was hot, a little damp and sweaty. She breathed in the scent of him. Intoxicating.

When had they changed their positions? she wondered vaguely. She'd started on top of him, hiding from Milly. Now she was pressed beneath him like a happy sandwich. She wanted to laugh at the silly thought.

He moved off her, and she felt the immediate chill of his absence. "Are you all right?" he asked, his voice a little stiff.

"Yes." She stretched lazily. "Wonderful." And strange. And weary but satisfied. She sat up, intending to kiss him, but he moved back.

"You'd better get dressed." Her dress flew out of the dark and landed on her.

Feeling suddenly awkward and unsure of herself, she put it on. She could hear him putting his shirt back on and buttoning his breeches—at least she assumed what those soft sounds indicated.

"Ready to return to my aunt's?"

She stared into the darkness desperate to read his face. Was that it? Really?

"I will escort you, of course."

"There's no need." She groped in the dark, found her shoes and slipped them on, suddenly feeling on the verge of tears. Which she refused to shed. "It's a few dozen steps."

"Nevertheless, I will—"

"No!" She moderated her voice. "Thank you."

She felt a cool draft as the door was opened. "Well then . . ." He hesitated and she waited for him to say something, anything that would banish this cold stranger and bring back the man who had taken her to the moon and back.

Leo stood in the doorway not knowing what to say to make it all right. But he couldn't. The damage was done.

"I'm sorry," he said finally. "I didn't realize. I should have . . . but I didn't." Didn't think, more like.

"Realize what?"

"That you were a virgin."

There was a short silence. He couldn't see her expression. "Why wouldn't I be?" Her voice was tight. Brittle.

Leo didn't answer. He had no idea what to say. "We'd better go. That wretched girl might return." It was a feeble excuse, but he couldn't think of what to say or how to react. "I'll escort you back to my aunt's house."

"I told you before, that's not necessary."

"But—"

"I'm perfectly capable of walking a few dozen yards by myself. Good night, Lord Salcott." There was no arguing with that tone of voice. She didn't want him anywhere near her. He couldn't blame her.

She'd been a virgin. He'd ruined her—and probably

hadn't even given her much pleasure in the process. While for him it had been glorious.

Back home, Leo stripped off and flung himself into bed. Sleep eluded him. Questions pecked at him endlessly—unanswerable impossible questions.

He hadn't come to the summerhouse intending to seduce Isobel. Belle. It had just happened.

And she'd wanted it as much as he did—she'd made that more than clear. He hadn't forced her. Seduced her maybe. Or maybe they'd seduced each other.

But one thing was crystal clear. He'd seduced a virgin, and Leo knew what he had to do: marry her. It was the honorable thing to do.

Izzy walked slowly back through the garden. An owl hooted overhead, mournful and lonely. She let herself into Lady Scattergood's, locked the back door behind her and walked slowly up the stairs.

Was this how it was for most women, their first time? This plummeting from joy to despair? Exhilaration followed by devastation?

Was this how it had been for Mama? Had Papa shown her a glimpse of heaven and then walked away as if nothing had happened? Acting like a polite stranger.

No, Papa was never polite, not unless he wanted something.

She would never have imagined that Lord Salcott was in any way like Papa. But she was wrong. She didn't understand him at all.

She let herself into her bedchamber, stripped off her dress, poured cold water into a bowl and washed herself all over. Every inch of her. Washing the scent of him from her body.

By the time she finished washing herself, she was shivering. And not with pleasure.

I'm sorry. I didn't realize . . . you were a virgin.

What had he expected? He knew her background, that she and Clarissa had never been anywhere, met anyone.

What had he thought, that she'd rolled in the hay with farm boys and laborers?

Anger stirred deep down inside her. But in the cold dark of night despair ruled.

She'd been too eager, too hungry. Too enthusiastic. Sluttish.

Women—ladies—were supposed to be reluctant. To hang back. To need to be coaxed, seduced. Not to writhe and moan and rub themselves against the man like a cat in heat.

Only men were supposed to enjoy it. Nanny had warned them about that.

So perhaps she wasn't a lady after all, because she had damn well enjoyed every bit of it. Until the end when he'd turned into a stranger. And she refused to pretend otherwise.

So she was a whor—no, she would not use that ugly word. She was a woman who enjoyed bed sports. Fine. And if he didn't like that, too bad. She was what she was, and she refused to be ashamed.

She pulled on her nightdress, climbed into bed and dragged the covers over her head. Wishing for oblivion.

L eo hardly slept. When morning eventually came, he rose, bathed, shaved and dressed with extra care. His duty was clear, and Leo always did his duty.

He crossed the garden and asked to speak to Miss Isobel in private. The butler informed him that Miss Isobel was just back from walking the dogs, and would be with him shortly. Mrs. Price-Jones and Miss Clarissa were visiting the shops.

Leo was glad. If that woman had insisted on joining

them, he might have had to throw her out of the window. He was tense, his temper on edge.

Honor demanded he do this thing.

When Isobel arrived, he scanned her face for signs that she, too, had spent the night tossing and turning. But there was none. No shadow of visible regret or distress; her eyes were clear and bright, her skin smooth and lovely as ever. Fresh as the first snowdrop of the season.

"Good morning, Lord Salcott." She didn't look like a virgin who'd been ravaged.

"I owe you an apology," he said gruffly after she sat.

She arched a brow. "For what?"

He barely heard what she said. He'd rehearsed his speech half the night. "And naturally I am willing to marry you."

A glint of something flashed in her eyes. He had no idea what it meant. "Why?" she asked eventually.

What did she mean, why? Wasn't it obvious? "I didn't know you were a virgin."

"You didn't ask."

"I didn't think I needed to. You came to me willingly enough."

Her lips tightened. "Bad blood, is that it? Tarred with my mother's reputation?"

He shrugged. The truth was he hadn't even thought about it. He'd wanted her and she'd let him take her. It was only afterward that he'd thought about it. And the implications.

Her eyes glittered with anger. "You know my mother slept with only two men in her life. And that she was seduced by my villain of a father at sixteen and didn't even know how babies were made."

"But you knew," he heard himself say. Why, he didn't know. Fanning the flames of his own destruction.

"Yes, because my mother made damned sure I knew. She didn't want me to be seduced by an unprincipled rake."

He flinched at the accusation, but couldn't argue. He said stiffly, "I have just offered to marry you."

"Yes, in the spirit of a man going to the gallows," she flashed. "Well, thank you, Lord Salcott, but I decline your so-handsome offer, so now you can take yourself off, heave a sigh of relief and congratulate yourself on a lucky escape."

Leo blinked. "You decline?"

"Yes. Unbelievable, isn't it? Such a prize you are, and yet I'm turning you down."

"But—"

"But what?"

"You're no longer a virgin."

Her look scorched him. "Thank you for pointing it out—again. I might have forgotten."

"What if there's a child?"

"Then I trust you will make him or her an allowance."

"I don't want to support a bastard."

"And I don't want to give birth to one."

"Then marry me."

"Why?"

"Didn't I just say why?"

"Sorry, not good enough." She shook her head. "I doubt I'll be with child, but if I am, then . . . we'll see."

"If you are with child, you'll marry me and no argument."

She gave him a hard look. "I said, we'll see."

He thought he knew what women wanted, but he didn't understand her at all. "I was under the impression you were looking for a husband."

"I am."

"Then . . ." He frowned. "Is there someone else?"

"Dozens of them."

His scowl darkened.

"Several gentlemen have made their intentions obvious. I'm considering my options."

"But you're no longer a virgin."

She gave him a hard look. "Really? Good heavens." She shrugged. "Naturally I will explain it to the gentleman whose offer I decide to accept. Along with the truth about my birth and my complete lack of any fortune, all of which I will tell him *before* I give him my answer."

"He won't want you if he knows."

"If he's that petty minded, I won't want him," she snapped. "But I hope I'm a better judge of character than that."

Leo didn't know what to say to that. "Who is this large-minded gentleman?"

She gave him a cool smile and rose to her feet. "That, Lord Salcott, is none of your business. Thank you for calling. I have a luncheon engagement shortly. Good day."

Leo didn't move. "Whoever he is, he will still call on me first, unless you intend to declare to all and sundry that I am not in fact your guardian."

She frowned. "But you will send him to me for the final answer?"

He shrugged. "If I think he is suitable."

"No! I thought I'd made it clear—"

He shook his head. "The kind of men you've been encouraging, anyone would think you're a fortune hunter."

"I am."

"What?"

"A fortune hunter. Oh, don't look so shocked, what else can I be? Or are you as hypocritical as the rest? It's perfectly acceptable for nice young society ladies to strive to make 'a good marriage'—to a man with the fattest fortune and the noblest title—but let an illegitimate girl of no fortune try and it's somehow underhanded and despicable." She snorted. "I'm just more open about it, that's all. If I fail to marry well, I have nothing to fall back on. Like my mother." She raised her chin, knowing he would be recalling how her mother survived her poverty.

And he was. The thought horrified him. "What about Clarissa?"

"At the moment Clarissa shares her income with me—we agreed to it long ago, as recompense for our father's failure to provide for me and my mother. But I have no intention of battening on my sister's generosity forever. So I must make the kind of marriage that will ensure security for myself and any children I might have."

Leo could see that. He didn't have to like it, but he had to acknowledge that her logic made sense.

"I thought all young ladies dreamed of falling in love."

She let out a huff of cynical laughter. "Strange how so many of them find it so much easier to fall in love with a man with a title and a substantial fortune—think about all those girls so very willing to fall in love with you, Lord Salcott."

She shook her head. "I'm not so hypocritical. I won't feign love, but I will make the man I accept an excellent wife. I am a bargain."

"A *bargain*?" The term offended him. "What the hell does that mean?"

She began furiously listing things off on her fingers. "I'm loyal—unlike many wives who make practical marriages, he won't ever have cause to doubt my fidelity; I will be a good and devoted mother; I will make his house a home, where he will be comfortable, a place where he will be proud to welcome his friends. His interests would be my interests. You see," she added with a small cool smile, "I understand all the requirements of good wifehood."

Somehow the recital of her wifely qualities disturbed him. He had no quarrel with any of them in theory, but it was as if she were, in some way he couldn't pinpoint, diminishing herself. Reducing herself to a list, squashing herself into a mold. As if she were applying for a job—which he supposed in a way, she was. But oh, he did not like it. She was so much more than that.

She hadn't even mentioned the qualities that were most likely to land her this theoretical man of substance—her beauty and vivacity. And they were only part of what made her special and desirable.

And she'd said nothing about the obligations of the husband. Would this fellow—Leo despised him already—be faithful to her? Leo doubted it. Would he treat her well, respect her, cherish her as she deserved to be cherished? No, he would not.

The kind of rich man who would choose a lovely young woman like Isobel Studley, a woman with no family to protect her, would no doubt treat her like a possession, rather than a woman. Or like a servant. He'd seen it before . . .

"I can see what this man might get from such a marriage, but what about you? What would you get from such a cold-blooded arrangement?"

She looked at him as if he were dense. "A home of my own. A place where I belong—mine!—where nobody could throw me out or move me on. A place to raise my children. A family."

"You could have all that with me." His voice cracked as he said it.

She shook her head. "You only offered for me out of a sense of obligation. Nobody dreams of being *an obligation*. And if I had accepted your offer, how long would it be before you were thinking I'd somehow entrapped you? I've seen how that ends up—with bitterness and resentment. No, better a cold-blooded practical arrangement, as you call it, where both sides know what's expected. Besides," she added after a moment. "I have no interest in a title."

Leo couldn't think of a thing to say. His thoughts were in turmoil. All he knew was that he desired her—lord, but he'd never felt such powerful desire in his life—but it was true that it was guilt that had prompted his proposal. And while he'd been shocked at her refusal, there was also a trickle of relief. And a great deal of confusion.

Only one thing was clear to him: he hated what she was preparing to do. Voices in the hall indicated the chaperone and Clarissa had returned from their errand. The door flew open and Mrs. Price-Jones stood in the doorway. "Lord Salcott, I'm shocked," she declared. "Calling on Miss Isobel when you knew I was out."

Leo rose to his feet. "And here's your precious charge, Mrs. Price-Jones," he said sarcastically, "uncompromised and untouc—" He broke off, recalling that he had both compromised and thoroughly touched Isobel last night.

Isobel made a noise that might have been a cough. He didn't look at her. Doing his best to ignore his reddening face, Leo bowed to the ladies and took his leave.

Izzy was furious, furious with herself for giving in and making love with him. Furious about what he'd said to her, and with the way she'd handled his proposal. Where had her common sense gone? Jeopardizing her future like that, without a thought.

One kiss and all her resolutions had washed down the drain.

He won't want you if he knows.

He was probably right. She brought enough disadvantages to any potential marriage as it was.

She'd been foolhardy and reckless, giving in to the impulse of a moment.

No, not a momentary impulse. Hadn't she dreamed of being in his arms, night after night? And so when the moment had come, she'd seized it.

And no matter how much she might berate herself, deep down in her secret heart, she couldn't truly make herself regret it.

Oh, she might regret the consequences, the ruin of her prospects. And what if she found herself with child . . . his child. She touched her belly and was shocked to find herself feeling a little wistful. Lord, but she was more like Mama than she thought. She'd even be happy to bear his child, though not to live as she and Mama had, never like that.

But then, what he'd said to her this morning. The way he'd said it. As if proposing to her had all the appeal of swallowing a frog. Oh yes, she was furious about that.

She paced back and forth, tense as a coiled spring.

Clarissa laid a hand on her arm. "What on earth did Lord Salcott say to you to get you into this state?" she asked softly.

Izzy glanced at Mrs. Price-Jones, who was giving instructions to Treadwell about something. "Not here. I need . . . I need a ride, 'Riss. Will you join me?"

Clarissa gave her a troubled look. "Of course. I'll send a note to Lady Tarrant, sending our apologies for luncheon. She won't mind. It was a casual arrangement."

O h, that's better," Izzy exclaimed as her horse drew up at the big oak that marked the finish of their impromptu race. They'd gone riding on the heath, just the two of them and the groom in attendance, who hung back a short distance, giving them all the privacy they wanted. The vigorous exercise in the fresh air had done her a power of good. "Like old times, eh, 'Riss?"

Clarissa laughed. "Yes, such fun. I've been missing our rides." Mrs. Price-Jones didn't ride, so most of their activities involved either walking or rides in the carriage. "Now, tell me what Lord Salcott did to put you in such a temper."

"Temper? I wasn't in a temper."

"No?" Her sister gave her a quizzical look.

"It's just that he's a big, thickheaded, honorable, blind, oblivious idiot."

Clarissa laughed and clapped her hands. "I knew it! You're in love with him."

Izzy stared at her. "In *love*? With that great, gormless, infuriating, boneheaded—"

"Definitely in love," Clarissa said.

"I am not."

Clarissa just looked at her. Izzy resisted for a moment, then sighed, deflated. "I did something very stupid the other night, after the Gainsborough ball."

"What?"

"I met Lord Salcott in the summerhouse."

Clarissa frowned. "After we got home, you mean? You went out there in the middle of the night? Again?"

Izzy nodded. "He said he wanted to talk to me in private—well, you know how Mrs. Price-Jones has been heading him off every time he tried to speak to me."

"And he asked you to meet him secretly? At night? Alone in the summerhouse? Oh, that was not well done of him. But you went anyway?"

Izzy nodded.

"He kissed you again?"

Izzy nodded.

"And . . . was that all?"

Izzy gave a tight little shake of her head. "Worse."

"A little bit worse or a lot worse?"

"All the way worse."

Clarissa's eyes widened. "You didn't! You made love with Lord Salcott? Oh, Izzy."

"I know," Izzy said wretchedly. "I don't know what I was thinking. I wasn't thinking at all. Stupid, eh?"

There was a short silence. And then Clarissa asked, "And was it wonderful? Oh, I am so envious."

"Clarissa!"

Her sister laughed. "Well, you were the first of the two of us to have a proper kiss from a handsome man, and now you're the first of us to make love—with the same handsome man. Of course I'm envious. So what was it like?"

"I didn't plan for it to happen."

"Of course not. But what was it like?"

"It was all Milly Harrington's fault."

"Milly Harrington?" Clarissa's voice rose almost to a squeak. "What on earth did she have to do with it?"

Izzy told her how Milly had come spying again and how they'd been hiding from her in the dark and how she'd tripped and ended up lying full length on top of him on the daybed.

"Lying full length on top of him in the dark. So shocking." Clarissa sighed. "It sounds blissful. No wonder you got carried away."

"Well, at first we were trying not to laugh because of the fuss Milly was making, and then he stopped my laughter . . . with a kiss."

Clarissa gave a rapturous sigh. "And then what?"

"One thing led to another."

Clarissa narrowed her eyes. "Izzy Studley, if you think you can get away with 'one thing led to another,' you've got another think coming!"

Izzy laughed. "It's very hard to explain, 'Riss. It was wonderful, and very . . . carnal. Very physical—more than I'd expected, really. But also . . . transporting. I mean, Milly was outside, banging on the door and trying to shine her lantern inside when he first kissed me, and yet, I just . . . forgot about her."

"You didn't—I mean not with Milly there, did you?"

"Oh no, by the time things got really serious, she'd long since given up and gone home." Izzy should have brought things to a halt then, the moment Milly had gone, but she hadn't been able to bring herself to stop the kissing and caressing . . .

The truth was, she hadn't thought at all.

"So, what was it like? Doing *it,* I mean."

"As I said, very physical. He caressed me everywhere— I mean everywhere, 'Riss. He put his mouth on my breasts."

Shivers rippled through her at the memory. "And touched me here." She indicated with her hand. "The sensations . . . I can't describe them. I forgot everything, everything except what was happening to my body." And she wasn't even thinking about that, not in any conscious way. Like being swept away on a wave of pleasure . . . and need. Just floating, drowning in sensation. Oblivious of everything except the intensity of the moment.

"Did you touch him in the same way?" Clarissa said breathlessly.

Izzy nodded. "He has a beautiful body—well, I couldn't see it, it was so dark, but it was hard and strong, and . . ." She shivered again. "Magnificent."

"Did he take off all his clothes?"

"No, just his shirt—which I pulled off him. And his breeches were half-off." She blushed remembering.

"And you took off all your clothes?"

She nodded. "I was wearing an old dress with nothing underneath."

"Izzy!" Clarissa gave a half-shocked laugh.

Izzy grinned. "I promise you I didn't plan it." She sighed. "But I don't regret it for a minute."

There was a long silence. Then Clarissa said, "Then what were you so upset about this morning when he came to call? I presume he offered for you."

At the question, a cold stone lodged in her chest. "He did."

Clarissa read her expression and her face fell. "Oh, Izzy, you didn't, did you? You refused him?"

"He only offered out of guilt, 'Riss. Because that's what an honorable man does when he's deflowered a virgin."

"But what does that matter?"

"I refuse to be a millstone around his neck."

"'Millstone'? What nonsense. You'd make a wonderful countess."

Izzy smiled. "You're biased. But no, what I really meant

was that he only proposed out of a sense of obligation, of guilt. Not because he loves me. I don't want to be anyone's obligation, and a forced marriage is a recipe for resentment and bitterness."

"But you love him. And anyway, I think he does care for you. He just doesn't realize it."

Izzy shook her head. "I won't risk it. Both your mother and mine loved a man who didn't love them back. And, married or not, they were both desperately unhappy. I would rather make a marriage based on liking and respect; at least then there is a possibility for love—or at the very least affection—to grow. But one-sided love . . ." She shook her head again. "It's too painful."

You only offered for me out of a sense of obligation. Nobody dreams of being an obligation.

Leo couldn't get the words out of his head. They made no sense to him.

Yes, he'd made his offer from a sense of obligation—he was honor bound to do it, after taking her virginity. What sort of a man would he be to ruin her and leave her to face the consequences alone?

But he didn't think of her as an obligation. Nobody could think of Isobel Studley as an obligation. She was a delight, an infuriating one at times, but nevertheless, a delight.

He thought about making love to her the previous night. She was also a glory . . . So open and giving and generous and . . . and loving.

Yes, loving. The thing he tried so hard to avoid. She'd given it anyway.

What was it that Race had said? *Love is the prize.*

And yet she was planning to offer herself up in a marriage of convenience, to one of those dreary fellows who were courting her. For the sake of a house. No, *a home.*

A place where I belong . . . where nobody could throw me out or move me on. A place to raise my children . . .

In other words the kind of security she'd never in her life experienced.

Leo could give her that—and more. So why refuse him?

Nobody dreams of being an obligation.

Was that what she imagined he thought of her?

He thought back over the conversation he'd had with her. He'd been nervous. And ashamed that he'd taken his pleasure of her without ensuring she had experienced her own pleasure. Her first time, too. Guilt flayed him. He'd wanted—no, he'd needed to make it up to her. And a marriage proposal was the only way—the only decent way—he knew to do so.

He hadn't even mentioned how he felt about her. But he'd been so on edge, so tense that, looking back, he realized he'd even implied that she was at fault, that she should have stopped him, that she was responsible for her own deflowering.

He closed his eyes as shame swamped him. *You came to me willingly enough.* Had he really said that? The age-old defense of men, blaming the woman for acting on the desire he had deliberately aroused. Just as her father had no doubt blamed her sixteen-year-old mother.

What an arse!

He wouldn't ever think of her as an obligation, and he needed to make that clear to her. He wasn't giving up on her yet.

Filled with resolve, he crossed the garden to his aunt's house.

"I wish to speak to Miss Isobel," he told Treadwell.

"I'm sorry, my lord, but she and Miss Clarissa have just left to go riding."

"Damn. I don't suppose you know where, do you? Hyde Park or the heath?"

"I heard Miss Isobel mention Hampstead Heath, my lord."

"Excellent. And they only left a short time ago?" He might be able to catch up to them.

"Ten minutes or so. However"—Treadwell stepped in front of Leo, blocking his exit—"Lady Scattergood wishes to speak with you. I was about to send the boy over with a note. Her ladyship is in the sitting room. Awaiting your immediate arrival," he added pointedly when Leo hesitated.

What on earth did she want? Cursing silently at the delay, Leo made his way to the sitting room. He needed to find Isobel and make it right with her.

His aunt greeted him coldly and bade him "Sit" in a manner strongly reminiscent of the way she talked to her dogs. Only more severely. Leo sat.

"Like many older people, I suffer from insomnia," his aunt informed him.

"I'm sorry to hear it, Aunt Olive." Though what she thought Leo could do about it was a mystery to him.

"When it strikes, I generally sit at my bedroom window, sip ginger wine and gaze out over the garden."

"I see."

"Do you? I certainly saw some interesting things last night. At half past two in the morning." She raised her lorgnette and eyed him beadily for a long moment. "Lights in the summerhouse."

"Ah." Leo suddenly remembered what it was like to be a schoolboy awaiting a caning.

She regarded him sourly, her mouth like a sucked lemon. "I saw young Izzy go in, then I saw you arrive. I saw that ridiculous Harrington gel prowling around trying to peer inside, and I saw her give up and go home again. And after a *very* long time I saw you leave, and then Izzy. So what was that about, eh?"

Leo told her, the bare bones of it, but hiding nothing. Admitting all responsibility.

"I presume you will make it right with the gel?"

"I proposed to her this morning. She refused me."

His aunt lifted her lorgnette again. "She did, did she? Hah! The gel's got spirit. But what sort of a man are you to give up at the first hurdle?"

"I don't intend—"

"Convince the gel that you mean it, boy! Woo her—or have you modern men forgotten how to do that? Scatter-good had to woo me for weeks, and I made him propose several times before I finally accepted him."

And two weeks later the man was on a ship bound for India, Leo thought. *And never returned.*

She pursed her lips. "I suppose when you proposed to the gel, you were all starched up and formal."

"A certain degree of formality is inevitable when making an offer of marriage." Leo was aware of where he'd gone wrong, but he didn't intend to discuss it with his elderly aunt. Especially all wound up as she was.

"Fiddlesticks! That's your father in you. He was a pompous windbag at the best of times—what your mother ever saw in him I don't know. And though she had all the morals of a bitch in heat, she had a heart, at least. Oh, don't look at me like that, boy, I can say what I like about my own relatives. And you're like neither of them—except occasionally when you sound distressingly like your father. But you were a warmhearted, affectionate little boy, and something or someone has encased you in ice. Well, chip your way out of it, I say. Young Isobel is a dashed fine gel—just the wife for you. A loyal and loving heart, good with dogs, and she'll stop you being stuffy and humorless like your father. So get out there and woo her and stop wasting your time bothering an old woman."

Leo rose. "That, Aunt Olive, is exactly what I came here

to do. I have no intention of giving up on Isobel." He bent and kissed her withered cheek. "But thank you for your support."

He sent for his horse, changed into his riding gear and headed out to the heath. But he'd left it too late. There was no sign of them. They could be anywhere.

Frustrated he rode home. He called in at his aunt's again, but Treadwell informed him, not without faint perceptable pleasure, that the young ladies were not at home. Leo didn't believe him, and was about to argue when Mrs. Price-Jones appeared. She briskly informed him that he was wasting his time. The young ladies were not receiving visitors. They were attending Lady Arden's ball in the evening, and since they had spent the afternoon in strenuous horseback riding, Mrs. Price-Jones had sent them upstairs to rest before they went.

Chapter Sixteen

Lady Arden was a popular hostess and a duke's daughter, and though her ball was not one of the truly grand ones, Mrs. Price-Jones informed Izzy and Clarissa, all the best people would be in attendance.

"I don't know what she means by the truly grand balls," Clarissa whispered to Izzy as they passed along the receiving line. "This is quite grand enough for me."

The ballroom was made up of three large rooms that opened onto each other. Chairs were set around the walls, and the room was decorated with swags of white flowers and lush green vines. The main dancing area was defined by a matching design of flowers and vines drawn in chalk over the floor.

"Look, Izzy, how pretty," Clarissa said.

"Shame it won't last past the first dance," Izzy commented.

"Lady Arden is known for her excellent taste," said Mrs. Price-Jones, coming up behind them. "Now, gels, let's see who is here. You won't want to miss a dance." She glanced around the room and pursed her lips. "Why is it that men always arrive late?"

Once the ball got underway, everything was delightful. Now that they knew so many people, Clarissa was much more comfortable in society and seemed to be enjoying herself, which left Izzy free to enjoy herself without worrying.

She'd danced with four of the men on the list she and Mrs. Price-Jones had been compiling, though it had to be admitted that none of them sparked any real interest. Still, they had all indicated their interest in her: a decision had to be made, and soon.

Lord Salcott was also in attendance, but when he'd asked her to dance, Izzy had pretended all her dances were taken. She could tell from his expression that he didn't believe her, but she didn't care. She refused to be his obligatory wife.

The dance had finished, and her partner, a Mr. Roberts, was escorting her from the dance floor when there was a stir at the entrance. A group of raddled-looking older gentlemen had arrived, somewhat the worse for drink judging by the noise they were making. Izzy glanced at them, and ice slid down her spine as she recognized her father's friend, Lord Pomphret.

If he saw her . . .

"Come to collect m'wife," Lord Pomphret slurred loudly. Izzy didn't even know he had a wife. "Leaving London tonight. Where is the woman?" He peered around the room, spotted Izzy and recoiled.

"Good God! It's Bart Studley's little bastard bitch! What the hell is she doing in respectable company?" Unfortunately, he said it at one of those moments at a party when a momentary hush occurs, just by chance.

After he spoke, however, the hush deepened. It was clear that at least half the room had heard him.

Izzy froze. So it had come, the moment they'd been

expecting—and dreading. She looked for Clarissa, but couldn't see her anywhere. Her first instinct was to leave the floor and then, somehow, vanish, but that would be disastrous.

No, she would stay and see this thing out.

Her gaze flew to Lord Salcott. What would he do? Disown her? Escort her out, never to be seen in this company again? He caught her glance and gave his head a tiny shake, as if he thought she might flee.

She put up her chin and met his gaze squarely. She refused to flee from that swine Pomphret. But what was Lord Salcott going to do?

Izzy was standing on the edge of the dance floor. She glanced at her partner, who was staring at her like a stunned goose. He disengaged her hand from his arm and took a step away, as if she were contagious.

There was a flurry of movement in the watching crowd, and Clarissa hurried across the floor. She linked her arm through Izzy's and said in a natural-sounding voice, "I'm parched, aren't you, Izzy? Let us get something to drink." Acting as if nothing had happened. Had she heard Lord Pomphret or not?

"Mr. Roberts, you don't mind if I kidnap my sister for a moment, do you?" she said with a slight but perceptible emphasis on the word "sister." Clarissa had heard Lord Pomphret, then, and this was a show of sisterly solidarity. She squeezed her sister's arm affectionately but didn't move from the floor. She needed to hear what was happening.

Lord Pomphret gestured in Izzy's direction and repeated loudly, "I tell you, that girl is Bart Studley's bastard. I'd know her anywhere."

"You're drunk, Pomphret." It was Lord Salcott. He'd crossed the room and was standing in front of Lord Pomphret. Looming over him. Funny, until now she'd never realized Lord Pomphret was quite short.

Pomphret glowered up at Lord Salcott. "'M not so drunk

I can't see what's in front of my nose—that's Bart Studley's bast—"

"We heard you before," Lord Salcott snapped. "But you're talking rot."

Lord Pomphret glared up at him. "'S'not rot. I tell you—"

"Offensive, drunken rot."

"Bart Studley was my good friend and—"

"And yet he chose to make *me* his daughter's official guardian—and I have the documents to prove it."

Izzy bit her lip. What was he doing? Perjuring himself? All he had was that dreadful letter her father had written about her.

Lord Pomphret said mulishly, "I tell you, that girl, the black-haired chit, is Bart's bast—"

"I said, *enough*!" Lord Salcott raised a hand in a threatening gesture.

Lord Pomphret staggered backward a couple of steps, shouting, "He struck me! You all saw that. He struck me!"

The men who'd entered with Lord Pomphret moved away, distancing themselves. A couple of them laughed uncomfortably. One said, his voice loud with disgust, "He never even touched you, Pomphret—get a grip, man."

Lord Salcott pulled off his gray kid gloves and said in a menacing manner, "If you continue to spout any more of this offensive nonsense, you will be answerable to me. Understand? As his daughter's guardian—appointed by Sir Bartleby himself."

Pomphret scowled and muttered something Izzy couldn't hear.

"What's that you said?" Lord Salcott said in a threatening voice. He slapped his gloves into the palm of his hand in an unmistakable gesture.

Izzy clutched Clarissa's arm. "He's going to call Pomphret out. Because of me. Oh, 'Riss, I can't let him do it. I have to stop this."

She tried to move, but Clarissa held her tight. "Don't. You'll ruin things."

"Ruin what? He could be killed because of me, defending my nonexistent honor."

"Hush. It's a brilliant move, and I think it's working. Pomphret is obviously drunk, and Lord Salcott has a reputation as an honorable man. He hasn't even told any lies. He hasn't claimed to be your guardian, just Papa's daughter's, which is me."

"But Lord Pomphret is—"

"A pig, remember? And we should—" Clarissa broke off with an arrested look. "I've just had the most splendid idea. Follow me." Towing Izzy with her, she headed toward a group of ladies, many of whom they knew from the literary society. They were talking in hushed voices, their eyes darting from Lords Pomphret and Salcott to Izzy and back.

Izzy hung back a little. "Come on, we must be bold," Clarissa hissed, pulling her on. Izzy blinked. It was the kind of thing she usually said to Clarissa.

"Good evening, ladies," Clarissa said breezily. "What a to-do! Of course that nasty Lord Pomphret always did drink too much, didn't he, Izzy?" To the ladies she explained, "He was an occasional guest of our father's when we were growing up." She wrinkled her nose. "Not our favorite of Papa's guests at all—we used to avoid him whenever possible, didn't we, Izzy?"

"Tried to," Izzy said dryly, wondering where her sister was going with this.

The ladies exchanged glances.

"Yes, he wasn't so bad when we were small, but when we grew older . . ." Clarissa pulled a face. "Of course, that's why he hates us."

"Hates you? Why?" one of the ladies asked.

Clarissa looked at Izzy. "Do you mind if I tell these ladies? In strictest confidence, of course."

Izzy gave a reluctant nod. She knew where this was going now. "In strictest confidence?"

"Oh, of course," the ladies assured her. "Strictest confidence." They moved closer.

Clarissa began. "As you all know, my sister is the beauty of the family. When she was fifteen—or were you sixteen, Izzy?"

"Not quite sixteen."

"Yes, she was not yet sixteen, but Lord Pomphret had already been making unwanted advances to her for some time. You know the kind of thing—lewd and suggestive comments, unwelcome touches."

"They started when I was thirteen," Izzy said.

The ladies made shocked-sounding exclamations.

Clarissa nodded. "Dreadful man."

Another lady added, "He has that reputation, I've heard. Cannot be trusted with young gels."

"But did your father not act to prevent this appalling behavior?" one lady asked.

Clarissa gave her an incredulous look. "Our father had no time for mere daughters. He cared more about his horses than us."

"But Lord Pomphret didn't interfere with Papa's horses, so . . ." Izzy said sardonically. She couldn't believe she sounded so calm. Almost all her attention was on the scene happening across the ballroom, but it was very frustrating. She couldn't hear what they were saying. The chatter in the ballroom had grown louder—no doubt everyone was discussing the incident.

"Anyway, as I was saying"—Clarissa's voice dropped and the ladies pressed closer—"one day when Izzy was almost sixteen, Lord Pomphret found her alone outside—he was drunk, of course, just as he is now—and he tried to . . . tried to ravish her—my younger sister in her own home!"

The ladies gasped and exclaimed in horror.

"I fought him, of course," Izzy said.

"But a young gel would have no chance against a grown man," one of the ladies said, and the others murmured agreement. They looked at Izzy in horror, the question hovering unspoken in the air, too polite to ask.

"I found them," Clarissa began.

"I was yelling."

"Yes, and kicking and scratching and biting. I tried to pull him off her but it was no good. He was too strong." Clarissa glanced at Izzy with a little smile. "Luckily we weren't far from the pigpen."

"The pigpen?" a lady echoed, bewildered.

"Yes, and the pigs were waiting to be fed. There was a large bucket of pig slops standing there—soured milk, vegetable peelings, grease, fish guts and more—so I grabbed it and tipped it over Lord Pomphret. And then I let the pigs out. They were very hungry."

"And in the confusion I was able to get away."

"Yes, we ran."

"But he was absolutely furious. His clothes were ruined—he considers himself quite a dandy—and some of the pigs bit him. Papa's other friends who were visiting thought it was quite funny."

"And so Lord Pomphret has never forgiven us. Which is why he's saying horrid things about my sister."

Izzy snorted. "We've never forgiven *him*. In fact, from then on we called him Lord Pig Slops. Just between ourselves, you understand."

"Except you did call him that to his face a couple of times, remember?" Clarissa reminded her.

"Papa was furious with us," Izzy admitted.

"We had to hide for the rest of that visit," Clarissa said.

There was a short silence. Then one of the ladies tittered. "Lord Pig Slops." Two more started sniggering, and soon they were all laughing and repeating, "Lord Pig Slops."

"But that's in the strictest confidence," Clarissa reminded them.

"Oh yes, *of course*," the ladies assured her. "In the *strictest* confidence."

"I never liked him," a lady said.

"Things haven't gone well for him recently," said another. "Gambling," she added.

"His poor wife has much to bear, I fear."

The group of ladies broke up then, circulating among the rest of the guests, as was only polite. As they drifted away, Izzy heard one lady say, "Ridiculous man. As if a man like Sir Bartleby would choose to raise his by-blow with his legitimate daughter. He was always frightfully toplofty . . ."

Clarissa giggled. "Because we never gave him the choice."

Izzy slipped an arm around Clarissa. "Thank you, love, that was inspired. At the very least it should sow some uncertainty into their minds. Though I doubt the story will stay confidential."

Clarissa laughed. "Of course it won't—why else do you think I stressed it?"

Izzy turned back to see what was happening with Lord Pomphret. She'd been so distracted by Clarissa bringing up the past that she'd almost forgotten her anxiety about a possible duel. To her relief Lord Salcott was now standing a short distance away from Lord Pomphret, leaning against a column with his arms folded, wearing a grim expression and watching the man. Daring him to step out of line again.

Lord Pomphret wasn't saying much, just downing glass after glass with a brooding air. The friends he'd arrived with were now nowhere to be seen.

"Don't look so anxious. I think it's going to be all right," Clarissa whispered.

Izzy shook her head. "I'm not so sure." She didn't trust Lord Pomphret an inch.

After a few minutes a drab-looking lady appeared and took Lord Pomphret's arm. His wife? He shook her off, then grabbed her hard by the wrist. He said something over his shoulder to Lord Salcott—Izzy couldn't hear what—and towed his wife unsteadily from the room.

He'd gone. Izzy felt suddenly hollow. And exhausted.

She gazed across the room at Lord Salcott.

She couldn't believe how he had stepped up to defend her reputation. Publicly and unequivocally. After telling her again and again that she wasn't acceptable to the ton.

Putting his own reputation on the line to save hers. And Clarissa's.

Being prepared to risk his own life in a duel—to defend a lie, to save Izzy.

The foolish, gallant man. Whatever had possessed him?

H ow do you think it's going?" Leo asked Race. His friend had been subtly circulating among the guests at the ball, picking up snippets of conversation here and there, gauging the crowd's reaction to Lord Pomphret's accusation and Leo's response.

"It's early days yet—people are still sorting out what they think," his friend told him. "But overall, I think the indications are positive. Apparently Pomphret's been making an arse of himself in other quarters as well, which is in our favor."

Leo raised a brow, and Race added in a low voice, "Word is he's drowning in debt. Lost a bundle tonight at the tables and by all accounts was damned unpleasant about it. Accused a fellow of cheating, but it didn't wash. Got quite nasty I heard. Members who witnessed it were so seriously unimpressed; there's talk he'll have his club membership withdrawn."

Leo's brows rose. "That is serious. Might explain why he was so anxious to leave London tonight. Not a good night to be on the road, though. No moon at all." He shook his head. He had no interest in Pomphret's traveling arrangements. "What are people saying about Miss Isobel?"

Race grimaced. "Mixed. Some are saying they always knew there was something about Isobel Studley—but they're the usual sort who seize on any little piece of scandal and wallow in it. But a surprising number seem to have dismissed it," Race said. "Partly a reaction to Pomphret's bad manners in casting a public slur on a popular young lady, and ruining Lady Arden's ball." He chuckled. "Though if I know the ton, Pomphret's outburst will have added a certain cachet to the ball. Everyone will be talking about it."

"Damn," Leo muttered. The gossip wouldn't help Isobel's situation at all.

"I wouldn't worry about it. I heard one woman telling her friends that Studley was so toplofty that he never once brought his wife to London because, according to him, she 'smelled of the shop.' Even though she was an heiress. So nobody can imagine him raising one of his by-blows in the same house as his legitimate daughter."

Leo nodded. That would help.

"And a lot of people seem quite impressed by the way the Studley sisters responded to Pomphret's allegation—not just Miss Isobel's dignity, which was in sharp contrast to Pomphret's drunken abuse, but also the way Miss Studley raced to her sister's side. It was a clear public declaration of support. That kind of loyalty . . ." Race shook his head in wonder. "Priceless."

"Impressive, isn't it?" He'd been so proud of the girls' reaction.

Race eyed him thoughtfully. "Speaking of impressive loyalty, you didn't do so badly yourself. No, don't dismiss it," he added when Leo waved that off. "Your firm repudiation convinced many."

Leo hadn't planned his reaction at all. But when that lout

had called Isobel *Bart Studley's little bastard bitch*—in front of half the ton—he'd seen red. Isobel hurt nobody by her presence in the ton: in fact she only added to it with her charm and sprightliness. And the obvious love of the two sisters for each other was something to be admired.

"One thing has me stumped, though," Race added.

"What's that?"

"Quite a few people are referring to Pomphret as Lord Pig Slops."

"'Lord Pig Slops'?" Leo repeated. "How bizarre. Why on earth would they call him that?"

"No idea, but it's pretty widespread. Might be some kind of school nickname, I suppose," Race suggested doubtfully. "I never did move in the same circle as Pomphret and Studley and that older generation, so I can't even make a guess at it."

"Lord Pig Slops? Not exactly complimentary." But Leo didn't care about Pomphret's strange nickname: he was more interested in how Isobel was faring.

He looked over to where she and her sister were standing in a small group of men and women. He'd hardly taken his eyes off her since Pomphret had left—but as Race had said, she seemed amazingly composed, sipping champagne and chatting quietly with several people. She even laughed at something one of them said, apparently quite unaffected by Pomphret's outburst.

A surge of pride rose in him. Nobody would believe she'd just been the focus of a nasty accusation—and worse, one that was true. She looked serene and lovely, as calm as the moon.

As he watched, the orchestra started up again. Some fellow bowed over her hand and led her out onto the dance floor. The ball continued as if nothing untoward had happened at all. Except that Isobel was the focus of many eyes, and most of the murmured conversation.

As Race had said, they weren't out of the woods yet.

* * *

"Well, what a night." Clarissa slumped back against the padded seat of the carriage. "I'm exhausted. Izzy you must be utterly shattered."

"I am," Izzy admitted. But it wasn't the exposure of her illegitimacy that had left her feeling so drained—she'd been mentally braced for that for weeks, though the suddenness of it had been a shock. Nor was it the effort of maintaining a tranquil mien in front of all those curious people, though that had been exhausting, too.

The thing that had truly overwhelmed her was the knowledge that Lord Salcott had been prepared to fight a duel on her behalf—even though he *knew* that Lord Pomphret's claim was true. He'd risked his *life* for her, for she was certain that had it come to a duel, Lord Pomphret would never have done the decent thing and deloped. And as a lifelong hunter, he would be a very good shot.

Besides, dueling was illegal. Even if Lord Salcott survived, he would have had to flee the country or face a gaol sentence.

All because she'd wanted to have a season with Clarissa.

If she'd known this might be the result . . . She took a deep steadying breath. It didn't help.

On top of all that, the amount of support she'd received after the incident, from all kinds of people—well, it humbled her. So many people had come up to her to ask her if she was all right, and then stay to say something disparaging about Lord Pomphret.

He was deeply unpopular, it seemed.

But what would have happened if the person who exposed her irregular birth had been popular? She didn't dare think about it.

"Wasn't Lord Salcott magnificent?" Clarissa continued as the carriage pulled out. "And what a surprise, after all his gloomy prognostications about the axe falling and all that. I felt sure his first reaction would be to hustle us out of there."

Izzy had expected much the same.

"What axe falling?" Mrs. Price-Jones asked.

Oh. Izzy swallowed. It was time she told their chaperone the truth. "I really am illegitimate," she said. "I'm sorry that we didn't tell you earlier. We thought it would be better for you if you didn't know."

"So that you couldn't be blamed for colluding with us if—when—it came out," Clarissa added.

Mrs. Price-Jones chuckled. "Oh, I always knew, my dears. Olive told me when she first wrote and asked me to come to London and take you gels about."

Izzy's jaw dropped. "And you didn't mind?"

"Not a bit. I don't hold with all that 'sins of the father' nonsense. And if you really think about illegitimacy, half the ton would be 'there, but for the grace of God, go I.'"

Clarissa beamed at her. "That's exactly what we think."

"One question intrigues me however," Mrs. Price-Jones said. "How is it that you two were raised together in the same house? It doesn't sound at all like Sir Bartleby. I knew him slightly in my youth and he didn't seem the fatherly type. Or even very responsible."

"He wasn't," Izzy said. They told her their story, finishing just as the carriage drew up outside Lady Scattergood's house.

Clarissa peered out of the window. "Oh dear, look who's waiting for us."

Izzy glanced out and her heart sank. What did he want? Surely tonight there'd been enough drama?

But there he stood on Lady Scattergood's front steps, waiting, arms folded, feet braced apart, looking grim and heartbreakingly handsome: Lord Salcott.

He stepped forward and helped them down the carriage

steps. He didn't say a word. Nobody did. In silence they entered the house.

Izzy knew why he was here. The very thing he'd predicted had come to pass, and he was here to say I told you so. Which she didn't need to hear. She still felt sick at the very thought of the risk he'd taken on her behalf.

"I wish to speak to Miss Isobel—alone," he told Mrs. Price-Jones firmly. It was not a request.

The lady tilted her head and regarded him thoughtfully.

"I will not take no for an answer." He looked very stern.

Izzy watched wearily, dreading the argument that was bound to follow. When would this night end?

"Well, and about time, too," the chaperone said. Izzy looked at her. What?

Mrs. Price-Jones linked arms with Clarissa. "Come along, dear, let's leave them to it." Clarissa hesitated, but Mrs. Price-Jones swept her along. As they rounded the stairs at the landing, Izzy heard her say, "Let that be a lesson to you, my dear. Nothing focuses a man so much as denial of what he most wants."

Izzy frowned. She had no idea what was going on.

Lord Salcott opened the door to the sitting room, and waited. Izzy entered. The sooner this was over, the better. She braced herself and met his eyes.

He gestured for her to sit. "You look exhausted." She took the sofa.

She shrugged. "It's been a long day." And it had. A rejected proposal, a quarrel, a long and vigorous horse ride, a ball and a public scandal, all in one day. And it wasn't over yet.

He remained standing, looking down at her, his expression somber. "You were magnificent tonight."

She blinked. *Magnificent?*

"I was so proud of you. Your sister, too, of course, but you, most of all."

Proud? Izzy didn't know what to say.

"Lord Randall is of the opinion that the majority have dismissed Lord Pomphret's claim. There will be some gossip, of course, and possibly the shadow will always overhang—"

"How *could* you?" she burst out.

He stared at her. "How could I what?"

"Risk yourself like that! You were that far"—she held up thumb and finger—"from facing that dreadful man in a duel. And he's a crack shot. And has no gallantry at all, so he would have killed you."

"Nonsense."

She jumped up and prodded him in the chest. "It's not nonsense *at all*. You could have been *killed*, and all to defend a lie—a lie about *me*! And I'm not worth dying for." She stared at him a moment, then her face crumpled. "And even if he didn't . . . didn't k-kill you," she sobbed, "you would have had to . . . to f-flee the country, because d-duels are il-illegal."

"Hush now." He drew her against him and she subsided onto his chest. "There was no chance of a duel—though I would have been glad of the opportunity."

"No! How can you say such a thing?"

He produced a handkerchief and started wiping her cheeks with it. "Pomphret is a bully, and bullies are invariably cowards. He certainly is one. The way he behaved tonight, even some of his cronies were obviously disgusted. It did his reputation—such as it was—no good. But I didn't bring you in here to talk about Pomphret, or even the events of tonight's ball. Apart from telling you that you were magnificent."

There was that word again. Izzy took his handkerchief, wiped her eyes and blew her nose, playing for time as she fought to master herself again. She despised tears, and was cross with herself for giving into them.

"What did you want to speak to me about, then?" she said in as calm a voice as she could manage. Which wasn't very.

She tried to move away—she was practically plastered against his chest—but his arm was firmly wrapped around her, and he made no move to release her.

She didn't try very hard. His body was so warm and so comforting.

"I need to tell you something."

"What?"

He took a deep breath. "I made a dreadful mull of things this morning."

"This morning?" She couldn't think for a moment. So much had happened.

"When I asked you to marry me."

"Oh, that." It felt like an age had passed since then.

"Yes, 'that,'" he repeated dryly. "I was an ass, a fool, a self-centered, oblivious, brainless clod when I spoke to you that way. I was swimming in guilt, you see—not thinking about you at all, but only about myself and how I'd ruined you. I couldn't even look you in the eye."

"I noticed." She swallowed. She hadn't expected this, not at all. "But I think you should know that I don't feel ruined in the slightest. I chose what we did last night—or have you forgotten? It was my responsibility." It was always the woman's fault.

"Nonsense. It was entirely mutual. And except for any consequences we might face, I don't regret it for a minute. It was a glorious experience and one I'll treasure for the rest of my life."

Did he really mean it? *Treasure for the rest of his life? Consequences we might face?*

He placed a finger beneath her chin and gently tilted her face up. "You really are exhausted, aren't you? I should undoubtedly leave you in peace and let you go up to bed, but I can't, I just can't." He gave her a rueful smile. "Besides, with you too tired to argue, I have a better chance of getting through the speech I've been rehearsing all week."

She stared up at him, bewildered. *Speech?*

"I've wanted to say this ever since I walked out of the room this morning, even before that—last night—and I cannot let another night pass without telling you."

"Telling me what?"

He gazed down at her for a long moment and sighed. "See, that's the problem. I gaze into your glorious eyes, and every coherent thought I ever had vanishes. It was quite a good speech, too."

She had no idea what he was talking about. "What speech? Speech about what?" For a moment all she could think of was a speech to Parliament. He was a member of the House of Lords, after all. But that made no sense.

He took a deep breath. "No speech. Just, I love you."

For a moment Izzy couldn't breathe. "What did you say?" she whispered.

"I love you." His lips twitched. "There it is, plain and simple, the words I've been wanting to say for so long, and failing miserably at it."

"You love me?"

"Yes." He took her hand and placed it against his heart. "I love you and I want to marry you—not because I took your virginity, not because I feel obliged nor any other of those stupid things I said this morning. Just, I love you and I'm proud of you, and I cannot imagine a life without you in it."

Keeping her hand in his, he went down on one knee. "So, Isobel Burton Studley—my lovely Belle—will you please do me the very great honor of bestowing on me your hand in marriage?"

Izzy stared down at him. She couldn't think of what to say. "But you're an earl."

"I know. Why? Is that a problem? You'll be a countess—if you say yes."

She tugged on his shoulders and made him stand so she could look him in the eye.

"You're not doing this because of Pomphret, are you? Or because I'm no longer a virgin? Because you didn't seduce or me, you know—I wanted it as much as you did." She couldn't bear it if this were some kind of gallant gesture.

"I doubt it. But no, none of those is important. I'm asking you for one reason only: I love you and I don't want to live another day without you in my life."

At his soft words, Izzy was melting inside. But she had to give him one last chance. "I'm a nobody, Leo. And a bastard. I would hate to be a millstone around your neck."

"You won't be—you could never be any kind of millstone. You will be my friend and my lover and my wife—and, if we're blessed, the mother of my children."

Izzy's eyes filled with tears. "Are you sure, Leo?"

"Sure of what? That I love you? Absolutely positive. That I want to marry you? One hundred percent certain." He took both her hands in his. "So, what do you say? Do you think you could take me on? As a husband I mean."

"Oh, Leo," she said mistily and threw herself into his arms. "Oh, Leo." She planted kisses over his face, working her way to his mouth.

"Does that mean what I think it means?" he said after a while. He was now seated on the sofa with Izzy on his lap.

"That I love you? Of course I do. I have for the longest time."

"You have? I thought you generally wanted to throttle me."

She smiled mischievously. "Oh, I did, often. But even though there were times I was furious with you, I still couldn't help but love you."

"Well, that's all right, then." He kissed her again, long and lavishly, then pulled back with a sigh. "I would give anything to take you to bed here and now, but I know I must resist."

She gave him a sultry smile. "Must we?"

"Minx." He kissed her again and stood up, adjusting his breeches with a grimace. "Shall we get married soon?"

She nodded. "As soon as you like."

Chapter Seventeen

The following morning Leo woke to a gray, relentless drizzle. He lay in bed, listening to the rain pattering against the window panes, trying to rid himself of a small niggle. Part of him wanted to smile and rejoice in the fact that Isobel—Belle—had agreed to marry him. But . . .

She'd been utterly exhausted last night. Was it fair of him to have asked her after the day she'd already been through? Had he pushed her into agreeing to wed him when she was in such a state? What if she'd changed her mind?

No use lying in bed wondering. Seize the moment. And think positive. He rose, bathed, shaved and dressed, and while he did, he outlined a possible plan with Matteo.

"It might not even happen, and if it does, you will have much to do and not much time to do it in. Do you think you can handle it, or shall I hire someone?"

"Hire someone? Hire some stranger?" Matteo drew himself up in indignation. "Never think of such a thing, milor'. Of course I can arrange everything. Is easy. Like this." He snapped his fingers.

"Well, if you're sure."

"Milor', is great honor you make me, and I will not let you down." Matteo laid his hand over his heart. "On my honor."

Leo was touched. "Matteo, you have *never* let me down."

Matteo flushed. "And I 'ope I never will, milor'."

Leo then sent a note over to his aunt's house, asking Isobel to meet him in the summerhouse at her earliest convenience. How long would it take her to dress and prepare herself? An hour? Assuming she wasn't sleeping late, which she probably was.

He couldn't wait that long, not with the uncertainty eating at him. He went straight to the summerhouse, where he paced anxiously, going over the events of last night, trying to decide whether he'd pushed her—he had—and how far.

Might she have changed her mind?

Did she truly mean it when she said she loved him? Or had she seen marriage to him as the only possible alternative after Pomphret had exposed her like that?

Of course, if she'd accepted him for protection, he would try to be content with that—he'd give his life to protect her. But he desperately hoped she really had meant it when she'd said *I love you.*

Isobel didn't keep him waiting long. She burst through the door and came to an abrupt halt. Her complexion glowed like damp silk from the cool air and the rain. Raindrops glittered in her hair like diamonds. She normally wore it tied back in a bun: this morning it spilled in a glorious ebony mass over her shoulders. Leo was enchanted.

As she looked at him, her smile faded. She stood motionless, suddenly pale, clutching the handle of the open door. "What is it?"

Rain spattered against the windows. Leo cleared his throat. Best to get it out in the open now, have no misunderstandings. "Last night I pushed you into giving me an answer, but I should never have asked it of you, not when you were exhausted."

Her grip on the door handle tightened. Her knuckles whitened.

He continued. "Now, the morning after, and in the cold—and drizzly—light of day, I'm wondering, are you having any doubts? Do you wish to change your mind? Because if you do . . ." He couldn't finish. He had no idea what he'd do if she had changed her mind.

He waited, his heart thudding so loud it was a wonder she couldn't hear it over the sound of the rain.

"Doubts?" Her face was like marble. "No. Why? Have *you* changed your mind?"

"Me?" His jaw dropped. "Good God no, marrying you is still my dearest wish."

Color washed into her pale cheeks. It was like watching dawn breaking. With a little smile, she carefully closed the door, turned and flung herself bodily across the room and into his arms. He caught her against his chest, staggered back and landed on the daybed, with Belle on top of him. His arms tightened around her.

She laughed softly. "Here we are again. Good morning, Leo." She peppered his face with tiny warm kisses. He buried his face in her hair and breathed in her fragrance. Rain and sweet warm woman.

After a moment she drew back and hit him lightly on the shoulder. "You gave me such a fright just then. Why would you imagine I'd changed my mind? Didn't you believe me last night?"

"I thought I might have pushed you into it."

She gave a gurgle of laughter. "Oh, Leo, when have I ever given in to your pushing?"

He gave a rueful smile. "True enough." He kissed her again. "I suppose once I marry you I'm in for an exhausting life under the cat's paw."

Mischief danced in her eyes. "Exhausting, certainly." She gave a little wriggle that sent hot darts through his body.

They were distracted then by a rapping on the door. Matteo stood outside, peering out from under a giant black umbrella. Rain poured off it in cascades. He shook the umbrella and stepped inside. "All good, milor'? We go ahead with everything?"

Leo nodded. "Yes. Everything. And deliver my note to Miss Studley. Eleven o'clock." He suddenly recalled that Race had planned to call on him this morning, to discuss the fallout from the Pomphret incident. "And when Lord Randall arrives send him out here, too."

Matteo bowed. "Very good, milor'." Wreathed in smiles he bowed again, even lower, this time to Isobel. "Felicitations, Miss Isabella. You make us all very, very 'appy." He closed the door and disappeared.

"Matteo is such a dear." Izzy tugged lightly on Leo's neckcloth, ruining its careful arrangement. She loved seeing him in slight disarray. He was normally so neat and stiff and buttoned up, but when the man let himself loose— she shivered deliciously—he was magnificent. She was determined it would happen often in their future. *Their future.* A thrill ran through her. "What is happening at eleven o'clock?"

"Breakfast."

"Oh, is that all?"

"Is that all?" He snorted. "You haven't had one of Matteo's breakfasts yet. He has found a superb Neapolitan chef. I don't know where he finds these people, but I'm very grateful."

She rubbed her cheek against his chest. "You know what I'd do if I had piles of money?"

He quirked an eyebrow. "No, what?" There was only

curiosity in his face, no hint of suspicion. He wasn't thinking of her as a gold digger. The thought warmed her.

"I would buy a hotel, put Matteo in charge of it and
make him an equal partner."

He didn't look too impressed. "I could, I suppose, but
then I'd lose his exclusive services."

"He's wasted just looking after you."

"Wasted?" Cupping her face in his hands, he attempted
a stern glare, but his flinty gray eyes were dancing, and his
dimple—the one he claimed didn't exist—was showing.
Oh, but she did love seeing that dimple. "Wait until you've
had one of his breakfasts before you make such an appall-
ingly ignorant judgment. And recall that in a short time he's
going to be looking after you, as well."

She laughed and kissed him. "How short a time?" She
still could hardly believe that she was going to marry this
wonderful man.

"As soon as we can arrange it." Leo's fingers slipped
slowly along her jawline and buried themselves in her hair.

She flinched self-consciously. "Oh, don't, it's awful—all
frizzy from the rain." She should have tied it back in a bun
as usual, but she'd been in such a hurry to see him again she
hadn't bothered.

"It's not frizzy, it's beautiful, like spun silk. Magical.
You have no idea how much I have longed to do this." He
lifted handfuls of her hair, buried his face in it and breathed
rapturously in. "Glorious." He smiled down at her. "Now,
where were we?" He bent to kiss her again.

The door opened and Clarissa came to a sudden breathless
halt in the doorway. She'd been running to escape the rain.
"Oh!" She looked at them in surprise. "What's going on?"

As she spoke, Matteo appeared bearing a large covered
tray. He was accompanied by a footman holding an umbrella over him and the tray. "*Scusi, signorina.*" Matteo laid
the tray down and whisked off the cover to reveal a bottle
of champagne, four glasses and a couple of dishes of tiny

exquisite pastries, crispy, golden and glittering with sugar crystals. "To start with, milor'," he said and hurried away.

"Champagne? For breakfast?" Clarissa said doubtfully.

"Call it a pre-wedding breakfast," Leo said.

"*Wedding?*" Clarissa exclaimed.

Izzy couldn't stop her smile from bursting out. "You're the first to know, 'Riss."

"Oh, Izzy, Izzy! I'm so happy for you!" Clarissa hurried across the room and embraced her sister in a fierce hug. "But when did all this—?"

"Last night. After the ball."

"So that was what he wanted to talk to you about, not—?" Clarissa had been thinking of Lord Pomphret. Izzy hadn't even given that dreadful man a thought today. All her thoughts were of Leo. And the future, a future she'd been almost too afraid to dream of.

"He surprised me, too," Izzy said softly.

"Let's drink to it." Leo poured the gently fizzing liquid into an elegant crystal flute. He handed it to Izzy, saying, "I seem to remember this stuff has a delightful effect on you."

She laughed, blushing as she recalled their first kiss in this very place, after the twilight party. "Is that why you arranged for us to meet here this morning? I never realized you were such a romantic."

He made a gruff kind of sound and frowned over the pouring of a glass for Clarissa and another for him. But he didn't deny it. So sweet.

Hasty footsteps sounded outside and the door flew open. "The windows are all steamed up—again! What are you up to now, Izzy Studley? Carousing with a man again?"

Izzy raised her glass at Milly in a silent, mocking toast.

Milly looked disgusted. "Drinking at this hour of the day? Is there no end to your brazen behavior?"

Milly then spotted Clarissa snuggling back comfortably in her favorite squashy chair. "Oh. Miss Studley? You're here, too?"

Clarissa raised her glass. "Good morning, Milly."

Before Milly could respond, Lord Randall arrived. "Pardon me, miss." He pushed past Milly, who was still standing in the doorway, and shook his wet head like a dog. Droplets of water scattered everywhere.

Milly jumped back with a squeak and pressed herself against a window, drawing her shawl tightly over her bosom, eyeing Lord Randall with a mix of dread and excitement as if he would pounce on her at any minute.

Lord Randall was oblivious. "Sorry about that, Miss Um. Morning, Miss Studley, Miss Isobel, must say you're both looking ravishing at this early hour. This wretched weather, Leo, why the dev—er, deuce did you ask me out here instead of staying warm and comfortable at your—" He broke off, spotting the champagne. "Oh, I say, put her to the question, did you? So glad, Miss Isobel. Pour me a glass, will you, Leo? Ah, here's Matteo with the food. Excellent, I'm famished."

Matteo and the footman began to set out a delicious-looking array of food. "More to come soon, milor'."

Milly watched, her eyes round. "What is all this? You *are* carousing." She glanced suspiciously at Lord Randall. "Is this an orgy?"

"We're celebrating our betrothal," Izzy explained.

Milly's eyes darted back and forth. "What? A *betrothal*? Whose?"

Leo lifted Izzy's hand and kissed it lingeringly. Milly's eyes almost popped. "You and Lord Salcott? But . . . but he's an earl, and you're a bas—" She broke off as four pairs of eyes narrowed at her. "A nobody. It's not fair. And you've never even *been* to Almack's!"

"I know." Izzy was so happy today she could almost feel sorry for the wretched girl.

Milly looked at Leo, aggrieved. "And my mama is second cousin to a *duke*."

Leo, missing the significance of this, nodded vaguely at

Milly. "Is she? Well, well. How nice for her." He turned back to Izzy. "More champagne, my love? And have you tasted these marinated strawberries yet? They're delicious." He picked up a strawberry and prepared to feed it to Izzy by hand. Milly's gasp of outrage was audible, even over the drumming of the rain on the roof.

Clarissa, whose manners were better than Izzy's, said, "Would you care to join us for some breakfast, Milly?"

She drew herself up. "No, I would not! This gathering is a disgrace. Mama will be furious when I tell her."

"Well, you run off and tell her, then," Izzy said, and parted her lips to receive another delicious morsel from her beloved's fingers.

S o, when is this wedding to be?" Race sat sprawled in one of the bamboo chairs, his long, booted legs loosely crossed. Breakfast was over—they were all stuffed full—and the men had moved on to fine Italian coffee while the ladies sipped hot chocolate.

Leo glanced at Isobel. "As soon as possible?"

She smiled and nodded.

"Special license?"

Leo was about to agree, when he thought better of it. "No, banns, I think. I want the world to know I am marrying Isobel." No hasty hole-in-the-corner wedding for his Belle.

Race nodded. "St. George's, Hanover Square, then."

Leo nodded. It was the most fashionable church in London, the parish church for Mayfair.

Clarissa turned to her sister. "You will need a new dress."

Isobel laughed. "So will you, as my bridesmaid." They both turned to Leo. "And your best man?"

Leo glanced at his oldest friend. "Race, will you do the honors?"

Race raised his coffee cup in a toast. "Delighted."

"So, we'll be married in just over three weeks' time. We'll marry in the morning, then a wedding breakfast, and in the evening a ball."

The two ladies sat up. "'A ball'?"

Clarissa clapped her hands. "Two new dresses."

Isobel stared at Leo. "In three weeks? You can't possibly organize a wedding and a ball in such a short time."

Leo shrugged. "Matteo assures me he can."

The two girls exchanged glances. "Then we shall help." They fell to discussing themes and decorations and ball dresses and other things that Leo had little interest in.

He turned to Race and said in a low voice, "Anything more on the reaction to Pomphret's announcement?"

Race shook his head. "It's going to take time—some are still doubtful, but no one is sufficiently engaged in the matter to investigate, and I predict the announcement of your betrothal will settle it still more. And once a new scandal takes its place, as is inevitable, people will forget all about something a drunk called Pomphret once said at a ball."

The following week Izzy and Clarissa were sitting downstairs with Lady Scattergood and Mrs. Price-Jones awaiting the first morning callers of the day. Since the news of Izzy's betrothal had been made public, the number of callers had trebled.

Izzy and Clarissa were poring over lists. Invitations for the Salcott ball had gone out, and acceptances were already pouring in. Any fears that society might shun Izzy were rapidly fading.

Mrs. Price-Jones was knitting and Lady Scattergood was, as usual, deep in her morning correspondence.

"Good God!" the old lady exclaimed. She looked up from the letter she was reading. "That villain Pomphret won't be bothering you or anyone else ever again, gels. He's dead." Everyone exclaimed over the news.

"How do I know?" She gestured to her little writing desk, which, as usual, was piled high with papers. "I might not leave the house very often, but my friends keep me up to date with all the goings-on of the world, believe you me."

She waved the letter at them. "Hush now and listen. According to my friend Gertie, Pomphret blew his brains out on the night of the Arden Ball."

"But that's when—" Izzy began.

"Don't interrupt." Lady Scattergood rattled the letter at her. "According to Gertie, he drove down to his country property immediately after the ball—no, Clarissa, Gertie doesn't even mention our dearest Izzy! Now, are you going to let me tell this story or not?" She sternly leveled her lorgnette at the girls, then satisfied of their complete attention, she returned to her letter.

"The very night he arrived home, he went straight to his library—without a word to his poor wife—and blew his brains out. Gertie says it is all over town that he'd come straight from some horrid gaming hell where he'd gambled away every last penny he owned, including his estates—which were already mortgaged to the hilt. He only went to the ball to collect his poor wife and go home—apparently so he could kill himself in comfort."

She snorted. "It's his poor wife I feel sorry for. I hope he's burning in the other place! Well, of course he is, along with the rest of that circle of which your father was one. All gone now and the world will be a better place for it." She glanced around. "Is there any more tea?"

Izzy, feeling a little numb at the news and not quite sure how she felt, jumped up to refill the old lady's teacup. This, then, would be the scandal Lord Randall had mentioned the other day, the one that would replace the scandal about her birth. How ironic.

She ought to feel sorry that the man was dead, but she couldn't. She passed the old lady her tea. "Here you are, Lady Scattergood."

The old lady eyed her sternly. "Isn't it time you started calling me Aunt Olive, gel?"

Chapter Eighteen

❧

I t's going to be a beautiful wedding." Clarissa sighed. "You'll look so lovely."

Izzy smiled and ran her hands over the exquisite wedding outfit spread out on the bed. Miss Chance had outdone herself with a beautiful, simple dress in ivory silk, tight at the bosom, then flowing in layers. And because the weather in London was so unreliable, and Miss Chance said that goose bumps weren't a good look for a bride, she'd added a lovely creamy long-sleeved spencer in silk velvet brocade, fastened down the front with pearls.

"And did you see what she sent you as a gift?" Clarissa pushed a small, flat distinctively embossed box forward. "She gives one to all her brides, she said."

Inside was . . . well, it was like no nightgown that Izzy or Clarissa had ever seen.

"Are you supposed to wear that to bed? It looks terribly improper."

Izzy held it up against herself. "Gorgeously improper. But

then a wedding night isn't supposed to be proper, is it?" It was beautiful, the palest, sheerest peach silk trimmed with lace and gauze. And a kind of a—well, you couldn't call it a dressing gown because it covered practically nothing, but oh, it was so pretty.

She couldn't wait to wear this for Leo. She tucked it away for later.

"You're going to need a maid," Clarissa said abruptly.

Izzy glanced at Betty and then realized Betty would be staying with Clarissa, of course. "Perhaps Matteo could find me one."

"We have an idea," Clarissa said breathlessly. "Betty and I."

"Go ahead."

"We thought we'd go down to the orphan asylum—there's one in Mayfair—and Betty and I could talk to the girls there. And select one to be your maid."

"The girls there are ever so good, miss," Betty said anxiously. "But most of them will end up in factories, or scrubbin' floors. Or worse. Like me, before you and Miss Clarissa brought me here with you."

"And while you're away on your honeymoon, we—Betty and I—can train her up a bit."

"Teach her how to do hair, and clean and starch and iron clothes and all that." Betty gazed at Izzy with almost painful eagerness.

A maidservant from an orphan asylum. Izzy never passed one of those places without thinking that there but for meeting Clarissa that fateful day, went she. She might have been the one toiling in a factory or scrubbing floors. Or worse.

"It's a splendid idea." She embraced her sister and then hugged Betty. "It will be a wonderful wedding present, thank you. Now come on, help me dress. I don't want to be late for my own wedding."

* * *

Izzy had never been to a wedding, and found the whole thing much more moving and emotional than she'd expected. Everyone she cared about had come: Clarissa, of course, Lord and Lady Tarrant and the little girls, half the ladies from the literary society—even Lady Scattergood, who'd arrived in her beloved palanquin. Even Milly and her mother, who'd sat prune faced through the ceremony.

But the look on Leo's face, the blaze that lit his smoky gray eyes—how had she ever thought them hard?—when Izzy entered the church and started walking down the aisle . . . She'd never forget it.

If she'd ever had any doubts about why he wanted to marry her, they would have dissolved then and there. Not that she had any doubts.

And then he'd taken her hand and the minister said, "Dearly beloved . . ." and the rest passed in a blur.

The wedding breakfast, too, passed in a happy, noisy, extravagant, delicious blur. Matteo and the cook, Alfonso, had outdone themselves. She recalled mounds of gorgeous, colorful, exotic-looking food, but she barely tasted a thing. She was floating on a cloud.

Finally, the guests departed, most planning a nap before dressing to return for the ball. Leo had led her upstairs to his big wide bed.

"Do you need a nap?" His gray eyes smoldered with desire.

She snorted. "Of course not. I just need someone to help me out of this dress—is there a maid? The buttons are down the back."

"I think you'll find I can perform maid service very nicely," he said, turning her to start undoing the dozens of tiny buttons that fastened down the back of her dress.

"I'll remember that for when I need my petticoats starched."

"Baggage." He kissed the nape of her neck, and she shivered deliciously.

Muttering under his breath about ridiculously tiny buttons, he finally lifted the dress up over her head and laid it carefully aside. He reached for the next layer, and she shook her head and stepped away out of reach. "Fair is fair. Off with that coat."

He removed his coat. She then allowed him to struggle with her corset while she wrestled with his neckcloth. Halfway through they stopped and looked at each other.

"You undress you and I'll undress me," she said.

"Agreed."

In minutes they were naked. Leo just stood and gazed. "Lord, Belle, but you're so lovely. How did I ever deserve you?" Izzy would have felt embarrassed, except for the look of almost worship in his eyes.

Besides, she was too busy staring at him. At that intensely masculine part of him, already standing proud and erect. "Did that really—" She broke off, blushing.

He gave her a slow, knowing smile. "Yes, and it fitted perfectly, remember? Shall I demonstrate?"

Izzy thought nothing could touch the magic of that night in the summerhouse, but the second time of making love with Leo was even better.

The third time was better still. Afterward they lay in his big wide bed, naked and spent. And blissfully boneless.

"That was . . . that was . . ." Izzy couldn't find the words.

"Practice makes perfect," Leo murmured.

"Good, you'll need lots more practice, then," she said sleepily.

"Minx." He leaned forward to kiss her. But she was asleep. "So, nap time after all, eh?" Rolling over he gathered her against him and dozed off.

*   *   *

S ome time later, Matteo knocked on the door. "Time to
get ready for the ball, milor'. I 'ave a bath prepared for
milady in the dressing room, and another for you in the
next bedroom. And Miss Studley and the maid Betty will
be coming soon to help milady attire herself."

Leo was very tempted to suggest they only needed one
bath, but then thought better of it. What he had in mind
would probably make them late, and the last thing he
wanted was for Belle to feel hurried or distracted preparing
for the first ever ball in her honor.

He woke her gently, and they went off to take their re-
spective baths.

Then Clarissa and Betty arrived to help dress Belle for
the ball, and Leo was banished to his own quarters.

But finally, the time came. Guests were already arriving
downstairs. Leo paced. He wanted everything to be perfect
for her.

Betty knocked on his door. "She's ready, m'lord."

He hurried to his bedchamber. Clarissa opened the door
with a flourish. And there stood Belle, ravishing in a dress
made of clouds. At least that's what it looked like to Leo.
Smoky ice blue in soft layers rising up her body to cup and
frame her breasts. Her eyes were shining. A lump formed
in his throat. His Belle. She was so beautiful.

She wore no jewelry—she needed nothing to adorn her
beauty, but Leo snapped his fingers and raced back down
the hall.

"What—?" Isobel stood, shaking her head in bemusement.

He returned in a few minutes with a flat box. He opened
it, scooped out half the contents, and handed the box to
Clarissa. "Turn around," he told Belle.

"Leo, what are you—?" She stopped as he placed a
necklace around her neck.

Clarissa gasped. "Diamonds? Oh, Izzy, they're magnificent."

"Earrings, too." Leo pulled them out and handed them to her. "And a bracelet. There's more—it's the Salcott Parure, but you won't need the tiara and the rest, not tonight."

The women moved as one to the looking glass, where Belle carefully attached the diamond drop earrings. She stared at her reflection and touched the diamond necklace cautiously. "It's stunning, Leo. But I can't wear something so expen—"

"Nonsense. They're perfect. You're perfect. You adorn *them*. Besides, they belong to my countess now—to you. So, are you ready to go downstairs and let me introduce you to all our guests?" He held out his arm.

She gave him a misty smile, stood on tiptoe to give him a quick kiss, then placed her hand on his arm. Side by side they walked slowly down the stairs. The floor below was crowded with guests, the cream of the ton, all glittering in their finest and talking loudly and animatedly, but as Leo and Belle descended the stairs, a hush slowly fell. All eyes turned to the couple they'd come to honor, Leo, Lord Salcott, and his new bride.

"Ladies and gentlemen," Leo said. "Let me introduce to you my pride and joy, my bride, my wife, my lovely countess."

Someone started clapping—it was Race, Leo saw—and in seconds the whole crowd was smiling and applauding. Leo glanced at Belle.

"I'm not crying, I'm not," she muttered, blinking furiously.

Laughing softly, he led her down to the ball, and to the rest of their lives.

Epilogue

❧

Bright sun pierced a gap in the curtains. Izzy stirred and stretched sleepily. Opening her eyes, she found a pair of warm gray eyes regarding her.

"Good morning, my lovely wife." Leo leaned over and kissed her, first her mouth, then her bare shoulder.

Izzy blushed, feeling a little shy. She was not yet used to waking naked in a bed with a large, handsome, equally naked man next to her. It was wonderful, of course; she was just not accustomed to sleeping naked. Nor was she used to being the focus of such warm approval. No, not approval— love.

"How are you feeling?" There was a faint anxious thread in his voice. They'd made love not long after dawn, the third time since their marriage the day before and her husband was clearly worried he'd used her too hard. He hadn't.

She rose on one elbow and kissed him. "I feel wonderful, Leo. I had no idea . . ." She sighed happily and fell back against the pillow. "It's bliss, isn't it? Like heaven."

He chuckled. "A little earthier than that, but yes, with you, it is indeed bliss." He kissed her again, then swung his legs out of bed. "We'll leave as soon as you're ready." They were traveling to Salcott, Leo's country estate that day.

"There's no hurry," he added as she sat up hastily. "Matteo will bring you breakfast in bed while your bath is being prepared." He bent, picked up her delicate, beautiful, almost transparent nightgown from the floor where he'd tossed it the previous night, then frowned down at the frivolous froth of fabric in his fist. "On second thought, if Matteo is coming in, you'd better not wear this piece of nonsense. Put this on instead." He took a man's dressing gown made of heavily embroidered silk from the wardrobe and passed it to her.

She hid a smile as she slipped her arms into it. It was miles too big for her, of course—practically a tent—but it smelled faintly of Leo's cologne and she snuggled it around her.

Leo left to wash and dress, and Matteo entered with a tray containing a pot of hot chocolate and a plate of delicious-looking pastries glistening with sugar crystals. "Your sister, she come looking for you earlier, milady."

"Clarissa? What did she want?"

"She no say. I offer her breakfast: pastries, chocolate, coffee—even a cup of good English tea—but she no want nothing, not even to wait in the house. She say to tell you she see you in the garden before you leave."

Wondering what Clarissa wanted, and why she didn't simply come up to Izzy's bedchamber as she always had before, Izzy raced through her breakfast, took a hasty bath and hurried downstairs to the garden.

She hastened along the gravel pathway, her feet aching a little from all the dancing last night. Her new shoes had pinched. Then she smiled to herself. Other, more unfamiliar parts of her body also ached a little, but they only sparked the memory of delicious sensations. Her body felt well used—and very well loved.

She found her sister sitting in her favorite spot—the rose arbor.

"You wanted to see me, love? And why didn't you simply come upstairs."

Clarissa blushed. "To your bedroom? That you share with your husband?"

Izzy laughed. "I didn't think of that. So what did you want? You didn't think I'd go without saying goodbye did you?"

"No, of course not. I just wanted . . . Oh, Izzy." Clarissa's eyes filled with tears. "You look . . . you look so . . ."

"What? What do I look like? And why are you crying?"

"They're happy tears," Clarissa said, dabbing at them. "Look at you, Izzy, you're glowing. As if you'd swallowed the moon and the stars."

Izzy patted her stomach. "I know, I ate too much yesterday, but that food . . ."

"Oh, stop it." Clarissa gave a shaky laugh. "You know what I mean. You look so happy. I don't think I've ever seen you so happy."

"That's because I am happy, happier than I ever believed possible." Izzy slipped onto the wooden bench beside her sister and linked arms with her. "And it's all thanks to you."

Clarissa looked at her in surprise. "Thanks to me? But I didn't do anything."

"You made me your sister. And fought to keep me."

There was a short silence broken only by the chittering of birds, and the distant sound of traffic.

"That day, ten years ago, you changed my life."

"And you changed mine," Clarissa said. "You have no idea how lonely I'd been before you came."

"It was more than that." Much more. Izzy couldn't imagine what her life might have been like had Clarissa not found her hidden in the shrubbery and decided to adopt her. All Izzy's current happiness, all her future security, she owed to that one incredibly generous act of Clarissa's. If she was bursting with happiness now, it was thanks to this quiet, shy, unassuming young woman who could become a tigress in defense of those she loved.

"Will you be all right while I'm away on my honeymoon? Because if you like—"

Clarissa cut her off. "Oh, hush. Of course I'll be all right—more than all right. I'm so much more confident in society now, and I know dozens of people. And I have friends like Lady Tarrant and Mrs Price-Jones and others."

"And there's no need to hurry about finding a husband. Take your time and be sure."

Clarissa gave a kind of half shrug, half nod. She was not nearly as confident as she pretended.

Izzy hugged her. "I promise you, 'Riss, you're going to be as happy as I am. You will find a man to love you as you deserve, I promise you."

Clarissa stood up and said briskly, "Izzy darling, this is no time to be worrying about me. I will be perfectly all right. Now, you're about to leave on your honeymoon and I don't want to delay you by even a minute. And look"—she pointed—"there's your handsome husband come seeking you. Cinderella, your carriage awaits."

At her sister's light-hearted words Izzy's eyes sheened with tears. Because she really was Cinderella; ten years ago she'd had nothing and no one, and now here she was, surrounded with love.

Izzy hugged her sister again. "You will find love, 'Riss. I promise."

Arm in arm the two sisters walked towards the waiting man, tall and serious and more handsome than any man had a right to be. Leo, Lord Salcott, the man she loved with all her heart. And who, by some miracle, loved her too.

ABOUT THE AUTHOR

Anne Gracie is the award-winning author of the Marriage of Convenience, Chance Sisters and Brides of Bellaire Gardens romance series. She started her first novel while backpacking solo around the world, writing by hand in notebooks. Since then, her books have been translated into more than eighteen languages, including Japanese manga editions. As well as writing, Anne promotes adult literacy, flings balls for her dog, enjoys her tangled garden and keeps bees.

CONNECT ONLINE

AnneGracie.com

Ready to find
your next great read?

Let us help.

Visit prh.com/nextread